Praise for Kate Clayborn and ~~her~~ ~~~

"Kate Clayborn once again plucks my heart from my chest and makes it dance to her tune. . . . This is a book for plunging into, a river of feelings with an inescapable current. Even as you are swept away, you know Clayborn's hand is safely on the tiller, steering you expertly through the rapids."
—*The New York Times* on *Georgie, All Along*

"*Georgie, All Along* is a sweet novel that reminds you going back is sometimes the best path forward . . . and that planning is never as rewarding as doing." —Jodi Picoult, *New York Times* bestselling author of *Wish You Were Here*

"Kate Clayborn's writing is magnetic and witty and expansive, and her characters feel as real and solid to me as my own limbs. The world is going to fall hard for this deliciously whimsical and captivating story, and I cannot wait to see it!"
—Ali Hazelwood, *New York Times* and *USA Today* bestselling author of *The Love Hypothesis* on *Georgie, All Along*

"Absolute perfection—this is the book you are looking for. *Georgie, All Along* is a tour de force, beautifully written and full of charming characters, rich emotion, and delicious spice. With it, Kate Clayborn solidifies her place in romance royalty."
—Sarah MacLean

"Kate Clayborn's writing is a study in syntax and rhythm; her storytelling is a perfect example of patience and pacing. With her trademark eye to detail of setting and scene, she has built a pitch-perfect love story, in a precious world-within-the-world setting, and honest-to-god the most delightful cast of characters I've met in ages. Tonally perfect, deeply romantic, and exquisitely crafted, Clayborn delivers a modern romance masterpiece." —*New York Times* bestselling author Christina Lauren on *Love at First*

"Kate Clayborn's luminously beautiful *Love at First* is playful, heartbreaking, wise, and wonderful. I adored this story about two souls finding their way out of loss and grief and forging their own paths to true love."
—Ruby Lang, author of *Playing House*

"A novel of lush complexity, one bursting with humor, a tender melancholy, and meditations on love, friendship, and life, any reader can find solace and inspiration in. It's lyrical and engrossing, a novel that possesses all the colors, idiosyncrasies, and range of the alphabet. Like the pages Meg designs, *Love Lettering* is a novel bursting with hidden messages essential to discover—long as we open our hearts to analyze the codes."
—*Entertainment Weekly*, A+ , on *Love Lettering*

"Quirky and winning."
—*USA Today* on *Love Lettering*

"Fresh, funny, clever, and deeply satisfying."
—*Kirkus Reviews*, STARRED REVIEW, on *Love Lettering*

"What if you and your two best friends all went in together on a winning lottery ticket? The romance between Kit, a no-nonsense scientist who dreams of her first real home, and Ben, a recruiter and builder (I promise, it works) is emotional and real. Plus, I adored Kit's strong relationship with her two best friends." —*O, The Oprah Magazine*, Best Romances of the Year, on *Beginner's Luck*

"Clayborn's characters are bright and nuanced, her dialogue quick and clever, and the world she builds is warm and welcoming." —*The Washington Post*, 5 Best Romances of the Year, on *Luck of the Draw*

THE
OTHER SIDE of DISAPPEARING

Other Books by Kate Clayborn

Georgie, All Along

Love at First

Love Lettering

The Chance of a Lifetime Series

Beginner's Luck

Luck of the Draw

Best of Luck

Novellas

"Missing Christmas" in *A Snowy Little Christmas*

THE
OTHER SIDE of
DISAPPEARING

KATE CLAYBORN

KENSINGTON
PUBLISHING CORP.

www.kensingtonbooks.com

KENSINGTON BOOKS are published by
Kensington Publishing Corp.
119 West 40th Street
New York, NY 10018

Special book excerpts or customized printings can also be created to fit specific needs. For details, write or phone the office of the Kensington Sales Manager: Kensington Publishing Corp., 119 West 40th Street, New York, NY 10018. Attn. Sales Department. Phone: 1-800-221-2647.

The K with book logo Reg US Pat. & TM Off.

ISBN: 978-1-4967-3732-8 (ebook)

ISBN: 978-1-4967-3731-1

First Kensington Trade Paperback Printing: April 2024

10 9 8 7 6 5 4 3 2 1

Printed in the United States of America

For my heart-of-gold Dad,
who taught me the meaning of an honest day's work

The Last Con of Lynton Baltimore

Transcript excerpt from Episode 1, "The Duchess"

Salem Durant: And yet you said nothing of what you had discovered about him, of what he had taken from you and your family. Not for months and months.

Duchess Helene-Therese Duchaussoy: This is true. I did not.

Durant: Because you thought he might return? You thought . . . perhaps you thought there would be an explanation for why he'd taken the painting, or an explanation for why he disappeared with it?

Duchaussoy: ::laughs quietly:: There could be no explanation. I said nothing because I was ashamed. I am still ashamed today. I speak to you now because you will speak about me even if I do not.

Durant: Well, we—

Duchaussoy: What is interesting about Thomas—no, not Thomas, of course. I apologize. What is interesting about Mr. Baltimore is not that he steals things from people he claims to love. What is interesting is not even that he disappears. What is interesting is that, when he does, he makes others wish they could disappear, too.

::long pause::

Durant: That is interesting.

Chapter 1

Jess

At first, I think my sister has run away.

I could be forgiven, I think, for the dramatic thought, could be forgiven for jumping to such a conclusion based on nothing more than a silent house, a set of keys missing from the shelf we keep by the front door. It could be something simple, after all: an errand she forgot to tell me she was running, a walk she didn't text to say she was going on.

It could be something totally simple.

But it's like I said.

I could be forgiven.

"Teeg?" I call out for the second time, but I know she's not here.

I can *feel* she's not here.

I take a breath through my nose, willing myself to settle, to ignore an old, familiar ache in the pit of my stomach.

It isn't that, I tell myself firmly, but still, as I move through the kitchen, my eyes dart unconsciously to the small, round table where Tegan and I ate dinner together last night. Where my mom and I used to eat dinner together every night.

There's no envelope there.

I close my eyes and shake my head.

I could be forgiven for checking.

When I open my eyes again, I'm more settled, more present. It's like that moment when you come fully back to reality after waking up, startled, from a bad dream. *I'm in my bed,* you think. *That wasn't real at all.* I remember that Tegan and I—despite the strange tension of the last couple of months, despite the big transition both of us are facing—had a great night last night, the best we've had in weeks.

There's no reason there'd be an envelope.

I let out a quiet scoff. It's private self-deprecation for my anxiety chased by a pang of sadness: not even three months from now, Tegan will be away at college, and I'll be walking into an empty house every day.

I'd better get used to it.

I clock the empty popcorn bowl and glasses we left on the coffee table last night. I'd fallen asleep on the couch, two-and-a-half episodes in to whatever season of *Friends* Tegan was currently streaming, and when she'd poked me awake a couple hours later she'd smiled and called me an old lady. I'd laughed and told her I wouldn't argue, since I could remember the days when *Friends* was on reruns after I got home from school. I'd waved her away from cleaning up and we'd both shuffled to bed, and before I shut off my light she'd called to me from her room.

"Love you, Jess," she'd said, and I'd felt a little clutch of emotion gather in my throat. It was good to hear her say it. I'd started to think—what with her sullen, sometimes sharp attitude lately—that maybe she didn't anymore.

In my bathroom, I find easily what I came all the way back home for, barely five minutes after arriving at work: my best pair of shears, the ones that hardly ever leave my station at the salon. That'd been, really, how last night's unexpected girls' night had started: yesterday I was halfway through my day, taking a quick break while a client's hair was processing, and I'd checked my phone to find two messages from Tegan, a voice note followed by a string of prayer-hands emojis.

"Jessieeeeeeeee," she'd whined cheerfully, in a way I hadn't heard her do in forever. In a way I'd smiled to realize I'd missed. "You have *got* to do something about these ends! It has to be tonight! I won't be able to *stand* it! Please, *please?* I know you hate cutting hair at home but what if!"—she paused dramatically—"I make you your favorite egg sandwich in exchange?"

I texted her back an eye-roll emoji for the begging and a thumbs-up for the request.

The truth was, I would've done it without the egg sandwich, which was actually not my favorite anything, but it was the only food Tegan could competently make, and I always made a big deal of praising her for it.

I made a big deal of it last night, too.

I pick up the shears, preparing to tuck them into their sleeve, but then . . .

Then I pause, that anxious, ominous feeling pulsing through me again.

It has to be tonight, she said on her voice note, and I didn't even think her hair was that desperate for a trim. I've never let it get unhealthy looking, not in all the ten years I've been taking care of her.

I swallow, drifting out of the bathroom with the shears held loosely in my suddenly clammy palm, snippets of Tegan's steady stream of cheerful, casual chatter from last night coming back to me. My nail polish color, her new favorite song. How the mail guy talks loudly on his phone every time he walks up the front stoop to our box. Tegan training a new co-worker at the coffee house where she's worked part-time for the last two summers.

But also:

What time do you work 'til tomorrow?

Have you by any chance seen my laptop sleeve?

I probably won't see you before you leave for work; I'm totally going to sleep in.

Love you, Jess.

It reminds me of something.

Her bedroom door is open, and I hesitate before I peek in.

I picture an envelope again. This time, left for me on a bed, or a nightstand. Maybe a small desk I saved for and assembled myself.

She wouldn't, I think. *She's not Mom.*

But when I finally gather my courage and look, I could be forgiven for thinking she is.

WHAT's clear is that she hasn't gone yet.

First of all, there's no envelope.

But there is a suitcase on the bed, looking fully packed, still unzipped. There's Tegan's faded, worn backpack resting alongside it. There's her open laptop on that desk I labored over, its screen dark in sleep, its power cord already coiled for storage. That sleeve I told her she could find in the front closet ready beside it.

Maybe she's written me an email, instead.

For a few seconds, I simply gape at the scene in front of me; I try to make some other sense of it. Maybe it's some kind of weird practice run for the only trip we have planned for this summer—the one where we'll get her set up at school.

But even I know a single suitcase and backpack isn't how a dorm move-in is meant to look.

My phone pings in my back pocket, and I rush to pull it out.

Sorry to bother you, it reads. **But your 10:30 showed up early. Should I tell her you're on your way? Sorry again, I know you're rushing!!**

I blink down at the text from Ellie, who runs the front desk and does shampoos sometimes when we're shorthanded. She's twenty years old and she's only worked at the salon for a month

and a half, and the two *sorrys* are typical. I'm quiet at work—
quiet everywhere, really—and I'm pretty sure Ellie thinks that
means I don't like her.

My reply won't help.

Cancel morning appts, I type out with shaky fingers, pressing send.

Anyone else, I know, would add something. An explanation,
an apology. *Family emergency*, anyone else might say, to make
sure everyone knew it was serious.

But I haven't been anyone else in ten years.

And no one gets to know about my emergencies.

I navigate to my text box with Tegan, but before I send out a
panicky **Where are you?** I pause and swipe to my email instead.

Just to make sure there's not an envelope waiting for me
there.

What loads, though, is the usual—a notification about auto-
payment on the electric bill, a promise for the sale of the season
at a place where I haven't shopped in years, a reminder from
one of my streamers that I still have episodes left on a mediocre
medical drama I gave up on a few weeks ago.

My heart is pounding in my ears.

Or . . . is that not my heart?

I press send on my text to Tegan as I move toward the sound
of knocking at the front door, and like so many other things
I've come across this morning, it could be nothing; it could be
totally innocuous. An inconveniently timed delivery or a sales
pitch for faster internet service.

But I don't really know if I'm really *in* this morning. Instead
my brain is a hot stew of a Sunday night when I was twelve years
old and a Saturday afternoon when I was twenty-one. My head
is full of the steam it lets off.

Tegan left, too, that steam whispers, even as I unlock the door.
*Everything you did, all the attention you paid. You missed it happen-
ing again.*

I know deep down that whatever is waiting for me on the

other side of the door will somehow have something to do with that laptop, that backpack, that open suitcase on the bed.

I just don't expect it to be a giant.

I gape at the man who seems to take up the entirety of my front porch, my stewy brain slow to process the sheer size of him, broad and muscular. Maybe that's why I take in his face, first: sandy-blond-stubbled and unsmiling, his jaw sharp-edged and his brow lowered in confusion. His green eyes narrow as they take me in.

He has to be at least six-five. He looks like he throws truck tires for recreation. Like maybe he throws the trucks themselves. I have never seen a man this built in real life.

But his voice is unexpectedly high-pitched.

"Hi! We're looking for Jess Greene?"

"What?" I say, blinking at him.

That's when I realize his voice is not, in fact, high-pitched. Or at least I don't know if it is, because he has not actually spoken. He's not alone.

Beside him—I could be forgiven for missing her—is a middle-aged woman whose head barely reaches the top of the giant's elbow. She has a mass of silver-brown curls and she is wearing black-framed glasses that are competing for size with her companion's massive biceps.

I cannot imagine—head full of steam or not—what these two people have to do with Tegan.

Or wait. With me.

I'm the one narrowing my eyes now, at the woman in the glasses.

"Who's asking?"

The giant shifts on his feet. The woman smiles. My phone pings in my hand.

Tegan, I think immediately, and look down at it. But it's only Ellie again. **Okay, sorry!!!** she's typed, and I recognize it's unfair, but I'm so irritated that she's gotten my hopes up for a reply from my sister that my fingers tighten around the phone in frustration.

I think the woman has started to answer, but I cut her off.

"Look, this isn't a good time. For . . . whatever." I gesture vaguely at them with my frustration phone-fist. I don't even remember when or where I set down the shears, but I don't have them anymore.

The giant's brow-furrow gets deeper, but the woman is undeterred.

"Well, we have an appointment."

"Not with me, you don't."

"Right. We have an appointment with Jess Greene."

That steam in my head—it's spread everywhere now, and I look down, trying desperately to ground myself. The woman's still talking, but I can't hear her. If I could only calm down enough to think straight, or if Tegan would just reply. If there was some sort of explanation for some appointment I don't remember making, if—

". . . Broadside Media, and we've been working with—"

"Wait," I say, something about what the woman has said finally getting through this haze of confusion and fear.

It's something familiar.

Not just *what* she's said, but *how* she's said it. Her voice.

I know that voice. Don't I?

Forget the stew, the steam. I am chilled straight through, remembering a time when I heard that voice—through my headphones, or through the speakers in my old Honda—week after week, on the wildly successful, wildly popular podcast everyone I knew seemed to be listening to.

Eventually—as everything in my life, in my sister's life, was falling apart—I'd thought that voice was somehow speaking directly to me. Pressing closer and closer to those fallen-apart pieces.

I'd never wanted to hear it again.

I look up, and the giant's watching me close. The woman with the familiar voice is waiting, just like I asked her to. In the space between them, behind them, I catch a movement on the driveway, a flash of white fabric, a familiar shock of red hair. Freshly trimmed.

It's my sister, carrying a plastic bag from the pharmacy around the corner, walking toward us quickly, her face flushed. Panicked.

"Jess," Tegan says, and the giant and the woman both turn to face her.

"Jess!" the woman echoes, friendly recognition in her tone.

But then her brow furrows, too, and she looks between us.

"*I'm* Jess," I say to her, at the same time Tegan says, "This is my sister."

The giant and the woman share a brief, concerned look. But she recovers quickly. She volleys her gaze between me and Tegan again and says, "Interesting," and my *God*, it is her. I'd recognize the way she said that word anywhere.

She used to say it at least once an episode.

Salem Durant. The woman whose hugely popular podcast series ended up being about something way too close for comfort.

Something way too close to home.

I've been working all these years to keep it far, far away. Especially from Tegan.

My sister and I speak over each other again. Me with a sharp, desperate, "There's obviously been a mistake," and her with a determined, unapologetic, "I can explain."

Salem Durant smiles again. A cat that got the cream. A story that just became twice as interesting.

She says, "I've come to talk to you about your mother."

Chapter 2

Adam

It's a shame I haven't learned to trust my instincts.

Because I had a feeling something was off.

Since last night, for sure, when we got off the plane here and I got recognized for the first time. It wasn't necessarily unusual given my past, but still felt like a bad omen for this particular trip, when I'm working so hard to put some distance between then and now.

Since six days ago, when Salem announced these travel plans in the first place, a light in her eyes I'd heard about from others, but hadn't once seen in all the months I'd been working with her, had appeared.

Since two months ago, when I first read a short email sent to the Broadside Media pitch account, promising new information on a story that was almost ten years old.

A story I knew Salem had never forgotten.

I had a feeling—even as I forwarded that email along—that there was something strange about it.

But instincts, I'd told myself, were not for thirty-three-year-old recent grads from J-School. They were for people further along in this career than me, for journalists who've been around on the actual job and who've seen more than I have. Instincts without experience, one of my professors once said to me, were a liability.

Salem has always been known for her good instincts.

Except on this story, I guess, which is why it's a shame I still don't trust mine.

Too late now.

There's a heavy silence between the four of us. The redhead who's just come up the driveway—the young woman Salem and I have known as Jess Greene for the last two months—is swallowing heavily as she stares at the woman who opened the door. Her sister, apparently, and also, apparently, the real Jess Greene.

Salem still has that light in her eyes, and for a second I wonder if she had an instinct something was off, too. If in fact we're here because of that instinct.

She speaks first, calm and unbothered. "May we come in?"

"No," says Jess, her voice sharp, impatient, and I can't help but look at her again. When she first opened the door, I'd had an instinct, all right, but it wasn't a professional one. I'd felt a strange thunk in my chest at the sight of her: big, blue eyes and the thickest blond hair I've ever seen, wavy and reaching well past her shoulders. Against her clothes—a loose black T-shirt, slim black jeans, black sneakers—everything light about her had been a curious sort of shock.

"Jess," says the other woman, the redhead, the person whose *name* we don't even know, and it at least pulls me back into the moment. A source who's deceived us, who's given us information that's probably useless to us now. This might be Salem's story, but I'm not trying to be involved in things she considers a failure.

I'm trying to impress her.

"Let them in," the redhead says. "I'll exp—"

Jess cuts her off. "Explain why you have a bag packed?"

The redhead flushes. I saw her a couple of times when I was sitting in while Salem did video calls with her. She looked older on the screen, and I wonder if she somehow altered her appearance for those calls. Worn makeup or clothes that'd make her seem more grown-up. Standing here, I wouldn't guess she is any older than twenty.

This is a disaster.

"Yes," she says, and I transfer my gaze to Jess, which is a mistake, because for a split second, a second that might be imperceptible to everyone on this front stoop but me—she looks as if she might cry. My chest aches. The wrong instinct. I'm supposed to be curious, determined.

I'm supposed to want to figure this out.

"You can explain that without them coming in," she finally says, no trace of tears in her voice.

"I don't think she can," Salem says, and then she turns her eyes on the redhead. Our source. "I think you probably have an explanation to make to me, too."

"Don't talk to her like that," Jess snaps.

Salem raises her hands in surrender. I cross my arms and look down at my boots. Maybe we ought to give these women some time alone.

The redhead clears her throat.

"Ms. Durant," she says, even though she's been calling her Salem for the last two months. "My name is Tegan Caulfield. I know I told you something different. I—"

"Are you recording this?" Jess says.

"No," I say, and Salem cuts me a look. I don't know why I answered. My job here isn't really to talk, at least not yet.

"We are not," Salem says pointedly, and I'm pretty sure some of the tone there is directed at me. She looks at Tegan. "Go on."

I expect Jess to intervene again, but whether it's shock or curiosity or some combination of the two, she doesn't, not yet.

"Jess is my sister. My half sister. I contacted you using her name because two months ago, I was still seventeen years old."

Oh, Christ. My fingers dig into my biceps. Salem betrays nothing. In my periphery, I think I can see Jess's chest rising and falling with quick breaths.

"But I'm eighteen now. And the information I've given you is good. It's—"

"Absolutely not," Jess says, finally speaking again. When I look at her, I can tell she's straightened her posture. She's lifted her chin, too. But her cheeks are flushed, same as her sister's. "Whatever this is, we're not doing it. You two need to go. Tegan, you need to come inside."

It's a knee-jerk, desperate response; I can tell. She feels powerless, confused, caught off guard. We may not have come for her, but whether she knows it or not, Salem's already thinking of her as a source, too. And Salem is good at cultivating sources. She's good at calmly sharing what she already knows; she's good at making every bit of the story she's working on seem like it's in the public interest.

People say you can't stonewall Salem Durant.

But I have a feeling Jess Greene might be an exception.

"I'm happy to share with you—" Salem begins, but Jess shakes her head.

"I don't know what my sister has told you. But whatever it is, it's a mistake. She doesn't know—"

"Jess," Tegan says, and if there were traces of regret or apology in her voice, she's stripped them out now. She sounds as harsh and as hard as her sister did only a second ago. She sounds angry.

For an uncomfortable stretch, the two stare at each other. This strange arrangement—the four of us standing here— we're a broken compass. Tegan and Jess at two poles, north and south. Salem and I, east and west. The needle spins frantically around, disoriented by all this tension.

Then Tegan speaks. "I found Mom's postcards."

I watch Jess turn white.

"And I know you know where she is."

Jess swallows. She tightens her fingers around her phone. And then she says, "You'd better come in."

My guess is, these two don't often have company.

The house is small, tidy, and spare. The round table in the eat-in kitchen where we stand has four chairs, but it probably only sits two comfortably. In the next room, there's a couch, but it's the kind an ex-girlfriend of mine used to have in her studio apartment, the kind where I alone would take over half the thing even if I stayed fully upright. Outside, through the sliding glass door off the living room, there's a small deck: two chairs, a tiny table in between.

I'm used to feeling huge in a space, but this is next level. Salem and I don't just seem like we've made it crowded; we seem like we've made it somehow unsafe. I shove my hands in my pockets, sweat blooming on my lower back.

I look over to where Jess stands by the counter, her arms crossed. Peeking out from beneath the sleeve of her T-shirt, I can see a network of thin, black lines—tattoos I'm too curious about. I caught myself, when she stepped back from the front door and I gestured for Salem and Tegan to go in before me, trying to make eye contact with her. Like I could somehow apologize for how upset she looked.

There's no reason for me to be noticing her tattoos, no reason to be apologizing.

I shift my gaze toward Salem.

"Shall we sit?" my boss says confidently, gesturing toward the table.

Tegan moves quickly toward it, pulling out a chair. "Oh, yeah—sorry! We should definitely sit."

I realize Tegan doesn't just look younger than she did on

those video calls. She sounds younger, too. Like she'd really become someone else during them. I'm sure Salem's already clocked the irony, given the story we've come to track down.

Salem and Tegan settle at the table, and at first, Jess stays put, her expression mulish. When her sister and my boss both lift their hands and clasp them atop the table's surface, though, looking as if they're settling in for a negotiation, Jess seems to break, resigned. She drops her arms and joins them.

Salem looks over at me meaningfully. She has to be kidding. There's no way I'll fit at that table. My knees will probably jam into all three of them.

"I'll stand," I say, and take up the spot by the counter Jess vacated.

"Why don't we start with introductions?" Salem says. "I'm—"

"I know who you are," Jess says. "Obviously Tegan knows, too. Let's skip that."

Salem glides right over this, gesturing to me. "This is my colleague, Adam Hawkins. Everyone calls him Hawk."

I try not to wince. She's not wrong, but I've never much liked the nickname. I used to try to correct people about it, but other than my family, only Cope ever listened.

But now's not really the time to think about that. Not until we get through this story.

So I nod in acknowledgment of the introduction, grateful that neither of them seem to recognize my name, and refocus.

I know what happens next matters: I know I'm about to see a side of Salem I haven't had a chance to yet, and I know it's an opportunity to learn. On her initial calls and video chats with Jess—no wait, Tegan—things were different. Sure, she wanted the information, but it was Tegan coming to her, not the other way around. Salem was friendly but cautious. In control. The addition of Jess—the *real* Jess—means she needs to change tactics if she wants to keep that control.

She looks directly at Jess. "Your sister has shared with me information about five postcards your mother sent to you in the months after she disappeared." She pauses briefly, then adds, "We believe with a man named Lynton Baltimore."

Jess's hands aren't clasped on the table; they're hidden in her lap. But I get the sense she's clutching them together all the same.

"I don't know where she is," Jess says, more to her sister than to Salem. "I don't."

"But you did, once. And you never told me," Tegan says. "Five different times you knew."

Salem watches them carefully, and it's strange, the pang of judgment I feel. I'm watching carefully, too, after all. I'm her shadow; I'm supposed to be learning this, and it's a privilege to be learning it from Salem Durant. Being a journalist as skilled as she is—this is what I've set out to do.

This is what I *need* to do.

"I won't talk about that now. Not in front of them," Jess says to her sister, before looking back at Salem. "We don't want to talk to the media."

"*I* want to talk to them," Tegan says, angry again. "I've *been* talking to them. I told them about Mom, and about Miles Daniels. Or Lynton Baltimore, I guess, whatever. I already *told* them."

Jess's eyes close briefly, and my chest aches again, so much that I have to look away. But Salem catches my eye, and man— those instincts. If they took a hiatus during her time talking to Tegan Caulfield, they're fully checked back in now, because I can tell she's seen me watching Jess. I can tell she somehow knows about that aching.

This job is about the truth, Hawk, she said to me a few months ago, when I'd first told her about my idea, the one that got me pursuing this career in the first place. *I'm not saying it's not about other things, too. But the truth has to be first, even when it's about your best friend. You need to figure out if you'll be able to tell it.*

I straighten, the memory of those words a talisman, a discipline. I cross to the table, pull out the last chair. I move it far away from the table, sparing everyone my knees. It creaks when I sit, but I don't cringe.

I'll be able to tell it.

This Lynton Baltimore story is just practice. A test.

Salem sits back in her chair, as though she's welcoming me into the fold.

"We don't want to intrude on a private family discussion," she says gently, and I know that's a tactic, too. She's not going to *let* Jess Greene stonewall her, not today, because she's not going to ask anything of her.

Not yet.

"It's clear that this is a shock, so let me sum up. Then Hawk and I will leave you to your discussion."

"But—" Tegan protests, a note of fear in her voice, because she can't tell this is a strategy. She's worried Salem's giving up on her.

"About ten years ago," Salem says, as though Tegan hasn't spoken. Right now, she's only talking to Jess. "I released a serialized podcast about a confidence man named Lynton Baltimore. You're aware of it?"

Jess swallows. A single, nearly imperceptible nod. I ignore the ache.

"So, you know that the final episode of the show was meant to be an in-person interview between me and this man, following his release from prison."

Jess doesn't bother nodding this time.

"And you're also aware that he never showed up for this interview."

"Because he came here," Tegan says, and I watch Jess's throat bob again. "He came here and met Mom."

"And then, sometime after that," Salem adds, keeping her attention fully on Jess, "He seems to have simply disappeared."

"*With* Mom," Tegan says, obviously bruised about not having Salem's full attention.

"We don't know that," says Jess.

"The postcards your sister found suggest—" Salem says.

"They don't. They don't say anything about Lynton Baltimore."

"Well," Salem says. "They wouldn't, would they?"

It's the first time Salem's cool politeness has slipped. Probably Jess and Tegan don't hear it, the edge of frustration in her voice, but I do. I know from these last couple of months that this is one of those *other things* for Salem, something beyond just truth-seeking for her story. She's never really forgotten it, that she's the namesake of her famous podcast.

As far as the world knows, Salem Durant—prepped and waiting for an interview with a man who never showed—is the last con of Lynton Baltimore.

She clears her throat.

"We want to find out the truth about him," she says, gentling her voice again. "About where he's been for all these years. We think your mother might be the key to that."

"Well, it's like I said," Jess says, new determination in her voice. She wants us out. "I don't know where she is. So we can't help you."

"We're going to find her," Tegan blurts, hasty and overloud, and Salem purses her lips. I can tell she was hoping to make a graceful exit before this part came up. "We've planned it all out."

"We're still working out the details," Salem clarifies, but that's a stretch. Out in the rental car, there's a binder of details that I put together. Maps, itineraries, contact information for a few leads. There's also the detail that Salem and I are scheduled to be out of the office for the next month, working on this story.

Jess ignores Salem and stares at her sister. I don't know if I've ever seen a face like hers—it's like looking through a window at a storm. There's rain, lightning, wind; there're trees bending and shaking with the force of it. Part of you is glad to be separate from it.

But part of you wants to press against the glass and get as close as you can.

"That's why you have a bag packed?" she says.

Tegan nods, but doesn't meet her sister's eyes.

"Were you going to tell me?"

There's a long, laden pause.

"I was going to leave a note."

That storm I'm watching on Jess Greene's face—it's a gale force in her eyes. I wonder if Salem is bending under its strength, too.

I brace myself, because what follows this can only be a crash, an explosion. A tree limb down, a transformer blown.

I think Jess Greene is about to lose her grip on the temper she's been holding since she opened the door to us, and something down deep inside me shifts. Maybe I was detached from this story before; maybe I was simply going along with whatever tasks my boss assigned me. Impress her and move on to the story I truly want to tell.

Right now, though? Right now I want the truth of this storm about as bad as I've ever wanted the truth of anything.

But I know the truth isn't so easy.

And I know Jess Greene doesn't want us—or her sister—to have it.

So instead of showing us her temper, she pushes back her chair and stands calmly from the table, saying nothing.

And then, she leaves.

The Last Con of Lynton Baltimore

Transcript excerpt from Episode 6, "The Sister"

::indistinct chatter fades in::

Durant: Do you have cream?

::sound of a refrigerator opening::

Gillian Baltimore: Milk'll have to do.

Durant: That's fine; thanks.

::sounds of dishes clinking, liquid pouring, the dulled honk of a car horn::

Gillian Baltimore: Well, I guess I'm ready, if you are.

Durant: Let's go back a ways, to start. Were you close with your brother, growing up?

[**Durant, voice-over:** You can't see it, but that was a shrug, a noncommittal one. I might even describe it as bored, and the truth is, on the surface, Gillian Baltimore seems bored by everything, including me. At this point, I don't have high hopes for our interview. I wonder if Lynton Baltimore's sister will prove to be as elusive as he is, even though I'm sitting right next to her.]

Durant: You two are close in age, though, only a year apart. Did you have a lot in common?

Gillian Baltimore: ::snorts:: Lyn didn't have anything in common with anyone. ::pauses:: Or I guess he had everything in common with everyone. It really depended.

Durant: Depended on what?

Gillian Baltimore: Probably on what he thought he could get out of you.

Durant: Mm.

Gillian Baltimore: You have any brothers or sisters?

Durant: I don't, no.

Gillian Baltimore: I'll tell you, then. They sure can break your heart. They sure can.

Chapter 3

Jess

It isn't as though I can go far. It isn't as though I would.

But I do make it out the back door, across our small, slightly shaggy lawn. I stomp through the fresh-cut grass of three neighbors' yards, and as I go, I imagine each of them watching. The stay-at-home mom in the split level on the phone with a friend, probably saying, "Oh my God, it's that rude woman who lives next door to me; she *never* wants to chat." The older couple in the colonial with all the garden gnomes, wondering if I'm some kind of daytime burglar. Those people on the corner lot who put out a political sign I deeply disagree with last year, probably lamenting the mere sight of a woman in pants walking around unattended.

None of them could have any idea of how it feels inside my head. My heart.

When I emerge from a side yard out onto the sidewalk, I stop, realizing my breath is labored, and I think of bending over, of setting my hands on my knees to recover. But it's not the walk that's done this to me. It's the shock, the fear. The throbbing hole of hurt I felt inside me when Tegan said it out loud.

She was going to leave me a *note*.

I push my fingers through my hair, clasp them together on top of my head. Surely staying upright is better. Staying upright is what I've always done.

I turn back to face the direction of my house, but I stay where I am for the moment. I don't think she'll leave now, mostly because I don't think Salem Durant and the giant—*Hawk*, she called him, and he watched me like one, brooding and silent and *knowing*—would take her with them. They might not feel as hurt as I do, but I'm sure they have to regroup. I'm sure they have to think about what it means that they'd been planning to take a teenager out to find Lynton Baltimore.

To find our mother.

I don't know how long I stand there, letting it wash over me, what's happened this morning. It isn't as though I spent the last ten years with Tegan fearing this *specific* thing—Tegan stealing my identity to contact Salem Durant? To plan a road trip with her and her—I don't know what, bodyguard?—but it isn't as though I haven't feared something similar. I've always worried someone would find out about the link between our mother and Lynton Baltimore. That if they did, Tegan and I would become the subject of the sort of rampant, reckless attention and speculation that followed so many of the people featured in Durant's podcast—Baltimore's family, his network of fellow grifters, and, most of all, his victims. The people he stole from, the people he conned. For months after the final episode aired, there were follow-up stories about them, intrusive and unnecessary, and every single one would make my gut churn with dread.

What if someone realizes, I'd think. *What if someone—one of those amateur online sleuths—realizes that your mother is somewhere out there with Lynton Baltimore right now? What if they turn you and Tegan into some piece of cheap entertainment?*

And I worried, too, of course, that Tegan herself would realize it. I worried about those five postcards I could never bring myself to throw away, all of them sent to me in the first six months after my mother left Tegan in my care.

But I thought I'd have more time before I'd have to tell her.

Or maybe I thought, when it came to this, that I could somehow stop time altogether.

I think of Tegan, eight years old. Sitting on the carpet in the living room of the house we still live in, the braid in her hair loose and sagging, her shoulders pink from the sun. She'd been playing with her favorite Barbie, having missed it all day while I'd taken her to the state fair. She'd practically run right to it when I brought her inside.

And I'd stood in the kitchen, my hands shaking as I opened the envelope our mother left for me.

Same as the one she'd left for my dad, nine years before—the first time she disappeared from my life.

It's that thought that gets me moving again—back toward the house, but now, I take the long way around. I don't think about whether any neighbors are watching me. Instead I think about the same thing I've thought about ever since I was twenty-one years old, ever since I opened that envelope.

Tegan.

Protecting Tegan, taking care of Tegan.

Never disappearing on Tegan the way Mom disappeared on me.

THERE'S no car in the driveway when I get back, not that I remember if there was one when I first opened the door to Tegan's . . . guests, co-conspirators, whatever. But the garage is still open from when I first came home, thinking this was just a regular morning where I'd made a simple mistake. Forgetting a pair of shears, not missing all the signs that my sister has spent the last two months on the precipice of blowing up our quiet, private lives.

I take a deep breath before I walk in.

She's standing at the fridge, getting out a can of water, and I think that's so insulting, for some reason. Drinking a sparkling water at a time like this.

"They left?" I say, clipped.

She pops the top on the can and takes a sip. "For now."

She carries her drink over to the table and sits in the same place she sat only moments ago. Before, when it was the four of us here, she seemed nervous, frantic, eager to please. But now, with only me, she's transformed, and it's not into the sullen, sometimes sharp teenager she's often been over the last few months—behavior that I guess now makes more sense, given that she found the postcards. No, this Tegan is different. She seems . . .

She seems so confident.

So grown.

Maybe impersonating a thirty-one-year-old will do that to a person.

It's that thought that propels me forward, newly desperate to get answers. I settle across from her, clasping my hands together on the table's surface until I realize that's the same posture Salem Durant took up. I immediately reposition, crossing my arms.

I take another breath.

"Teeg," I say, before I realize that I don't even know where to begin. I settle for a simple, stunned, "*How?*"

She flicks at the tab on her water can, and it's a curious sort of relief to see her fidget. She presses her lips together and rolls them inward, a habit she's always had when she's trying hard at something. This is how she looked when she flipped my egg sandwich last night. I'd thought it was sweet.

She shrugs. "I set up an email account. I sent an email."

"Using my name."

The *ping* of that can top again. "You kind of made it easy."

I blink across the table at her. "*I* made it easy?"

It's a ridiculous thing to say. Anyone who's ever dared criticize how I've raised Tegan over the last decade has always said the same thing: that I'm overprotective, that I helicopter, that I never learned, as she got older, to let go a little. I ask her too many questions about her day; I pry about the details; I'm vigilant about monitoring her social media. Sure, Tegan has more independence now, is alone when I go to work, but I still always—

But that's not the point, I know. Not now.

"How did I make it easy?" I say, gentling my voice as best I can.

She takes another sip of water before speaking again.

"They weren't really going to be able to check easily if I was you. You don't have any social media. No photo on the salon website. You won't even get into other people's pictures."

That last part, she's said with an edge. I remember the evening of her senior prom a couple of months ago, a gathering in the gorgeous front yard of one of her friend's parents' houses. Photo after photo of parents flanking their kids, getting in their own shots before dates and friend groups started being the focus.

I'd hung back, tried not to be overly blunt as I passed on well-meaning offers to photograph Tegan and me. We'd already taken a few selfies together back at the house.

As always, I'd asked her not to share them anywhere.

I stare at her, my stomach uneasy. The irony of my obsession with privacy backfiring on me in this way.

I don't like my photo taken because I think I look so much like my mom.

Because someone might see me, and connect me with her. Connect me with Lynton Baltimore.

"But you're . . . you're a *teenager.* How did they—"

She lifts her chin. "I look mature for my age."

Something on my face must show my doubt. I'm sure I'm biased, given that I've raised her, but Tegan doesn't look any older than she is. Some days I still see the face of that eight-year-old in her, playing with her favorite Barbie before she realized Mom had gone.

"I wore a lot of makeup. And I downloaded a filter for my webcam that helped."

I shake my head, ignoring a wave of nausea, of guilt. I guess I haven't helicoptered enough. Been vigilant enough.

"But when they got here, of course they were going to see—"

"I just needed to get them here," she interrupts. "I needed to turn eighteen, and I needed to get them here. I knew—I *know* they'll take me anyway."

I lean forward in my chair, setting my elbows on the table and running my hands through my hair, bowing my head. "Teeg. You can't—"

"I don't know why you're getting to ask *me* questions," she says sharply. "Now that you know about this, maybe you should answer some of mine."

When I look up at her, she's shoved her can away, putting her elbows on the table, too. But she's not sagging into it the way I am.

She's pressing in. Determined and angry.

"Did you know Mom disappeared with Lynton Baltimore?"

"No," I answer quickly, but then I pause. I'm giving her the answer I would've given to Salem Durant, had she asked the question so directly.

I swallow. "Not at first, no."

Tegan interrupts with a scoff, as if it'd be ridiculous for me to finish, to say I'm not sure.

She's so confident in this, so certain. I have a terrible thought. Did he contact her somehow? Did Mom?

"How do you know about him?"

For a second, I think she won't answer. I think she'll say, *I'm asking the questions now.*

But finally she gives in.

"A couple months ago, I read a listicle online. 'Best True Crime Podcasts of the Last Decade.'"

A fucking *listicle*. *"Best" True Crime.* What a world.

Of course, I'd listened to Salem Durant's podcast, too.

I was *entertained* by it.

"*The Last Con of Lynton Baltimore* was on it, with . . . there was a photo of him. His mug shot."

I know that photo. It was featured on the podcast's title card. Black and white, a little grainy. I never connected that photo with the man I knew as Miles Daniels until later. He hadn't looked the same to me, not even a little, which I guess was the point.

And anyway, I only met him a couple of times, always briefly. "Brief" was basically all I'd allow when it came to time with my mother back then.

"I recognized him," Tegan says. "I knew right away. That was Miles."

If I thought the guilt was bad before . . . it's nothing to hearing my sister say this, to the reminder of how I was mostly absent from Tegan's life for those last few months before Mom left. Tegan would've been around Lynton Baltimore all the time, because my mother wanted Miles Daniels around all the time.

I stand from my chair, restless and newly nauseated.

"And then I just . . . I don't know. I got curious. I listened to the episodes. I worked out the timeline. Mom met Miles a month after Lynton Baltimore got out of prison and ghosted Salem Durant."

I don't know if I nod. For a few seconds, I don't know if I do anything other than clutch at the counter I've found myself at, right in front of the kitchen sink. I flip on the tap, run my wrist under the cool water. I'm desperate to get rid of this hot, sick feeling. Ten years I've spent, being the best I could for Tegan. Responsible, protective, *present*. Only to be undone by my paranoia over my photograph being taken and a callous listicle. Undone by my past absence.

When I flip the water off again and look up, she's watching

me. Waiting for me, I guess, so she can be sure I'm paying attention to her for this next part.

"And then I went looking through your things. Mom's things."

She reaches beneath her chair and grabs at the backpack I saw on her bed when I first came home. From it she pulls a plastic zippered pouch, pale pink with a gold *T* on the bottom left corner. Before she graduated she kept pencils inside it. I ordered it for her last summer.

She takes out the five postcards and sets them on the table. They still curl slightly from the way I'd stored them.

She arranges them like we're about to play some kind of game. Match these cards to a terrible memory, maybe, and I could do that easily. Every one of those cards came on a day I was drowning: when I was washing Tegan's sheets for the third time in a week because she'd wet the bed again. When I was arguing with my dad and my stepmom, Bernila, for even gently suggesting I let someone else take care of Tegan. When I was sick with shingles—stress, the doctor at the urgent care had said—gasping with pain every time my T-shirt rubbed against my back. When Tegan's principal suggested she be held back a grade. When the state social worker came for a scheduled home visit and interview, an expression like she'd smelled something bad on her face the whole time.

"You did more than go looking," I say, because they weren't simply put away. They weren't with any of the other things Mom left behind, which I'd boxed up carefully and stored in the garage. They weren't with things I considered personal—a memory box from high school, my bank information, the advance directive and will I had done when I officially became Tegan's guardian.

I'd *hidden* those postcards.

"Inside a curtain rod," she says. "Smart."

God. She makes me sound like a criminal. Like I'm Lynton Baltimore himself.

"I planned to tell you about them."

"*When?*" She slaps her hand on the table, and the cards scatter. Two on the floor. Three to the edges of the table.

"Don't talk to me like that," I say, because . . . don't I have to? Don't I have to be in charge here? Don't I have to somehow take control of this, the way a parent should?

She stands from her chair quickly, nearly knocking it over. She points down at the cards.

"She talks about me." Her voice is shaking with tears, with rage. With some combination of the two. "She said she was thinking about me."

"And I told you that, Teeg. I never kept that from you."

"You know that's not what I mean."

I *do* know. I told her things like, *I know Mom thinks of you all the time,* or *I'm sure she's missing you.* I told her those things as if they were an obligation, a hope, a probability. But I never told her the specific things in those cards, things that I thought were painful and selfish and so grossly detached from the mess Mom had left behind. That selfishness, that detachment—*that* was the mom Tegan had been too young to truly see.

I'm sure you're doing fine with Tegan. I saw wild horses the other day! I know she loves horses.

"You have to understand. That time, after she left—that was such a hard time. It was confusing for both of us, and—"

"I'm not a kid anymore!" she shouts, and there's a unique pain to this. To know how fully she means it, and to know that, to me, it's so fully untrue. Isn't she still a kid? Haven't I worked so hard in order that she could stay one?

But seeing my sister like this, her light eyes like fire, her delicate skin flushed with frustration—it's the first time in all these years I've felt, down deep, that all the work I did was wrong. That I messed up, miscalculated. That my choice to not tell her about those postcards—about my suspicion that the man we knew as our mother's boyfriend was someone else—was the worst one I could have made.

That it would push her straight toward the things I've tried to protect her from.

"Salem is giving me a chance," she says. "To find out all the things you never told me."

That cuts like a knife. Right down the center of me.

"Tegan," I say, my voice strangled. "There's not—I don't *know* where she is. I didn't tell you about the postcards, but there's nothing else. I've never heard anything else."

It's true, but I can see that right now, to her, it doesn't matter. I've betrayed her. Failed her. She trusts Salem Durant and a man named Hawk more than she trusts me, and I guess, when it comes to this, that's what I deserve.

"I'm going with them, Jess. And if they don't want me to go anymore, that's fine. I'll go by myself."

"You can't."

She bends down and calmly gathers the two postcards from the floor. Reaches across the table and slides the other three toward her, stacks them all in a tidy pile, zips them back into her pouch. She clutches it tight as she looks at me.

"I'm an adult now. So I definitely can."

For long minutes after she walks away from me, down the hall to her bedroom—where she shuts the door firmly behind her—I stare at the spot where she stood. Stare at the spaces where those postcards were set and then scattered.

I cannot let this happen.

I cannot let Tegan go on some podcast-sponsored road trip with Salem Durant without someone there to look after her.

I cannot let her go out there by herself, either.

And I cannot—I could *never*—let her face our mother alone. Even if I doubt whether she'll ever find her.

So I stare at that table for a little bit longer, until it settles into me what I know I have to do.

Protect Tegan. Take care of Tegan.

Never disappear on her, even if—right now—I've made her wish that I would.

Chapter 4

Adam

The morning after I first meet Jess Greene, I make my way over to a small diner that's barely a block away from the slightly shabby, slightly suspect hotel Salem and I booked yesterday.

It's vaguely familiar, this particular end of town, not all that far from the Horseshoe, where I played two of my best college games. But there's Ohio State gear pretty much everywhere you look, signs of the proximity to campus, and I admit, it's adding to the uneasiness I've already been feeling about how things went yesterday. I don't have a problem with this place or this campus or that stadium specifically, but of course I've got problems with all the stuff it reminds me of.

Cope, mostly, and all the reasons he's gone.

I take a breath through the pang of grief I feel and decide the diner's a nice opportunity. I'll get a stack of pancakes in Cope's honor. We always ate pancakes after a big win.

Not that anything that has happened in the last twenty-four hours could be described as a win.

When I open the door to the diner, I see Salem's already

there, in a booth at the back. She's got her glasses on top of her head while she looks down at her phone, her thumbs moving rapid-fire across the screen. She's probably writing, or maybe texting her husband. At her elbow is a cup of coffee I bet she thinks is too weak.

When I sit, she doesn't acknowledge me beyond pushing a plastic menu across the table's surface and saying, "The coffee's basically water."

I know better than trying to open a conversation with her while she's on her phone, but the truth is, I'm not sure I have anything worthwhile to say. Yesterday, after Tegan Caulfield sent us away with promises to be in touch as soon as she "got things settled" with her sister, Salem and I made our way to a nearby café to regroup, but that basically amounted to the decision to take the rest of the day off while we waited to hear something. Unless Salem's holding out on me, we still haven't, and I can't decide whether I'm relieved or disappointed.

Because I know I've been thinking too much about Jess Greene.

That blast of blond hair. Those lines on her arm. That look on her face.

It's the look that's haunted me the most, though I'll admit— in a weak moment last night, as I scrubbed a small amount of hotel shampoo through my short hair, I wondered if a woman with a head of hair like hers would have to use the whole bottle. Since that line of thinking involved a someone I don't know taking a shower, I'd been pretty mad at myself, but it's not as if returning my curiosity to that storm in her eyes had made me feel any better.

If anything, after seeing her leave her own house the way she did, it made me feel worse. Like I was being predatory, intrusive. Uncaring.

I'm trying to pursue the kind of journalism that's the opposite of that.

Maybe I should tell Salem we ought to leave these two sisters alone.

But by the time the server comes over, she's still ignoring me in favor of her phone, so I pass on the offer of coffee and order a stack of blueberry pancakes, extra syrup. The server's waiting for Salem's order so I clear my throat.

Without looking up, she says, "Two eggs, scrambled. Whole-wheat toast."

She's definitely writing.

Guess I'll keep debating with myself then.

I wonder if those tattoos go all the way up to her shoulder, I think, and then clench one of my fists on the table. Obviously that's not a topic I'm meant to be debating.

For the next ten minutes, I avoid my own phone and instead run through the mental catalog I've been keeping about the Baltimore story since I got that first email from . . . not-Jess. Back then, I was still getting the lay of the land with Salem, having basically been the last person available for assignment after all the other senior producers at Broadside had picked their preferred staffers for their latest projects. Up until I showed her that email, she'd mostly seemed indifferent to me—to the job in general, if I'm being honest—but after that, she'd barraged me with emails and texts, links to leads and information I should catch up on. One week she dropped ten worn paperbacks on my desk, all of them about famed grifters—Abagnale, Rocancourt, Chikli, Lustig, de Valfierno, more. I'd read them all, and had been interested.

But do I think Lynton Baltimore is the same as those guys? Do I think it matters if he is?

The truth is, I didn't get into this work to do true crime.

Or to make someone hurt like I think we might've hurt those women yesterday.

When our food arrives, Salem finally sets down her phone, but whether she's interested in talking now, I couldn't say, because these pancakes look fucking great. Steaming and fluffy and I'm pretty sure that's real maple syrup covering them.

I'll think about the story later.

Except as soon as I open my mouth to take my first bite, an unfamiliar voice interrupts.

A nervous-sounding, "Hey."

I pause, looking up, my fork midair. I know before the guy speaks again. Salem smirks across the table at me, having already seen a version of this back at the airport.

"You're Adam Hawkins," he says, and then stumbles into an unnecessary correction. "The Hawk."

I set down my fork. Arrange my face into something neutral.

"Hey, man," I say, and hold out my hand. It's a practiced strategy, this offer. If they take it, that usually means it's going to be the good sort of encounter with someone who recognizes me. If they don't, I better brace myself. It'll be the bad sort.

He takes it. Pumps my hand enthusiastically. That's a relief, but it isn't as though I always enjoy the good sort, either.

"Oh, wow. Oh, wow."

I smile, hoping it looks natural.

"I saw you play here—I don't know. A dozen years ago now?"

I nod. "Sounds about right."

"Man, you were amazing. I saw you absolutely *flatten* a guy."

Salem sips her coffee, overloud.

"Sure," I say, because he's probably right. Flattening was my specialty. Most tackles for loss in my conference, all four years I played. He's still shaking my hand. I loosen my clasp, and he takes the hint, releasing me.

My hand, at least.

"And, uh," he begins, and I know we're about to get into the next thing I'm known for.

The bigger thing I'm known for.

"I just wanted to say, I think it was great. You know, all that stuff you said about Copeland Frederick. About . . . you know, how people treated him while he was alive."

I swallow, spare a glance at Salem. She's picked up her phone again and has started scrolling, I'm pretty sure as a kindness. She sips her coffee quietly now.

"Appreciate it," I say, and I do. But the tips of my ears are heating. It's not fair to call it embarrassment, because I'm not ashamed of the string of viral social media posts I sent out over five years ago now, just after Cope passed, when I was torn apart by rage and grief and frustration.

By the loss of the best friend and teammate I ever had.

Everything I said back then was true; everything I said was something I'd meant and still believe.

But I'd say it different now.

I'm pursuing this entire career because I'm trying to learn how to say it different.

"My little brother, he's had some struggles in life. With his mental health, I mean. Your posts, they meant a lot to him."

I nod, my expression serious. Gentle, I hope. "Thanks for telling me that. He doing all right?"

"Yeah, he's good these days. He won't believe I saw you, oh man! He's gonna be jealous."

He wears an expression I recognize. He's considering asking, and I'm going to spare him the trouble.

"You want to get a photo for him?"

The guy lights up.

"Would you?"

"Sure." I slide out from the booth, trying not to look ruefully at my pancakes. They don't really matter, not in the face of this. I know that stuff I said helped a good number of people, for all the people who ended up hating me for it.

"I'll take it," says Salem, holding out her hand for the guy's phone. When I stand, he laughs a little, gets another one of those *oh wow*s in. He's maybe a head and a half shorter than me.

We stand together while Salem snaps a few photos, and then the guy swipes through them, deciding which one to send to his brother first. Somehow seeing those pictures seems to give him more confidence, and he's got another favor to ask, wants to know if I'll hop on the phone and say a quick hello to the brother. I do it, because the guy seems so genuine, and once he's on the line, the brother's so thrilled he can hardly form a complete sentence. It's probably ten minutes before I get it all wrapped up—the call and the thank-yous that follow. I must say "No problem" and "Happy to do it" about twenty times before the guy finally walks away, shaking his head in cheerful disbelief and typing on his phone.

I cram myself back into the booth.

"Your pancakes are probably cold," Salem says.

"That's all right."

But I admit. I'm bummed about the pancakes.

I try not to make a disappointed face as I chew, because I can tell Salem is watching me.

"You know," she says, "it's too bad the real Jess Greene isn't a football fan."

I do a closemouthed cough. It sounds guilty. Damn me for having that thought about how much shampoo she uses in the shower.

"Maybe that would've made her more amenable to our presence yesterday."

I take a sip of my water, clear my throat. I guess I should take this as an opportunity to tell her my reservations, even if I'm worried about what she'll think of me for it.

"I don't think anything's going to make her more amenable."

"Oh yeah?"

There's a doubtful tone to her voice. It makes me wonder if she's already heard something from Jess Greene. But when I meet her eyes she shakes her head as if she can read my mind.

Then she makes a gesture with her hand, a *go on* gesture.

I set down my fork again.

"It seems risky. Our entry point into this was a teenager. The sister—that's her guardian, I'm pretty sure—doesn't want us around. Was hostile to having us around."

Was hurt by having us around, I don't add.

"This from the guy who . . . what'd your friend say? *Flattened* people?" Salem says.

She's teasing, but my ears heat up again. I don't want her to think I've misunderstood one of the most fundamental things about the kind of journalism I want to do, and that's that it takes tenacity, perseverance. More perseverance than flattening guys on a football field. More tenacity than sending out a series of scathing, off-the-cuff social media posts about the kind of shit that happened to your best friend on and off of that football field.

"It's not really that. I know it's important to push sometimes."

She raises her eyebrows. "But you don't think it's important to push for this?"

I swallow, shift in my seat. I can hear in her tone that she's annoyed, defensive, and I can't blame her. Around the office, I've heard the snarky remarks: that the Baltimore story is "too dead now to even attempt reviving," that Salem must be "running out of original content." It's like everyone's forgotten what they owe to Salem, to the Baltimore story—the serialized podcast that started the fashion for that sort of storytelling. On our last day in the office, during a meeting about download numbers across our platform, another senior producer—one who has made his career on serialized, narrative true crime over the last five years—had wished us luck on our "goose chase" before reminding us not to go over our per diem. As far as he's concerned—as far as everyone in the business is concerned, maybe—the Baltimore podcast wrapped up compellingly, if not neatly. The man primarily known for grifting powerful women disappearing on one again. In a way, it was a fitting conclusion, even if Salem's never let it go.

"Because it *is* important," she says, before I can even attempt an answer.

She pushes her plate out of the way and leans forward, setting her elbows on the table. "Let me ask you something, Hawk."

"Sure," I say, like I'm agreeing to another selfie. But Salem never makes small requests, never asks small questions. I listened to the original Baltimore podcast, and that's what had made her so good.

"Where's football fall on a list of the top five problems facing our country right now?"

Harder than a selfie.

But not too hard, because I've spent a lot of time thinking about this.

The three years I spent mostly hiding out, after I sent those posts out into the world and they exploded onto people's feeds in every corner of this country and beyond. The two years I spent getting my master's in journalism, once I finally got my head together. The months I've spent as a new hire at Broadside, getting my feet wet, trying to find a way into the kind of opportunity I need to tell Cope's story.

"Doesn't make the top ten. But I'd say it's got something to say about stuff that's on that list, actually."

"Yeah?"

I nod. "Masculinity, and how people define it. Mental health. Corporate greed. Appetites for violence. Nationalism, and not the good kind. If there is such a thing."

She smiles, approving.

"Right. And so, this story you have in mind. The podcast you want to do about what happened to Copeland Frederick. Do you want people thinking it's a ten-episode series about some dumb jock who lost his way? Some guy who couldn't handle all the success in the world? Someone weak who wasted talent that other people would kill for?"

I don't really have to answer. I know what she's getting at. For all those nasty remarks I've heard about Salem over the last couple of months, I'm certain she's heard worse about me. That *I'm* some dumb jock, some roided-up former athlete who let loose his temper once on social media and now thinks he can be a journalist. That I've only got one idea, one point of view, and it's better suited to a cable sports network than it is to anything that's *true* human interest.

That there's nothing to me beyond who my best friend was, and why he died.

"No," I say anyway.

"Right, well, the Lynton Baltimore story isn't just about a grift. It isn't just about him moving around, changing his identity, making new selves everywhere he went. It isn't even about him making off with artwork or jewelry from some minor royal family's collection, or about any of the other heirlooms or money he managed to wheedle out of the various women he was involved with over the years."

She pauses, points her index finger down at the table, pressing it into the surface to emphasize her point.

"It's about the *stories* he tells those women. It's about how he creates a certain self to suit them, how he makes promises to them about all the things they've been taught they need from a man. Protection, affection, respect. He tells them the same story society's been telling them, in one way or another, forever. And then when he leaves them, he takes away so much more than their money. *That's* what the Baltimore story is. And it's important."

I nod, doing my best to mask the surprise I feel at how passionately she's said this. Maybe people at work would've talked less shit if she showed this kind of heat about why it'd be worth it to continue working this story all these years later. But she never did. Instead she talked about download numbers for the original Baltimore series, or about the places it'd shown up in the news the past few months as it comes up on its ten-year anniversary. She connected it to the success of any number of other current series—podcasts, documentaries, biographies—about grifters.

For the first time since I saw that storm on Jess Greene's face, I get curious again. In a different way, sure—one that doesn't feel as if my heart is about to beat out of my chest.

But in a way that I know is better for the job.

Still, when I open my mouth to speak, I can't be sure if I'm talking about the story.

"I still think the sister will be a problem."

Salem raises an eyebrow.

I clear my throat, try to forget about the storm.

"She doesn't want to talk, and she doesn't want her sister to talk. Tegan still seemed determined in front of us, but who knows what their relationship is behind closed doors. Families are complicated. Theirs more than most, I'm pretty sure."

"Oh, I'm pretty sure, too."

Salem says this as if she's excited about it. But for the first time since yesterday, she looks worried, too. She's down to the dregs of her coffee and we've been in this diner for nearly an hour, which means we're looking at almost a full day since we showed up on Jess Greene's doorstep. Every hour that passes where we don't hear from either her or Tegan doesn't bode well.

I take another bite of my cold pancakes, trying to stretch it. After this, we don't have much of a plan, and as bad as that is for Salem, it's probably just as bad for me. If we go back to Boston with nothing, I can't see how I don't get associated with failure on the first big job I've been put on since I started at Broadside. I can't see how my chances of getting to tell Cope's story there don't take a pretty big hit.

Salem's trying to catch the eye of the server—probably to get our check—when her phone vibrates on the table between us.

We both look at it—a local number—and then at each other.

She reaches for it, and I can't decide if I'm relieved or disappointed that she doesn't put it on speaker.

"This is Salem."

It feels like a long time while she's listening, but I don't think it's more than a couple of minutes. Whoever's on the other end—and I think I know already—I'm pretty sure she's not interested in letting Salem get a word in. I'm pretty sure she worked out exactly what she wanted to say before she called.

I try not to feel like I'm pressing against a windowpane.

"I'm happy to hear that," Salem finally says, and then, after a second, she pulls the phone from her ear and looks down at the screen.

"She hung up."

I don't know why that makes me want to smile.

"That was Jess Greene," she adds, unnecessarily.

"A problem," I repeat, shoving another bite of cold pancakes in my mouth.

Salem sets down her phone. "They're in, though."

I finish chewing, swallow. "It doesn't mean she'll talk."

"It doesn't. Especially to me."

I look up at her, and once again, she's watching me close, her lips set in a small smile.

"What?"

She shrugs and looks away, waving at the server. She doesn't look at me when she speaks again.

"Hawk," she says, casual-as-you-please, as if she's not about to change my relationship to this story—to the woman I was up half the night thinking about—entirely.

"If you get Jess Greene to talk to us about her mother, I'll produce your podcast myself."

The Last Con of Lynton Baltimore

Transcript Excerpt from Episode 2, "The Inmate"

Automated Voice [fading in]: This is a SimLink Global pre-paid call from

Baltimore: Lynton Baltimore

Automated Voice: An inmate at a Georgia correctional facility [fading out, intro music plays]

[**Durant, voice-over:** Ten years ago, when I was just starting out as an investigative journalist in public radio, a colleague of mine took a big risk, the kind that can change the course of an entire career. In this case, the risk was eating a box of takeout in his refrigerator that was long past its safe-to-eat date. The career that got changed was mine, because I was suddenly assigned the very unexpected task of interviewing my first head of state: a man whose recent election to his country's highest office had been shrouded in controversy, in claims of criminality. He was in New York City, and I was slated to meet him in a small conference room of the hotel where he and his team were staying. When I walked in, I remember thinking that I would never be able to ask this man the questions my colleague had prepared. He had eyes like a snake's, a voice like the edge of a butcher knife. Every second of my four-and-a-half minutes in his presence felt like a risk to my life, as though the man giving me clipped, noncommittal answers was simply cataloging everything he would need to know about me in the event that I reported on him in a manner he would find distasteful. In the event he would need to find me again, and hold me to account for it.]

::sound of a deep breath, indistinct whispers::

Automated Voice: Will you accept this call?

[**Durant, voice-over:** But that interview was nothing compared to my first conversation with Lynton Baltimore.]

Baltimore: Where would you like to begin?

Chapter 5

Jess

Adam Hawkins even looks big in a much bigger house.

My father's house, that is.

I'm discreetly watching from the kitchen as he attempts to settle himself on the sleek, cream leather couch in what my stepmother Bernila calls "the front room." I've never really seen the point of this room—with its uncomfortable-looking seating and weird art pieces and its bulky coffee-table books about the history of marble sculpture or some other boring thing that Bernila likes. But now, I get it: It's a room designed for a conversation with a near stranger. It's a room where you put someone when you don't really want them to know anything about you.

It's perfect.

I thought a lot about this meeting before I made my call to Salem Durant this morning. Where I wanted to have it, who I wanted at it, what I wanted to say. In the small hours of last night, after Tegan had finally fallen into a snoring sleep on top of her covers—more exhausted than she'd ever admit, I think, both from our tense conversations throughout the rest of the day and from keeping her secret for so long—I'd paced back and forth across my own bedroom floor, working it out.

Tegan may be eighteen, and she may have forced my hand into going on this trip.

But I'm the *real* Jess Greene.

And surely, Salem Durant would think I have value to her awful podcast, too.

I knew I needed to use that value to protect Tegan as best I could.

So I called Salem, and I set up this meeting. I chose my dad's house, only about ten minutes from mine and Tegan's, because I won't talk about any of this in a public place, and because this house, which my dad and Bernila bought after I moved out of their previous home when I turned eighteen, reflects nothing of me or my history. And I chose Adam Hawkins—I'm not calling him Hawk; what a ridiculous suggestion—because I don't trust Salem not to try to use this meeting to get information about or an interview from my dad, and also maybe because I'm not ready to face her just yet. I told her I had conditions, and we wouldn't be going anywhere until I got to lay them out.

It's possible—given Tegan's determination, her *righteousness* about all this—that I was bluffing about that last point. But Salem hadn't argued.

And she's sent Adam Hawkins here.

I finish filling another water glass and watch him fidget with the binder he walked in with. He sets it beside him on the cushion but then seems to reconsider, which I guess I can relate to because that couch probably gets dirty just from someone looking at it. I can tell he's thinking about putting it on the coffee table, but then he'd have to move one of the books about marble sculpture out of the way, and that's to say nothing of the big, oval-shaped ceramic platter that's full of actual sculptures (non-marble), that I guess are supposed to look like avant-garde pine cones. He cocks his head to the side as he looks at them, settling for putting the binder on one of his muscular thighs.

I admit. He's very attractive.

My dad clears his throat and I almost drop the water glass.

"I'll be out back," he says, gesturing to the French doors that lead to his and Bernila's patio. He's looking at me with a familiar expression. Part confusion, part frustration, part pity.

Part affection, too, but sort of . . . a sad kind. An *I love her, but* kind.

I guess that's because I'm making him sit outside while I have a meeting I've told him only very basic information about for now—that there's a journalist interested in the man Mom left with ten years ago, that there's a possibility of finding her after all these years. He knows, at least generally, that Mom sent me a few postcards after she left, so I didn't have to go through explaining that again, and it isn't as if he pressed for more details. He didn't even do that when she first sent them, probably because he knows I wouldn't have told him anything anyway. My dad may not be quite as reticent as me, but he's quiet enough—contained enough—that he seems to understand the instinct, even when it worries him.

So, I'd asked him to wait outside while I had this meeting, and he'd frowned at me, but still, he'd agreed. Because of the affection. The *I love her, but* feeling. Probably the pity, too, which he's had ever since that day my mom left an envelope for him. *Brent and I need some time on our own,* her letter had said. *Once he and I have a solid foundation, I'm sure I'll send for Jessie.*

She hadn't. Dad had taken care of me for all the months she was gone. And for all the months after, too, when she finally came back. No Brent, but Tegan in her belly. My relationship with her changed forever.

"Thanks," I tell him, trying to gentle my voice, and he nods and ducks out the door to where Bernila waits for him.

I head back into the front room, where Adam Hawkins waits for me.

"Here," I say, holding out a glass of water. He didn't ask for one, but once I opened the door to him, I needed an excuse to walk away for a minute. Without Salem, he is much more . . . noticeable.

And it isn't as though he was hard to miss yesterday, even when I was halfway to a panic attack.

"Thank you." He takes the glass about as awkwardly as I offered it. His eyes drift to the coffee table, but there are no coasters there among the avant-garde pine cones.

I sit in a nearby chair. It's more of a stiff, upright hammock than a chair, but I do my best to make it look natural. I don't have anywhere to put my glass, either.

He clears his throat, but since I spent basically the entire day yesterday getting caught off guard, I don't want him getting the jump on me even in conversation. I speak first.

"Mr. Hawkins—"

"You can call me—"

"I'm not calling you Hawk," I snap. "This isn't . . . I don't know what. Basic training. Or a locker room."

He blinks at me. "I was going to say . . ."

He trails off, swallows. I think this means we're abandoning the issue of what to call each other for now, which is probably for the best.

"Tegan tells me you've had an itinerary set for some time," I say quickly. "I want a copy."

Because she didn't ask for her own copy. Because she is naïve; because she is a child; *because she has no idea what she was doing,* I don't add, even though things like that keep threatening to burst forth from me. Yesterday, with Tegan, I kept having to bite the inside of my cheek to stop myself. There's a small sore there now.

He awkwardly opens the binder with one hand, and from the front pocket, slides out a stapled-together stack of pages.

"I could also AirDrop it to—"

"No."

As if I'd ever be searchable on AirDrop. As if I'd ever be searchable to him in any way, ever.

He hands the itinerary over, but the way he's tilted his head slightly—I might as well be a pine cone sculpture. I duck my head, desperate to avoid his green, green eyes.

They make me feel searchable.

I concentrate on breathing slowly through my nose as I look over the first page of the itinerary: an overview, I guess. Five cities, in the order the postcards came from.

Chattanooga. Pensacola. Tulsa. Sante Fe. Olympia. I can't picture anything from the front of those postcards. No pretty landscapes or landmarks. But I can see in my mind's eye what she wrote on the back of each one.

"The first four stops, we'll do by vehicle," he says. "Then Santa Fe to Olympia, we'll fly. We have someone back at the office helping us work on some schedule changes for that."

"It's not clear that they actually *stayed* in these places." My tone is irritating even to me. It sounds like I'm trying to score a point.

"The next few pages explain what we think are reasonable places to look into nearby, if we need to." He clears his throat. "Based on some of the content of the postcards. And what we know about Baltimore."

He has a nice voice. It doesn't sound like point-scoring, but it feels like it all the same.

I don't flip to the next page. "I'll review this later. For now I want to talk about my conditions."

He adjusts slightly on the couch. He's wearing jeans and a light blue button up and I have the strangest urge to ask him where he buys his clothes. Does he have to get them custom-made to go across shoulders that wide?

"All right," he says, but there's a slight note of confusion in his voice. I think maybe I left too long a pause there, thinking about a man's tailoring.

I lean forward and set the itinerary on a small empty edge of the coffee table. To keep it in place, I set my water glass on top. Then I straighten in my hammock chair.

"First, I don't—" I narrow my eyes at him. "Do you want to write these down?"

"I have a good memory."

It doesn't sound smug; it sounds simple. True. *I have wide shoulders. Green eyes. A nice voice.*

I don't know why I'm thinking of any of that. My mind grasps for a thought that will keep me more grounded. That will make him feel less true.

"Is that because you're recording right now?"

He frowns. "What?"

"Do you really have a good memory, or are you recording this?"

He shakes his head. "I'm not recording this. I'm never going to do that without you knowing."

"Will Salem?"

"No," he says firmly. "You'll always know. She'll always ask."

"And with Tegan, too. She always needs to ask her first. That's one of my conditions."

"Got it."

"I also don't want Salem speaking to her alone. If she's doing an interview, if she's getting recorded, I need to be there."

He doesn't immediately respond to that one. He takes a sip of his water, then follows my lead and sets his glass next to mine. It's not as if I can complain about water stains on the itinerary I'm not letting him AirDrop to me.

"Salem's spoken to her one-on-one quite a bit already," he says, by way of answer.

"No, she hasn't. She's spoken to a pretty poor imitation of me."

I pressed Tegan for details during one of our talks—fights, thinly veiled battles, whatever—yesterday. What *had* she told Salem Durant, when she was pretending to be me? But Tegan had only said she'd stuck to the facts as much as possible: that at twenty-one, she'd come home from an outing with her younger half sister to find a letter of goodbye from their mother. That she'd been raising her half sister since. That their mother, in the months prior to her leaving, had been seeing a man named Miles Daniels. That she knew, in hindsight, that Miles Daniels was Lynton Baltimore.

The truth is, if Salem Durant had been pressing me, I probably wouldn't have said much different, so maybe Tegan's imitation was spot-on. But it still hurt, somehow, to hear her tell it. For ten years, I've told myself I'd do anything for Tegan; I'd let her have anything that was mine.

But I guess the truth is, her having my story—her telling my story to someone I never would have trusted with it—is a boundary between us I didn't know existed.

Adam—that's what I've decided I'll call him in my head, though I'll keep it formal to his face—presses his lips together.

Then he says, "There may be things she wouldn't want to say in front of you. About her own experience with your mom. The time before your mom left."

The time when I was hardly around, I think guiltily. *The time I lived with my dad.* But Adam doesn't need to know that. I want to say something clear, sharp, forceful. Something like, *Tegan and I don't have secrets from each other.* But of course, what Adam already knows is that this is a lie.

"Tegan and I already talked about this condition. She agreed to it, as long as she can be present for any information I might provide."

I'm making this agreement sound a lot less fraught than it was. In reality, it might as well have been a hostage-taking between us, both of us holding something at gunpoint.

Something changes in his expression, those green eyes going sharper.

"Does that mean you plan to speak to us about your own memories of—"

"I said *might.* No guarantees."

No chance, I'm thinking.

He nods, but I think I notice those broad shoulders lower the smallest amount.

"What else?" he says.

"We give you three weeks, and that's it. Tegan starts college at the end of this summer. Three weeks is all we can give you."

"It's only the beginning of July. She goes to school at the end of this month?"

This time, I cock my head at him, fix him with what I hope is a scolding gaze.

"I also have a *job*," I say, though no one at the salon will really push back, so long as I do all the necessary rescheduling. I've barely ever taken a sick day.

"The only itinerary you need to concern yourself with is"—I gesture at the coffee table—"that one. I said three weeks. After that, it's none of your business what my sister and I do."

"I'll talk to our team," he says, and I shrug my shoulders. I don't care what their "team" says. I'm not spending the last month I have at home with Tegan doing a fucking *podcast*. Probably now I'll spend the last month I have at home with her cleaning up whatever mess this podcast causes.

I take a deep breath through my nose, steeling myself for this last one. I've tried to do it subtly, but I think Adam notices. He abandons whatever care he had for the couch and sets his binder beside him, then rests his elbows on his thighs, clasping his hands loosely in the space between them. It's a leaned-forward, listening posture.

"*If* we find her," I say, glad that my voice sounds the same as it did for all my other conditions, "whether she's with Lynton Baltimore or not, Tegan and I talk to her first. No recording. Alone."

He looks at me for a long time, and I don't want to be the one to break first. That means I'm stuck looking back, and there's a strange, small riot happening in the center of me. It isn't that I don't regularly find handsome men attractive; it's just that, for the last ten years, I've only found them so when they lived, for example, on my television screen, or maybe inside the pages of a book that has particularly vivid descriptions.

But Adam Hawkins is *right here*, and he's not a client sitting in my salon chair, or one of the boring, slightly sleazy divorced dads from Tegan's school who have hit on me before. He's right here and he is not a convenient person to find handsome given he is part of something that is exploding my life. My sister's life.

He says, "Have you really never spoken to her in all these years?"

I blink at him, stunned that he's asked. Sort of . . . intrigued that he's asked.

No, wait. I'm *angry* that he's asked.

I have to stay angry.

It's the only way I'll get through the next three weeks, I'm pretty sure.

"That's not really your job, is it?"

He furrows his brow. "What isn't my job?"

I huff. "Asking me that. Aren't you . . ."

I trail off, wave a hand. I have that strange, looming sense of dread that sometimes happens when small talk goes awry. Maybe I ask a client a banal follow-up question about their son's recent wedding and all of a sudden it's fifteen minutes on the new daughter-in-law being "too outspoken" and "obsessed with her career," and I spend the whole haircut wishing I hadn't asked.

"Aren't I what?" Adam says.

"Uh," I say, and I *hate* the way that dull, uncertain syllable makes me sound, hate it enough that I push past the bad small-talk feeling and blurt out a bit of my first impression of Adam Hawkins, from back when he seemed—to me at least—to silently stand guard over Salem in my kitchen.

"Aren't you . . . security, or something?"

As soon as I've said it, I realize how ridiculous a thought it was, how ridiculous it sounds now that I've said it out loud. Why would Salem Durant have *security*? For her work on a podcast about a totally nonviolent grifter? For her meeting with *me*—or, who she thought was me?

It gets worse when I notice how still Adam has gone. His ears are pink, and he blinks down at his lap, unclasping his hands and setting them on his thighs.

When he looks up again, it's not searching in his eyes. It's not leaned-in or listening. It should be exactly what I want from him, because I'm allergic to curiosity when it's directed my way, and obviously what he's here to negotiate with me about goes well beyond curiosity.

But it strangely does not feel like what I want.

"No. I am not security."

"Ah," I manage, swallowing thickly.

He doesn't offer any additional information, and I guess I can respect that.

Stay angry, I tell myself, but it doesn't work, because Adam's ears are still pink and he's standing from his spot on the couch, one of his knees knocking the edge of the table as he rises. Nothing falls, but the water in our glasses ripples and the abstract pine cones clink together.

I stand, too, because I'm not sure what else to do. I don't think it'd be a good idea to stay in my hammock-chair and feel like Adam Hawkins is standing guard over me.

He clears his throat. "Any more conditions I can pass along to Salem?"

I cling to those conditions, shoving away the embarrassment I feel. The regret I feel over the embarrassment I'm pretty sure *he* feels. I don't owe Adam Hawkins anything.

I run through them in my head: *No recordings unless we know. No recording Tegan without me present. Three weeks. If we find Mom, Tegan and I talk to her first.*

"I think that's it," I tell him, but the truth is, I can't be sure now that things have gone off course.

Ironically, I should've written them down.

He waits a beat, as if to give me time to be certain. I don't want to think about what a kindness that is, or whether I deserve it at this moment. I smooth the front of my T-shirt—black, again, always—and look anywhere but at him.

"Don't forget your binder," I say, gesturing toward the couch.

He turns, bends slightly to pick it up. When he looks back at me, the pink at the tips of his ears has faded, and there's a beat of silence where neither of us seems to know how to end this. For the next three weeks, I'll be with Adam Hawkins every single day, and somehow, in this moment, that feels riskier than every other part of this trip. This entire situation.

"I'll be heading out," he says, and I nod gratefully, stepping to the side so he can pass me on the way to the front door. When I open it for him, I feel an anticipatory relief over him being gone. I can already picture what I'll do next: stand here in this foyer by myself until I get my bearings enough to go face Dad and Bernila in a way that will make me seem tough, unruffled, ready. I'll say, *Well, that's done*, and I'll ask if my dad can stop by our house a few times over the next three weeks to check our mail. I'll answer their questions vaguely. I'll say I need to get home to pack.

But instead of going, Adam pauses in the doorway. He looks down at me with those same searching green eyes as before.

"One of your conditions," he says, and I stiffen, no longer anticipating relief. If I have to fight him on any of these, I'll do it. But I was hoping I wouldn't have to.

"You could consider requesting that we don't use your voices. That we re-record any interviews later. With actors. Sometimes people prefer that. For their privacy."

I hardly know what to say. I settle for a shocked, inarticulate, "Oh."

He doesn't give me any extra time to answer, or to be certain. He says, "See you soon," and ducks out the door and down my father's front steps.

And when he's gone, I wonder why I feel so small.

Chapter 6

Adam

The next morning, I'm driving to Jess's house in the rented minivan I'm going to spend a good portion of the next three weeks inside, Salem in the passenger seat, our bags tidily stacked on one side of the trunk. I've got a worried knot in my stomach I'm trying to ignore, and I know even before we pull into the driveway what we're going to find when we get there.

Jess and Tegan already outside on their small front porch, bags at their feet, the house locked up behind them.

"Efficient," says Salem when I'm proven right, but I don't agree with her. I know better now. Twenty minutes inside Jess Greene's father's house, and I know better.

This isn't efficiency.

It's privacy.

She's out here because she doesn't want us inside her home again.

I pull into the driveway, shutting off the engine. I'm pretty sure Salem is looking over at me with the same blend of curiosity and doubt she's leveled at me ever since we met up in the hotel lobby after my meeting with Jess. I'd told her all the conditions I'd been given, though for now I left off mentioning the one I suggested myself. I still can't really admit to myself why I did it, especially not after Jess treated me like I'm some kind of heavy. But I had a feeling if I'd told Salem, she'd admit it for me.

She'd know.

"Come on. You can help with their bags."

I stifle a groan. It isn't that I don't want to help with their bags; it's practically in my DNA to want to help people with their bags or their flat tire or the too-big box a delivery man left outside their door.

It's that helping with their bags is going to make me look like I'm *security*.

And I'm grown enough to admit: that makes me feel insecure.

If Cope were here, he'd get it. In a different way, but he'd get it. For a long time, not a lot of people really believed Cope when he said he was struggling; not a lot of people thought someone as good-natured and fit and talented as him would be struggling, at least not for long. With me, it's more—it's more that most people look at me and think there must not be room for a brain. Most people think I'm built for flattening.

Most people including a whole lot of my teachers, my coaches. My classmates in graduate school. Probably even Salem, when she first met me.

Jess Greene.

Still, I get out of the car, knowing I'm going to head straight for those bags.

Salem's saying hello as if this whole setup hasn't been ten kinds of tense, because that's how she is. We're on the path to the story she wants now, so it doesn't matter what happened to get us here. I guess I should take a lesson.

"Morning," I say, approaching them. Tegan is smiling, something victorious in her expression, and that's fair enough, given she got one over on us and her sister. Beside her, Jess is ramrod straight in basically the same outfit I've seen her in the last two days: black sneakers, black jeans, loose black T-shirt. In the sunlight, her hair is spun gold against her shoulders.

I bend down to pick up their suitcases.

"I can get it," says Jess.

It sounds pretty much the same as everything else she's said either to or around me: tight, impatient, final. But when I look up at her, I think I see something different in her expression. It might be regret.

"It's all right," I say.

I heft a bag in each hand and head straight for the back of the van, hiding from that look on her face. Bad enough I ended yesterday by giving her a tip, even though I know Salem wouldn't ever argue with a request to use voice actors. Worse if I start mooning over every look she gives me.

I'm here to do my job, and that job isn't worrying over a woman who probably hates me, even if she does feel a little bad about thinking I'm some kind of security detail.

In fact, my job is to somehow get her to talk.

"Jess needs to sit up front," says Tegan as I'm closing the rear door. "She gets carsick in back seats."

So of course I look over at her again. Chin slightly up, jaw tight. *And what about it?* this look says.

"Great," says Salem, which seems a little insensitive. "Tegan, we'll sit in the back and talk a bit."

Tegan's eyes drift to Jess's immediately, briefly. An instinct for permission. But then just as quickly she snaps her gaze back to Salem.

"Great!" she echoes, all unbothered excitement.

When we pile into the van, though, I wouldn't say anything feels particularly exciting, at least not to me. Salem and I booked this van because we figured it'd be more spacious than an SUV, and it's a quieter ride, too. But with Jess next to me the front seat feels close, and I can hear it when she sucks in a shaky breath. I hate being part of anything that makes someone this nervous, and I guess that doesn't bode well for me in the long term of this job.

I back out of the driveway slowly, as if I'm giving everyone, including myself, one last chance.

But behind me, Salem and Tegan seem focused on settling in: Salem points out a cooler we put together this morning, full of water and some snacks; Tegan says her tablet is loaded with word puzzles. Their friendliness toward each other is pointed enough that I have the feeling it's more of a performance for Jess's benefit than anything.

Somehow, I can tell she's not buying it.

When I turn right out of the neighborhood onto a main road, I start to calm down, or at least to lean in to the reality of this. It's just under seven hours until our destination, according to my phone's GPS, and I'm counting on one stop for fuel, lunch, and a bathroom break. I know Salem has a plan for this leg: light conversation, casual topics, nothing threatening. Trust-building stuff. Tonight, she's hoping to do some recording if Tegan's up for talking, and all signs point to Tegan always being up for talking.

"Oh, wait!" says Tegan, and I automatically take my foot off the gas. "Hawk, I googled you last night!"

I clench my back teeth, ease back on the accelerator. This is not the fast track to light conversation.

"I only found out your name was Adam Hawkins the other day. Salem always only talked about you as 'Hawk' on our video calls!"

"Right," I say, trying to sound casual. Trying not to mess up the plan. Trust-building, I know, involves giving something of yourself, too.

But it'd be easier if I didn't have to give the stuff that comes up on Google.

"Jessie," she says, and I can *feel* the way Jess stiffens next to me, as though this nickname, said in this space, is some sort of violation. "Hawk was a big-deal college football star."

Jess says nothing. Not even a flicker of interest. The silence should maybe be more insulting than her thinking I work security, but strangely, it's not. She's stonewalling again, but this time, it's as if she's doing it on my behalf.

"Jess hates football," Tegan adds, I guess to Salem. "She thinks it's barbaric."

Okay, well. Maybe she's not stonewalling on my behalf. Maybe she just thinks I'm barbaric.

"And then he—"

"Tegan," Jess says, her tone cool. "Let him pay attention to the road."

In the rearview, I see Tegan flush, chastened and probably more than a little angry at the light scolding. At eighteen, that kind of talk from your parent in front of someone else is uniquely humiliating.

Jess adds, more gently, "At least until we get on the freeway."

I keep my eyes straight ahead. Thanking her would be too revealing, I know, but I want to. There's no world where I want to start a road trip—a *work* road trip—talking about what I'm internet famous for.

Salem smoothly takes over, as if she's been given a handoff. She asks Tegan to see the word puzzles, and within a minute, they're doing the trust-building without us. Light and casual and nonthreatening. Tegan's explaining a game I know Salem's played before, and it seems they'll keep up with this well after we get on the freeway.

I wonder if Jess realizes she's just played teammate to a woman I'm pretty sure she's planning to work against for the next three weeks.

I slow as I approach a busy intersection, the light ahead yellow. But as cautious as I'm being, the guy in the lane next to me isn't—he speeds ahead, and before he's gotten much past our front end, he slides in front of me and promptly hits the brakes.

So I hit mine, too.

And—like millions of moms and dads and generally careful drivers before me—I stick out my right arm like it's a steel bar, keeping safe the person in the seat next to me.

Jess Greene.

It's not a crash, but it might as well be one—the feeling of any part of her against any part of me a jolting impact. When her body naturally reels back into her seat, the hair that had fallen over my forearm brushes back across it in soft, electrifying trails. One of us sucks in a breath. I think it might've been me.

We turn to look at each other, both of us frozen until I slowly lower my arm. I'm pretty sure she felt it, too. That jolt between us.

"You okay?" I say, low and quiet.

She blinks across the console at me, her blue eyes wide. Something so much softer than a storm.

"Yeah. Thanks."

I'd probably keep looking at her but for Salem speaking up from the seat behind me.

"Goodness!" she says brightly, tapping at Tegan's iPad. "Let's hope we don't have any more moments like that between here and Tennessee!"

Jess drops her eyes, folds her hands primly in her lap.

I turn to face the windshield. To focus on the red light in front of me.

Yes, I'm thinking, that knot in my stomach something different now. *Let's hope.*

Two hours in and I was wrong about Tegan, who is not in fact always up for talking, because pretty much as soon as we hit a speed above sixty-five, she falls asleep and stays asleep. And it's not a light nap, either: I can hear her softly snoring. In the rearview, I see her head drooping to the side, her mouth slightly open. I used to travel for games with guys who slept this way. Lulled by movement even if they weren't tired. Even if they'd already slept for hours.

And probably Tegan's had a few sleepless nights lately, given all this.

Other than the forgettable sounds of some adult contemporary satellite radio station I have playing on a pretty low volume, it is *brutally* silent in this car. I think Jess and Salem are in some kind of no-speaking standoff, and I can't think of anything to say because I'm still too fixated on how my forearm feels.

Her hair was really soft. It reminded me of—

"My daughter is exactly the same way, you know," says Salem, finally blinking first and breaking the silence, and also my train of thought. "She can't stay awake in a car ride to save her life."

Jess doesn't respond, but I don't think Salem expected her to. She expects *me* to. Even if Jess isn't talking to her, she wants Jess to hear her talking about casual stuff, light stuff.

I clear my throat. "How's she doing?"

"Oh, you know. Fifteen and she's figured out the entire world. She thinks her father and I are the most embarrassing people to ever exist. You know how they are at that age."

That, too, is for Jess's benefit—for the benefit of someone who has recently raised, is *still* raising a teenager. In my periphery, I see her adjust her hands, which she's been keeping in her lap. It's her only reaction, and I'm not sure if it even counts. She might be the most contained person I've ever met in my life.

"Sure," I say, relying on the knowledge I've gained from working with Salem these last few months, the steady way you build a certain kind of insight into your co-workers' lives. "Is she still dancing?"

"Oh yes. Practice five nights a week in the summers. It's running Patrick ragged, but better him than me."

She laughs lightly, but I'm pretty sure Patrick being run ragged with dance class pickups isn't a light topic between them. I've overheard more than one tense phone call between them about Salem's work hours lately.

I think she might stop there, but instead she takes a risk.

"My daughter—her name is Penelope—is a very talented contemporary dancer."

This time, she's very clearly directing it at Jess—an explanation, an inclusion.

An invitation, and it'd be rude to turn it down. Salem's set it up that way: Jess doesn't have any reason to hold something against a fifteen-year-old kid who's into contemporary dance, but if she doesn't respond, it'll seem as if she does.

"She's been going to the same studio in Boston since she was seven," Salem adds.

There's a long, tense pause. I'm holding my breath.

Jess finally says, "That's nice for her."

I figure this is about as closed off of a response she could've given to Salem. *That's nice for her, but I don't care what it means for you*, she might as well be saying.

But Salem obviously figures something else. She's never seen something closed that she doesn't want to open. The Baltimore story's been closed for a decade to everyone else, but here we are, trying to pry it off the hinges.

"Does Tegan do any activities outside of school?" Salem asks.

And that does it. I can't look over to see if there's another storm on Jess Greene's face, but I feel it nonetheless. An atmospheric shift.

She turns her head toward the seat behind mine, a flash of that spun gold I now accidentally know the texture of. I have a stupid thought about my forearm: Would there be any trace of the smell of her shampoo left there?

I don't have time to dwell on it.

"We made a deal, Salem. My sister doesn't talk unless I'm around, and I don't talk unless she is. *This*"—I can only assume she's gesturing to a sleeping Tegan—"doesn't count as her being around."

I don't dare turn my head, even though I want to. Instead, I check the rearview. Salem looks calm, unbothered.

"I hope it's clear I'm not attempting to start our work with this conversation."

"Oh, you're starting it," says Jess, her voice so *knowing*. It's as though she's been doing battle with people like Salem for years.

"It's a long way to Tennessee," Salem says. I can hear the shrug in her voice.

I resist the urge to tell Salem it's not all that long now. And anyway, I've got a feeling that Jess can stonewall someone for a lot longer than four and a half hours.

After only a few seconds, though, it's clear that something about this exchange has rattled Jess. Maybe she's so insulted by the veneer of friendliness, or by Salem's confidence, or by the last two days in general, that she simply can't hold back.

"You know, we don't know anything about Tennessee. We've never been there. Our mother had never been there. We don't know anyone there, and never have, and that postcard she wrote from Chattanooga is probably the vaguest one of the five. So if you're expecting to find out something helpful from us about why she and Lynton Baltimore went there, between now and the time we arrive, you're out of luck."

I grip the steering wheel tight in my hand, my knuckles going white. I wish I could have put out my arm for Jess just then, because she doesn't realize what she's just crashed into: information Salem has that she doesn't, uncovered only a day before we left Boston to come on this trip. I would've told Jess about it, had she given me the chance yesterday, but she'd barely been interested in the itinerary. She wanted those conditions secured and then she wanted me to go.

The pang of guilt I feel is instant, and the only thing I can think is that I better get used to it.

Because I'm probably going to feel this sort of guilt for the next three weeks.

I don't dare look in the rearview, in case Salem catches my

eye and sees right through me. But I can hear her shuffling back there. I'm pretty sure she's taken a book out of her bag.

She's about to win this standoff, and I know it's going to hurt the woman sitting beside me. Doesn't matter if I have an arm out for her or not.

"That's fine, Jess," Salem says. I can hear her turning pages, finding her place. "Hawk and I already know who we need to talk to in Tennessee."

Jess doesn't move for a few seconds; she's still turned toward Salem's seat. Probably she's trying to strike her with the lightning from her eyes. She must want to ask who it is; she *must*.

If she does, though, she wrestles the impulse back under control. Contains it.

She slowly faces forward again.

But she doesn't clasp her hands on her lap, at least not right away.

Instead, she reaches one out toward the van's stereo and gently adjusts the volume, turning up the music.

And I can't help but notice. Her fingers tremble the smallest, saddest amount.

The Last Con of Lynton Baltimore

Transcript Excerpt from Episode 4, "Confidence Games"

Professor Stephen Weir: There's so much misunderstanding about men like Baltimore, and what he does. People think, oh, he's a criminal; he's a con man.

Durant: But he is a con man. Isn't he?

Weir: He's—well, yes. But we use this term so freely now, it's lost its meaning, really. Baltimore isn't making crank calls, asking for an old woman's Social Security number. He's not putting himself on dating sites. That kind of scam, he would find distasteful.

Durant: Distasteful how?

Weir: A confidence man—a true confidence man—he's an artist, not an instrument. He's studied. He comes from a long line; he knows a long set of traditions. He speaks a language that is unique to other artists of his kind; he only works with other artists of his kind. It's aristocratic, really.

Durant: You almost seem to admire him.

Weir: I wouldn't say that.

Durant: He has victims. Innocent people who have been hurt by him.

Weir: A man like Baltimore, a man who does his kind of work, would say that there's no innocent mark. He would say . . . well, he would say what confidence men have always said.

Durant: And what's that?

Weir: ::chuckles:: He would say that you simply can't cheat an honest man.

Durant: Well. Well, I suppose I have to wonder about that. Since not everyone, of course, is a man.

Chapter 7

Jess

At 6:30 a.m. in the bathroom mirror of a hotel room just outside of Chattanooga, I look about as disoriented as I feel. My hair half out of the bun I put it in last night after my shower, evidence of how much I tossed and turned on the room's too-soft bed and too-crinkly pillows. My skin sallow looking, because even in the front seat of that van I sat in yesterday, I fought what felt like motion sickness but what might have actually been nerves. My eyes red and dry, because I spent most of the predawn hours staring up at the ceiling and the blinking light from the room's smoke detector, wondering how in the world I ended up here.

Of course I know, in the abstract, how I ended up here: the man I knew as Miles Daniels, Mom's postcards, my sister's ingenuity, Salem Durant's obsession with the still-untold ending to a story she can't let go of. I know I had no choice but to be in this hotel room, Tegan sleeping in the queen-size bed next to mine, her phone's alarm set for a half hour from now.

But the abstract is nothing compared to how this feels.

How it feels to be getting further and further from home,

where I've worked hard to be fully in control of my life—and Tegan's life—for the last ten years. How it feels to have Salem studying me from the back seat of the van, getting one over on me. How it feels to sit next to my sister on a picnic bench in a public park while she answers questions about what she remembers about the man our mother disappeared with.

How it feels to have Adam Hawkins see it all, when I think he can see right through me.

I lift a hand and unwind what's left of my bun, letting my hair fall heavily onto my back, my shoulders. From my travel kit, I take out my boar-bristle brush, fitting it into my right hand in the way that feels perfectly familiar. I use the handle and my left hand to separate the length into sections, and then I start: one hundred strokes per section, from scalp to ends. Professionally speaking, I know the advantages. I'm conditioning my hair; I'm helping it shine. I'm massaging my scalp; I'm helping keep my follicles healthy.

Personally speaking?

Personally speaking, my mom used to do this for me.

We're like twins, she used to say, standing behind me while she brushed. *I'm so glad you got my hair.*

I'd been so glad, too. I loved those moments when she was at my back, brushing tangles away. Even for a kid—and a restless one, at that—it had been meditative. The brush pulling the busy, nagging thoughts away from my brain.

When my mom left the first time, I started doing it for myself. Twelve years old. Pulling away my confusion. Pulling away the way I missed her.

Now, I work through it section by section, detangling: I tell myself that I can stay in control, even far from home. Salem can't get the better of me again: yesterday's brief flare of anger in front of her was regrettable but not necessarily repeatable. And Tegan—who talks about Lynton Baltimore as nothing more than a more-normal-than-most boyfriend of our mother's— seems to be doing fine so far.

But Adam Hawkins, I admit, is like hitting a snag.

Honestly, given what he already knows about me via my sister, it has to be only fair I googled him. Not, in fact, after Tegan mentioned it in the van yesterday, but actually the day before, when I'd still been standing in the foyer at Dad and Bernila's house, watching him drive away, still smarting from that awful moment when I'd called him *security*.

And from that gentle moment afterward when he'd tried to help me anyway.

As soon as the results on his name had loaded, I'd gone slowly back to the hammock-chair, trying to take it all in.

Former All-American Blasts NCAA, NFL

Frederick's Former Teammate Goes Scorched Earth on Social Media

Adam "The Hawk" Hawkins Says Copeland Frederick Sought Help

No One Safe from Hawkins's Screed: Coaches, Teammates, Administrators Implicated

Since I've never followed football a day in my life, it'd taken a few clicks to put it together: Adam had once been the best college linebacker in the country, an apparent savant at memorizing plays. He shocked pundits by declining to go pro—first in his junior year, when everyone was fairly certain he would be a first-round draft pick, and then again in his senior year, when everyone was *absolutely* certain. He was vague about his reasons: "Injuries," he sometimes said. "Other interests," he sometimes claimed.

Probably he would've been left to comfortable obscurity had that been the end of his life in the public eye. But five years later, he became the headline again, for a tragic, terrible reason: His former college teammate and longtime best friend—a man who had found massive success in the professional league Adam never went into, a man who was big like Adam, with dark blond hair and a bright smile and kind eyes in all the photos that popped up online—drowned on a summer holiday weekend, not far off the coast of Southern California.

Alone on a small boat he'd rented. A cocktail of substances

in his system. A past full of mental health challenges that Adam eventually claimed football exacerbated and forced him to ignore.

I admit it: I followed a few of the links to his social media posts before I closed my browser.

Adam Hawkins in raw, roaring pain in full view of the world, calling out every person who could've helped Copeland Frederick, but didn't.

I'd felt awful for looking. Like I'd spied on him, even though there was nothing private about what he'd done.

Afterward, I resolved not to let it preoccupy me anymore. It was terrible, what happened to Adam's friend, truly devastating. But I had my own mess to worry about, and it wasn't as though Adam had been a neutral party in helping to make it.

Of course, then Tegan had brought up his past in the car, and my resolution went out the window.

I just . . . I didn't want him to have to talk about something painful. I didn't want to violate his privacy.

Obviously, it makes no *sense*. The same way it doesn't make sense that I can still feel the strength of his arm across my chest, or that I can still see his green eyes watching mine as he asked if I was okay.

There's a knock on the bathroom door as I'm on stroke number whatever—I lost count a long time ago—and when I open it, Tegan stands there in sleep shorts and her senior class T-shirt. For a second, it's as if she's forgotten that she's still mostly mad at me. She smiles drowsily and says, "Gotta pee," so I duck out and wait for her to finish.

When she's done, she opens the bathroom door again, sticking her head out.

"You can come back in."

I guess she's remembered—there's some of that arctic chill back in her voice. Last night, after her interview with Salem, she barely spoke to me, told me that she was "all talked out" when we got into our room and I tried to engage her.

But her inviting me back in, that's an opening, and I stand next to her at the vanity, watching her in the mirror as she picks up my brush for her own use. She does it the same as me: sections, strokes. Unfortunately, I can't think of anything at all for an opening.

"Are you going to keep interrupting me today?" she says, meeting my eyes in the mirror.

I blink back at her. I don't know what she means. It nearly killed me, but I was a statue during her interview with Salem yesterday.

So was Adam Hawkins, come to think of it.

Not that it matters.

"I didn't interrupt."

She loudly and dramatically clears her throat. Then she says, "Does that sound familiar?"

I can't help but smile. Tegan gets a lot of joy out of dragging me.

"No," I say, but I guess it does. I can think of a few specific throat clears. *He was actually so nice to her, compared to some of her other boyfriends,* she said about Miles Daniels . . . or Lynton Baltimore. *Our mom basically always wanted men to love her,* she'd said. *She was a fun mom, but she could get distracted.*

"Well," I say, ceding the point, "I don't really think you're supposed to do much talking on our outing today, so I won't do any throat-clearing."

She shrugs, noncommittal. I'll probably need to keep on with the throat-clearing.

Today, Tegan and I are going with Salem and Adam to meet the person Salem smugly—and vaguely—mentioned yesterday during our tense exchange in the van. Later, when Tegan was awake, Salem made a real production of revealing a few more details.

"Now that you're both . . . *around,*" she said, cutting me a subtle look, "I'll tell you a bit about Curtis MacSherry."

A man Salem is certain Baltimore knew well, and so probably a person he saw when he and our mom came here. Another career confidence man, apparently, and likely an associate of Baltimore's in more than one grift. I asked whether Salem and Adam could simply go on their own to talk to this guy, if we weren't needed, and Tegan had basically turned me into an iceberg with her eyes.

"I'm here to find out about *Mom*," she said, an accusation. A reminder, I guess, of what Salem's offering her that I haven't. That's what this trip was all about for her.

So, we're going.

Tegan pulls the brush through another long section of her red hair. We don't look much alike. From what I remember of her dad, who wasn't around for all that long before my mom ran off with him, and never again once she came back, Tegan favors his features, though sometimes, when she smiles, I see my mom there.

"You also interrupted me with Adam yesterday," she adds now, even as she keeps up the brushing.

On instinct, I snap my eyes over to look at my own face instead of hers. It's as though I'm checking for guilt in my expression. But in the mirror, I look the same as I did a half hour ago, just with smoother hair.

"He has a really interesting story," she says, and even though I *want* Tegan to talk to me, even though I want to have something to share with her that's not this massive, messy thing involving our mom and the man she left us for, I'm afraid to let it be this. I don't want to think too hard about why.

But I still feel his arm across my chest, holding me back. Strong and sudden.

"I thought maybe he wouldn't want to talk about it."

She pauses, midstroke. I can feel her looking over at me, but I've busied myself with my makeup bag.

"You looked him up?" She sounds about as surprised as she should be. About as surprised as I still am.

I mimic her noncommittal shrug. I pretend I'm digging for something in this bag, but really there's only maybe five things in it. Concealer that won't help with these dark circles. Some mascara. A stick of cream blush, ChapStick, brow gel. I'm so distracted by waiting for Tegan's response that I doubt I could manage putting any of it on.

After what feels like forever, I hear the *swish* of the brush through her hair again, and I let out a breath.

A snag, I tell myself firmly, grabbing the concealer. *Adam Hawkins is only a snag.*

And today, I'm resolved to pull him out.

LIKE most things, it's easier said than done.

Tegan and I eat a free continental breakfast in the hotel lobby, me trying to restrict my coffee intake so I don't turn into a throbbing exposed nerve in front of everyone, and Tegan loudly proclaiming her delight at being able to eat as many mediocre croissants as she wants, because we've never stayed anywhere with a free continental breakfast before. I'm grateful Salem and Adam haven't shown up to see this display. I can only imagine the little notes they'd write about my poor sister's deprived childhood.

But when I see them walk into the lobby, I'm inexplicably annoyed that they've clearly been out somewhere for breakfast without us, probably working. Salem's talking on the phone through her earbuds, but she's also frantically typing at the screen, which is something I see her do a lot. Adam has his trusty binder and a laptop under one arm, and with his other hand he's typing on his phone, too.

My mind snags on a bunch of things about Adam Hawkins I've resolved not to be curious about: *What are you typing? Do you have someone waiting for you at home, someone you text every morning? Someone you tell about all those things you stopped putting on your social media?*

It's so disorienting to wonder.

"Oh, here they are, finally!" says Tegan, rising from her chair.

"Teeg," I caution, because I don't want her to seem so eager.

It's so risky to do that, when someone wants something from you.

But she's already walking away, so I drink down the rest of my coffee and follow her.

When I catch up, Tegan's already telling Salem—who I'm pretty sure is still on the phone—that our bags are behind the front desk and we're "totally ready to go." Salem takes it as an invitation, and guides Tegan over there. I clench my fists by my side in frustration at this show of camaraderie between them.

"How are you this morning?" Adam says.

I look over—and up—at him. Yesterday, in the van—I guess as part of my efforts to avoid the snag—I tried hard to avoid looking his way. Except for that near-collision, I thought I'd mostly succeeded, but when I look at him now, I'm disconcerted to realize his features are already familiar to me. He must've shaved this morning: the jaw I've seen covered with stubble now smooth, the line of it looking even more cut. His hair is darker when there's no sunlight streaming through a windshield.

The tops of his ears are pink again, but I haven't said anything rude yet. Maybe he and Salem ate their breakfast outside, and he has a little sunburn. I blink away, watching Tegan at the front desk, Salem beside her, still on the phone.

"Fine," I say, which is all I ever say when people ask me that. Everyone except my sister leaves it alone.

"I was hoping you didn't feel unwell from all the driving."

I'm tugging desperately at that snag.

"I'm fine," I repeat, but also, I'm obviously not. I'm about to spend the day with a career criminal who has met my mother and the notorious boyfriend she abandoned us for. My sister is standing next to a woman who wants it all on tape.

And here I am, thinking about who Adam Hawkins texts back home.

When I look back at him, I catch his eyes looking lower than they usually are.

I clear my throat—it's getting to be my signature move—and

he snaps his gaze back to my face. His ear-tops are blazing red now. He opens his mouth to speak, but then closes it when Salem's voice cuts in.

"Are we ready?"

For a second I think she's genuinely done something helpful for once by interrupting this strained moment, but then I realize she's wheeled my bag over. Obviously I should say thank you, but really I want to shout *Don't touch my stuff!* and run screaming from this lobby.

It's possible my face telegraphs the sentiment, because she hands it over.

By the time we're piling into the van, though, I'm pretty sure that Salem holding my bag for fewer than sixty seconds has, in fact, turned out to be helpful. In a way, it's oriented me again: I don't want her touching my stuff literally mostly because she's trying to touch my stuff metaphorically, and today I need to be focused and unflappable, no matter what this guy says about Lynton Baltimore or my mom. I need to be focused on being there for Tegan.

Who of course remains eager.

We're not even out of the parking lot before she's pulled out the Chattanooga postcard.

"Okay, so what we didn't talk about yesterday," she says, in a voice that reminds me of all the times over the years she told me about a day at school, or a birthday party she went to, or someone she had a crush on, "was how this postcard has anything to do with . . . wait, what was his name again?"

"MacSherry," says Salem, who is still on her goddamned phone. "Curtis MacSherry."

"Right, MacSherry. How do we get from this"—I can see her, in my periphery, waving the postcard back and forth between her and Salem—"to him?"

I swallow, bothered by how completely *I* don't know the answer—how completely this part of my and Tegan's past has been blanketed by my own survival instincts over the last decade. I know those postcards well, but it isn't as though I wanted to investigate them. Mostly I wanted to forget them.

We've been having such a wonderful time, that postcard says. It had been so insulting that I hadn't ever wanted to think about it again.

Now that we're on this trip, though, I see how uncomfortable it is to be caught flat-footed.

"That's Hawk's doing," Salem says. "Hawk, you tell it."

I don't look over at his face. But I see his knuckles whiten again.

"You can."

Salem's still typing. She doesn't bother responding to him.

I think he might quietly sigh. He really doesn't seem like the sort of man who'd go scorched-earth on social media.

But I'm not meant to be focusing on that.

"There's a line in the postcard that mentions 'learning about Miles.'"

I know just what he means. *For the first time,* my mom had written, *I'm really learning about Miles, and it's been so important for our future.*

I don't see how that reveals anything other than my mother's selfishness, writing that to her daughter, whose entire future had been upended by her leaving.

"Okaaaay?" says Tegan, the teenaged expression of my doubt.

Adam clears his throat. "In one of his interviews with Salem, Baltimore says that a great confidence man is mostly unknowable. Unless you know other confidence men."

"That wasn't in the podcast," Salem says, probably for Tegan's benefit, but I listened to the podcast, too. Salem just doesn't know it. "It's one of the bits I cut."

"I figured, if he took Charlotte—" He breaks off, mumbles an unnecessary apology, I guess for using our mother's name. "If he took your mom somewhere where she felt she really learned about him, maybe it was to someone else who was in a similar line of work as him. So I did some research."

Salem snorts. "More than a lot! Hawk probably knows about every living confidence man in the country by now. But I guess we're taking advantage of that Ivy League education he's got!"

This time, I break and look over at him, and it's because I already know what I'll see.

Tips of his ears: pink.

"Didn't you go to some gigantic state school?" asks Tegan.

"Not for graduate school! He got his master's in journalism at Columbia," Salem chirps. It somehow sounds judgmental. "Were you the oldest in your class, Hawk?"

He shakes his head. I know I'm still staring, but I can't seem to stop yet. The words from my mother's postcard have been shoved back into the forgetting parts of my brain. The only questions I seem to want to ask are, once again, about the man sitting next to me.

But it's funny, how he is. How he looks straight ahead and doesn't offer anything else.

It's funny how he reminds me of me.

Did he stand in front of his hotel mirror this morning, sectioning off his face to shave?

"MacSherry's only agreed to talk to us for two hours," he says, so clearly not wanting to talk about himself. "The address he's given us is for a place in Signal Mountain, but I don't think he actually lives there."

"Of course not," Salem snorts.

"This morning Salem and I discussed how we'll use those two hours."

It's the most he's talked in front of Salem since I met him—the first time I've seen him take the lead about the story.

It's difficult not to notice the shift that takes place inside me when Adam is at the wheel of the process: It's an arm out across my chest. A safer feeling I've had in relation to this thing since it started. I shouldn't trust it, but it's also difficult to ignore it.

He's like that. Gigantic in his effect on me.

"MacSherry hasn't worked in a few years," he continues.

"We've told him we want to talk with him about some of his most famous jobs. We haven't focused on Baltimore in our preliminary contact with him. We haven't mentioned our questions about his possibly meeting your mom."

Again, it feels good, calming. Like something I can handle going in, something I can feel in control of. At this point I'm pretending Salem isn't even in the car.

But my sister is, and I don't think she means to, but once again she punctures that sense of control.

"Good luck with that," says Tegan, her voice sarcastic.

I turn my head, see Salem stop typing and look over at her. "Why?"

Tegan shrugs and meets my eyes.

I know what she's going to say before she speaks. After all, I was just thinking of it this morning.

"Because if he's met our mother, you'll know it as soon as he sees Jess. They're like twins."

Chapter 8

Adam

I asked her if she wanted to stay in the van.

I tried to do it quietly, subtly, when Salem was gathering her things in the back and Tegan was already opening her door. I tried to do it without looking again at what I saw, thanks to her sleeveless shirt, in full view for the first time this morning: the black-ink tattoos on her right shoulder, fine-drawn flowers with long stems and slender leaves. I tried not to embarrass her.

On all counts, I'm pretty sure I failed.

Salem certainly heard.

This time, I noticed that one of the flowers had a lovingly curved petal falling, right along her tricep.

Jess said, "I'm fine" again, and opened her door, too.

By now, there's no ignoring the way I want to spare her. I don't want to see her hands shake, or to have her feeling car-sick, or to have her ambushed by Salem or her sister or a career criminal who will recognize her face.

I don't *want* to get her to talk.

At least, not for this.

Not for anyone else but me, if I'm honest with myself.

I need to tell Salem about how I feel; I know I do. But this morning, with this particular interview on the schedule, seemed like the wrong time. MacSherry is my get, after all, and I figured that doing an impressive job with him might help grease the wheels with Salem. I do a good enough job, follow all the plans Salem and I set at breakfast, and it's another point in my favor for getting my future story off the ground.

No getting Jess Greene to talk necessary.

But as soon as Curtis MacSherry steps out onto the wraparound porch of a run-down ranch deep in the woods of what must be one of the few remaining undeveloped tracts of land in Signal Mountain, pretty much all those plans go out the window.

Because he does recognize her.

I can see it right away: His lean, tall form—aided in its uprightness by a slim, polished cane—stills, and he stares long at where Jess stands on the dirt path leading up to the house.

She looks back, chin up, mulish again. A dare.

He smiles, and from beside me—frankly, I forgot she was there—Salem says quietly, "I see how he got the nickname."

The Cat, he's sometimes called. Because of that bright-white, easy smile. A Cheshire grin, knowing and mischievous.

He takes a step down off the porch, and I step forward.

"Mr. MacSherry," I say, because I don't want him approaching her. Not with that smile on his face. Probably not at all.

He looks over at me, keeping the smile. He's dressed as though he's going for dinner at some warm-weather, by-the-sea resort: loose but unwrinkled linen pants, a short-sleeve patterned shirt that's open at the collar. His salt-and-pepper hair is neatly trimmed, his skin strikingly unwrinkled for a man his age. He wears three gold rings on the hand that holds his cane.

"The Hawk," he says as he extends his hand to me. I've always referred to myself as Adam when I've communicated with him, but I'm pretty sure this is a tactic, a reminder. Both of us with our silly nicknames, given to us by other people. Something we have in common.

"Adam," I correct, shaking his hand firmly. Probably more firmly than is necessary.

He's still smiling, but when I release his hand, he looks over at Jess briefly before turning his gaze back to me.

"You seemed too earnest for an ambush, Adam." He's said it casually, almost like a joke, but still—I detect a note of censure there.

"In fairness," Salem cuts in, "she was a surprise to us, too."

She holds out her hand and introduces herself, and I take the opportunity to look over at where Jess and Tegan stand, several feet away. For the first time since I met them together, Tegan seems to stay deliberately close to her older sister. On the ride here, she made the remark about Charlotte and Jess looking alike casually, almost a little cruelly. But now, she seems reluctant to leave Jess's side.

They're complicated, the two of them. The love between them as obvious as the tension. I wonder if they know how clearly they show it.

"—and so we had actually been speaking to Tegan, when we thought we were speaking to Jess," Salem is explaining, when I finally refocus, and I don't see why we have to give him that information. I don't see why we can't at least try to stick to the plan.

"Is there a place you want us to set up?" I interrupt.

I think of that curved petal along Jess's tricep. I think about wanting to catch it in my cupped hand.

MacSherry looks at me calmly. Even when he's not smiling, he somehow is. He turns and walks toward Jess and Tegan, as though I didn't speak. I get an old urge to do some flattening, which is definitely not part of the plan.

"I'm Curtis," he says to them smoothly, but he doesn't extend his hand this time. I get the sense he knows he'd be rejected.

Jess doesn't even blink. She may be trying to flatten him in her own way.

But he doesn't seem bothered. He doesn't even wait for either of them to reply, though Tegan looks like she's about to.

He simply takes over, making a plan of his own.

"And you're Charlotte's daughters."

"She was very friendly," MacSherry says, sipping idly from his iced tea. "Very funny and charming. She seemed to love the area here."

He gestures with his glass, all around us.

We're around the back of the ranch house, on a large stone patio overlooking the thick woods. When MacSherry led us here, he gestured to a grouping of mismatched chairs, all arranged around a brick fire pit that does not look professionally constructed, and invited us to sit as though he'd just brought us to the luxury by-the-sea resort he's dressed for. He offered us drinks: sweet tea or Coke. He said he had cheese and crackers inside.

Salem and I had exchanged a confused, surreptitious glance—*this* is the man who once secured two-and-a-half million dollars from a Greek shipping heir for a painting that turned out to be a forgery, and a pretty bad one, at that? The man who once successfully impersonated an MI5 agent for at least a year in the 1980s?—and then we started setting up some of our equipment as best we could on the rickety fire pit.

Now, he's holding court, reclined with one slim leg crossed over the other in a faded lawn chair as if it's a throne. If he's bothered by being ambushed, he doesn't show it. He's been blowing smoke for at least the last forty-five minutes.

"At the time," he continues, his voice taking on a wistful quality, "my mother was still living. She and Charlotte got on very well during the visit, and—"

"Mr. MacSherry," I interrupt, because every time he says the name Charlotte, I can somehow *feel* Jess get more tense. Twice he's mentioned the "remarkable resemblance" between them. He's taunting her.

"It might be helpful if you could talk more about the nature of that visit. If you could talk to us about your relationship to Baltimore, and why he might have come here."

I don't look over at her, but I'm pretty sure Salem approves of this. She favors a loose style when interviewing, but MacSherry is more than loose. He's liquid.

"Relationship!" he echoes, laughing. "I wouldn't call it that."

"What would you call it?"

He looks over at me, and I guess I owe it to the nickname, but I think of a video I saw on the internet once: a house cat sitting on the edge of a desk, casually swiping items off its surface. A knowing glint in its eyes. A cup of pens, a tape dispenser, a stapler.

"Probably I'd use a term you're familiar with, what with your . . . *history*." He smiles, turning his taunting toward me now. "We were teammates."

Jess clears her throat. It's so loud. The only thing I don't like about it is the way it draws MacSherry's attention back to her. His eyes catalogue her face as he smiles, smiles, smiles, and I swear: If he says "remarkable resemblance" again, fuck the plans.

It'll be flattening time.

Lucky for him, he gives up and turns back to me.

"Do you know what a roper is?"

Salem snorts. Obviously I know what a roper is, being on this job. I did my research.

"I don't!" says Tegan. She's leaning forward in her chair, excited.

"Ah," says MacSherry, clearly thrilled, and if I were writing copy for the intro to this interview, I know exactly what I would say. I would say that this is a man who loves to hear himself talk. A man who longs for a captive audience. I'd say I'm pretty sure that it's the talking that keeps MacSherry grifting, rather than whatever it is he goes after in the grift.

"A roper is a"—he slides his eyes toward me briefly—"a *team-mate* I sometimes have. He might, after quite a lot of careful work, facilitate an introduction for me. To someone that I wish to know better."

Tegan blinks at him. "I mean," she says flatly, that excitement from before muted with annoyance, "I can just look it up on my phone, if you're going to be like that about it. All *mysterious* or whatever."

I almost—*almost*—laugh. Instead I snap my gaze toward Jess, just in case she does.

Just so I don't miss it.

I see the barest, most beautiful quirk at the corner of her mouth. It's a syrup-drenched stack of pancakes. It's nowhere near a laugh, but still. I could eat off that quirk for days and days.

Salem actually *does* laugh this time, and whether it's authentic or tension-breaking, I can't really tell. I do know that Mac-Sherry joins in, and while I could be overthinking it, it seems . . . reluctant. A saving-face laugh, an *I'm not going to let a teenager get the better of me* laugh.

He looks back at Tegan, doing a quick but somehow still menacing pass of his gaze over her features, and says, "Now *you*. You may not look like her, but you're *much* more like your mother in spirit."

Whatever's the biggest thing on the proverbial desk, The Cat has just swiped it off, and the crash is deafening. I catch Salem, her laugh trailing away, shake her head shortly at me. A warning, maybe, but I look away from it and focus on Jess again.

I've seen this expression on her face before—the storm behind glass—and I half expect her to stand up and walk away again, taking Tegan with her.

This time, though, she cracks the window.

"Let me ask you something, Mr. MacSherry." Her voice is a

pelting, icy cold rain. "How long did our mother stay in this house?"

It's a good question, one Salem and I eventually planned to ask. But I'm pretty sure Jess doesn't share our motivations, and she definitely doesn't share our tactics. Still, if he answers, Salem will probably be thrilled.

MacSherry tilts his head at her. He's probably thinking about another labyrinthine, obfuscating way to respond to a simple request.

But maybe he doesn't enjoy being this close to a storm, because after a tense few seconds, he merely says, "Five days."

No smile.

She nods coolly, then basically lightning-bolts his face off.

"Well, good for you. But my sister and I both knew—*lived with*—our mother for years, so I hope you don't think your *five days* provides you some kind of special insight. If we have questions about her, we'll ask you. For now, why don't you answer the ones Adam has already put to you, and stop wasting our time."

I know it's MacSherry who's been struck by this electricity from her, but I feel a current move through me all the same. In my gut, up my spine, buzzing in my chest. She sounds fierce, protective. Absolutely immune to bullshit. It's somehow better than a stack of pancakes.

Also, she said my *name.*

Adam, she said.

I feel warm all over.

It's so goddamned unprofessional.

The part of me that can still recognize this snaps back to attention, and I'm pretty sure it's not self-preservation on my part. I don't even look to see if my actual boss has noticed my reaction. Instead, I look to MacSherry, because Jess is trying to deflect his attention from her sister to me. It's for her—not for my career and my future hopes for it—that I want to take it.

I expect to have to intervene, somehow—to see him having recovered his smile, readying himself for a smooth comeback.

But watching him now, I can see that a tension has settled over him. He's turning one of the rings on his hand; he's flexing the foot of his crossed leg ever-so-slightly up and down.

I think of what Salem said to me back in the diner the morning after we first met Jess and Tegan: that Baltimore's grifts are really about what women have been taught they need from a man.

But Curtis MacSherry looks like a man who's just met a brick wall.

A wall that's not impressed by or fearful of his charm, his power, his elusiveness. That cares nothing for what he has to say, that needs nothing from him. He's clearly so unused to that.

He may not answer any of our questions at all.

"So Baltimore was your roper?" I say.

He meets my eyes, and it's hard to explain what happens: It's as though he's deciding to rearrange reality so that I'm the only person here. Salem is desperate enough for information about Baltimore that she'd be the friendlier audience, but I guess it doesn't matter to this guy. I guess she gets confined to the same box he's now put Jess and Tegan in.

It's labeled, *People Who Don't Think I'm the Most Interesting Man in the World.*

I do my best to fake an interested expression.

MacSherry laughs, recovering himself.

"Oh, he'd hate to hear that. No, no, not consistently. Mostly, he worked alone. But this once, he'd done me a favor. It involved . . . ah. Chemistry, let's say?"

He's testing me, seeing what I know. Judging by the way he looks at me, and by that *teammate* shit he said before, he probably thinks my brain is made of bricks.

But I know what he's referring to. A few of MacSherry's biggest grifts involved wine forgeries: brokering huge deals for what enthusiasts and collectors thought were rare, antique bottles. Apparently, these were pretty easy touches. Marks who wanted to seem sophisticated, elite. Marks who rhapsodized about vintages and blooms and flavor profiles. And the best part, for MacSherry, was that they were reluctant to admit it when they couldn't tell the difference between an eighteenth-century red and a mixture of three different wines from a grocery store.

So they never did. And MacSherry kept the money he made.

If I say any of that on the recording, he won't acknowledge it. So I simply nod.

"I owed him a share. That's why he came here. To collect it."

He slides his eyes briefly toward Salem before looking back to me. "For several months before that, he'd been . . . unavailable."

The seven months Baltimore was in prison, he means. His only stint, ever: a class-one misdemeanor charge for impersonating an officer. It's during that time he talked to Salem.

I can sense she's wound tight over there, torn between wanting to take over and not wanting to disturb whatever fragile link is keeping MacSherry out here after he got dressed down so thoroughly. But I think she can tell we're on short time, now—that MacSherry won't want us here for much longer.

So I have to get what I can in the time we have.

"And did you give it to him?"

I'm really fucking sick of that smile.

"Of course I did. I'm a man of my word."

Without looking, I know it's Jess who huffs out a breath. Sardonic and dismissive, and *noticeable*. It's terrible timing, but I can't blame her. Probably I'll congratulate her for it later, if I can get up the courage to talk to her without weirdly asking her to say my name again.

MacSherry's eyebrows lift briefly. Time's up, I think.

"It took me a few days to pull it together," he says. "*Five*. As I mentioned."

Salem gets desperate, interrupting. "And while Baltimore was here, did he—"

MacSherry stands, cane in hand. "I've just remembered another engagement. I'm afraid I'll have to cut this short."

"No, wait!" Tegan bolts upward from her chair, her voice overloud. "*I* wanted to ask things!"

"Teeg," Jess says softly, in a tone that's so different from the way she talked to MacSherry.

"You said you wouldn't interrupt me again."

"I didn't say that." She's still using that soft, gentle tone. "Today isn't—"

I don't get to know how she's going to finish that sentence, because this time, it's Tegan who walks away. It's not the silent, controlled stride Jess left her house with a few days ago; it's Tegan shoving her hands into her hair and letting out a frustrated, teenaged, "*Argh!*" before stomping off the patio, presumably back around front to where the van is. Obviously that's not the way to get her questions asked, but I'm pretty sure she's not thinking straight.

MacSherry's all Cheshire cat again. Pleased as punch. "Well! Wasn't this a dramatic morning?"

Fuck off, I want to say, but hold my tongue. Salem begins an apology, but I can't listen. He doesn't deserve one. What he wanted was two hours of us stroking his ego over the clever crimes he's committed and never been punished for. I don't feel even a little bad that he didn't get it.

Instead I look at Jess, whose jaw is set tight as she watches her sister's angry retreat.

". . . what if you and I—" Salem is saying to MacSherry.

"We're done here," Jess cuts in, and Salem maybe doesn't have lightning-bolt capacities, but she's no slouch, either. She looks so mad at Jess that I instinctively step toward the fire pit and shut off the recording.

This is a goddamned mess. Right now, *we're* the story. The broken compass, on display.

It's the opposite of the plan.

Salem takes a deep breath, clearly stifling the urge to snap back at Jess. She's gearing up to do more placating of Mac-Sherry, but Jess stops her before she can speak again.

"We don't need him. I know why they went to Pensacola."

MacSherry turns to her. The fastest I've seen him move all day.

"Pensacola?" There's a knowing lilt to his voice. His smile transformed.

"Do you know something about Pensacola?" Salem says.

He laughs again, then pauses, seeming to consider something. Finally, he shrugs. A sort of *Why not?* shrug.

"You may want to visit a little gift shop there. Sea . . . something?" He waves a lazy hand.

Helpful, I'm sure. In a literal seaside town. What if I did just a minor flattening?

"Is there anything else you can tell us about that, Curtis?" Salem says. "This gift shop?"

He inhales deeply through his nose, smiles out toward the woods.

"Oh, I don't think so." He taps his cane once on the patio, an obvious farewell. "Just keep in mind. Even the best of us don't work *all* the time."

The Last Con of Lynton Baltimore

Transcript Excerpt from Episode 9, "Mistakes Were Made"

[**Durant, voice-over:** Baltimore is understandably reluctant to speak about his misdemeanor conviction. His reputation has for so long depended on his shape-shifting that I can only assume he would have rather had his—until recently—spotless record marred by almost anything else. Wire fraud, forgery, even theft. But whether he's open to talking about what got him here, he doesn't seem at all to mind talking about the fact of being incarcerated.]

Baltimore: I've always made the best of my circumstances. This one isn't any different.

Durant: I doubt that.

Baltimore: Why do you doubt it?

Durant: I can't imagine there's a lot of opportunities for you to do what you do from where you are. I can't imagine you're enjoying yourself in a place where you have no freedom of movement, where you can't be anyone else but whatever your inmate number is.

Baltimore: ::laughs:: I thought you were the storyteller here! You're having a failure of imagination, I think.

Durant: ::laughs, slightly uncomfortably:: That's interesting. Maybe I am.

Chapter 9

Jess

When Tegan was nine years old, she brought home an invitation to something called a "Mommy & Me" birthday tea party.

It was a girl from her class who was having it, or, I guess it's more accurate to say, the mother of the girl from her class was having it, because I don't think there are that many nine-year-olds who are excited to drink hot tea or eat cucumber sandwiches. Tegan brought the thick cardstock invitation home and showed it to me as though the Queen of England herself had sent it.

She'd said, "I can't believe she invited *us.*"

Obviously, I did not want to go, but also, obviously, I *did* go. It'd only been eight and a half months since Mom had left, and Tegan was as fragile as spun sugar, barely showing excitement about anything. I would've eaten a million cucumber sandwiches for her.

I would've curtseyed to the Queen of Fourth Grade.

At the party, it was pretty clear to me that we were a pity invite. I'd heard more than my fair share of *the mother ran off* or *the sister is really her only family* whispers over the previous few months, had endured concerned and curious gazes. By that point—so soon after Mom's departure, and still close enough to the whirlwind popularity of Salem Durant's podcast—I was still in the height of my furious, panicked fear that someone, somehow, would put it all together, and I'd barely let myself be seen by other parents at innocuous things like school drop-off. Clearly, that strategy had worked in terms of avoiding questions, but not in terms of rousing sympathy. So when we walked in, women greeted me with exaggerated tongue-clucks followed by versions of "How are you doing, *really?*" They looked down at my black knit dress and settled for compliments like, "Very classic!" or "I love a simple dress!" They called Tegan *honey* and *sweetheart.*

We were, predictably, seated at a table in the back, six of us in total: a cousin and aunt of the birthday girl, and another obviously unpopular girl from Tegan's class. Conversation was stilted but mostly harmless, right up until the cousin—while her mom was taking a bathroom break—told Tegan the story about the kitten.

"Yeah, so I heard them arguing about it in their room. My dad was asking her whose kitty it was, and then my mom said it was *her* kitty. But then he kept asking her a bunch of times, and—"

I froze in my seat, hoping against hope this was going in a different direction.

"So then finally she said it was *his* kitty, and then they were quiet for a while, well like mostly quiet? I think something is broken in their room. But like, where is the kitten, you know? I thought maybe I would get it for my birthday, but—"

I locked eyes with the other mom at the table. I thought maybe she'd be in the same state of shocked paralysis as me, trying to stifle an embarrassed laugh, but she wasn't. She looked at me as though it was somehow my fault—the black-dress wear-ing, tattooed twenty-two-year-old—that she'd gotten stuck at a table with a kid whose parents were into dirty talk.

Tegan was saying, "I don't get why your mom and dad would be calling it a kitty," when the cousin's mom returned to the table.

That, I'd always thought, had been the most painfully awk-ward experience of my adult life.

That is, until I took a car ride from Chattanooga to Pensa-cola.

Six hours of almost-silence.

Six hours of everyone mad.

It's nearly midnight now, Tegan's asleep in our room, and I've escaped to a place where at least the quiet feels less heavy: the hotel's pool area, which is technically closed but also the kind of closed where there's poor signage and no lock on the gate. Plausible-deniability closed. It's so humid that the slats of the lounge chair I'm lying on stick to my legs, but there's at least a faint, if warm, breeze. The rise-and-fall sounds of crickets and frogs and cicadas aren't as recriminating as Tegan's cold shoul-der or Salem's barely leashed frustration.

As Adam's careful, contemplative quiet.

I shouldn't feel guilty about what happened at Curtis Mac-Sherry's house. I shouldn't feel guilty for wiping that sleazy smile off his face; I shouldn't feel guilty for not trusting him to give Tegan a straightforward answer about anything. I knew, deep down, that if she'd asked him questions about Mom, he would've kept up with his slick, dodging answers. He would've made her feel confused and unsure of herself.

He wouldn't have told her anything worth knowing.

But I can't help wondering if I should've just let her see that for herself.

I thought about telling her. I thought about saying that I was sorry, thought about telling her how it made my stomach feel queasy to hear Curtis MacSherry say Mom was funny and charming, that she was a nice companion for his elderly mother.

It wasn't that I thought he was lying.

It was that I thought the opposite.

She *was* funny and charming. When she paid attention to you—really paid attention to you, for however many moments you could catch her attention—you thought you were the most important person in the world.

It hurt to be reminded that she was still all of these things to other people after she left. That other people had always been able to catch her attention for longer than I ever had.

When I tried, though—when I opened my mouth to make my apology, my explanation—I felt a stone lodge in my throat. I've spent so many years never talking to Tegan about how I feel about Mom that I don't know how to start, and anyway, I don't know if I should.

It's Tegan who hurts the most from what Mom did, not me.

I run my hands over my face, part of me wishing I could let out a great big, gusty *"Argh!"* to the sky, same as my sister did in Curtis MacSherry's backyard.

When I hear the quiet clink of the unlocked gate, I'm so annoyed by the interruption to my solitude that I contemplate pretending to be a hotel employee in charge of policing the joint. However, since I'm lying on this chair in my pajamas, I guess it'll be a tough sell. Instead I lower my hands from my eyes and hope whoever it is won't notice me.

Of course, it's Adam Hawkins.

And he notices me.

"Oh," he says, stilling where he is. "I'm sorry."

I push myself more upright so I can see him better. He's wearing athletic shorts and a soaked-through T-shirt. He's sweating. Breathing harder than normal. His hair is damp and sticking up in all directions, windblown. He's the in-real-life version of every movie star who does some cheesy magazine cover story about how they bulked up to play a superhero, except in real life, it's not cheesy at all.

This is terrible news.

"The pool is closed," I blurt.

"I was just cutting through." He gestures to the bank of rooms beyond us.

Then I think he . . . I think he maybe . . . laughs? Quiet and low and brief. A chuckle.

My pajamas are normal, shorts and an old T-shirt. I don't think I have anything on my face, not that he could see it in the dim, watery light. I don't see what there is to laugh about.

"What's funny?"

He shrugs those big shoulders. "You sound like you're working security."

I blink up at him. I can't believe I want to laugh, too. I don't, because that seems risky—acknowledging that he and I have an inside joke. But maybe I smile a little.

Silence falls over us again, but it's not the same as before— it's not the standoff of the van. This is a tentative silence, an inviting silence.

"Can't sleep?" he says finally, keeping his voice quiet. He stays in his spot by the gate, waiting to see if I'll take him up on answering this simple question.

There's no stone lodged in my throat now, and there probably should be.

"No. I'm guessing you can't either?"

He shrugs, coming a few steps closer and crouching at the edge of the pool. He cups a hand and dunks it in, then brings it up to the top of his head, letting the water drip down and cool the back of his neck. I cross one leg over the other, mortified by my quick, hot, pulsing reaction to this, to him: his face, his body, his breathing. The way he rises from his crouch and sets his hands low on his hips.

The way he says, "Are you doing okay?" as though all he cares about in this whole world is how I am.

It's so disarming.

"I'm sorry," I say, before I can change my mind. "I'm sorry I ruined things today."

He drops his hands and looks at me for a long time. The rippling water from the low-lit pool plays across the parts of his skin I can see. When he comes closer and gestures to the chair beside me, a question in his eyes, I'm powerless to do anything but nod.

"Sorry if I stink," he says as he sits, not reclining. But he doesn't stink. He smells like saltwater and wind and delicious sweat, and whatever deodorant he wears. All I want is to get closer to it.

I should *not* have let him sit down.

"You didn't ruin things."

My only answer is a look. A *yeah, right* look.

Adam shrugs. "He was always going to be difficult. And he was trying to rile you and your sister. That's not your fault."

"It's my fault for letting him."

God, it'd made me so *mad*, hearing him talk about Mom. It'd made me so mad, to have him look at me like I'm her carbon copy.

I shove the thought away, focusing instead on my apology. On the man sitting next to me, his breathing slowing by degrees with every second that passes.

"You were—you did a good job." It sounds as though I'm being forced to say it. I try to soften my voice, but it doesn't come naturally. "You seemed calm. Nothing he said got to you."

I can see him swallow, but he doesn't respond. Usually, I don't have any problem being the one to let the silence stretch. In fact, usually I prefer it.

But tonight I feel different. Raw and sad and uncertain of myself.

"I hope I didn't cause problems for you. With Salem, I mean."

One side of his mouth hitches up. "You hope that, huh?"

I think from anyone else, it might sound snarky, maybe even censuring. I've made no secret of not wanting to participate in this, and it'd be fair enough for Adam to think the way I acted today was about sabotage, about me derailing this thing I never wanted to do. Somehow, though, Adam doesn't seem to mean it that way. Or if he does, he doesn't seem to mind it.

"She'll be fine," he continues, waving a hand. A single, cool drop of pool water from his fingers flicks onto my calf and it feels so nice I barely suppress a hum of pleasure. I'm halfway to thinking about how it would feel if he would set his hand to my thigh and run it down to my ankle, cooling the whole length of my leg, before I stop myself.

I can't be thinking of Adam Hawkins this way.

Right?

"And Tegan?" he says, which does the work of refocusing my attention, and answering the question I posed to myself. I stiffen in my chair—automatic, defensive. I know he notices, and when I meet his eyes, there's something soft and understanding in his expression.

He adds quietly, "Is she okay?"

I gust out a sigh and tip my head back, staring at the dark, swaying shapes of the palm trees above me. I want to pretend, just for a little while, that he's *not* Adam Hawkins. I want to pretend that he's a stranger whose job doesn't have anything to do with my past, my sister's past, my mother's past. I want to pretend like I wasn't just thinking of his hand on my leg.

So I don't look at him when I answer.

"I don't really know if she's okay. She won't talk to me."

It's not much of a confession. Adam was in the car, after all. And when we stopped for a meal, Tegan announced—to Adam and Salem, not to me—she wanted to sit by herself. I'm sure it wouldn't surprise him to know she ghosted me in the hotel room we were sharing, too.

"I guess I deserve it," I add.

To the palm trees, I lie to myself. *You're talking to the palm trees and the pool and the night air.*

"You were just trying to help."

A palm tree would never say that, obviously. But I'm still pretending.

"I don't think she sees it that way. Right now I don't think she sees anything I've ever done that way."

My head is a highlight reel of mistakes I've made with Tegan. It's not even hiding the postcards from Mom or snapping at Curtis MacSherry. It's wearing a black dress to a Mommy & Me tea party. Not knowing what to say when she announces she wants to sit by herself.

I can understand why Adam goes palm-tree silent. When have I ever given him any indication I want him to press me on anything, to ask me a follow-up? When have I ever, in the days since I've known him, *offered* him any information?

I turn my head toward him without lifting it from the chair. I'm reminding myself, I guess, who he is. I've given him an opening for any number of questions I'm sure he wants the answer to.

What was it like for you, to take over Tegan's care?

What kind of relationship did you have with Tegan before your mother left?

Do you regret not telling Tegan sooner, what you'd realized about who your mother left with?

But he doesn't ask any of that, because he knows I won't respond.

He just says, "Teenagers, right?"

And it is the perfect response. The most knowing response. Probably the only response that would not make me feel embarrassed or threatened or angry. It isn't a prodding, inauthentic effort to bond, like the clumsy one Salem made in the van on our first day of this trip.

It's offering me a way out.

"You have a lot of experience with the species?"

He chuckles again, shakes his head once. "Not really, I guess. I was one, once. Spent a lot of time around other ones while I was."

Of course that's true for pretty much every person who lived through their own teen years, but I get the sense Adam means more than just classmates and friends. He was an athlete, after all, and a good one. Part of a complicated network of guys his own age, for years and years.

I think of MacSherry saying that word to him, *teammates.*

I hated that.

"Your sister," he says, a note of caution in his voice, "She's a good one. Smart, curious. Independent."

I make a noise, not unlike the one that blew up our meeting with MacSherry earlier. Smart and curious and independent is what got us here, and it's not as if we've been having a great time.

But also, I'm warmed by the compliment to her. Tegan *is* smart; she *is* curious. She's grown into herself, is sure of herself.

I've always loved it, when people see Tegan's strengths.

"That doesn't happen on its own," he adds, and I can tell by the tone of his voice.

He means me.

He's saying Tegan is all those good things because of *me.*

This time, I don't have it in me to make a snort of dismissal. In fact, I have to turn my face back up to the sky, because I feel an alarming and sudden press of tears behind my eyes. I won't let it go any further than that. Crying is for the shower, which is basically the unlocked pool gate of locations for having emotions. You can maintain a lot of plausible deniability about the moisture on your face in there.

Still, it opens something in me, to hear him say this. The truth is, ever since I walked into Tegan's room and saw her bags packed, I've felt slingshotted back in time to ten years ago, when I was barely an adult myself, trying to figure out how I was going to raise my sister on my own. I've been *living* in that highlight reel of mistakes, seeing nothing but all the things I'm certain I've done wrong, the things that would've made it okay in Tegan's mind to write me a note and leave for weeks while I was off at work one day.

Probably Adam is giving me more credit than I deserve, probably he's doing his best to be nice to me so I don't go off the rails again, wrecking whatever interview comes next. But right now, I'll take it.

I'll take anything.

"Thank you."

I'm relieved when he doesn't take advantage right away. He seems to be letting me live in this palm-tree pretending moment, where I can simply lie here and take the compliment. Press pause on the highlight reel. I'm so desperate to stay that I do something unexpected.

I ask him a question.

"Do you normally go running at midnight, or is this a special occasion?"

I don't look over at him, because I don't want to see it if he's pulling a shocked face. That's probably what the extra beat of silence is before he finally answers.

"Not normally, but . . ." He trails off, and I hear the lounger creak beneath him. "I get sore from driving. My back, my legs. Old injuries. It helps me to get out and move."

Because of the football, I imagine saying, but don't. *You said injuries were a reason you didn't go pro,* I imagine saying. *I read about it.*

But obviously, I don't.

"Helps me think."

I close my eyes, blocking out the palm trees. It's a good compromise, because I don't want to look over at him for what I'm pretty sure he's going to change the subject to. I'm pretty sure I know what he needed help thinking about.

"So, tomorrow."

I don't open my eyes. "I already told Salem what I know about Pensacola."

It was one of the few things I said, after we left Curtis MacSherry's. I told Salem that Mom had a friend from high school with a condo here, or at least she did when I was sixteen, Tegan three. She wanted to take us both there for a week in the summer, a "girls' trip." When I went to her house for my weekly visit, which my dad still insisted on, she showed me pictures of the condo, of the beach view. She said her friend Julia was so nice to let us use it. She said Julia had married very well.

I told Salem we never ended up going.

I didn't tell her why, and I think she was still too mad about the MacSherry interview to ask.

But the why is pretty boring, anyway. Mom got a new boyfriend that summer, a guy named Glenn. He didn't want to go to Pensacola, so we didn't. Tegan was too young to care. I remember being relieved.

When Mom sent me the postcard from here all those years ago, I thought for sure she must've come to that condo, thought she must've gone to see her friend Julia. She'd written, *It's as beautiful here as it always looked in the pictures! Miles and I are reconnecting with loved ones. I'm thinking of you both.*

After what Curtis MacSherry said, though, I'm less certain about what that postcard meant.

But that's not really my problem.

"I won't get in your way. Or in Salem's way. I know you have to look at all these gift shops or whatever."

I wonder if he notices I don't make any promises about Tegan. Maybe I should, but when I think of it—when I think of her earlier today, desperate to get information from a dirtbag grifter—the stone lodges in my throat again.

I'm having such trouble letting go.

Adam clears his throat. "What if we split up?"

He's said it differently than he says most things. There's not necessarily a slowness to the way he speaks usually, but there's a . . . carefulness. A calmness, like what I tried to compliment him on from the meeting with MacSherry.

Now, though, he's spoken quickly. Rushing it out before he can change his mind.

I finally open my eyes and sit up. I almost swing my legs over the lounger but stop when I realize that would definitely result in my bare legs touching Adam's. That would be disastrous. I can *feel* the way it would be disastrous.

"Split up?"

"It's . . . not a small number of gift shops."

I stare at him, uncomprehending. "Tegan and I can't just . . ." I trail off, try again. "We wouldn't even know how to—"

"Not you and Tegan."

"*Not* me and—?"

He interrupts me before I can finish.

Stuns me.

He knows exactly what I've been having so much trouble with, I think.

"Tegan and Salem," he says. "And you and me."

Chapter 10

Adam

"She better not change her mind."

It's the first thing Salem says to me when she gets out of the second rental car we're just back from picking up. I've been waiting for her by the van in the hotel's parking lot, knowing she stopped off on the way back to get coffee. It's just past ten a.m. and already brutally hot, even though I've been standing in a shady spot. Salem doesn't even seem to notice the temperature. The paper cup of coffee she's got in one hand is comically large.

"She won't," I say, but honestly, I'm not sure.

I haven't been sure of anything since I met Jess Greene.

When she left the pool last night, after we'd reached our tentative agreement, I sat by myself for another twenty minutes, part of me wondering if any second I'd wake up in my uncomfortable hotel bed, having dreamed the whole thing: the sight of Jess in shorts by the pool, the conversation we had, the deal we made.

I thought, *I can't believe she said yes.*

I wish I could say I had the idea earlier, that I'd thought of it sometime between leaving Curtis MacSherry's place and the moment I'd left my hotel room—achy and irritated—for a head-clearing run. But the truth is, I didn't think of us splitting up until I sat next to her. Until I saw that flash of emotion in her eyes after I tried—clumsily, probably, but truthfully—to compliment her about Tegan.

She looked up to the sky and I saw her throat bob in a heavy swallow. I saw her close her eyes tight before opening them again, fixing her gaze on the trees above. Gathering herself.

I only wanted, in that moment, to give her a break. From Salem, from her sister. As much of one as I could manage, while still doing what I needed to do for my job.

She was desperate for a break; I could see it.

That's how I got the idea.

Salem comes to stand next to me in the shade, lifting the lid off her coffee. It is steaming hot but she takes a big sip anyway, then makes a noise of satisfaction. Thank God. She has not had a good thing to say about a cup of coffee she's had in days, and I can't say that's been helping matters.

"Hawk," she says, after a few seconds, and I can hear in her voice the caffeine's already working. She's starting to feel more human. In the office, she barely talks before about nine thirty, and this morning, I woke her up with a call just before six, to tell her about the plan.

To tell her what Jess had agreed to.

"Yeah?"

"You did well yesterday."

I turn my head and look down at her. She's watching the hotel's front doors, blowing on her coffee.

"You had good focus with MacSherry, even though things went wrong. He's not an easy interview."

Probably I should be happier to hear this. In fact, I should have been more worried, all day yesterday, about how pissed

Salem seemed with the way things had ended up. I should've been focused on the story, the consequences to the story. The consequences to how Salem would see my work.

But mostly I hadn't been.

Mostly, Salem's compliment about my work means nothing compared to the grudging one Jess Greene gave me at midnight by the pool.

"Thanks."

"And whatever you said to Jess last night—I wish you'd recorded it, honestly. It's good that it worked, because right now those two are like cats in a bag with their fighting. Except one of the cats is determined to keep them both in the bag forever."

I feel a prickle of annoyance on Jess's behalf. The comparison feels pretty incomplete, pretty unfair.

We're the bag, I want to say. *This story is the bag.*

"I don't know how you did it."

I shrug. "Just tried to keep it simple."

It hadn't been simple; it'd been like defusing a bomb. Like looking at a bunch of wires all tangled together, all but one ready to cause an explosion. I didn't know Jess well enough to know about her wires, so it has to be that I got lucky.

It's really the only explanation.

"I know it probably doesn't seem like it," Salem says, "but yesterday was good practice for you. Both things."

"What?"

"The people you're looking to talk to for the Copeland Frederick story—they'll have things in common with MacSherry, and with Jess, too. There will be people who have lawyers and PR people in their ears, and they'll be like MacSherry—too slippery to talk. And then there will be people like Jess. Too hurt to talk."

It's the first time she's mentioned my story in a couple of days, and guilt nudges me. For years, my focus has been Cope. I've worked on other stories—when I was in school, when I was an intern, and in the time I've been at Broadside, too—but I've always managed to see them as stepping stones to my bigger goal.

Now, with that goal in sight—with an actual, if conditional, promise from Salem to help make it happen—I'm losing touch.

It isn't that I'm not thinking about Cope; I'm thinking about him all the time. In fact, I thought of him last night, when I sat down next to Jess and apologized in advance for maybe smelling bad after my run. I could practically hear his laugh. I could practically hear him say, *You have no game, Adam,* in that teasing way he had, and he would be right. Just seeing her long, bare legs made me flush with a heat that had nothing to do with my run.

I wish he was here to rag me about that.

Salem's phone pings and she pulls it from her back pocket. I'd be more relieved by the distraction from talk of Cope except that when she looks down at her screen, she rolls her eyes and mutters something in clear frustration. I've always known Salem to be tied to her phone, but that's not unusual for the people I work with. On this trip, though, it's been unreal—not just constant, but also seemingly stressful to her.

"Everything all right?"

"Don't ever get married," she says, which . . . is a lot. We do not have that kind of relationship.

I figure I ought to not respond, in case she forgot that for a second.

"I don't mean that," she says, once she's sent off a text reply.

"Sure."

"And anyway, *you'd* never have this problem. No one's saying anything about you going on a three-week business trip."

That's true, no one is. In part because I'm single, but more importantly, because of the bigger thing I'm smart enough to know Salem is talking about.

"No one would text you to ask where we keep the snack packs for recital days. No one would expect you to remember where the drop-off area is."

I open my mouth to agree.

"Never mind," she says. "Here they are."

I look toward the doors and see Jess and Tegan coming out, Tegan a couple of steps ahead, dressed for Florida seaside gift shopping in a bright pink tank top and jean shorts. Jess is in her usual.

Beautiful, as usual.

She puts a hand on Tegan's arm before they cross the parking lot, stopping her. Then she reaches into the bag she has over her shoulder and holds out something to Tegan, a white bottle with an orange cap. Tegan shakes her head and starts walking again, but Jess tugs at the small backpack Tegan wears, stopping her. She shoves the bottle inside while Tegan stands impatiently.

It's sunscreen, I think. She was remembering to give her sunscreen.

"Remember the conditions," I tell Salem, keeping my voice quiet. It was important to Jess, last night, that we go over them. That we make sure the rules stay the same even when we're not all together. It's what she needs to keep this new plan for today safe for her and Tegan.

My boss sighs heavily. "Sure. Hugely unnatural conversation, all in service of one person's demands."

"There's other things you can talk to Tegan about, besides her mother."

As if I'm a real hero at conversation. As if I won't feel that full body flush again as soon as Jess and I get in the van together, alone.

"And, we call each other if we find something. *Before* we do any further talking to anyone we might find."

She clucks her tongue. "Whose story is this?" she says, a joking note in her voice.

Jess's, I think. *Tegan's.*

Not ours.

But that isn't what she means.

"You *are* doing well, Hawk. I'm impressed. Of course, you know how I'd be even *more* impressed . . ."

She trails off meaningfully, raising her eyebrows, but I don't respond. I know that half the reason she's excited about splitting up today is that she thinks I'm doing it to get Jess to trust me more, to get her that much closer to talking. I still haven't told her any different, haven't told her that how I feel toward Jess isn't good for getting her to talk.

"Good morning!" says Tegan, as she approaches us with a big, bright smile. You'd never know she spent most of yesterday sullen. She's got that teenaged emotional elasticity that's as exhausting as it is admirable.

Jess says nothing, but she does catch my eyes. No smile, but still, I think it's a greeting.

From somewhere, Cope is telling me I'm wasted for this woman who probably has the power to get me fired. He's right, again.

"So! Do we know where we're going?" Tegan says.

Mindful of the *Whose story is this?* remark, I keep quiet and let Salem take over. She explains some of the research she managed to do in the van yesterday after we left MacSherry's. There're only two gift shops within twenty-five miles that have the word *sea* in the name, but ten years ago, there were more. We've made a plan to hit eleven shops total. We'll ask around about shops that have closed, or changed names. We'll add in some other shops with names that relate to water, just in case MacSherry was misremembering or misleading. We've got photos of Lynton and Charlotte ready to go. We've divvied up the map. We're hoping we find something today, but if we don't, the plan is to try tracking down Charlotte's friend Julia tomorrow.

Tegan's so excited it's as if she's had two of Salem's coffees. When Salem says "Are you ready?" to her, she practically leaps out of her skin.

When they turn to walk away, Jess speaks for the first time this morning. "Teeg."

Her sister pauses, only halfway turns around.

"Just . . . you know. Be careful."

Tegan waves a dismissive hand and turns away again, and I tighten the muscles in the middle of my body automatically. As if I could take this punch for the woman standing next to me. I watch as Jess tracks Tegan and Salem. When they duck into the rental, closing their doors, I can see that she's stricken. She wants to change her mind about this whole thing.

When she looks over at me, part of me expects that there'll be something harsh, judgmental in her eyes. A *Why did I let you talk me into this?* look. I expect I'll be getting it from her all day.

Instead, her expression is soft, a little sheepish. I want to remind her of what I said last night: that Tegan is smart and confident. That Jess taught her well.

Right now, though, she probably doesn't remember any of that. She probably only remembers what came after, me selling her on this idea she's still not sure about.

But as it turns out, I'm wrong about what she remembers. She sets her hands on her hips and looks me over, painting me with the warmth of a concerned gaze I've only ever seen her offer to her sister.

Then, she holds out one hand and says, "How about you let me drive today?"

She's different without Tegan and Salem around.

Not notably different, not the kind of different that most people would clock. She's still contained, still quiet, and not shyly so—more like purposefully so. In the stores we go into, she doesn't touch anything; she keeps her hands close to her sides. When people casually welcome her in and ask how she's doing, she still answers with a quick "Fine," closing the door on further questions.

But I'm not most people.

I notice, for example, that when she drives, she taps one finger on the steering wheel in time with whatever music we play in the car. I notice that she's less inclined to keep her gaze straight ahead—she looks around, not just at what we pass as we make our way through our mapped-out routes, but at the shelves of the shops we go in. I notice she doesn't so quickly contain her expressions: when she sees a jokey bumper sticker about "Florida Man," she offers up that quirking corner of her mouth. When a shop owner I'm talking to makes an unprompted, aggressive remark about his devotion to the Second Amendment, she rolls her eyes. When another shop owner—this one a kind-eyed older woman whose entire store's aesthetic might be called flamingo-core—asks if we're married, Jess coughs in what I can only assume is appalled surprise.

All of it is small, but also, I know none of it would have happened if we were with Salem and Tegan.

Obviously, a catalogue of Jess Greene's microexpressions is not the intel I'm supposed to be gathering, but so far, everything else has been a dead end. I've had some nice conversations, have gotten some good tape of people who recognize the name Lynton Baltimore from Salem's podcast, and who have opinions on what happened to him. That would make for nice filler on a new story, but only if we actually end up finding something. If we don't, it's just a record of me hitting a wall. Since we haven't yet heard from Salem or Tegan, I'm guessing they're not having much more luck.

"This is our last one?" Jess says, as she pulls into a parking spot outside of an unassuming but well-tended strip of shops.

This is different, too—she's spoken to me more freely as the day has worn on. It doesn't matter if nearly everything she's said has been about logistics: a question about directions or background information on a store we're heading into, a reminder when I almost leave the van without my phone, a brief ask about whether I'm more comfortable in the passenger seat.

The fact that she's just used the word *our* feels monumental.

"Yeah."

I unhook my seat belt and take a second to open the Notes

app on my phone, where Salem and I are sharing a collation of the details we gathered about various shops. For the previous four visits, Jess hasn't given any indication that she cares whether I tell her the basics before we go in, but I still tell her anyway.

This one is a long shot, seeing as how it's never been inside Pensacola proper. And a decade ago, it was even further away, in a different location, with a different name: The Sea Spot. Now, if I'm judging by the slick website, it's less gift shop and more gallery. It's called Sandbar Studio & Design, and six years ago its ownership transferred from someone named M. Acosta to an LLC under the store's new name.

"Okay," Jess says after I finish, which is the same thing she's said every time. So it's a surprise when, instead of opening her door and getting out the way she usually does, she stays put and says, "Do you like doing this work?"

I turn to look at her. She pulled her hair up a couple of hours ago, high on the top of her head in a haphazard bun, and the fact is, I've avoided most eye contact since. Her neck is long and smooth and she has two slim, gold hoops in the cartilage of her right ear. I thought seeing her legs was bad, but this?

This is brutal.

I try for levity. "Do I like spending my day looking at shell souvenirs in the Florida Panhandle?"

There's that quirk again.

"This just—" she begins, running her finger along the bottom edge of the steering wheel, staring out the windshield at the shop. "It's frustrating. It's hours of work, and we have nothing to show for it. I keep thinking about how many cuts and colors I'd have done by now."

She pauses, then adds, "I do hair."

"I know. Tegan told us."

"Right." Her tone is sharper than before, and I could kick myself for bringing it up. She offers up a piece of information about herself and I remind her of her sister's betrayal? I use one of those collective pronouns she only just started using to refer to me and her, to instead refer to me and Salem?

I'm desperate to recover.

"I do like it. It's a lot of false starts, when you're first trying to track down information. But even the little pieces you find sometimes end up being worth something, once it's time to put it all together. This kind of stuff"—I gesture out the windshield—"it's hard to see it as part of the story. But even if there's nothing here, it'll matter. It's one of the angles you tried. To get the final picture."

As soon as I finish, I'm worried I've made another error. The final picture I'm out here trying to get, after all, has to do with her and her sister. And isn't that the same thing that had me feeling annoyed at Salem this morning?

But Jess doesn't say anything, not right away. She tilts her head to the side slightly, lengthening that line of her neck I'm definitely not looking at or thinking about setting my lips to. And when she speaks, she doesn't say anything sharp.

"A shell souvenir," she says quietly.

"What?"

She shrugs. "I don't know. It's like—collecting a bunch of little shells from the beach. Individually, they're nice, sure. But if you want to remember your trip, you do something with them, the way these shops do. Put them in a jar, or glue them to a frame. Coat them in something that's probably toxic and make a keychain. Stock them on your shelves for selling. A souvenir."

Then she opens her door and gets out.

I blink at her vacated driver's seat for a good three seconds before I can move again. Did she just compare investigative journalism to cheap shell keychains?

Worse, did it somehow make sense to me?

I catch up to her as she's walking in the door of the shop, and I have to stop myself from asking her to wait. I want a break.

I want to get back in the van and turn on my recorder and ask her to say that exact thing again. I want to ask her to compare a hundred other things from my life to something else— whatever her mind offers up.

But already a blast of air-conditioning is hitting me in the face, and I know I have to focus enough to get through this last dead end. The previous four shops we visited were pretty densely stocked—lots of aisles and displays to get through on the way to whatever point-of-sale counter was set up. In those places, I'd make my way straight there, while Jess hung back among the merchandise for a while.

In here, though, Jess and I both stop right inside the doorway, taking it in. It's bright and uncluttered, and there's not really an aisle in sight. Instead, the room we're in is set up similarly to a museum space: large and small frames holding abstract art hung on the white walls, a few pedestals with sculptures of what I think are waves. There are three shelving units along one wall lined with colorful blown glass. Another shelving unit with delicate, handmade jewelry.

"No shells," Jess whispers.

It's so quiet in here—a soft, mechanical bell sound played when we came in, but so far, no one's come out to greet us. Obviously, talking to someone is what I'm here for, but honestly, some of this stuff looks pretty cool. I might as well look around uninterrupted while I have the chance.

Jess must have the same idea, because she wanders away from me, back toward where the jewelry is. I get lost in a couple of those wave sculptures, which, when you look up close, have the tiniest pieces of gold foil set into their crests, like sunlight. I don't know how long I look, but it's long enough that I consider calling Jess over. I want her to see this, too.

She beats me to it, though.

"Adam?"

When I turn I don't see her by the jewelry anymore. I feel a strange pulse of unease in my gut, both because I can't see her and because when she says my name, there's something different about her voice. It's certainly not the sound of someone who's found secret gold foil in a sculpture.

I move toward the rear of the space and realize there's an entrance to a back room here—more of a studio than a display area. There are metal drawer units, long tables, shelves full of supplies. A sign hanging on the back wall says ART IS FOR EVERYONE.

Jess stands with her back toward me, facing another wall. I don't know how I can tell something's wrong, but I can. The set of her shoulders. The way she holds her hands at her sides.

I come closer, until what her back has been blocking me from seeing is revealed.

I stare at it in dumbfounded shock. The only words I can think of aren't my own.

In fact, they're words that just yesterday, I was ready to do battle over.

Remarkable resemblance.

If I didn't know better, I'd say I'm looking at a painting of Jess Greene.

But I do know better.

And this is a painting of her mother.

Chapter 11

Jess

"Is that better?"

Adam's voice is low and soothing, the hand he has on my back warm and perfectly weighted. I take another sip of cool water and nod, staring out of the front window of the shop we're still in, waiting for Salem and Tegan to arrive.

In a back room only a few feet away from me, there still hangs a gorgeous, photorealistic portrait of my mother, the artist still—for the next few minutes, at least—unknown to us.

But right now, the only thing I seem able to think about is the man standing beside me, and all the things he's done for me in the moments since I first saw it.

First, the calloused hand at my elbow, steadying me against the unexpected rush of dizziness I felt looking into her face that way, painted and unsmiling.

Second, the soft way he whispered two simple words—*Hey, now*—as he'd taken in whatever expression I'd been wearing, using that hand at my elbow to guide me back a couple of steps.

Third, how he smoothly and so calmly handled the young,

frazzled studio employee who'd emerged from a rear break room, apologizing profusely for leaving us waiting alone.

She'd taken one look at me and snapped her eyes to the painting. She said, "Wow," and Adam took care of everything after. A succinct and carefully vague explanation of our presence. A question about the painting's artist. A request for a glass of water for me. A quick text to Salem, and, ever since—steady, patient waiting at my side.

"I'm sure it's the heat," I say curtly, which we both know is a lie. But he doesn't call me on it. He only moves that hand in a soothing, small circle on my back.

I don't just feel it there.

I feel it everywhere.

Spine, neck, the sensitive skin behind my ears. Stomach and thighs and in between them, too.

It must be some kind of stress response. It must be that I don't want to think yet about the artist of that portrait—the owner of this studio, apparently—who is on his way here, phoned by the frazzled employee who greeted us. It must be that I don't want to think yet about Tegan seeing it, or about what Salem will say.

It *must* be.

Because there's no other explanation for the way I want to turn toward Adam's broad body and have the whole of mine folded into his. To have all that comforting calm control surround me. It isn't right, the way I want to be close to him—the way I want his affection, his attention.

It isn't *me.*

Wanting those things makes me feel like the woman in the painting. Like I'm being selfish, like I'm putting myself at risk, or Tegan at risk.

Still, I don't tell him to move his hand, or step away from him. He may not even realize he's still touching me.

"We don't have to do this right now. I'll tell Salem."

I turn my head toward him and look up. His jaw is rough again with new stubble, and there are faint, lovely lines at the corners of his eyes. When he looks at me, I don't think he sees that portrait. I hope he doesn't.

"You would, wouldn't you?" My voice is quiet. Not even a lick of curtness in my tone.

"I would."

I nod and look down at my cup of water. It helps to know he would. It . . . opens something in me, makes me feel curious in a way I haven't been on this entire trip. Maybe not in the last ten years. Suddenly, I want to see the portrait again, to take it in without the initial pulse of shock. I want to find out who painted it, and why.

And I want to have Adam's hand on my back the whole time.

"Here they are," says Adam quietly, and I raise my eyes to see Salem's rental car pulling into the parking lot.

Instinctively, I step away from him, that temporary opening in me narrowing again, though not closing completely. When Tegan gets out of the car, I watch her, same as I used to when she'd get off the bus after school. I could always tell how her day had gone, just from looking at her come down those school bus steps.

I wonder if she, too, will feel disoriented when she sees the portrait, if she'll feel hot in her face and cold in her limbs.

"Jess."

I keep my eyes on my sister, ignore the way him saying my name feels like him rubbing a small circle on my back.

"Just say if you want to take a break from this today. Say it, or pinch me under the table, or tug on your ear. Anything you want. I'll stop it, anytime."

I can't help but look at him as he says it, and God. It *has* to be a stress response, the way I hear this offer. Like we're not talking about an interview at all.

I step away from him, toward the front door. I hold it open for Salem and my sister, and it obviously reads as extremely abnormal. Salem looks at me as though I've been body-snatched.

Tegan, at least, is either too excited or still too annoyed with me to even register my flustered presence.

"Is he here yet?" Salem says to Adam, at the same time Tegan says, "Ooooh, this stuff is *nice*," as if we're here to do some shopping.

I follow her over to one of the sculptures she's bent to get a closer look at. I don't know how much Adam told Salem in his text to her, and I also don't know how much Salem told Tegan about whatever the text said. I feel obligated to give her a heads-up about the portrait, but I'm still not sure what to say.

It's Mom, and she looks like the cover of a magazine?

It's Mom and she'll be looking right at you?

"So in the back there's this portrait," I begin quietly, but I don't get to finish. The young woman who greeted Adam and me bursts back into the main room, trailed by a short, middle-aged man. He has thick, jet-black hair, and he's wearing paint-splattered cargo shorts and a bright green T-shirt. He looks a little frazzled, too, but happily so. As though it's his natural state.

"Okay, he's here!" the young woman says. "Everyone, this is Luís, the owner of the studio. The painter!"

Luís looks first at Adam—I can't blame him there, the man does overwhelm a room—and then at Salem. He's smiling broadly at them, apparently thrilled to be called into work unexpectedly. Then he looks toward Tegan and me. I brace for his smile to drop, or to turn into something strange and false, like Curtis MacSherry's.

But it doesn't. It widens, his cheeks rounding and his eyes lighting. Oddly enough, I don't feel compelled to shrink from his recognizing gaze, but I do wish I still had Adam Hawkins's hand where it was before.

Salem starts to speak, but Luís is practically vibrating with excitement, and he blurts out a single, surprising word.

"Finally!"

*   *   *

IF it were possible for someone to design my literal, exact opposite when it comes to meeting strangers, talking about oneself, or receiving surprising news, that person would, I think, be a lot like Luís Acosta.

The friendliest person alive. The most comfortable person alive.

The calmest person alive.

We're back in the art studio, all of us—except for Luís's employee, Asha, who's gone out to watch the front of the shop—gathered around one of the tables that, Luís has cheerfully explained, usually gets used for the various classes he hosts throughout the week. Mondays, watercolors; Wednesdays, oils; Fridays, clay sculpture; Saturday mornings, still-life sketching.

He's told us all about it, excitedly and in detail.

He hasn't even seemed in a hurry to know about what we're doing here.

Yesterday, this might've made me angry or frustrated; it would've seemed to me—like I'd told Curtis MacSherry—a waste of time. But in the first place, Luís isn't like Curtis Mac-Sherry. And in the second, I keep thinking of the things Adam has said to me.

Even the little pieces you find sometimes end up being worth something

It's one of the angles you tried

Just say if you want to take a break

All of it, somehow, seems to help.

Sitting next to him helps. Tegan not having bad-day-at-school-face helps.

Also, not facing the painting helps.

"So you're *not* here to take it?" Luís says, once Salem has finally managed to coax him back around to it.

Salem pauses meaningfully, catching me off guard by looking my way. "Jess? Do you want to . . . ?"

She gestures behind me at the portrait. I'm not sure if she's manipulating the situation or if she's trying to be deferential to the fact that I'm the one who showed up here to see my own face on a gigantic canvas.

Beneath the table, Adam's knee presses lightly into my thigh, a question. *Anything you want,* he said.

"Well, obviously, that's our mom," I blurt.

Inelegant, but Luís doesn't seem to mind. He nods encouragingly.

"But we—my sister and I—we didn't know about this painting until today. We only knew that our mom was in this area around ten years ago." I decide I shouldn't mention any tips from MacSherry, so I say, "We've been checking out places we thought she might have visited when she was here."

Luís lifts a hand and strokes at the thick stubble on his chin, his brows lowered in thought.

"Ten years ago is about right, for when I did it. I've got the date on the back of the frame. But you're saying Libby never told you it was here?"

Libby? I think, at the same time Tegan actually says it aloud.

Luís sits back in his seat, for the first time looking confused. "Is that not . . . ?"

"Luís, if you don't mind my stepping in and providing you with some background?" Salem says, and as she starts—as she tells him her credentials, and her interest in Lynton Baltimore, a name Luís clearly doesn't recognize—I feel Adam's knee against my thigh again. He's checking in. He wants to know if, already, it's all I can take: finding out my mother used a fake name when she was here. When she sat for that painting.

I'm so grateful that I do something that later, I'm sure I'll think is absolutely off-the-rails.

I set my hand on his leg. Close to his knee. I don't pinch, because I know that's the signal for stopping. I sort of . . . pat. Once. An *I'm okay* pat. He has a really nice leg but I definitely know I can't keep my hand there.

Except . . . except then, Adam sets his hand on top of mine. Warm and weighted, exactly how it was on my back. I can't help but look over at him, but nothing on his face betrays this secret communication between us beneath the table. He's watching Salem talk to Luís as though it's his sole focus.

It's so private.

It's perfect.

Across from me, Tegan is rapt—her eyes bouncing between Salem's face and Luís's, as if she can already sense that today's interview is going to be so different than yesterday's.

I don't move my hand even a little. I want him to keep his right where it is.

"You're saying, Libby is Charlotte, right?" Luís says.

"Right," says Salem.

"And the man who paid me to do the painting, that's Lynton Baltimore?"

Salem takes out her tablet, and after a few quick swipes, slides it across the table to Luís. Even from here I can see it's the mug shot. Luís looks down at it, squinting.

He shakes his head, and at first I think it's because he doesn't recognize the man in the photo. But then I realize the head-shaking is more of an accompaniment to a disbelieving laugh, quiet and breathy.

"Man, that *is* him."

Salem's eyes light in something close to victory. "Okay, great. Can you tell us a bit about him? About his visit here, or about why he had you do this painting?"

Luís is still looking down at Salem's tablet. He taps a finger against the just-dimmed screen, lighting the photo fully again before he does another laughing headshake. Under the table, Adam's hand gently squeezes mine, solid and reassuring.

"I guess I should tell you the big thing first," Luís says. "Which is that this guy"—he slides the phone back across the table—"is apparently my biological father."

UNDER the circumstances—the circumstances being that Salem Durant's decade-old true crime story about Lynton Baltimore ended up being connected to my own mother—I haven't listened to a podcast in years. From what I gather, the biggest ones still have the broad strokes of what put Salem on the map: serialized, suspenseful. Not simple, but not so complex that you'll lose the thread if you drift away for thirty seconds during your commute.

But I don't really know the details of them anymore; I don't know their textures. I don't know if they use more music than Salem did, if they have lots of ads or just a couple, if the episodes are peppered with multiple interviews or if the focus is tighter. I don't know if the hosts talk a lot or a little, if they make themselves part of the story the way Salem often did, or not.

I don't know all that, but I still feel certain that Luís Acosta's story would make for a pretty good podcast episode.

He tells it easily, smoothly—one step at a time, not too overwhelming. He tells us about John Harold Tygart and his fiancée, Libby Mitchell. Their visit to his mother's old gift shop, the Sea Spot. John Harold, Luís's mother had told him, was an old friend who'd kept in touch over the years. She'd said she'd always bragged to him about Luís's art; she'd said that John Harold was in the area, and wanted to see it for himself.

He says John Harold was so complimentary. Sophisticated. A person who knew a lot about art. Friendly, but not overly so. Nothing suspicious about him.

"I couldn't believe he asked me to do a portrait of Libby," he tells us, and then he looks meaningfully at the recording equipment that's set up in the middle of the table.

"Should I call her Libby, or Charlotte?" he asks, and the nice thing is, he directs the question to me and Tegan.

"Whichever!" says Tegan, totally enthralled, and probably yesterday, I would've cleared my throat.

But yesterday, I wasn't basically holding Adam Hawkins's hand beneath a table.

Luís looks at me, a question in his eyes, and it's such a nice thing to do that I simply repeat after my sister. "Whichever is fine."

Luís nods and goes on.

"I'd been experimenting with portraits in my training that year. I had this whole idea about 'realistic saturation.' I wanted the brightness of a Warhol portrait, but the realism of the old masters. Libby loved the ones I showed them. She went on and on."

She would have, I know. I can practically hear her. She gave the most elaborate compliments for the most mundane things: your outfits, your handwriting, your skill at folding laundry. I can only imagine what she said about something as impressive as Luís's art.

"So, this John Harold guy, he says they'll be in town for a week. He tells my mother he'll pay—" He breaks off, shaking his head again. "This part is probably going to be hard to believe!"

"I doubt it," says Salem, in a tone I'm sure will sound good on the recording. Weary and knowing. It'll be comic relief for her listeners, the ones who have the sense that they know her, who feel like they're on a journey with her.

Without thinking, I turn to look at Adam, and he turns to look at me. Our little team from today, shell collecting. Sharing a secret, private glance about what we found.

Tegan clears her throat, and Adam and I both snap our eyes away from each other.

Like we've been caught passing notes in class, or whispering during a church service.

Holding hands beneath a table.

I slowly—so no one can tell, I hope—slide my hand from beneath his. I don't know what I was doing, letting that go on as long as it did.

Nothing is private in here.

"Fifty thousand," Luís rushes out, as if he's embarrassed by the number. I look over at Salem: No doubt she sees the same shell I see, no doubt she's thinking that fifty thousand must be at least some of what Lynton Baltimore picked up from Curtis MacSherry before coming to Pensacola.

"Keep in mind, at that time, I'm twenty-five years old. I'm doing art on nights and weekends and working part-time at my mom's shop—that was the Sea Spot—and part-time at a deli. I'd never done a commission in my life. I thought he must be joking."

"That's a life-changing amount of money," Salem says, encouraging.

"Yeah, and my mother, she knew it." He gestures at his green T-shirt, smiling in good-natured self-mockery. "I know I look like a responsible business owner now, but I wasn't too bright back then. I think she was pretty concerned I'd blow it all on a fast car or a sport bike."

He pauses, and when he speaks again, his voice has a new tone of fondness. "She was real overprotective."

"Tell me about it," mutters Tegan.

A victory: I don't react. But my hand twitches, cool and lonely, in my lap.

Adam shifts slightly in his chair.

"So what happened?" Salem says. "She didn't let him pay that much?"

"Oh, she did. She was no dummy!" He laughs. "We had some . . . let's call them back-and-forths about the money. All week, while I was having Libby sit for me and doing preliminary sketches, my mom was saying we were putting that money straight in the bank. I'm not saying I was arguing for a sport bike, but I'm not saying I was arguing for anything a whole lot better.

"So anyway, end of the week comes, and I've got everything I need to work on the portrait. I figured it'd take me at least a couple months to do the painting, and John Harold and Libby say that's fine; they'll come back for it. Turns out, that gave my mom a pretty good upper hand with the money issue."

I'm pretty sure all of us make some expression of confusion. Since you can't hear those on a tape, obviously, Salem prompts him again. "What do you mean?"

"Well, John Harold insisted on paying up front. All fifty grand, at the end of the week. When he left, my mother said, 'We're not touching that money until he picks up the painting.' I don't think she trusted him."

He pauses again, tilts his head thoughtfully.

"Which I guess makes sense, if he was this Baltimore guy."

"Do you think she knew that?" Salem asks.

"If she did, she never said. All she ever said about him was he was an old friend, someone she knew back when she first moved here. It's not until the day she passed on—she had heart disease, at the end—that she told me about him being my father."

"Was that hard for you?" I could almost admire it, the way Salem changes her tone to ask this—the way she injects it with such convincing concern.

Luís shrugs. "Not so much as most people would think. Always, it was only me and her. If I ever missed having a dad, it must not have been for long, or not so bad that I remember it. She was a good mom to me." His eyes turn shiny. "The best mom. By my side for everything."

I look at Tegan, who's leaned forward, her elbows on the table. She's not watching Luís; she's looking at the painting of a woman who wasn't by her side for anything over the last decade.

My heart aches. I think about reaching out and pinching Adam's leg. Or I guess tugging on my ear, which would be the safer, non-contact option for stopping this.

But just as I'm about to, Tegan looks away and her gaze catches mine. Instead of doing what I expect her to do—roll her eyes, maybe, or worse, blink and blank out my existence for being so *overprotective*—she offers me a small, slightly embarrassed smile before turning back toward Luís.

My heart aches again, in a different way. It's stretched huge with how I love her.

Luís sniffles once, gathering himself. "And if she had any complicated feelings about the guy, she didn't show it while he was here. She treated him like an old friend. She treated Libby like a new one. I wouldn't have ever guessed she had that kind of history with him."

"You didn't want to try to find him again? Once you knew?"

"Once I knew, I was focused on my mom. Grieving for her, and doing right by her. She was right about putting that money away. Invested it, in fact. So when she passed on, she left me a good amount of money, and her shop. She always wanted me to have my own studio, so that's what I did."

Not even an hour ago, I was thinking of Luís as my opposite, but when he says this, I think he and I might share something fundamental in common. I knew how to focus, too. When Mom left, everything was for Tegan. If I'd never heard the name Lynton Baltimore again, it would have been fine by me. A cheap price I would have paid for keeping Tegan safe from this story, this mess.

"So do you still have the original fifty thousand?" Salem says, which strikes me as the crassest possible question. Not the shell I would've picked up, if I were the type to go gathering.

Luís opens his mouth, pauses, and then closes it again, looking—for the first time—a little uncertain.

Adam reaches a hand to the middle of the table and stops the recording.

He's good at this, I think, but I'm not sure exactly what *this* is. Building a podcast episode, or protecting people from them?

Luís looks at him gratefully.

"I don't know how much I should talk about the money. If that money's from something bad, I don't want trouble. I have a wife, two little ones at home."

"Of course," says Adam, before Salem can object.

"I always figured, after my mother passed—I've done what she would've done. I've kept that painting in case he ever came back for it, in case anyone asked what that money was for. But mostly I figured, maybe he came here that time because he got a conscience about child support, or something. Maybe he was just paying a debt, and the painting was his way of doing it."

"That might—" Salem begins, but she's interrupted by a shrill ring from the phone she's had facedown on the table since Luís passed it back to her. She grabs for it quickly, muttering an apology. "I thought I had it on 'Do Not—'" she looks down at the screen, then stands. "I'll just be a moment."

When she rushes out of the studio, Adam looks after her, obviously concerned. Of all the people in this room who might've interrupted this interview, I'm sure he would never have guessed Salem.

Luís seems relieved for the break, though, something in his posture loosening. He looks between Tegan and me, and then at the portrait.

"You could take it, you know. I'd be okay with that. I think Libby—uh, your mom, I mean—would be okay with it."

Once he's said it, I can tell he rethinks it almost immediately, worried he overstepped. I didn't say, after all, where our mom is now. I said we didn't know about the painting, but I didn't say all the other things we do or don't know.

"Oh!" Tegan says, sounding excited. Sounding hopeful. "Did she talk about us, then?"

Luís's face falls, and my stomach turns over. Tegan's eyes dim in disappointment by slow, painful degrees.

I hate myself for not tugging on my ear a dozen times before now. For not pinching Adam Hawkins's leg until it bruised.

But before Luís can give her the official *no* we all know is coming, Salem runs back into the room, her face pale.

"I'm sorry," she says quickly. "I'm going to have to fly back to Boston."

Chapter 12

Adam

We don't take the painting.

Probably we wouldn't have, even if we hadn't had to leave Luís Acosta's studio so suddenly, Salem half-frantic, half-frustrated. It'd been her husband calling, and not about snack packs or the drop-off area.

He'd been calling because their daughter had been in an accident on her way home from today's recital.

She's okay, thank God, or at least as okay as a talented teen-aged dancer could be with two broken ribs and a fractured tibia. But Salem had been as rattled as I'd ever seen her— obviously desperate to get to her kid, and also obviously ready to tear Patrick's face off for letting their daughter ride home from her recital with two of the older girls from her troupe, the driver only having recently gotten her license.

That had not, apparently, been the plan.

Even Jess, I think, felt sorry for her. She offered to help pack up some of the recording equipment. She said, "I hope your daughter is okay," just before Salem drove away for the airport in the extra rental we only just picked up this morning.

Tegan, though, had been surprisingly more reserved. In the parking lot, watching Salem's car get smaller and smaller in the distance, Luís asked whether we wanted to come back in, have another look at the portrait, talk more. Jess looked at me, her eyes uncertain, but it was Tegan who spoke up.

"I think I just want to go," she said, and then she sort of . . . drifted over to the van, her shoulders curved in defeat, leaving Jess and me to say our goodbyes—well, goodbyes for now, at least; we'd exchanged numbers—to Luís.

I knew, as I stood there, that I needed to get back to the hotel; I needed to make a plan. The next time I talked to Salem, I needed to be able to tell her what we'd take care of in her absence. Would we stay here, talk to Luís again? Would we go on to Tulsa, me fully taking the lead in Salem's absence? Obviously, I didn't want Salem's daughter hurt, but I also knew that Salem's leaving gave me a professional opportunity.

I knew that what I did during the time Salem was gone would matter to my future. At Broadside, and for my story.

But once I was back in the van, I took one look in the rearview at Tegan—her lips pressed in a firm line, her eyes staring blankly out the window—and I knew something else, too. If we went back to the hotel, both she and Jess would have just as bad of a night tonight as they had last night, maybe worse. I imagined Tegan giving Jess the cold shoulder. I imagined Jess alone by the pool again, staring up at those trees as though they'd have an answer for her.

So instead of going to the hotel, I've taken them out to dinner.

I didn't really ask, but in the end, no one really objected, either. I pulled into a spot outside a well-reviewed oceanside restaurant I'd programmed into my phone's GPS and looked over at Jess, and before she could even give me a shrug of resignation, Tegan slid open her door and got out.

It's a way nicer restaurant than I should've picked, both based on what we're all wearing and also based on my allotted per diem for meals. But in the first place, dress codes in the state of Florida in general seem open to interpretation. In the second, I don't really care about the per diem. This one, I'll pay out of pocket. I didn't do two cheeseball commercials for local businesses in my Missouri hometown after I graduated college for nothing. Apparently, I did them to sit at a candlelit white-tableclothed table with an ocean view, and to watch two sisters pick unenthusiastically at their fancy food while I forget about my journalism career and worry about the both of them.

Tegan, obviously bruised from what Luís didn't even have to say out loud—that her mother never *had* mentioned her, that whole week she was here.

Jess, desperately—and so far unsuccessfully—trying to draw her sister out of this wounded silence.

"Teeg," Jess says quietly from her seat across from mine. "Want to try my potatoes?"

She turns her plate slightly so her still-mostly-full serving of fingerlings faces Tegan. It's such a small, trying-so-hard gesture, and I hate that I'm not sitting next to her. That I can't cover her hand with mine again.

Tegan rebuffs her with a tight shake of her head, not even looking at the potatoes.

I watch Jess turn her plate again, back to how it was before, her lashes lowered. Briefly, I wonder if anyone's ever stood up in the middle of a restaurant to ask if there's a therapist in the room.

I look down at my own plate—it's an impressive arrangement of red snapper and roasted vegetables—and realize I'm not doing much better than Jess and Tegan on making a dent in my food. I'm pretty sure this dish was at least thirty-five dollars. Maybe if I'd done three commercials instead of two I'd have been fine with not cleaning my plate, but as things stand, I better get back in there.

But right as I'm picking up my fork and knife again, Tegan sets hers down.

She says, "So, Adam," and it's pretty similar to when I was about to eat my first bite of beautiful pancakes back in that Columbus diner a few days ago. My red snapper will be at room temperature by the time I get back to it, probably, but at least she's talking.

"Yeah?"

"What's it like to go viral?"

I guess it's not all that similar to that day in the diner a few days ago, because Tegan's spoken with a sharp edge to her voice, as though she's spoiling for a fight.

I slide my eyes toward Jess, wondering if she's going to come through with one of her absurdly loud throat-clears, but she seems a little too shell-shocked. She's staring at her sister, eyes slightly widened. I bet going viral is Jess's worst nightmare.

No, I bet *Tegan* going viral is Jess's worst nightmare.

I set my fork and knife down, too, and look back at Tegan. If she wants to level all her hurt and frustration from today at me, that's fine. I can take it.

"It's pretty shitty, honestly," I say. "Especially when your best friend just died."

Tegan blinks, obviously surprised at my blunt answer. I wouldn't sugarcoat it, no matter who asked. Still, I feel a pang of regret at the way her cheeks flush. I didn't mean to embarrass her.

I add, with a shrug, "But I brought it on myself, so."

She shakes her head. "I don't really think so. All those people, posting empty statements. Condolences they probably didn't even mean—they deserved to be called out for it. I think it's brave, what you did."

I can still see some of those statements, most of them accompanied by old press photos of Cope on the football field. *Copeland Frederick was one of the toughest young men I ever had the honor of coaching*, one of the first to hit the internet had said. I'd screenshotted it and posted my own response.

You called Cope a pussy in front of the entire locker room at the half of the national championship game. You told him you were ashamed to have a "fucking nut job" on your team. You said he could check into his "padded room" after we won the game.

Over and over, I took those phony, synthetic-sounding statements to task. I wasn't going to let anyone who'd betrayed Cope during his life play the hero after his death. I wasn't going to let them rewrite the story.

Eventually, though, I realized.

I'd made myself the story.

"It wasn't brave," I say. "It was angry."

"So what?" Tegan says, with the kind of righteous indignation of a person who really, really wants to be angry. At her mother, at her sister, at Lynton Baltimore. At the world. "You had a right to be."

"Sure. But I probably should've just gone for a walk, instead."

I steal a look at Jess, who's watching me close. I remember her on the day we met, that storm in her eyes. Standing from the small table and walking right out the door, before she could do any more damage. I wish I could tell her how much I admire her for that.

"You don't think it's what your friend would've wanted you to do?" Tegan asks, drawing my attention back to her.

This question, it's different from her first one—she's not spoiling for anything right now. She's just asking. Calm and interested. Probably she's picked up a few things from Salem. It's a good question, so I take a second before responding. Make sure I'm giving her an honest answer.

"I don't know what he would've wanted me to do. That's a hard thing about losing him. It wouldn't be fair of me, to guess about what he would've wanted, especially about this. He's not here for me to ask."

He's not here for me to ask so many things. I miss him the same way I've missed him since the day he died. A ragged tear inside me that I know won't ever get patched or stitched up.

I don't dare look at her again, but I can feel Jess watching me still. It's wishful thinking, I'm sure, but if she were sitting next to me right now, maybe this time, she'd set her hand on top of mine. It's too small to patch the tear, but I think it'd help all the same.

"Do you ever—" Tegan begins, then stops herself, shakes her head. "Never mind."

All the fight's gone out of her now, and anyway, it was all bluster in the first place. Whatever she was going to ask, I know it's got something to do with how she's feeling about today.

"It's all right. Whatever it is, you can ask."

She fiddles with the narrow handle of her fork.

"Do you ever feel mad at him about that? I mean, that he's not here. For you to ask."

God. It's such a vulnerable question. I'm not sure if Tegan knows that, between the two of us, she's the brave one.

"I don't, no. I feel mad at myself, sometimes."

I swallow, a familiar press of emotion at the back of my throat. But I'm used to it. I don't hide it.

I can take it.

"I think about if I'd gone to visit him more, or if I'd called him more. I think about times I should've paid better attention to the texts he sent me, or the times I got frustrated with him for not taking better care of himself."

Cope, I'd say. *You can't drink like that; you know you can't.*

I'd say, *You gotta stay talking to your doctors, man.*

Tegan nods gravely, and I lower my eyes, pick up my knife and fork again. I may not be embarrassed about the fact that I got a pretty noticeable voice crack during that, but I still don't want to look over at Jess. If I do, I suspect I might beg her with my eyes for the hand-holding thing. I suspect I might simply ask her out loud.

After a long, uncomfortable silence, Tegan speaks again.

"I get that," she says. "But it, like, *definitely* wasn't your fault."

I look up at her, that hard teenaged toughness crumbled away now. She looks so young and sensitive and sad, as though all the weight of what Luís couldn't tell her today has settled again on her shoulders, and I have to admit. I understand why Jess would offer her every single fingerling potato on her plate. I understand why Jess protects her so fiercely.

"Thanks," I tell her. And then, even though I know it's a risk, I add, "And it definitely wasn't yours, either."

An hour later, I'm still at the candlelit white-tableclothed table.

Except now, Jess and I are alone.

Tegan's taken her dessert—a very elegant-looking ice cream sundae—out onto the restaurant's expansive deck, since the sun's about to set and the server promised spectacular views. With the edges of her mood smoothed out after our brief foray into the worst time of my life, Tegan turned into a friendly dinner companion to both me and Jess. She took some of those potatoes, finally, and told me about how she'll be attending Allegheny in the fall, a small college in Pennsylvania where she's gotten a big scholarship. She asked about what I did before I went back to school for my master's, and I told her about my mostly aimless and unsatisfying few years as a sales rep for a national sporting goods company. When her ice cream arrived at the table, she even invited her sister out for the sunset, and I thought for sure Jess would go. I figured I'd take a few minutes to text Salem, to get my head on straight again, to give the sisters some alone time after such a big day.

Instead, Jess had stayed.

"I'll be out in a few minutes," she told Tegan, and now it's only the two of us. The check paid, the table clear but for the candle and the cup of decaf Jess ordered, which she hasn't taken a sip of yet.

I am trying to remind myself that I'm not on a date. It isn't easy, what with the candlelight. With a purple-pink-orange sky outside, a whole ocean reflecting its glory.

It isn't easy, with Jess Greene across from me.

She clears her throat, gentle and nervous. Not an interrupting effort. More of a courage-gathering one. I figure she's maybe about to bust my chops for saying what I did to Tegan, though she hasn't ever needed courage for that sort of thing before.

"I'm really sorry about your friend," she says, so quickly that it takes a second for the words to register.

I'm oddly overwhelmed by them from her. She offers so little of herself that an expression of sympathy, even a quickly spoken one, feels powerful. Honest and fully meant.

"I knew about it, but I didn't want to say," she continues, her thumb rubbing back and forth nervously on the tablecloth. "I didn't know if I should know about it, I mean."

I want you to know about it, I think. *I want you to know about me.*

But obviously, I can't say that.

"Thanks. And it's okay that you know about it. I'm used to that."

She nods down at where her thumb still rubs, back and forth, back and forth. "Tegan is—well. She's a much more open person than I am."

I smile. "You don't say."

Teasing her, it could go either way. I'm definitely date-nervous. Date-with-Jess-Greene nervous, which is exponential nervousness.

When she raises her eyes to mine and slowly smiles back, it suddenly becomes the best date of my life, even though it is not a date at all. Her smile is the same as her condolences. Rare. Honest. *Meant.*

"You sound just like her," she teases back, her eyes dancing. Probably it's the candlelight, but still. They're dancing.

"How was my delivery?"

"Try rolling your eyes next time."

We both laugh—tentative and quiet, a secret we're keeping from the rest of this restaurant. It is strangely, strikingly intimate to share this: *Look at what we've had to endure from this teenager*, we're saying to each other. *Look how we've persevered together through her attitude.*

I may not have asked many personal questions of Jess in the time since I've known her, but I still know she doesn't share anything—with anyone—often. And my suspicion is confirmed a few seconds later when she says, as though it's a correction, "I mean, I'm not making fun of her. I'm not—"

"I know. You're just letting off steam. I get it."

She lifts her cup of decaf, takes a sip. I'm afraid she'll go back to being closed off and quiet, but she doesn't. She blows out a sigh and speaks again.

"It's hard, with her. It's always been hard one way or another, but this week . . ." She trails off, turns her head to look toward where Tegan stands on the deck, and suddenly, my stomach sinks, because the professional part of me knows that in that trail-off, she's left me an opening. An opportunity to prompt her. To say, *How has it been hard?* or *What's it been like for you, to raise her alone?*

But if I prompt her, aren't I betraying her?

It occurs to me how fucked I am, how *stuck* I am. I put off telling Salem how I've been feeling toward Jess, and now Salem's gone. I'm sitting here alone with Jess and she finally seems to trust me enough to invite conversation, and I can't bring myself to take her up on it.

After a long, painful silence—one in which I repeatedly contemplate how rude it would be to excuse myself from this table and call Salem right this second, when she's in the middle of a pretty serious family crisis—Jess lifts her cup again and takes another sip of her coffee.

I missed the window. The way she opened it just a crack.

"Do you think she'll come back?" she asks, her voice back

in that distant, not-quite-polite tone. "After she deals with this thing with her daughter?"

I don't know what she hopes this answer is, but I give her the honest one. I know Salem well enough to know. Or at least I know her devotion to this story enough to know.

"She will. She won't let this story go, and she knows your timeline. She'll get things settled at home, and then she'll be back."

Jess nods, looks out again at Tegan. "What do we do until then? More of"—she breaks off, carefully uses her mug to gesture around at the air—"this?"

I'm pretty sure she doesn't mean candlelit dinners, though I'd have a million of them with her. I'm pretty sure she means days like today, and days like yesterday. Research, interviews.

It's what Salem would want me to do in her absence.

Jess still isn't looking at me, which means I can look at her. Her nose turns up slightly at the end, and I don't know if I've ever noticed that detail before. There's so much research I want to do.

None of it to do with the story.

I have a traitorous thought: Salem didn't say what she wanted me to do.

It's a cracked window, too, this thought, and once that little bit of air gets in, I breathe it: Shouldn't we wait to get going again until Salem is back with us? Wouldn't it be unfair to go ahead without her, when this story means so much to her?

Doesn't Tegan need a break after today?

Hasn't Jess needed one for so much longer?

I speak before the window slams shut again.

"We could take a detour."

Jess snaps her eyes to mine. "A detour?"

"Yeah. I'll call your mom's old friend Julia, confirm that there's nothing there. Then we can take a few days off. While Salem figures out her stuff at home."

Jess looks dubious. "Take a few days off . . . here?"

I shake my head. "Not here. Somewhere away from all this."

Away from the story, is what I mean. Away from anything having to do with her mother. I want to give her that so bad, I can feel it in my bones.

She looks at me, assessing. This isn't like last night at the pool, where I made her a careful argument about why we should split up—where I made everything personal about my idea sound professional. Where instead of talking about the dark circles under her eyes, or the growing tension between her and her sister, I talked about covering more ground, about compatible interview styles. I'm not going to say anything like that.

I'm just going to let her look at me, and decide whether she wants to trust me with this.

It's a lifetime before she answers.

"That sounds good," she says, her voice soft again. Almost as if she's keeping a secret from herself. "Where would we go?"

Definitely I should have had a place figured out first, but I didn't. So the only answer is the one that comes immediately to mind. The place where I've always, always gone when I needed a break.

"We could go home."

The Last Con of Lynton Baltimore

Transcript Excerpt from Episode 7, "Young Lynton"

Baltimore: I thought this was an interview.

Durant: It is.

Baltimore: But you're telling me things, not asking me them.

Durant: I'm telling you what I've learned about you, through my research. What I've learned about your parents, your sister. How you grew up, what your experiences have been. You're welcome to correct the record.

Baltimore: I'm not in the business of correcting the record.

Durant: Mr. Baltimore, you're in prison. You're not currently in the business of anything.

Chapter 13

Jess

Adam Hawkins—huge, strapping, hard-working Adam Hawkins—grew up on a farm.

A *farm.*

Since I've lived in Ohio my whole life, I am *familiar* with farms; I have certainly *driven past* farms. I've thought to myself, while looking out my car window on rare drives that took me outside of Columbus, *Wow, that sure is a big farm* or *Look, that farm has cows.*

But also, I have never *been to* a farm. I have never known someone *from* a farm.

"It's under a hundred acres," Adam is saying, as we bump down a long dirt drive. His tone is almost apologetic, and I don't have the heart to tell him that neither Tegan nor I know the difference, in practical terms, between one hundred and one thousand acres. Both sound like a lot.

"It used to be bigger, but my mom and dad sold off a lot of acreage before I was born, and my oldest sister and her husband sold off some more when they took over five years ago.

So now it's just the vegetable crops, and the flower business my sister has started up. That does pretty well, actually, because she's ended up supplying for a lot of florists. But mostly the—"

He breaks off, cuts his eyes over to me, and then, a second later, up to the rearview. I don't have to look at Tegan to know she's got the same look on her face as I do. I've been sneaking looks over my shoulder at her for at least the last twenty minutes, as Adam's very determined farm chatter has picked up in speed and detail. We keep trading these little smiles, these *Isn't this adorable* suppressed grins at each other as he talks, and every time it happens I imagine something healing between us.

I know it's just a break; it's just a detour.

But already, I'm so grateful for it.

"Are you laughing at me?" Adam says. "Is that what's happening here?"

"Oh no," says Tegan lightly. "We would *never.*"

Adam looks at me again.

"Never," I add solemnly.

He scoffs, but there's a laugh behind it, because . . . because I guess it's what the three of us do now.

One nice seaside dinner where Adam Hawkins bared a little bit of his soul for my sister's benefit.

One loose end tied up—my mother's old friend Julia had definitely not heard from her ten years ago, and never since—so that we could leave Florida like we planned.

One leisurely twelve-hour drive from Pensacola to a little place outside Springfield, Missouri, a couple of stops along the way.

And now, we actually laugh together.

It might be more accurate to say that Tegan and Adam laugh together, and I occasionally don't succeed at hiding my smile, but still.

"A farm is serious business," Adam adds. "This farm has been in my family for four generations!"

"Oh my God," laughs Tegan, and once again I don't succeed.

It's partly because I love the sound of her laugh, and partly because I know Adam is hamming it up for her.

Helping her.

At least I tell myself that this is what he's been doing since we left Florida before dawn this morning, when I saw him pack the small bag of recording equipment in the trunk, rather than keeping it where Salem did, between her and Tegan's seats. When he asked Tegan if she wanted to plug her phone in and pick the music. When he listened to her earnestly talk about K-pop—including the concert I took her to two years ago, which she said was the best birthday of her life—until she fell asleep (again). When I pulled into a rest stop at the halfway point and he rhapsodized about the "disgusting" candy he was going to buy, and then encouraged both of us to do the same.

I tell myself he's working so hard to give her a real break. I have to believe he's not doing it for me, because whenever I suspect that he is—when I catch him watching me with that same tentative softness I saw in his eyes at the restaurant, telling me he knew I was just *letting off steam*, telling me we could go *away from all this*—I feel warm and wonderful all over, an unfamiliar flutter in my belly.

"There's the house up ahead," he says, interrupting my thoughts, and I squint out the now-dusty windshield, Tegan leaning forward from behind me. "My dad and my sisters and I built the screened porch on the side ourselves."

Neither Tegan nor I tease about that, and I think that's because both of us are more than a little stunned as the house comes into view: two-story, bright white siding, pretty cornflower-blue shutters and a gigantic front porch that's lined with overflowing flower boxes. There are flags waving from the porch posts flanking the front door—both of them, I'm pretty sure, floral printed. Our house in Columbus—the one that my mom and dad lived in together before they split, the one she got in their divorce and that I eventually moved back into so

I could take care of Tegan—is nice enough, and I know how lucky I am to have it. But any sane person would describe it as plain, nondescript. A small lawn I mow myself, squared-off hedges I only have to trim once a year. There's nothing I've planted or added. I don't even have a welcome mat on the front stoop. This past spring, when neighbors started setting out personalized congratulatory banners for their high school graduates, I'd thought, *Why would I put Tegan's name in our front yard?*

"It's nice," Tegan whispers, and I don't know if I can explain what happens to me when I hear her sound that way. It's like when you hear about hypnosis, when some smooth-voiced doctor-type says, *And on the count of three, you'll awaken with no memory of this time.* I hear Tegan say *It's nice* with that note of soft wonder in her voice and all of a sudden there's no trace of warm and wonderful anymore.

I don't want to pull up to this house, don't want to open this car door and get out to see Adam Hawkins's family step off that gorgeous, decorative front porch and open their arms to him, don't want to meet a group of people who were kind enough to produce a man who knows why it'd be relaxing to tease someone about their favorite candy, a man who knows to pack the recording equipment way in the back. I don't want to stand in this Hawkins-huge expanse of fresh, alive color in my black jeans and black top, don't want a fucking *flower farmer* to see these half-done tattoos I got three days before my mother upended my life by leaving home with Lynton Baltimore.

I want to turn to Adam and say, *This is too big, too open; I'm scared of this.*

For once, I don't think about Tegan first—don't think about her inevitable disappointment if I stop this now, if I say I've changed my mind.

"Adam," I say, and he looks toward me, and whatever I was going to say dies on my lips, because he looks so . . .

He looks so *happy* to be here. To be home. He looks as though he's going to get out of this car and finally step into a space that's big enough to fit him.

"Yeah?"

He'd do it; he'd turn the van around. The same way he would've stopped Salem, Curtis MacSherry, Luís.

The same way he took us out of Florida, as soon as he got the chance.

I swallow heavily, face the windshield. Stare at that nice house again.

"Never mind," I say, even as I have the sinking feeling that, at least for me, the break is already over.

ADAM must've given everyone instructions.

Detailed ones.

Over the course of the next couple of hours, Tegan and I meet more than a few members of the Hawkins family. His oldest sister, Beth. Her husband, Mace. Their three kids—Sam, Katie, Ginny—all under the age of eight. Adam's mom and dad, Claire and Adam Senior, who drive over from the small home they now live in on the north end of the property. Adam Senior's mother, Margie, who gets picked up by Mace two days a week from her retirement community to spend time with family. At one point, Adam's other older sister, Carly, FaceTimes Beth from St. Louis, where she works as a pediatric surgeon.

Not a single one of them mentions Salem, or the podcast. Our mom. Lynton Baltimore.

Not a single one of them mentions why we're all here in the first place.

They simply . . . welcome us in. Serve gigantic casseroles around a big dining room table. Talk about themselves, their (to me, at least) faraway neighbors, the farm. They laugh—and sometimes scold—at things the kids do. They argue about changes to area farmers' markets. There's a long diversion about irrigation. We hear about how Beth does most of the hands-on farm operations, and Mace does most of the business side of things, and the child care. We learn Adam Senior hates being retired, so he still mostly works all day, and that Claire has gotten into painting. Even at the mention of this—*painting*, for God's sake—no one brings up that we've basically come straight from a painter's studio, that a painting was a break in this big story the three of us are chasing.

Maybe Adam's told them nothing. Maybe this is just the most insular—but still somehow incredibly friendly—family to ever exist.

But I doubt it.

I doubt he left anything to chance.

It all should go a long way to easing the feeling that settled over me when we got here. I should be relaxed, at ease, enjoying the pound cake Beth's just brought out and the conversation no one seems to expect me to participate in. I should love the way Tegan is always either laughing or lit up as she listens, and I should feel great that no one's looked askance at my tattoos, especially since this house has at least one bright, full-color bouquet in every room I've seen so far.

I don't, though.

I'm confused and awkward and overwhelmed. I'm watching a play that's been staged only for me. I'm the toughest crowd to ever show up for the performance.

"Excuse me," I murmur, wiping my mouth on my napkin and rising from the table. I don't think anyone hears me, but then Beth calls out with directions to the restroom, and all I manage is a nod before I head that way.

A bathroom break isn't really enough, and when I re-emerge, instead of returning to the dining room, I take a left and move toward the front of the house. At first I think I'll step out onto the front porch, but at the last second, I decide I can't face it—that big, open stretch of land outside. So before I reach the front door I go to the right, ducking into a dimly lit room that

I'm guessing—from the tidy desk and old steel file cabinet—serves as Beth's office.

Perfect, I think, liking how everything's safely tucked away.

Except when I turn to take a load off in a comfy-looking chair near the window, I'm instead confronted with a wall of shelves, and unfortunately, they're not lined with closed-up books. Instead, they're decorated with pictures and trophies and framed certificates, featuring or for Adam.

All-Missouri Defensive Player of the Year. Butkus Award. *USA Today* High School Defensive Player of the Year. All American. Bednarik Award. Wuerffel Trophy.

In his photos, he looks bigger than he is now. Harder. No neck to speak of, and his hair a lot shorter. I prefer the way he wears it now, not that it's any of my business. Also not my business is that in the rare pictures where he's smiling, it's not the same smile he smiled at me over dinner last night, or over the center console today.

Maybe tonight would've been easier if I'd been sitting next to him. Not holding hands, which surely needs to be a one-off. But next to him, at least.

There's a knock on the jamb of the open door, and it's him standing there. Neck, nice hair. No smile, but still—a softness there when he looks at me.

"I'm sorry," he says.

I lower my brow at him, signaling my confusion over this apology.

"They're a lot. I know they are. Things will be quieter tomorrow, I'm sure. The kids will be—"

"Adam," I interrupt, embarrassed by how transparent I've obviously been. "Don't be sorry. It's not them; it's me. I'm . . ."

I shrug my shoulders. I don't know what I am.

Ask me, I think. *Ask me what I am.*

He doesn't, and I suppose I only have myself to blame. Or thank. I don't know which anymore.

"If it was too much to bring you here, we can go."

I shake my head. "No. No, it's—they're really nice. This was nice of you, to bring us here. Tegan's having a great time already. It's good for her."

There's a long pause, and then Adam takes another step into the room, tucks his hands in the pockets of his jeans.

"I wanted it to be good for you," he says finally. Quietly.

God. That warm and wonderful feeling. I have to look down at my feet. I let my hair slip over my shoulders, convenient curtains for my flushed cheeks. I think the right thing to say, the polite thing to say, would be something like, *It is good for me*.

But the problem is, I can't tell if it's a *true* thing to say. I can't see past how overwhelmed I am—by being around this family and not knowing how to *be*, by seeing, as if from a distance, how locked down I keep myself in even the most harmless, welcoming of circumstances. Away from home . . . no, away from home *and* on this break from the Baltimore story . . . it's as though those locks inside me are rattling themselves in frustration.

When I don't respond, he comes to stand beside me. Facing the shelves, his hands still in his pockets. It takes a good long while, but I wait until my face has cooled before I look up and over at his profile. His eyes course over all those photos and trophies and certificates.

"You must've really loved football," I say, relieved to ignore the rattling for a little longer.

He shrugs. "You'd think that."

"You didn't?"

"I loved parts of it. But really, it was sort of that I was built for it, at least around these parts. When I was a kid, it was a given. I was tall from a young age. I put on muscle easily; I was fast. Of course I'd play football, everyone knew that. So I did, and I was good at it. I committed to it. It brought me a lot of opportunities. Free college, and a job right after. Trips to a lot of places. My best friend."

Without thinking, I take the smallest step sideways, closer to where he stands. My shoulder barely brushes against the side of his arm. I doubt he even feels it, whereas I feel it everywhere.

"Why'd you stop playing?"

He looks at one of those no-neck photos.

"The parts I hated, I hated. And there were more of those parts, after a while. My body hurt. I was hurting other people's bodies. I was afraid of the life I'd have in ten, twenty years if I kept playing. I was afraid of the person I'd be."

I nod, inexplicably emotional. I'm probably overtired, but also . . . he's such a *big* person. He contains multitudes, I think. Why would anyone think a hugeness like his would only be good for football?

"Adam," I say, and same as when we were in the van, his eyes go right to mine. But this time I'm not going to *Never mind* him or not answer him. For once, I'm going to be honest with him.

"It's not that it's not good for me here." I fight the urge to look away, to put my eyes on something else as I finish. I fight to hold his gaze, and I win. "It's that I'm not sure I know what's good for me anymore."

As soon as I say it, I realize that in spite of my earnest effort, it's still not quite the truth.

Because I'm pretty sure that being near him is good for me.

He's quiet again, and there's a clutch of embarrassment in my stomach as I come to another uncomfortable realization: Other than various versions of *Are you okay?* and *Why in God's name would you pick sour gummy worms?* Adam hasn't asked me a single personal question since I told him not to, that day in my father's front room.

I gave him instructions, and he's followed them to the letter.

I can't believe I'm even contemplating it, but maybe I should bring things back to football, which is a thought I never expected to have in my life. At least it'd let him off the hook.

But as I open my mouth to ask something, anything—what's a Butkus Award, how'd you grow your neck back—Adam rushes out a sentence that makes me stiffen where I stand.

"I need to tell you something."

I blink up at him, that embarrassed clutch in my stomach transforming into something heavy at the serious expression on his face. I don't even realize I've taken a step away from him until he gestures toward the chair by the window, offering me a seat.

I shake my head, cross my arms. My brain kicks up into an anxious, irrational register: *This has been some kind of trick. There's something about Mom or Lynton Baltimore here. This wasn't really a break at all.*

He looks as though he can read my mind.

"Everything's okay."

"Don't tell me everything's okay," I snap, tightening my crossed arms. Pressing them against that heavy feeling in my stomach. "Just *tell* me."

He nods and crosses to the chair, sits in it himself. He clasps his hands loosely between his spread knees and looks up at me. Whatever he has to say, he's sorry about it. I can tell already.

"I'm at Broadside because I want to do a story about what happened to Cope."

He pauses, his fingers flexing and unflexing.

"About other things, too. Young men and their mental health, and football and head injuries and . . . it doesn't matter."

I'm sure it does matter. Maybe it'll even matter to me, if he doesn't tell me something shitty in the next thirty seconds.

"Salem said if I get you to talk on the record about your mom, she'll produce it."

So, something extremely shitty then.

A trick, after all.

"That's why you've brought us here?" My voice sounds too high to my own ears. Overloud. "That's why you've been so . . . so . . ."

I'm at a loss. The only words in my head are *warm and wonderful.*

"Did you *agree*?" I finally say.

He shifts in his seat. "I didn't disagree."

I start for the door. I'll get Tegan. I'll steal that fucking van if I have to. I let him *hold my hand.*

And all he wanted was for me to *talk.* My past, my pain in exchange for his goddamned podcast.

"Jess, please. *Please.*"

I don't know why that should stop me even for a second, but it does. Maybe it's that voice crack again, the same one I heard in the restaurant last night. I don't look back at him, but I stay put. I can tell he's standing up again. There's a burst of collective laughter from the dining room, and I can pick out Tegan's even from here. I close my eyes, wishing it could calm me down.

"Is Salem's daughter even hurt? Has this been—did you and she have some kind of plan? I'd talk more if she was gone?"

"Jesus, no." He has the nerve to sound shocked, and I whirl on him.

"Don't do that. Don't you dare suggest I'm crazy for asking. You pretended you were on my side, but all this time, you were on your own."

I snap my mouth shut, surprised at what I've said. Since when have I needed anyone on my side? Since when have I even wanted it?

He lowers his head, runs a hand over his brow. I don't feel an ounce of sympathy for him. However, I do think I might cry, which is mortifying. I'm sure my shower later will be a real *where's-the-water-coming-from* guessing game.

"I'm on your side," he says. "You have no reason to believe me, I know that. But I am. The other night at the pool, last night at the restaurant. Just now, Jess, when you said you don't know what's good for you anymore. You have no idea the things I want to ask you about your life. The things I want to know about you. Not about your mom, or Lynton Baltimore. Only you, because I—"

He breaks off, swallows and shakes his head before speaking again.

"But I don't ask you. And I won't, not for this. I'm telling you now because I can't go another second not telling you. I just wanted—I wanted to give you a break. A real break. That's why I brought you here. No other reason. I swear to you."

I shouldn't believe him. I know I shouldn't. He's no one I know. He's just a guy with a job that puts me and my sister at risk.

He's no one to me, no matter how he's made me feel over the last few days.

I should go get Tegan.

Take the van. Leave here and go home. Convince her to forget everything about this trip, convince her to focus on her future. Stay on my own side, forever.

"Because you what?" I say instead.

"What?"

"Why do you want to know things about me, if it's not for Salem? If it's not about my mom? Why only me?"

He blinks at me, clenches his jaw. Football-photo face.

For a tense few seconds I think he won't answer, and I want to scoff in frustration. I want to tell him he owes it to me. I want to say, *You held my hand.*

Except that would be so revealing, and I'm not going to reveal anything to Adam Hawkins, not anymore.

"Because I—" He's struggling again, a swallow and another shake of his head, a breath through his nose. I don't feel any sympathy for him.

I *don't.*

"Jess, I've had the wrong instincts about you from the first time I saw you. You opened your front door and I saw your face and half of me wanted to close it again for you. Spare you Salem, and the story we were coming to get. Except if I did that, I'd miss my chance to look at you, or hear your voice, no matter how little you used it. I'd miss my chance to be near this . . . this storm I saw inside you."

I drop my arms from where they cross against my body. I

want to ask him, *What storm?* But also, I'm pretty sure I don't have to. I know what storm. I've lived with it since Mom's first letter, leaving me with Dad.

I just don't know why it seems to have quieted down now.

Why it goes silent when Adam speaks again.

"I know it makes me a shitty journalist. It probably makes me a shitty person, too. But this is the truth, Jess. I don't want to know you for the story. I want to know you for myself."

Chapter 14

Adam

"Wow, you are fucked."

My sister comes to stand next to me at the table saw where I've been cutting—or, I guess, in this case, miscutting—narrow beams for the geodesic greenhouse domes we've spent the whole day plotting out and building. This is a big step for a new floriculture education project Beth envisions for the farm, and now I've slowed her down. I step back and set my hands on my hips, shaking my head at myself.

Wow, I am *fucked*, I think, with the same heavy dread that's been haunting me since last night.

Instead I say, "Shut up. I haven't done this in a while."

Beth snorts. "Please. You were never good at carpentry. I should've brought Katie out here; I probably wouldn't have had to check her work as much."

I gently shoulder-check her, cracking a smile for the first time in hours. But just as quick I go back down to frowning at my most recent cut. Too short. I'm not paying attention.

"Anyway, I'm talking about something else," Beth says, shoulder-checking me back.

I don't look over at her, but I don't really have to. Beth and I are only thirteen months apart, and we've always been close. When Cope died, and I came back here, Beth was the only person I could bring myself to talk to some days, even if it was just to say I didn't want to talk. She'd go for long, silent walks with me, even though she was hugely pregnant at the time. In the middle of the night, she'd come downstairs and sit with me on the couch when she'd hear me get up, restless with grief, still checking my social media feeds constantly, scrolling through the wild swings of praise and vitriol being sent my way. She knows me well enough to know I'm upset today, and she's probably got a good guess as to why.

"Yeah," is all I say.

"I mean, she was a little aloof last night," she continues, as though I've admitted it. "But this morning she was an ice castle. Surrounded by a nuclear moat." She pauses, *hmm*s to herself. "Does that metaphor work?"

"No."

But actually I think it does. Jess *was* an ice castle this morning. Cold and fortified, all through the awkward breakfast we all sat through together. The nuclear moat part might be a bit of an overstatement, but still. She wasn't going to let a single person around that table see her hurting.

See that *I'd* hurt her.

Beth shrugs. "You were the English major. Come on, we need to quit for the day."

I know she's right—the sun's about an hour from setting, I'm pretty sure—but still, I drag my feet at gathering up our supplies. This morning, after breakfast, I packed us a big cooler of drinks and sandwiches and snacks; I asked Mace if it'd be all right with him if Beth and I stayed out for the whole day. He looked at me curiously, because he knows me pretty well, too, and I lied and said I could use a good long stretch of time outside.

The truth was, I promised Jess I'd give her time today. That I'd stay away from her.

"You had a fight with her?" says Beth, as I'm folding up the table saw.

"I'm not talking about it."

I promised her that, too.

But it's hard not to tell it all to my sister: the devastation on Jess's face when I told her about Salem's offer to me, followed by the sort of seething anger and suspicion I'd gotten used to not seeing in her eyes. Her shocked expression at everything I said next—about that storm inside her, about the way I wanted to know her. *Only* her.

For a second, I thought she . . . I don't know. I thought she softened to it; I thought she was glad to hear it. My body had been vibrating with hope, with anticipation. I thought, *She's going to open the window all the way this time. She's going to let me in. Only me.*

Instead, she slid it shut again. She told me she needed to think, that she and Tegan needed to be away from me. The only success I had was in convincing her not to leave right then. I let her list out the same sort of conditions as she'd once given me while we were sitting in her father's living room, back when we were total strangers to each other.

I feel Beth staring at me. "Leave it," I tell her.

"If you don't talk to me, I'm just gonna *extrapolate*."

"Go right ahead, Boop," I answer, using her old childhood nickname. "I won't tell you either way."

She *hmm*s.

"Obviously, you're falling in love with her."

It is unbelievably difficult not to react. My respect for Jess—ice castle, nuclear moat, never-reveals-anything Jess—increases exponentially, which I might've figured was impossible.

"And I think she might have a thing for you, too."

I swallow. That's bait. I know it is. *Do not react,* I tell myself firmly. *Do not ask what she means. That would be a betrayal of Jess.*

My brain is desperately trying to coach my wayward heart from the sidelines.

"I think she wanted to sit next to you at dinner last night," Beth adds.

I'm sure that'll never happen again. Still, how did I miss she wanted me to sit next to her? Now I'm stuck replaying the evening in my mind, every cue I might have missed. I'm imagining it going another way. If I'd been next to her, if I'd set my hand on her leg. Would it have been good for her here then? Would everything after—my overdue confession to her—have gone better?

"Still," Beth says, grunting with effort as she hefts a toolbox into the truck cab, "despite her questionable taste in people she wants to sit next to, I like her."

I roll my eyes. But also, I'm glad Beth likes her.

Jess deserves to be liked.

I'm on the verge of saying that, at least, when my phone rings with a particular tone: Salem's.

"Shit," I mutter, pulling it from my back pocket.

It isn't that I don't want to hear from Salem, really—in fact, I'm hoping for a good update about her daughter's condition— but also, I have no fucking idea how to deal with the fact that I probably just blew up her story because of my feelings for Jess. I'd tell her, except that I promised Jess I wouldn't, and also, I don't want to pile on when she's in the middle of a major family crisis.

Again: I am fucked.

"Salem, hey." I give my sister a wordless signal to hang on a minute.

"How's farm life?" She sounds completely normal. I'll give her this: She is resilient as all hell.

"Good," I say, even though my day has been pretty much the opposite of good. "Quiet."

"Well, I hate that," she says, referring to . . . quiet, I guess.

"Where are you?"

"Cafeteria. The coffee is—"

"Terrible?"

"No." She sighs. "But also, yes. Like tar."

"How's Pen?"

There's a slight pause. Not good news, I take it, but Salem doesn't provide any detail.

"I'll probably need a couple more days."

"It's fine," I tell her, even though I have no idea if it's fine. In a couple more days from now Jess might be back in Ohio with Tegan, having done all the thinking she needs to decide she never wants to see me again.

"I'm working on Tulsa," she says, back to business. "Reviewing some of the initial leads we had about Baltimore's connection to that area."

I suppress a wince. There weren't any promising leads about Baltimore's connection to Oklahoma. She's reaching.

"And the postcard for this one, it does mention something about a 'tough few days,' but obviously that could be anything. Have you asked Jess and Tegan about it?"

I clear my throat. "Not yet. Maybe tomorrow."

The truth is, I haven't even thought about Tulsa. Not since we left Florida and decided to come here.

"Well, they might help narrow things down."

"Yeah, sure," I say, but there's no curiosity in it.

"If things aren't wrapped up here in two days, go to Tulsa without me. I'll meet you guys in New Mexico. I trust you."

Christ. I feel as low as the dirt beneath my feet. "Salem, I—"

"Listen, you had a lot of injuries when you played football, right?" she interrupts, her voice quick and tight. It's a rare show of vulnerability from her, and I have a strange thought.

Salem and Jess probably have more in common than either of them would ever guess at.

"I had some, sure."

Not the kind Salem's daughter has—I was uniquely lucky in never having broken a bone, and I never needed surgery. But I had overuse injuries, too many to count. Compression in my spine. Sprains and strains that felt as bad as breaks, made worse by the way I played through them. Two concussions, both mild.

"And you've turned out fine."

"Sure," I repeat. I'm glad I've never told her about the pain I get when I sit for too long, or any of the other half-dozen complaints I have about parts of my body on any given day. I'm glad I never mentioned the inflammatory ulcers I got from taking too much ibuprofen for years at a time, or that "mild" is pretty much a misnomer for any sort of brain injury.

I picture Salem alone in the hospital cafeteria, probably putting on a show of looking busy and irritated, sucking down tar-flavored coffee while she worries desperately about her daughter and doesn't show it to anyone, even the husband that I gather she's not talking much to.

"She's young," I add. "She'll recover."

There's silence on the other end, and then Salem says, "You're a good one, Hawk. I'll see you in a couple of days."

Then she hangs up, and I hang my head.

"Jeez," Beth calls. "I didn't think it was possible for you to look worse."

She's standing over by the truck, all packed up, waiting. I'd tell her to shut up again, but she just did all that extra work while I was on the phone. I settle for a grunt of annoyance.

She shakes her head at me in a big-sister mixture of sympathy and annoyance.

"Come on. Let's go cross that moat."

By the time we pull up to the house, I'm pretty much expecting the worst. The van's still out front, so at least one of my most-feared options hasn't come to pass, but I'm still fairly certain that I'll get inside to find Jess and Tegan packed up and ready to leave. And even though I spent hours today turning over last night in my mind, I'm still not sure what I could ever say to Jess to get her to forgive me. I've broken something so fundamental to her.

My stomach is sick with nerves.

But when Beth and I get out of the truck, we're both treated to the delighted, high-pitched shrieks of Sam, Katie, and Ginny, and I can't help but smile.

"Oh, God," Beth says. "They're on the trampoline. Mace is probably a wreck."

I give her a curious look, and she rolls her eyes.

"He hates that thing. Didn't talk to me for three days after I ordered it, even though it's got the safety net around it. He'll probably need to go to bed early from the stress."

Poor Mace. When I met him, the guy reminded me of a stone bust in the library, he was so stoic. But one wedding to my sister and three daughters later and it's like looking at a big, beating heart with legs growing out of the bottom.

"I'll go relieve him," I say, and tell myself it's not about putting off the inevitable.

"I'll come. I love to see the fun they have on it. It makes up for the times Mace emails me links to stories of trampoline accidents."

We fall in step beside each other, making our way around to the back of the house. I'm soothed by the sounds of my nieces laughing and shouting, wishing I could borrow even a fraction of their levity. But as we turn the corner, I hear two other voices mix in.

One in particular.

Jess's voice.

Jess's *laugh*.

I've never heard it before, her full, loud laugh.

I've never heard it, and yet I'd know it anywhere.

Barely fifty yards away, and I can see her. She's up on that trampoline, her huge, gorgeous mass of spun-gold hair swirling in the air as she jumps, holding on to Ginny's hand.

I still where I'm standing, struck dumb. I don't even notice that Beth's kept on walking until she turns back and waves her hands in front of my face.

"Oh, yeah," she says, moving to nudge me forward. "You're fucked."

I register that Katie's on the trampoline, too; I register, in a vague sense, that Tegan and Sam are cheering them on from the ground or maybe just calling out for their turn. But as we get closer, I can't focus on anyone other than Jess—the way she turns and takes both of Ginny's hands, the way she keeps her jumps small for Ginny's sake at first and then makes them bigger and bigger, bringing my gasping, thrilled youngest niece along. I watch as her smile comes into full view—and then *I'm* a beating heart on legs, unimaginably worse off than I was before I heard her, saw her like this.

If she goes now, I doubt I'll ever recover.

"Now would you look at this!" Beth says, using a particular mom-voice I recognize. A mock-chiding tone, one that'll make the girls excited to act as if they've gotten away with something.

"Mama!" Katie calls out, kicking out her legs and bouncing on her butt, which makes Ginny laugh and laugh, even as Jess slows her jumping, gradually bringing them to a stop.

"Where is your daddy?" Beth says, setting her hands on her hips, a mischievous glint in her eyes.

"He's lying down!" shouts Katie, and Ginny adds, "He hates the trampoline!"

Sam says, "Jess can do a *flip*!"

"Can she?" says Beth, but I'm pretty sure she's looking at me instead of Jess. Doesn't matter, I'm looking at Jess enough for everyone out here. Probably enough for the whole entire world. She's mostly still now, just the occasional wobbly wake of Katie and Ginny's movements toward the safety net's opening. Her hair is a wild, wavy tangle, one sleeve of her T-shirt pulled up high on her shoulder.

She raises her eyes to mine and I'm pretty sure I stop breathing.

Please don't go, I want to say. *Please let me find out how you learned to do a trampoline flip.*

"Should we go check on him?" I hear Beth say, overloud, which means I've probably missed out on a good chunk of conversation. But I don't want to take my eyes off Jess, especially not when she's got hers on me.

"Brownie!" screams Ginny, a non sequitur as far as I can tell, but kids are like that.

"Hmm," Beth says, tapping her chin. "Is it too late for brownies?"

"NO!" the girls scream, and Jess's lips quirk.

"I *also* want a brownie," Tegan says, but there's a little something in her voice, an abrasive texture I recognize—usually reserved, in the van and in our interviews, for her sister. It's enough to get me to look away from Jess, if only for a second.

But when I catch Tegan's eye, I realize that the tone is meant for me. She's got her eyes narrowed at me as if I've been hiding postcards in a curtain rod for ten years. Probably in any other circumstance, I'd feel uncomfortable, but instead, I'm strangely glad. I want Tegan on Jess's side, even if that means I'm their common enemy.

Katie and Ginny are on the ground now, greeting me quickly and bounding off again, as though I'm just another springy part in the jumping chaos of their evening. Beth herds them toward the house, sparing me a quick eyebrow-raise before she goes, and then it's just the three of us—me and Jess and Tegan, missing one of our original compass points, but still spinning with a strange, million-things-unsaid energy.

Tegan crosses her arms and continues staring at me even as she speaks to her sister.

"Jess, do you want a brownie?"

"I'm good."

Her voice sounds different, slightly breathless. A relic of her laughter and movement up on that netted-in trampoline. Now it seems like a cage. Keeping her in, or keeping me out. I wipe my palms on my jeans. Tegan's looking at me as if she's sitting in a recliner with a shotgun in her lap.

"I'll be in, in a few minutes," Jess adds, but Tegan doesn't move right away.

I follow her eyes to Jess, who gives her a short nod, and then Tegan's looking back at me with an *I've got eyes on you, pal* shotgun threat in her eyes. Given what I know about Tegan's priorities up to this point, that look might be less about protecting Jess and more about the Baltimore story and her desperation to continue searching for it.

But I have the feeling it's both, and I mimic Jess's short nod even as Tegan turns and stalks past me, following Beth and the girls back to the house, leaving an icy chill in her wake.

I'm weirdly proud of her. Weirdly happy she's learned some things from Jess, after all.

We both wait in silence until we hear the back screen door bang shut behind them, and then it's only us—night nature sounds coming to life in the air and grass and trees, me staring up at Jess through the black net she stands behind. I imagine myself as a defendant in court, her the judge.

Adam Hawkins, I imagine her saying, *this court finds you—*

"Do you want to come in?" she says, and thank God for that. Obviously my imagination has leaned fully into my sleep-deprived, stressed-out state of mind.

"Uh, yeah," I say, but then hesitate. She smirks.

"Are you *also* afraid of the trampoline?"

"No."

But actually, sort of. When it comes down to it, I'd rather be on firmer ground for this conversation.

Still, I move toward the net's opening, toeing off my boots and tucking my socks inside, and mumbling a quiet thanks as Jess holds the flap back for me. It's not the most graceful thing, being a grown man—a taller and more-built-than-average grown man—getting up onto a trampoline. Frankly it's a little lowering, which maybe is the point. The springs around the edge creak as I hoist myself up, and I wish I'd read a few of those articles Mace keeps an eye out for. Maybe they mention something about weight limits.

Once I'm on—in, whatever—the moment grows impossibly more awkward, both of us standing here on a surface that's meant for play, for joy, for the opposite of being serious. Are we going to . . . jump? Is Jess going to . . . do a flip, and then tell me she's leaving?

"Jess, I'm sorry," I say, hoping to head off either of those other options.

She doesn't say anything. She just lowers herself into a seated position and looks up at me, invitation in her eyes. So, no jumping or flipping. Only sitting, and as soon as I do, I guess I see that there's sort of a Jess-specific poetry about it. Surrounded by the net, it's contained, private. It's not really a closed door, but there's a carefulness about how open it is.

I watch as she folds her legs, crisscross style. Her feet are bare and beautiful. She clasps her hands in the space left between her legs and takes a breath through her nose, big enough that I see her chest expand with it.

"It hurt because I trusted you."

Quiet but clear.

A damning use of the past tense.

"I'm so—" I begin, but she holds up a hand, and that's fair enough. I'm just trying to stall the verdict, anyway.

"I don't trust anyone. Probably not really since my mother left the first time, when I was twelve, but definitely not since the second time, when I was twenty-one. If you were to ask me who my closest friend in the world is, I'd tell you it's Tegan, but I know Tegan isn't my friend. She's not even really my sister most days, because instead I'm the closest thing she has to a mother, and she can't see me as her sister when I'm taking away her phone for two nights because she lied about doing her calculus homework. If you were to ask me about my father, I'd tell you that I don't really trust him, either, because when my mother left the first time, I could tell having me full-time was an inconvenience to him, no matter how nice he acted about it. If you wonder about the people I work with, I'd tell you that I pay the rent on my chair at the salon every month on time and I attend every meeting I'm required to and I keep my book fuller than anyone else, but I've never attended a single happy hour or holiday party with any of them. Dating? I don't do it. I had a boyfriend when my mother left the second time and he lasted a week and a half in my new life as the twenty-one-year-old guardian of an eight-year-old before he told me things had gotten 'too real' for him. There isn't anyone, Adam. Not *anyone*."

I can barely process how it feels to hear Jess say all this: to hear her speak this much, to hear her reveal this much. In the moments I've let myself imagine a more open Jess, a Jess who'd speak about herself freely, I think I still imagined reticence: words instead of phrases, phrases instead of sentences, sentences instead of speeches. I feel like she's stood up on this trampoline and jumped hard enough to catapult me into the air.

But I also feel like I've taken a helmet straight to the stomach. I doubt I could catch my breath if I tried.

"Do you know why I'm telling you all this?"

I swallow thickly.

So I know how much I hurt you.

So I know how much I lost, losing your trust.

I can't make my mouth say either thing out loud. I can't do anything but look at her, in case I won't have the chance after tonight.

She doesn't smile when she says the next part. She says it as serious as she's said almost everything to me, ever since I met her. She says it so I know she means it.

"I'm telling you all this because I decided I'm going to try trusting you again."

Chapter 15

Jess

I know he's going to ask. Of *course* he's going to ask.

I get a moment of grace before he does: a moment where Adam Hawkins—brawny, beat-up-looking Adam Hawkins, who has dark circles beneath his eyes and who has been clenching his jaw for the last five minutes at least—swallows thickly and lowers his head, reaching up to run a hand through his disheveled hair as he blows out a breath. It's relief, I think, or maybe gratitude, and as soon as he does it, a weight lifts from my chest, too, as if my body knows I've made the right call.

Even if my brain put me through the wringer about it. All last night, and almost all of today. Back and forth about whether we should go.

Whether I should ever see or speak to this man again.

"Why?" he says quietly, the question I expected. Why would I decide to trust him again, after what he told me? Why would I decide to trust him, when I've just told him about how I've kept my trust from the world for years?

As soon as he asks it, I'm back in that wavering place—not

about the decision itself, but about what I should tell him about the reason I made it.

For what must be the millionth time since last night, I think of his words to me in that quiet front room, the distant sounds of his family and mine in the background. The catch in his voice when he said them. The look in his eyes.

I'd miss my chance to look at you, or hear your voice, no matter how little you used it.

I don't want to know you for the story. I want to know you for myself.

"This is so important to Tegan," I blurt, because if I don't, I might say so many other things that have nothing to do at all with Tegan and her need to know where our mother is. I might say things I can't be certain are true, because the truth is, I only *feel* he was telling me the truth. I *feel* he never meant to hurt me, that he wanted to tell me sooner. I feel safe with him, different around him, and when he's beside me, the prospect of finding out where my mother has been all these years doesn't strike me as the very worst idea in the world.

And I feel a flutter in my middle when I think of what it would be like to have Adam Hawkins know me for no one else but himself.

I watch as a flash of disappointment passes over his face, and I try desperately to talk right over it.

I can't focus on that flutter.

"We've come this far. With the story, I mean. And Tegan, she—"

"She'd leave," Adam interrupts, and I blink at him. "She would leave here, and leave this, if you wanted her to. I saw her just now, Jess. Whatever you told her about us last night—she'd do what you want her to do now."

That softens me, and I can't help but smile, though I direct it down to my hands. Tegan *had* defended me, hadn't she? Not just a few minutes ago, when Adam and Beth had returned from their day doing God knows what, but also last night, when she found me upstairs in the guest room Beth had set us up in when we first arrived. I'd been sitting on one of the narrow twin beds, my bag open beside me, my stomach turning and turning. I can't imagine what expression I must have had on my face to inspire such a quick reaction in my sister.

She shoved my suitcase out of the way enough to sit beside me. "What happened?" she said, with a note of pure, unselfish concern, and it was the first time in a long time I had the sense that she *saw* me. Not as the person who takes care of her.

Just . . . as a person.

So I told her the truth: that Adam had made a deal with Salem, his own podcast in exchange for me talking about Mom on the record. I hadn't expected her to react, really. If anything, I expected her to take his side—to say, *Talk about Mom, then,* or maybe, *You can leave, but I'm staying.* I was thinking of her that day at the kitchen table, those damning postcards spread out before her, anger written all over her face.

But she surprised me. She said, "That *sucks,*" and then she said that Adam was supposed to be "the nice one."

I stared at her in openmouthed shock, and she shrugged.

"He acts more like our friend than Salem does."

In that moment, I felt an incongruous pang of gratitude for the exact same man I was so mad at, if only for getting me and my sister to agree on something.

"She would," I say to Adam now, and in response, he tilts his head ever so slightly at me, a question in his eyes.

If she would, then why aren't you leaving?

"I don't want to be part of any deal you've made with Salem."

"I don't want it that way," he says quickly. "I don't want *you* that way."

That flutter in my middle takes up firm residence again. Blood rushes to my face, warm and revealing.

"I mean—" he stops, clears his throat. "You know what I mean."

The space between us is heavy with the possibility of that shy, cautious *you know what I mean.* I think he means what he said last night—that he wants to know me only for himself. But right now, in the fading light of the summer evening, all alone out here where I'm certain no one from the house can see us, what Adam Hawkins truly means by knowing me for himself seems as huge and as strong as he is.

My mind pulses with a hundred inconvenient images, all wrong for the moment: Adam's big hand on the back of my neck, both of mine gripping his biceps. Adam's chest rising and falling with breaths that come fast. My damp forehead against his bare shoulder. Our legs tangled together on a big bed.

I blink, desperate to clear them.

We are on a *trampoline*, for God's sake.

"When I talk to you," I say, trying to get back to the point, though I admit—my voice sounds suited for one of those inconvenient images. I try clearing my throat, too.

I start it over, in a safer place this time.

"*If* I talk to you, that's for you, Adam. That's not for the story. I don't know what that means for your job, but—"

"I don't care what it means for my job."

I let that hang in the air. Every small expression on Adam's face at any mention of his best friend, every word he's ever said about him in my presence, and I know it's not so simple as *I don't care what it means for my job.*

His job matters to him. His best friend matters to him.

He lowers his head again. "I'll talk to Salem. I was going to talk to her. We'll figure it out."

"How?" I ask, even though I know he can't possibly have an answer. *I* don't have an answer. That day at my dad's, I had all those conditions for Adam; I thought I could set every boundary in advance. Now, those boundaries fold in on each other, blurry and confusing. I'm staying on the story for Tegan's sake, but I'm still not talking. Except when I am, but that won't be for the story. Adam's staying on the story, because it's his job, but if he ever hears me tell my perspective on it, he has to keep it separate from Salem, from the story she's out to get.

And all that? All that is to say nothing of the *you know what I mean* of it all; all that is to say nothing of those crystal-clear images of us together in my head.

I doubt there's a *how* for those. There probably *shouldn't* be a how.

He blows out another breath, this one gusty and frustrated. When his body shifts with that frustration, the trampoline surface beneath us wobbles, and I list slightly to the side, catching myself on an outstretched hand. Adam and I both make the exact same Midwestern exclamation of surprise, quiet *ope*s as we steady ourselves, and it's impossible not to meet each other's eyes and smile, some of the tension scattering in the warm night wind.

"It's really hard to be serious on a trampoline," he says.

"Maybe that's okay. Maybe we need the break."

The whole reason we came here, after all, and neither of us has had much of one yet. At least my day included baking brownies and playing with some pretty good-natured kids while hanging out with my not-currently-mad-at-me sister. I'm pretty sure Adam hasn't been so lucky.

His smile fades, his face turning solemn again.

"Salem says if things with her daughter aren't settled in the next two days, we should go on to Tulsa. Without her."

I'm strangely unaffected by the prospect of it. The Tulsa postcard was an odd one, the cheerfulness from Mom's first two missives pretty muted. She mentioned the horses she saw in one line; in the next, she wrote of a tough few days, without any detail. She signed off by reminding me to go to my dad for help if I needed it, as though it was the first time it'd occurred to her to imagine I might be having some extremely tough days of my own.

A week ago, thinking of it would've made me feel that storm brewing in my chest. Right now, though, I can't summon it. Maybe it's because I've already been on two stops of this strange, searching road trip and survived them. Or maybe it's what Adam said: It's hard to be serious—stormy—on a trampoline.

"Okay."

He almost looks more surprised than when I told him I wanted to try trusting him again.

"Okay?"

I nod. "Two more days here. Tulsa after."

"Last night, I meant what I said, about wanting this break to be good for you. I still want that. I want you to have whatever you want, while you're here."

More inconvenient images, layering over the first set. Adam as I saw him after his late-night run, but this time, he peels off his sweat-soaked shirt and stands so close to me. He backs me into the hallway bathroom and puts a finger over his lips, reminding me to be quiet, as if I'd ever need to be told not to talk. His shoulders barely fit in the narrow shower, but they're perfect for me to hold on to, anyway.

"Jess?"

I startle enough to ripple the trampoline again.

"Sorry, I was—" No good ending to that sentence, so I redirect entirely with a boring, blameless lie. "Actually, I think right now I want a brownie."

I don't even like brownies.

He stares at me for a beat, obviously not buying it. But then he nods. "All right."

Neither of us moves.

He clears his throat, looking uncomfortable. "Need help?"

I smile, remembering his awkward clamber up here. "Do *you*?"

He laughs—a quiet, embarrassed chuckle. "Probably."

I stand easily, no wobble, but honestly, not laughing as Adam gets to his feet—a sort of crouching, crooked affair, with at least one full-on tip to the side—a Herculean effort. I give in when he cuts his eyes to mine and laughs at himself again.

"This thing wasn't made for a man of my size," he grumbles, when he's finally up, and I cannot help myself. I do a little hop.

Adam raises his arms to the side, doing his best to balance through my teasing trampoline-wake.

"Hey now," he scolds, but he's on the verge of laughter, too.

"I thought athletes were supposed to be graceful."

"I'm retired." He narrows his eyes at me, suspicious of me doing it again, but it's good-natured. It's practically an invitation.

I decide to hold out for now. Catch him by surprise, maybe.

I can't believe I'm being so playful.

"How'd you get so good at this, anyway?" he asks. "Doing . . . you know. Trampoline flips, or whatever."

There's a beat where we both realize the significance of this. Not the question itself, but the fact that he's asking it. It's this new trying to know me, with the promise that it's for him alone.

I flex my feet against the tightly woven, plastic-y surface beneath me. It's strange, how hard it is to answer. Didn't I just tell Adam things about my life—the big, scary, lonely things about my life—that I don't share with anyone? Shouldn't it be so much easier to say something small?

"I had this friend," I finally say, just when I think he's about to tell me not to worry about answering. "We met in our third-grade class. She had one of these at her house."

"Nice," he says, as though that was a really interesting piece of information, as though the small things matter just as much as the big ones.

"I wanted to be a gymnast," I blurt, before he gives up on me. "Like . . . an Olympic one. Obviously I get now that I would've had to start long before third grade. And also that doing flips on a trampoline isn't . . . you know. What gymnasts do. But at the time . . . I thought that would be so amazing, to be able to be one of those girls. Those sparkly uniforms they wore, the way they did their hair. The way they could just *fly*, you know?"

He smiles. Crooked and lovely and flattered.

"It's hard to picture." His eyes track over my black T-shirt and jeans. "You in sparkles."

I smile back, but cross my arms as if I'm offended. "It's hard to picture you hulking out over a little leather ball while wearing shiny leggings."

He snorts. "That's fair enough."

The silence stretches, as taut as the mat beneath me. It's an odd feeling, to stand on a trampoline and not jump. It's not built for standing still.

"I used to love sparkles. On everything. My school supplies, my clothes. My face, when my mom would let me put them there. Bright pinks and greens and blues."

Ask me, I'm thinking, the same way I was last night. Now that we've done this—had this conversation, made this new deal with each other—I could answer so many things.

"How come it's 'used to'? How come"—he tips his chin up at me, a gesture to what I'm wearing now—"it's this?"

I drop my arms back to my sides, tip my head up toward the still-darkening sky. The color I like to cloak myself in.

"At first, it was kind of a *fuck you*, I guess. To my mom, when she came back after the first time she left."

I close my eyes briefly, remembering those surreal first days after her return. She didn't tell me right away, about being pregnant with Tegan, but I thought something looked different about her all the same. Her face somehow a different shape, her lips and nose always slightly puffy. Late at night, I used to lie awake and think: *Maybe it's not really her. Maybe my real mom is still somewhere else.*

"I didn't want her to know me anymore." I look back at him, offer a slightly embarrassed smile. "I went a little Goth, I guess, at first. And then later—" I break off, aware that I'm approaching the part of this story that comes closer to what brought me and Adam together in the first place.

"Later, I wanted to keep things simple. Easy to buy clothes, easy to figure out what to wear. Easy to be . . . nondescript. I wanted to blend in."

"You don't blend in. Not to me, you don't."

He's said it so forcefully, but it lands like a caress. Soft and so disarming. It makes the steady posture I have to keep on this unsteady surface almost impossible to maintain. I should be lying down when I hear Adam Hawkins say something like this.

The images that accompany this thought—they're too intimate to contemplate.

So I bend my knees and jump.

Adam barks out a laugh as he flails to steady himself, and then he joins me, jumping back. Obviously, I've made a grave mistake, because once Adam commits to it, I'm the one flailing and laughing and caught completely off guard. I gasp and yell his name, forcing myself into a bouncing rhythm of my own, and that's how we stay for the next couple of minutes—two overgrown kids, jumping and laughing as though we haven't just had the heaviest, most personal conversation of our entire acquaintance. I think of third-grade me, making a study out of someone's backyard playground, imagining myself covered in sparkles on a grand Olympic stage. I'm so different now, but then again . . .

Then again, this laughter and play and silliness . . . it's still familiar to me, even if it's been years and years since I embraced it.

When Adam and I accidentally knock into each other, my shoulder catching him lightly in the sternum, we both reach out, an automatic instinct to keep from falling, and that's how it happens—my hands clutching his thick, corded forearms, his palms settling on my hips, both of us staring at each other as our goofy smiles fade. Another thing I haven't had in years and years—being touched this way by a man, by *anyone*—but it's not familiar. It's brand-new, its own thing, sparkles beneath my skin, at the backs of my knees, between my legs.

Up close Adam's throat is a column of temptation; his mouth the most crossable line in the sand.

His eyes drop to my lips.

Ask me, I think. *Please, please ask me.*

"Jess," he whispers, followed by an endless, throbbing pause. "Can I ki—"

I press onto my toes, already nodding. He doesn't finish his question.

He wraps his arms around my waist and lifts me to him.

Then he sets his mouth to mine.

He kisses like the most impossible dream, a study in perfect contradiction. Soft and firm. Searching and assured. Eager and patient.

He kisses like Adam: this huge, hard slab of a man who is somehow the most gentle person I've ever met.

When my tongue traces the lush curve of his lower lip, he tightens his hold and makes a low sound from his chest that rumbles through me, settling between my legs. I press as close as I can; I slide my fingers against the short hairs at the back of his head.

Either my kiss is magic or Adam has had a miraculous recovery from his earlier unsteadiness, because as his tongue slides against mine, the lines of his body transform in some ineffable way—he's planting himself, growing roots that go straight through the surface of the mat and deep down into the ground. It's the most obvious display of strength I've ever felt from him, and having it against me is intoxicating, a shot of something totally pure to my bloodstream. For a second I think I must be dizzy with it, losing my balance, but no—that's just Adam, bending his knees the slightest, sturdiest amount and running his big hands lower on my hips, around to the backs of my thighs.

In a smooth second I'm up and then around him, my ankles hooked at the base of his spine, and then he lowers us both to the mat in a slow, steady squat, somehow keeping our mouths fused, somehow keeping our teeth from knocking awkwardly together.

When we're settled in it—me in his lap, his thighs and knees a cradle for my back, my smile breaks through the kiss, a clumsy interference after all those perfectly executed moves.

Adam murmurs his curiosity against my mouth. "What?"

"That was so athletic," I say, then kiss him again, through his quiet chuckle.

"I came out of retirement for you."

He ducks his head and shoves his hands through my hair roughly, tilting my head back and pressing his face against my throat. I know he feels my answering laugh, the happy vibration of it down the column of my neck. He opens his mouth against it, his tongue tracing up, and it may be absolutely impossible to be serious on a trampoline, but it is not at all impossible to be sexy.

At least it's not impossible for Adam Hawkins.

When his mouth meets mine again, we kiss with new intensity, something so . . . *determined* about it. Maybe it's that we've got to keep ourselves mostly still to keep this from turning ridiculous; maybe it's that we're worried what we'll start thinking of if we stop. It is so fully the best kiss of my life that it must be the only kiss I've ever had, and I guess, in a way, it is—ten years since my last one, and ten years ago I was a different Jess.

This is my first kiss fully grown, fully an adult. It's not an experiment or a distraction or a forfeit for a night out.

This kiss is a *choice*.

It is hot and perfect and all mine.

Until that screen door bangs again, and Adam and I freeze. Clutch each other and stop *breathing* freeze. If that's Tegan, I don't know what I'll do.

I don't know what I've done.

"Uncle Ad*aaaaaaaaaammmmm*!" comes a bright, extraordinarily loud voice—Ginny's voice, if I'm recognizing right from all the delighted screaming she did before Beth and Adam showed up here. She sounds as if she's been sent on a mission, and that must mean we've been out here longer than anyone expected us to be.

I push myself off his lap.

And sure, I bounce.

But suddenly, I don't feel all that funny anymore.

"Mom says you hafta come in here and help Daddy with the—!" Ginny breaks off, and I look at Adam.

He's looking at me as if he hasn't heard a thing. As if my heavy breathing is the only sound in the world.

"I forgot what!" Ginny screams into the night, and then the door bangs again, leaving us in stunned, serious silence. I drop my eyes away from Adam's searching gaze.

Apart from the heat of his body, the pressure of his mouth— I'm returning to factory settings. Little mechanisms inside me turning and locking down tight. It's the opposite of a choice.

It's just what I *do.*

I look up, words at the ready before my brain can even really consider them. *This doesn't mean anything. Obviously we can't do that again. I can't mess this up for Tegan.*

But Adam's expression has shifted, too. If these are *his* factory settings, then I can see why he was so good at football, because he looks . . . he looks almost . . .

Is he *angry* at me?

"Don't say it," he says, his voice tight. "Don't say whatever you were going to say. Not now."

It is so exactly the opposite of anything Adam has ever said to me.

It is also, inconveniently, very reminiscent of that hallway bathroom fantasy I had a few minutes ago. The place between my legs practically vibrates with frustrated longing.

Before I can think of how to respond, he moves: one knee and one hand on the mat, that slow and intentional stiffening again. When he stands, it's not like he's on firm ground, but it's not like he's on a trampoline, either. He's mastered himself, somehow, and those locks inside me go loose again.

I doubt I could get up right now if I tried.

He turns and slowly makes his way toward the net opening,

his steps careful, his shoulders impossibly broad. I want to say something, to call his name, to call him *back*, but that is definitely not something I do.

Just as I think he's about to jump down without another word, he pauses, keeping his back to me, his hand clasped around the net he holds open. He turns his head the slightest amount.

"Jess." His voice is so low I wonder if I'm imagining it.

"Yeah?" I am, embarrassingly, still short of breath. All anticipation.

"I want these two fucking days," he says.

Then he jumps down, bending to swipe his discarded boots off the ground in one smooth movement before he stands tall and walks—barefoot—toward the house.

Leaving me wet and breathless and wobbling.

And more speechless than I've ever been.

The Last Con of Lynton Baltimore

Transcript Excerpt from Episode 3, "The Baltimore Trap"

Durant: You look happy in these photos, Natalie.

Natalie Basham: I was happy.

Durant: I mean that you both look happy. You and Lynton. You both look very much in love.

Basham: I guess he was good at looking like that. I guess that's how he got us all.

Durant: Was there ever a time where you doubted him? Where you thought, something doesn't feel real about this guy?

Basham: He doesn't really give you time to think that. He doesn't really give you time to think at all.

Chapter 16

Adam

When I first wake up, I wonder if I've gone back in time.

I'm on the couch in the basement of the house I grew up in—a green and navy plaid monstrosity that has always been, for me at least, as comfortable as it is hideous. I can stretch all the way out on it, my feet not even close to hanging off the edge, and the cushions are firm enough to feel the right sort of soft for my body.

When I was a teenager, this is where I slept after every Friday night football game—the perfect spot for the comedown I always needed. I'd watch TV or play video games for a while, too keyed up to sleep right away and trying to keep my noise away from the rest of the family. Eventually I would nod off and doze until I got ravenously hungry again—I ate all the time back then, trying to keep weight on—then I'd make my way quietly up the steps and rustle around in the fridge, usually finding leftovers my mom set aside for me, or sometimes my favorite roast beef sandwiches that she'd made in advance. A few times, when I was in my junior and senior years, I'd spend at least a couple hours after home games on this couch with Emily, a girl in my class who I had an off-and-on thing with, mostly during the season, since she sort of seemed to lose interest at other times of year. Looking back, I can't say I blame her, since what we did here was pretty clumsy and quick, me too naïve and hair-triggered with postgame adrenaline to be any good at fooling around.

This morning, I've got a teenaged-Saturday-morning feeling. Hungry, hurting, and with a definite hard-on. Wishing I could go back and instant replay the night before.

But not for any of the teenaged reasons.

Only one reason, really, and I haven't seen her since last night.

I lift my hands and scrub them over my face, suppressing a groan as memories come back to me. The good ones, first: Jess jumping on that trampoline, Jess's laugh and smile, Jess telling me she'd trust me again, Jess telling me so *much*. Jess's lips, her tongue, her whole body on mine. Her hair tangled in my fingers, her neck bared to my open mouth.

The five or so best fooling-around minutes of my whole entire life.

Then, the not-so-good ones, or maybe just the one that's been haunting me most.

Had I . . . had I sort of . . . *yelled* at her? Had I said, *I want these two fucking days* and then walked off without another word into the night to calm down the thudding in my chest and the pulse down the length of my cock?

I swing my legs onto the floor and sit up, an answering pang flaring in my lower back, which either means that I am now officially too old for my favorite couch in the world or I tweaked something while I was jumping on a trampoline with a woman I can't stop thinking about. Amazing.

I tap the screen on my phone and wince at the time. Eight goddamn thirty, on a farm. If my dad is over here helping out with chores this morning, I'm going to get dragged to hell. I can't very well explain to him that I didn't fall asleep until well after three a.m. because I was absolutely fixated on the idea that Jess Greene might tiptoe down the basement stairs and give me what I growled at her I wanted. I can't very well say that once I did sleep, I dreamt of having my hands all over her body, my mouth between her legs. The sound of her panting breath in my ear, the feel of her skin damp with sweat against mine.

I make a pit stop in the small half-bath down here, brush my teeth and splash some ice-cold water on my face before pulling on a pair of jeans and a clean T-shirt. I don't hear much going on upstairs, so maybe I'll get a couple of minutes of blessed privacy before I find Jess and try to do a better-than-Neanderthal job of talking to her in an adult way about what we did last night.

Except when I get up to the kitchen, her sister is sitting there.

Big bowl of cereal in front of her, spoon halfway to her mouth, a smirk on her face when she sees me.

"Morning, Hawk," she says cheerfully.

"Adam," I say, not cheerfully. I head straight for the coffee. Mace keeps a pot on pretty much all day, which, now that I think of it, probably doesn't help with his anxiety. Maybe I'll mention it to him when I'm not pathetically grateful for the fact that this coffee exists.

"You just missed your dad."

I think about opening one of the cabinet doors onto my head. Repeatedly.

"He's *real* disappointed in you."

I keep my grim silence until I've got a full cup, and then I move back over to the table, sitting across from her. "Doesn't seem you're an early riser, either."

She shrugs. "I'm a guest. You like, *work* here."

"I don't work here," I grumble, which is honestly the same tone I would've used on my dad. Maybe I did wake up back in time. Another dimension.

Tegan crunches at her cereal loudly, scrolling on her phone.

She acts as though we have breakfast together every morning. I am somehow both embarrassed that she's witnessing me in this rattled state and also strangely, nonsensically accustomed to it. She doesn't even seem like a guest.

"Where is everyone?" I say, shrugging off the weirdness of it all for the moment and simply leaning in to the familiarity.

"Your dad and Mace left to do mowing. Beth's taking a shower before she's gotta take the girls over to their camp."

She takes another big bite of cereal, chews slowly. She knows who she's leaving out.

I'm about to call her bluff and take out my own phone, fake interest in my email or the headlines, or see what new episodes Broadside has released in the past few days, when I hear noise outside—my nieces, first, loud and laughing, and then Jess's muffled voice. I'm obviously still too tired, still too uncaffeinated, still too in my head to stop myself from looking immediately out the window.

I want these two fucking days, my brain howls again.

I'm sure Tegan notices. Her ongoing cereal-chewing is a judgment.

Outside, Jess seems to be on some kind of backyard tour, all three of my nieces vying for her attention. Her hair is up again, a thick, loose bun near the crown of her head, and it's so much of her neck that I have to jam the pad of my thumb into the always-sore spot at the top of my left kneecap to keep other parts of me from reacting.

She smelled sweet there, but against my tongue, she was salty.

She crouches, getting at Ginny's eye level. Knowing Ginny, Jess is looking at a bug right now, but she doesn't seem grossed out. When I met her, I guess I wouldn't have figured she'd be good with kids. I would've figured they were too chaotic, too nosy, too pushy. But looking at her now, she seems totally at ease. Everything that can read as harsh and censuring about her silence around Salem and me seems to have settled into a kind of kid-specific patience and tolerance.

"That's how she used to be," Tegan says, interrupting my thoughts.

I turn my attention back to her, but I hide my curiosity in my coffee cup.

"Before my mom left, that's how she was with me," Tegan continues, swirling her cereal around. "She was really fun when she came to visit me."

It isn't that I hadn't known this detail—that Tegan and Jess didn't live in the same house together until after Charlotte Caulfield left with Lynton Baltimore—but hearing Tegan say it this way somehow makes the knowledge more striking. *When she came to visit me.* It must've been such a big change, when all of a sudden Jess was there every day. All the time, and in circumstances that were the opposite of fun.

"The coolest big sister," she adds, a wistful note in her voice.

"She's still cool."

My defense of her is automatic, and—judging by Tegan's smile—pretty revealing. I'm tempted to look back out the window, get a glimpse of Jess to ground me. But before I can, that smug and knowing smile on Tegan's face fades.

"I really want to find my mom. That's why I wanted to come on this trip."

I lower my brow, confused. That's not news. It's what she's said from the jump, even when she was pretending to be someone else.

"I want to know why she left and why she never came back, and what she's been—"

"Let's get your sister." I'm not fucking this up worse by breaking any of the rules. No one talks to Tegan about this stuff unless Jess is around.

"No," Tegan says, the sharpness in her voice from last night back again. "And don't bring up the 'conditions,' or whatever, because I'm pretty sure you and Jess have already talked about my mother when I wasn't around."

I could argue, I guess. I could say that Jess has said very little about Charlotte to me. *I didn't want her to know me anymore*, she said last night, but that was basically the extent of it.

But Tegan looks so serious, so desperate to get this out.

"And anyway, what I want to say to you isn't about my mom. It's about Jess."

I swallow. That five minutes is surely written all over my face.

"So I want to find my mom for my own sake, of course I do. I'm going to college in a matter of weeks and I *need* to know about this. I need to at least try. I want to meet new people and be able to tell them about myself without having this big question mark about my life in the background. That's what I want, before I go out there on my own. As an adult."

I know better than to tell an eighteen-year-old in Tegan's circumstances that real adulthood is probably still a ways off, or that the shit that bothers her at eighteen is, annoyingly, going to bother her for a fair number of years yet, if not forever. I channel the kind of patience I saw Jess showing to Ginny out there on the back deck, when all I really want to know is what she has to say about her sister.

"But I want to find her for Jess's sake, too. Because in a couple of months when I'm not home every day, when she doesn't have me to take care of, I have the feeling that a bunch of stuff she's ignored for a lot of years is going to catch up with her. I may be mad at her for what she hid from me, but at the same time, a person doesn't hide five postcards in a freaking curtain rod if they have a healthy relationship to their trauma."

If it were any other day, in probably any other circumstance—any other circumstance where I haven't gone ass over feet for this young woman's older sister—I'm sure I'd be hearing these words in a way that'd interest me from a professional perspective. Tegan speaks in a way I recognize from a lot of people in her generation—the phrase "healthy relationship to trauma" trips easily off her tongue; she's steeped in a language that makes it possible for her to talk about pain. I've thought a lot about it in the past few years, since Cope died. I've wondered if things could've been different if he'd had that kind of vocabulary. If *I'd* had that kind of vocabulary.

But I can't make this thought more than fleeting at the moment. I shouldn't have had this coffee on an empty stomach. Especially not if I was going to have to hear about Jess Greene as a thirty-one-year-old empty nester.

All alone with her trauma.

"My sister likes you. I think you know that, but I definitely knew before you did. I've never seen her watch someone the way she watches you when she thinks no one is looking."

"Tegan—" I attempt, not sure if I'm trying to protect Jess or myself at this point.

"And I don't care that she does. I don't care that you obviously like her back, because you watch her, too, like you're dry ground in a drought. In fact, I think you could be good for her, if she'd let you be."

I could be, I want to tell her, as if I've had this thought in my head all along—how I'd be, if I got to know Jess outside of this shitty story that defined her life against her will. I'd take her out, let her talk or not talk. Plan trips that have nothing to do with family secrets. Let her sleep late. Make her pancakes any day she wanted them, every morning an opportunity to celebrate. I'd do all the things for her I bet she's spent the last ten years doing for someone else. Laundry, meals for the whole week, the shitty, boring errands that wreck your entire Saturday.

I could be that.

"So be with her, or don't be with her," Tegan says. "But remember what I said, okay? She does need to know about our mom, even if she doesn't think so right now. Don't mess this up. Don't hurt her again, because she's been hurt enough for a whole lifetime."

Unlike when I first woke up this morning, I'm nowhere near back in time now. I'm ruthlessly present. I want to make Tegan a million promises I have no right to make. Not without talking to Jess.

Or my boss, I guess, which is a sobering thought.

"Oh my God." Beth's voice cuts through the silence as she bursts into the kitchen, hair hanging damp, her face scrubbed pink-clean.

"I took a *twenty-minute shower.* That is the longest shower I have taken in years." She points at Tegan. "I *love* you and your sister."

Tegan beams. "We're really *lovable.*"

I'm pretty sure that's directed at me. My ears are on fire, so it's perfect timing that the girls burst through the back door right then, Jess bringing up the rear. Our eyes meet and I'm exactly what Tegan said I was.

Dry ground in a drought. Last night was a shower, when what I really need is a downpour.

Beth claps sharply and calls to the girls to get their packs and get to the van, and it's chaos for at least the next two minutes, the girls running around looking for things called "Squishmallows" and shoes other than the ones they're currently wearing. Ginny says Mace called me "Uncle Lazy Bones" before he left the house and Katie decides to make up a song about it, and Beth can't find the keys to the van and Tegan announces that she needs a new toothbrush, and can she ride along to camp drop-off?

And I know I should be paying attention—to whether Squishmallows are the things I bought my nieces for Christmas last year, to how mad Mace is at me for not being awake for mowing, to the lyrics of this song that I'll probably never live down, to the fact that I saw the keys next to the coffeemaker a few minutes ago, and that Tegan probably doesn't need a new toothbrush at all.

But I'm not.

I'm paying attention to Jess and she's paying attention to me, and we keep our eyes on or almost always on each other until the door out to the garage closes behind everyone and the van starts up and drives away.

Until we're alone.

Briefly, she drops her eyes to her feet, and when she raises her gaze to mine again, her cheeks go pink, and her full lips press together briefly in what I hope is the same sense memory as the one I'm having right now. I think about saying something like, *Sorry if I yelled at you on the trampoline* or *Hey, your sister said you like me* or *I don't usually sleep this late.* I think about simply standing up and getting her over my shoulder, fireman-carrying her back down those basement steps to where I slept so fitfully last night and taking advantage of whatever few, private minutes we have before this house fills up again.

I'm weighing which one of these barely thought-out options is the least unhinged when Jess speaks again.

"I want the two days, too," she says, fast and maybe a little overloud for the fact that she's only a few steps away from me. My heart squeezes in my chest, hard and half-painful, at this small sign of her nervousness.

Her courage.

Jess Greene, trying to trust me again.

Everything Tegan said to me only moments ago comes back to me now, fresh and clear and important. I can't do barely-thought-out with this woman who's been hurt enough for a whole lifetime. I can't do naïve and hair-triggered on an old basement couch.

I realize, with a startling sort of clarity, that I'd cut out my own heart before I treated hers carelessly.

So I set down the coffee mug I forgot I was still holding and cross my arms over my chest. I'm making myself a million promises in my head about the next two days, but to Jess, I keep it simple.

"I'd like to take you out today."

She blinks at me, the pink flush in her cheeks deepening. "Oh."

If I'm not mistaken, there might be the smallest note of disappointment in her voice. Like maybe she wouldn't have minded the fireman-carry, the few minutes of privacy, at all. Like maybe she was hoping for exactly those things.

I admit—I briefly reconsider my plan.

But ultimately, I stick to my guns. Remember my promises. I smile across the space at her, and she presses those perfect lips together again.

"Like . . . on a date?" she says.

I shrug, feigning a nonchalance I'm nowhere near feeling.

"Whatever you want to call it. Just you and me. I'll text Beth and let her know."

She tucks her hands in the pockets of her jet-black jeans, and I know I'm watching her the way Tegan said I did. Practically praying for rain.

And she makes me wait for it. A long stretch where I guess she's deciding whether going out with me today is a bigger deal than making out with me on a trampoline.

I want to tell her that I mean for it to be bigger.

I mean to make it so the next time I touch her, she doesn't have any doubts about me or herself or this thing that's between us.

Instead I keep waiting until I see the long line of her bare throat bob in a courage-gathering swallow.

"Okay. Let's go out."

Chapter 17

Jess

In general, I'm not one to exaggerate.

But it's the best two days I can remember having in years.

It isn't that I haven't had good days in the last decade of my life. If I think back, I can count a lot of them, in fact. Tegan's first day of sixth grade was a great one: in the class she wanted to be in, with the teacher we'd hoped she'd get, wearing an outfit she'd loved, smiling huge and happy when she'd gotten off the bus in the afternoon. Mid-May five years ago, there was a day where I got a return big enough to pay off our property taxes for the year, and Tegan and I had ordered takeout for an entire week in celebration. The day Tegan got accepted to Allegheny with a scholarship package that made me cry—in the shower, of course—with relief.

And there's smaller ones, too, little victories of life that I know I don't think about or appreciate enough. There's times when Tegan and I have laughed together until our stomachs hurt or times when she's rested her head on my shoulder or thanked me earnestly for some everyday service I've done her. Times when I've watched her do something smart or kind or generous or funny and felt a swell of pride and love so big that it almost took my breath away.

But those days, they're different from these two.

It starts with Adam Hawkins doing exactly what he said he'd do: He takes me out.

Midmorning in small-town Missouri, me and him in the minivan alone, windows down and driving past places that he tells me about as we go: the fields where he first played peewee football, the diner that still serves his late grandfather's favorite apple pie with a slice of melted cheddar cheese on top, the chain pharmacy his mom refuses to go to because it replaced her favorite local place over fifteen years ago. We go to what has to be the most sophisticated farmers' market I've ever seen, and a woman who sells beautiful, delicious-smelling loaves of bread pinches Adam's lean, stubbled cheeks and looks at me as though I belong right there beside him. We drive back to the house with three bags of fresh food and together we make the kind of lunch that Adam says will get him forgiven for missing chores in the morning.

In the afternoon we go out again, this time with Tegan and Beth to the hardware store. We buy a bunch of stuff for a project Beth says Adam ruined yesterday, and they rag on each other good-naturedly in a way that makes Tegan and me smile at each other in sheepish envy. We get the girls from camp, take turns jumping on the trampoline again, eat a noisy dinner all together at the huge dining room table, and the whole time, things feel so easy between Tegan and me, easy like our best days at home, or maybe even easier.

That night, Adam and I sit beside each other in the family room while a kids' movie I can't pay attention to plays—the girls climbing all over Tegan as they watch and react, Beth and Mace asleep against each other fifteen seconds into the first musical number, and, most distractingly, Adam's arm slung along the couch behind me, his fingers occasionally brushing the back of my neck softly, perfectly, teasingly.

When we all go to bed for the night, I get the barest but somehow still extremely satisfying experience of my hallway bathroom fantasy: I step out from washing my face and brushing my teeth and Adam's leaning against the wall opposite. He pushes off and takes two steps forward, setting the whole of his warm palm against the nape of my neck, those fingers that teased me on the couch curling along the curve of it as he tips his head down and presses his lips once against mine.

"See you in the morning," he says quietly, as though we do this every single night, and it's simply incredible that I manage to walk back to the room I'm sharing with Tegan, what with all of the bones in my legs turned to putty.

When I wake up after a delicious, dreamless night of sleep, the sun's streaming through a slice of open curtains and Tegan's not in the bed beside mine, but it doesn't jolt me with concern because we're here and for some strange reason, here I know she's okay. The house smells buttery and sweet and divine, and that's because Adam Hawkins got up early enough to make pancakes for all eight people staying in this house.

But when I sit down at a chair he holds out gallantly, I think maybe he's made them only for me.

It's hard to explain how it's all so perfect. In the abstract, I can see that everything we're doing is so simple, so everyday. But to me, it doesn't feel simple or everyday at all. It feels like Adam—who maybe at first glance doesn't look the type to be so careful, so graceful—leads us through the most beautiful, complex dance, one where he's resetting all the positions we were put in when we first met. He puts himself on the spot so I don't have to be; he opens himself up about the small, silly details of his life so I can find room to do the same. He guides me through the steps until it doesn't feel as though I'm doing steps at all; I'm just . . . I'm *dancing*, talking easily about what my favorite foods are or what music I like best or why I'm well-known for doing the best balayage in all of Franklin County.

It's nothing about Mom or Lynton Baltimore; it's nothing about how I took over custody of an eight-year-old when I was barely an adult myself.

It's nothing about all the things that aren't me but have ended up defining me.

With Adam, during these two days, surrounded by his family and mine, I'm more myself than I've been in ages.

I can admit, though, that by sunset on our second evening— our final evening here, before we need to get back on the road to whatever we'll find in Tulsa—I'm restless with thoughts of what we haven't done, what we're running out of time to do.

In quiet moments, my mind drifts to that kiss on the trampoline, to Adam's rough hands and his firm mouth, his warm breath against my skin.

To the ways we don't know each other yet.

And I think Adam knows it; I think he catches me at it.

I think it might be part of the dance.

Other than that kiss in the hallway, every touch has been like the one on the couch—soft, sort of secret, something he makes an effort to ensure no one else notices. They stack up inside me, warm, smoldering coals that I want to feel ignite fully. Those factory settings I felt certain about on the trampoline the other night are an illusion to me now, or maybe I simply recognize them as having been installed by someone, something else.

So, when the sun is fully down and another family movie is playing, and Adam and I are in the kitchen quietly putting away the last of the dishes we volunteered to do, I barely let him finish his softly spoken, "Can I take you out again tonight?" question.

I say yes as though he's asking me if I want ten million dollars or to leave the tenth circle of hell. As though it'll be my last chance to say yes for this entire trip.

Adam only smiles at me in response, and those warm coals inside me flare with heat.

And I have to wonder.

I have to wonder how many more *yes*es I have in me tonight.

"You like it?"

It's not as easy to say yes as I thought.

And not because I don't like it.

Because I *love* it.

I'm sitting in the bed of a pickup truck Adam borrowed from the farm's garage, the hard, ridged steel beneath me barely a bother since Adam has covered it with two layers of thick, freshly laundered blankets. Beside me, the firm length of his body is warm and a little restless as he continues to fuss with this nest he's made for us.

The sky above us is the darkest navy blue, dotted with pinprick stars and bearing a curved slash of white light in the form of the crescent moon.

And in front of us, rolled out like a magic carpet, are rows and rows and rows of flowers, their blooms gently waving with the night wind.

I can't name them, because I can't see them clearly enough in the dark.

But I can smell them, fragrant and lovely, all around me, in a place where we're finally—*finally*—all alone.

It's overwhelming. The only truly romantic gesture I've ever experienced in my life. I hardly know how to process it.

"Jess?"

I realize that Adam has stilled, no more fussing. He's waiting for me to answer. There's a look in his eyes I recognize from all the times during this trip I've been caught off guard by some new revelation about my mother—that same cautious concern blended with his innate protectiveness.

He's worried I don't want to be out here with him. That I've changed my mind.

I love it, I know I should say, but I'm still too overwhelmed to get it out.

So instead, I lean in—fast and desperate—and fit my mouth against his.

At first, it's exactly what I've been waiting for. Adam responds how I need him to: immediate, intense, *grateful*. He makes a noise at the back of his throat and finds my hips with his big hands and practically yanks me against him, all that *I want these two fucking days* energy back in full force. I don't know how he gets me back to straddling his lap; I just know I'm there when I feel the thick, hard length of him against the center of me.

But then those smoldering coals in my middle—they seem to catch the same breeze that's rustling the flowers out there, and suddenly flames are licking up my ribs, my chest, my neck. It's the igniting I thought I wanted, but when I rock my hips against him, I'm almost alarmed by how hot and impatient I feel—a strange, panicked desperation I don't remember experiencing on the trampoline. When one of Adam's thumbs grazes the underside of my breast, I arch into him suddenly, electrified by even this incidental over-the-shirt contact. It feels incredible but also shamefully immature—too close, too soon, my body a live wire I don't know well enough to control when there's another person involved in giving it pleasure.

Anxious thoughts nag at the periphery of my mind: *How much time do we have left, what if I've forgotten how to do this, what happens tomorrow, what if I've been irresponsible, what if Tegan isn't okay* . . .

Adam stills and pulls his lips from mine, shifting his hand to rest on the curve of my upper arm, and I know those flames inside me must be congregating in my face, turning it tomato red with embarrassment. I was moving too fast; I was out of control.

His gaze searches mine, and if there's a comfort, it's that his breath is heavy, too, his length beneath me still rock-hard.

"You okay?"

Once again, the easy *yes* gets caught in my throat. I barely manage a nod, but Adam doesn't press. He keeps his thumb stroking over that spot on my arm, slowing its movement in time with his breathing and my own.

When I'm calmed down, cooled down enough to focus again, I notice that the way he's touching me is more complicated than a simple up-and-down or back-and-forth over my skin. Instead, he runs his thumb up in a line, then traces a circle. Moves a little to the right, does it again. Over and over, inner arm to outer edge. A pattern.

After a few seconds, I realize: He's tracing along the lines of my tattoos.

As though he's memorized them.

I sigh out a shaky breath, sagging a little as the last of my anxious thoughts recede, and he leans in, putting his lips close to my ear.

"I brought you out here because of these."

At first I can't do much more than shudder from the feel of his breath against the skin there. It's warm and patient and perfect.

"Because of my tattoos?"

He nods, giving me a teasing scrape of his evening stubble.

"Flowers," he murmurs.

I think of first driving up to this farm, the shock of shame I felt, imagining Adam's family seeing my line-drawn imitations of all these bright, alive things. When we first came here, I was afraid of being seen, being open.

But now I'm reminded: Adam sees me. Adam has *opened* me.

Adam is trying to know me for himself.

"They're not finished. I never got the color done."

"I like them this way."

He moves again, leaning back and maneuvering me slightly to the side so my center is no longer pressed directly against him. He takes my tattooed arm and lifts it, setting my wrist on his shoulder. Then he draws closer, moves his lips in that same pattern his thumb traced, and I feel it everywhere. Heat spreading evenly, perfectly, slow enough that I can savor it.

"This field at night. That's what your tattoos remind me of."

He gently nips at the skin of my inner arm.

My hips roll against his thigh. His breath catches, the hand at my waist tightening before he presses his face in the crook of my neck. I think he might say something about a couch, but I don't catch it, and it doesn't matter. This small show of desperation—even as he's trying to reset this, to get us in a better position for it—makes me feel so wanted, so powerful.

Like I'm in exactly the right sort of in control.

I dip my chin and whisper to him.

"I'm named after a flower."

He lifts his head and settles his back against the truck cab, pushing my hair over my shoulders before trailing his hands down again to hold my waist. He watches me, curious and patient.

"Jessamine," I whisper. "I don't know if Tegan already told you that. When . . ."

I trail off, not wanting to bring it up, that time before Adam knew me at all.

That time before he knew me like this.

"She didn't. It's a beautiful name."

"I like Jess."

He nods. "Me too. But it's nice knowing what it comes from."

I kiss him again, and it's better now: smooth like the trampoline, *rooted*, steady and shared and so good. When we pause I whisper his name—a prompt, an invitation. *Tell me about your name, too.*

"Not much of a story there," he breathes. "First son, father's name."

"It's a good name." I trace my tongue along his neck, up to the lobe of his ear. He groans, and I file that sensitivity away.

Knowing him.

For myself.

"I like you saying it. I always wanted you to say it, from when we first met."

Smoothly, swiftly, he moves me again, rolling me so I'm on my back. The view is perfect: half Adam, half wide-open sky.

Make me say your name a hundred times tonight, I'm thinking. *I'll introduce you to the stars.*

"I called you Adam in my head. Never Hawk."

He leans down and says "Good" against my mouth, and our kisses grow heated again, our tongues tangling and our hands roaming over each other.

And that's how it happens. That's how Adam and I find the right rhythm between two kinds of knowing.

The perfect dance.

He slips a hand beneath my shirt and says, *I have to know how much shampoo you use*, and I answer him with a gasp as he moves his thumb across one of my nipples.

I rub my palm over the front of his jeans, pressing against the hard bulge there, and say, *Where do you buy all your clothes*, while he groans out a response.

Do you know your mouth tilts right here—his tongue at the corner of my lip, his hand sliding effortlessly beneath my underwear—*when you're trying not to laugh*

Do you know—my hand finding the hot length of him—*the tops of your ears turn pink when you're embarrassed*

His fingers stroking between my legs, spreading my wetness

Do you like it this way

Can I take these off

Is it good

My face against his neck, my teeth against his humid skin

How come you smell so good when you sweat

His hips pulsing in time with my hand, his jaw tight with restraint

How come you smell so good all the time

We're quiet for a good long while when bare skin meets bare skin; we stick to the one kind of knowing. I find out that Adam's body underneath his clothes is as impressive as it is when he's in them: sharp planes, firm packs, sturdy curves. He finds out that

I've got another tattoo, a small and clumsily drawn feather on the right side of my rib cage that I got the day I turned eighteen and that I've always regretted until Adam sets his lips against it. I learn that Adam likes when I grip his hard length tight, tight enough that he has to say *when*; Adam learns that I want his teeth on the soft underside of my breasts.

I know I've got more questions to ask, know I've got more things to learn, but at a certain point I become incapable of anything except making demands. I'm telling him

Do that again or

Come up here or

Show me

And Adam listens—he's such a good listener—every time he makes me come.

When I make my last demand—more of a gasping, desperate plea, really—Adam stills over me, a foil square waiting in his hand and a question in his eyes, on his lips.

"I'm sure," I tell him, because I am—sure about right now, even if I'm not sure about tomorrow or how much time we have left or whether I'm being totally irresponsible out here in the open air in the back of a borrowed truck.

"I'll stop anytime," he says as he rolls on the condom, his voice soft and serious, an echo of what he once said to me in a tiny art gallery in the Florida Panhandle. He says it as though I didn't know, as though he hasn't shown me this same thing in some form or another since the day I met him.

I reach up and set one of my palms against his cheek at the same time I slide my other hand down to guide him against me. I use the head of his cock to tease my sensitive flesh; I make the now-sheathed surface of him wet with what I have to offer.

I look in his eyes and watch them shut tightly as he tries to harness his control.

I spread my legs a little farther apart. I open myself to him. I whisper to him again that I'm sure, that I don't want him to stop.

I gasp as he pushes inside me, his big body so perfectly suited for this—for leveraging his weight into thrusts that start slow but are still forceful, for giving me places to hold on to, for making me feel fully sheltered beneath him.

And my *God*, do I feel like I know him. His weight, his heat, his sounds. His lungs a bellows, his heart a drum. His mouth busy and seeking, even though the difference in our heights makes it difficult. His focus when he moves us so he can make it better for us both, me on top again. His eyes watching me move, his hands gathering my hair and tugging when I move over him a certain way, when I clench tight from the inside to tease him.

I know when he gets close, his grip on me tighter, his gaze going unfocused.

I lean in, get my mouth next to his ear. I say

Yes

Yes

giving him the permission I know he needs, and then I feel him stiffen, drawing me close as he does—a hold so tight as he groans his release that in any other circumstance it'd be confining, stifling, intrusive.

But there's nothing intrusive about Adam Hawkins, not when we're like this, maybe not ever, really, and as he sags into me, head heavy on my shoulder as his breath slows and his body softens, I can't stop thinking about how it's been ten years since I've let anyone into my body, ten years since I let anyone know me in this way, and having it now makes me feel like it's been more than ten years.

More than ten years since anyone's known me in any way at all.

I wait for it to come, the fear I expect to follow this realization. All these years I've locked myself down and the man I give the key to works for a woman who wants a piece of my history I haven't ever wanted to give out.

All these years and it's not a one-night stand, someone whose last name I don't know, someone who I'll never call again and who'll never call me.

It's not scratching an itch, unless the itch is in my heart.

In my most private, protected self.

But there's no fear yet. No thought of Mom or Lynton Baltimore or Salem and her podcast. There's no thought even of Tegan at this moment, and that's a first for ten years, too.

There's only Adam's strong arms, holding me together, keeping it all at bay. He presses a kiss to my sweat-slick shoulder and repeats himself, his voice thick and raw with exertion and emotion.

"You okay?"

So I repeat myself, too. My last one of the night, my last one of this trip, maybe.

I say *yes* as if saying it will somehow keep us here forever.

The Last Con of Lynton Baltimore

Transcript Excerpt from Episode 8, "Winning Streak"

Baltimore: It's boring to talk about.

Durant: It's boring to talk about the things you stole?

Baltimore: Salem, you know me better than that. I never stole a thing. Let's talk about you, instead.

::long pause::

Durant: That's not how this works.

Baltimore: ::chuckles:: You're a tough nut, you know that? Well, you can't blame me for trying. I'm only human, you know.

Chapter 18

Adam

"All ready to go?"

My dad steps up beside me as I'm distractedly packing the trunk of the van, quietly pleasing myself by deliberately setting Jess's suitcase right next to mine. It's a pretty sappy move, I know, but I'm practically marinated in sap at the moment.

Thoughts of last night coat every part of my brain: Jess above me, beneath me, beside me. Her words whispered against my skin, her drowsing sleep and her reluctance to part outside her bedroom when we finally came back in from the fields.

Her pleasure, her laughter, her trust.

"Pretty much," I say to Dad, stepping back from the trunk, raising an arm to close its door. I use the extra second to arrange my face into something slightly less sap-struck.

I don't know if I succeed, but looking at my dad is enough to bring me back down to earth for now.

He's pretty much the earthiest guy I know.

It's barely eight a.m., but he's been up and at it for a while—fresh mud on his boots, his jeans smudged with dust, one of his old navy-blue bandanas tucked messily into the front pocket of his work shirt, as though he's already taken it out multiple times to wipe his gray-stubbled face.

"Good, good."

He shifts his feet on the gravel drive, looking off into the distance. Since I've been seeing my dad do this stance for as long as I can remember, I know he's gearing up to make his version of conversation, which is most often monosyllabic. He's a quiet guy, an undemonstrative guy. Beth says his parenting style is "loving brick wall."

I turn and lean my shoulder against the rear of the van, waiting him out. It hasn't been all that long since I was home—I visited back in April for my mom's birthday—but I haven't had any one-on-one time with either of my parents on this particular trip. Most times, Dad and I keep our conversations confined to simple stuff: how work's going, how the farm is doing, how Grandma's faring. It used to be that we'd talk a lot about football, but those days are done.

He'd never say, but I think he misses it.

I watch as his eyes track over the fields. When it's been at least a full minute of silence, he settles on a simple, "You doin' all right?"

For a loving brick wall, these four words are about the deepest expression of concern imaginable, and I'd know, because Dad said them to me a lot when I was back here after Cope. Multiple times a day, no matter if we were sitting in front of the TV or out doing chores or driving around doing errands Mom would send us on, her effort to keep me off my phone as much as possible. *You doin' all right?*

Sometimes, if he was really worried, he'd add a *bud* at the end. So I'm familiar.

But I'm surprised to hear them this morning, of all mornings.

The morning after what's got to be one of the best nights of my life.

"Yeah, Dad. I'm good." I say it with a smile, a genuine one. I'm better than good.

But he doesn't look convinced. He takes out the bandana and sets about folding it neatly.

"She's got problems. Jess, I mean."

I straighten, my body stiffening. "Got problems" is my dad's code for a lot of things he doesn't know how to talk about it. He said it about my sister Carly, when she went to a therapist for a year and a half because she got bullied at school after she came out. He said it about Cope, too, when he got blackout drunk during his first visit here, nearly starting a fire in the kitchen because he got a two a.m. craving for a tuna melt. He said it about me, after I blew up the internet.

He even said it about himself, in an early morning conversation I can still remember, not long after Cope died. *I still got problems, you know. About losing my brother. Some days'll be worse than others.*

I'd known, of course, that my dad's only brother had died in a car accident when he was sixteen. But that morning was the only time I'd ever heard him talk about it directly.

So when my dad talks about "problems," he means loving-brick-wall business.

But hearing him say it now puts me immediately on the defensive. First, for Jess, because I don't want anyone talking about her out of turn. I've become as protective of her privacy as she's always been. And second, selfishly, for myself, because I don't want anything I've had with Jess over the last two days tainted by what my dad's saying.

"Everyone has problems, Dad."

"I like her. Don't get me wrong."

I stare at him. It doesn't matter if he likes her. *I* like her.

I more than like her, but I've been trying since last night not to focus on how much more.

I know it's too soon for that.

"Can't fix her," he adds.

I clench my back teeth, annoyed. He's barely had two meals with her.

"She doesn't need fixing."

He shrugs, and I take a breath through my nose. When I was a kid, I thought I'd grow up to be exactly the same as my dad. Stern, strong, and spending my whole life working on this farm. After I went to college, after I met new people and saw more of the country, after the things I went through with Cope, I know I started to see Dad differently. Not negatively, but still . . . differently. I started to see the way he mostly kept his distance from things that were complicated, saw that he kept his curiosity pretty limited to the most local of issues.

I can recognize that he's being protective, but any way I look at it, it chafes. If he's being protective of me, he's insulting her. And if he's being protective of her, he must not think anything good about me.

An unbidden, unwelcome thought comes into my head. Tegan at the breakfast table, telling me Jess has been hurt enough for a whole lifetime.

I really did prefer the sap-brain to this.

Then again, I can't forget that my brain has been doing more than reliving last night in the hours since I brought Jess back to the house. In fact, I spent a good deal of time making plans that are all about how to make sure she doesn't get hurt, and while I'm not going to stand here and tell my dad about them, it still makes me feel better to remember them.

Tulsa today, and Salem arriving there tomorrow. I've already texted her to say we need to talk when she arrives, and when she does, I'm going to tell her I need to take a step back. I'll say I'm too involved with Jess to go forward on the story, but I'll keep the details vague. I'll offer to be chauffeur, meal-planner, hotel-organizer, whatever; I'll insist on paying my own way, paying back whatever my share has been so far.

I'll say I'm too close to be responsible for getting Jess—or anyone—to talk about anything for this story.

I'll hope she doesn't fire me.

But if she does?

If she does, I'll find a way to stick with Jess and Tegan for the rest of this, however it goes. I'll follow them all in a separate car, if I have to.

I'll be the security guard Jess once suspected I was. I'll protect them both.

And I'll still find some other way to get Cope's story told, after all this is over.

My dad's got that thousand-yard stare again, so maybe he's gearing up to say something else. But when the front door opens and Jess and Tegan come out—followed by Beth and the girls—he moves his gaze to me again. I don't expect any big goodbye because that's not brick-wall style.

But he does pat me roughly on my shoulder and say, "Take care of yourself, bud," before walking toward Jess and Tegan.

I hear him say a short, gruff, "It was nice to meet you," and I try not to let it bother me that he's said it as though he never expects to see either of them again.

Instead I focus on Jess: her hair still damp at the ends, her cheeks dewy pink. I like to think her lips are a little swollen from our kisses, but probably the sap in my brain is making me imagine things. When Beth and the girls surround her and Tegan in a round of chaotic, enthusiastic hugs, she looks so surprised that I want to cancel all the plans and keep her here for longer. Convince my dad about her. Surround her with my sister's and my nieces' messy affection. Take her out to that flower field for as many nights as she'd let me.

But when she meets my eyes over Beth's shoulder and smiles softly, the trust and determination in her eyes also tells me it'll be okay for us to get on the road and keep going with this.

That things are different for her now.

And it's funny, what I realize then.

I brought Jess here to give her a break from this story Salem's been chasing; I brought her here and was honest about what Salem wanted me to get from her. I brought her here and I must've known deep down that I would've blown up my whole job for her.

I did all that, and now, for the first time since I met her, I think she might finally be ready to be a part of figuring out what happened to her mother.

And that's what Salem wanted all along.

Jess insists on driving.

"I'll take the first leg," she said to me, holding out her hand for the keys, and then she gave me a meaningful look, a look that said she remembered what I'd confessed to her late last night—after she'd let me taste her for the first time, begging me first to be gentle, then begging me not to be—about the collective effects of that old plaid couch and the imperfectly padded truck bed on my back and my knees.

I wouldn't have told her except that, when we'd set our feet back on the firm field ground, my body had basically made a sound like a bowl of Rice Krispies. Jess looked at me with wide eyes and still-rumpled hair, and half of me was embarrassed, but the other half of me felt strangely thrilled by the privacy of it. The intimacy of it.

This is how my body sounds, I wanted to say, *when I get out of bed in the morning. This is what you'd hear if you slept with me there.*

Now, I look over the center console at her, knowing I shouldn't be picturing it: Jess in the California king I have at home, way too big for my small apartment, but worth every square inch. I have white sheets, but maybe I should get black. Her skin, her hair, all a contrast. Her tattoos, to match.

Yeah. Black sheets.

"Quit it," she says, barely loud enough to hear over the music she has playing from her phone through the van's speakers, but there's the quirk at the side of her mouth.

"I didn't say anything."

"Your brain is loud."

I snort. She doesn't know the half of it. I shift slightly in my seat, trying to ignore that the black-sheets daydream gave me a semi. Jess's eyes flick up to the rearview.

"Out cold," I say, and I'm not exaggerating. Tegan took the bench seat in the way back when we set off, proclaiming herself "totally wiped" from the time with my nieces. She'd put on a pair of noise-canceling headphones, casually shouted, "Behave!" at us, and then she was asleep before we even cleared the edges of the family property.

That "Behave!" made Jess's neck flush. But I know she's not keeping this thing between her and me a secret from Tegan, not after all the secrets that brought them to this point. She may not have told her sister about last night—that, I'm pretty sure, is only for Jess and me—but she's not hiding that we're closer, either.

"Those girls ran her ragged," Jess says. "They couldn't get enough of her."

I don't miss the pride in her voice.

"She was good with them."

Jess doesn't volley back right away. Instead she chews on the inside of her lip and lowers her brow.

I'm about to ask her what's wrong when she blurts, "I didn't let her babysit, you know."

"I didn't know that, no."

I say it as if that makes sense, as if it's something I might have occasion to know, when in fact—even though I spent part of last night inside this woman—every new thing I learn about her, about her history, is a precious, perfect shell I've collected. One I never want to coat in something toxic.

"She wanted to. Her friends at school did. But then I would

worry. What if no one hired her, because of . . ." She trails off, waves a hand in the air. "Whatever people thought about me, or us as a family? Or what if people did hire her, and asked her questions about Mom?"

I know exactly what Salem would ask right now. She'd say, *And that's because you already had figured out who your mom had left town with, by this point?* She'd ask, *Did you worry people would make a connection, somehow, between the boyfriend your mother left with and Lynton Baltimore?*

I say, "That was probably smart."

She cuts her eyes to me, quirks her mouth. She can maybe see the sap.

But also, I mean it: It was probably smart. It was probably smart and difficult and Tegan surely gave her hell for it. It was probably the kind of lousy, fraught decision Jess must've spent the last ten years making while she did the best she could to protect her sister.

I'm desperate to put a hand on her. The back of her neck, her thigh. Anywhere I could reach to offer her some kind of recognition or comfort or promise that I always want to hear anything she's willing to tell me.

But then the ring of her phone cuts the music that's piping through the car's Bluetooth, and she startles, her eyes darting to the dash display.

Dad, the screen reads.

"Oh," she says, something flummoxed in her voice, and I realize that she's debating whether or not to answer, whether or not to take a call from her dad when I'm in the car to hear it.

I figure it'll always be a little like this: her making calculations in her head about what's okay to reveal, and when. Opening up and then closing down. I think briefly of what my dad said, and shove the thought away.

Beside me, Jess sets her jaw.

And then quickly reaches out a finger and presses accept.

"Hi, Dad."

I wonder if he can hear the effort in her voice that I can.

I turn my face toward the window, my small effort at making this feel less uncomfortable for her.

"Everything okay?" she adds, and that's revealing. My guess is, they don't do much calling each other unless there's news.

"Sure, sure. I haven't heard from you in a couple of days is all."

I realize I have no idea if her dad actually knows where exactly she is, or what she's doing, or even what she told him about my visit to his house.

"Sorry about that. We took a . . . uh. We took a break after Florida."

There's a beat of awkward silence, and again: I have the feeling that's pretty typical between them. I may have been annoyed with my own dad this morning, but I don't think any conversation we've ever had has been this strained.

"Well, the house looks fine. No important mail so far."

"That's good. Thanks for checking that."

"I am going to get someone over there to do your gutters, though. I think you're overdue."

I chance a look over at her and see the pink in her cheeks.

"Dad, that's okay."

The give in her voice—it reminds me of the first time we were in this van together, her quiet *thanks* when I set my arm in front of her after hitting the brakes hard.

He clears his throat and says, "So, where to next?"

I think that means he's still going to get the gutters done.

She purses her lips, probably because she thinks so, too.

"Oklahoma." She pauses, sliding her eyes to mine before adding, "I don't think we have any idea why, though."

That's an offering, I know—more to me than to her dad. She's not shutting the conversation with him down; she's showing me she can handle me being here while she has it.

But then there's another long pause on the other end of the line, and it's . . . weighted. Jess cuts her gaze to the screen, as though staring at the numbers ticking off the duration of this call could tell her something about what's coming.

"Oklahoma," he finally repeats. Slow and cautious. "Whereabouts?"

There's a specter of Salem in the back seat. I can almost feel it leaning forward in ghostly determination, catching the scent of this. A new piece of information.

"Tulsa," Jess says. "Why?"

My shoulders tense when he doesn't answer right away. If I wasn't certain before that I needed to take a step back from this story, I sure am now. It can't be right that I'd rather put a fist through that dash display than have Jess find out whatever piece of shitty news I suspect she has coming.

"We had a friend in Tulsa. Your mom and me, I mean. Years ago. When we were younger, before we had you."

He doesn't offer anything else, and I realize something about where Jess gets her reticence. It's from more than circumstances surrounding her mother.

It's from her father, too.

Jess clicks her tongue. It's as if a piece of that misty Salem-specter has settled right in the center of her.

"What friend?"

In the back, Tegan stirs, and I turn my head to see her sitting up groggily.

"Jess," I say in quiet warning, but her dad answers at the same time.

"I went to college with him. He was my roommate sophomore and junior year. His girlfriend at the time and your mom and I used to double date together."

"And he lives in Tulsa now?"

"I'd guess he still does, though I haven't been in touch with him in twenty years, probably. He was from there. Moved back after he finished . . ." He trails off.

Tegan's contorting herself awkwardly to move up a row, pulling her headphones off.

"Jess," I say again, but she ignores me.

"Finished—?" she prompts.

"Medical school. He's a doctor."

Tegan thunks herself into the seat behind me, leaning forward. "What's happening?"

"Hi, Tegan," comes the voice through the speaker again, a different tone than he uses with Jess. Friendlier, but somehow less familiar.

"Hey, Bill," Tegan says cheerfully. "Who's a doctor?"

Instead of answering, he clears his throat again, and I think he must be waiting for a signal. Did Jess sit across from him one day ten years ago and gave him a list of conditions, too? About when he was allowed to talk to Tegan, about what he was allowed to say to her about their mom?

Beside me, Jess has shaken off that specter, at least for the moment. She looks almost the same as she did before I brought her home to the farm. Tense and stricken.

She doesn't like the sound of this, a doctor in Tulsa.

But when she flicks her eyes to the rearview again, catching Tegan's gaze, there's something else there, too.

A courage-gathering, or maybe a resignation.

"Someone he knows in Tulsa," Jess answers for her father.

I hear her saying those words from only a few minutes ago—*I didn't let her babysit*—and feel a clutch of renewed affection and admiration for her.

She's trying so hard at this.

It takes gladiator-level strength for me not to reach a hand across the console. Instead I watch her throat bob in a heavy swallow, and I'm pretty sure I mimic it. I also don't like the sound of this. I don't like her dad's renewed silence, which somehow manages to be cloaking and ominous.

"Did Mom know him?" Tegan says, but almost as soon as she's finished speaking it's as though the cloak has covered her, too, and in my peripheral I can see that her easy, just-waking-up expression has transformed.

She doesn't wait for him to respond before she asks an entirely different question.

"What kind of doctor?"

"Teeg," Jess says gently, at the same time Bill says, "I'm sure there's lots of reasons to stop through Tulsa. College town. Lots going on there."

For the second time this morning, I know exactly what Salem would do here. She'd know we were on the cusp of something big, that the answer to *What kind of doctor?* is going to take this whole tale to a new emotional register. She'd make a gentle suggestion. She might say, *Let's continue this conversation somewhere more comfortable,* or maybe she'd address Jess's father directly, encouraging him in that firm way she has. *Bill,* she might say, *it's really important we go into Tulsa with as much information as we can.*

I realize, with no small amount of discomfort, that *I* might as well be the Salem-specter. That the promises I've made to myself—that I won't still work this story, that I'll keep my hands off it, that I'll be here for Jess and Tegan's protection only—are all belied by what I've spent the last few years of my life studying, training for, practicing.

That no matter what way I feel toward Jess now, the way I first met her will always be tied up with this.

Something that's toxic to her.

But I can't think about that now. I can only think about how her knuckles have gone white on the steering wheel, her face paling to match. All the tension I worked out of her body last night is taking her over again.

She steels herself, and then she does Salem's job for her.

Or my job for me.

"Dad," she says, flicking on the van's blinker, "let me pull over for a minute so we can talk."

Chapter 19

Jess

In the end, I asked Adam to do it.

I asked him to arrange the video call with my father and the surgical oncologist who was once his college roommate. I asked him to take us somewhere where there were two coffee shops close to one another, and then I asked him to drop Tegan and me off at one while he took himself off to the other.

I asked him to find out, without me and Tegan there, whether my mother was sick when she left with Lynton Baltimore.

I asked him to come tell us once he did.

It's been a tough few days, she'd written in her postcard.

Make sure you call your dad if you need anything, she'd written.

The funny thing—not, of course, *haha* funny—was that Tegan didn't fight me, not even a little. I blurted my suggestion to Adam shortly after that first call with my dad ended, a pit in my stomach and panic in my chest.

I said, "You should do it, Adam," and Tegan immediately added, "I agree."

It was a knee-jerk response, I know. It was, in principle, hugely contrary to all those initial conditions I'd set when this trip first started. But as the seconds ticked by and Adam slowly looked between Tegan and me, as though he was waiting for us both to come to our senses, I realized I didn't want to take it back.

I realized there were reasons for this way of doing it.

Reasons that weren't just my huge—and hugely unexpected—fear about what we might find out.

"You have more professional experience," I said, trying to ignore the way his eyes searched mine, knowing and soft, "talking to a physician who probably has privacy obligations."

"Yeah," said Tegan, nodding too enthusiastically. Almost desperately.

"And it's not as if my dad and I have an easy conversational style. He might feel more comfortable with you there instead of me."

"Or me for sure," added Tegan.

I could tell from the look in Adam's eyes that he was about to tell me no, that he was about to remind me of my conditions.

"I trust you," I said, preempting him, and in spite of everything Adam and I had been through over the last couple of days together—in spite of the fact that I'd woken up this morning with tender skin on my neck from his stubble, that I'd had the most intimate night of my entire life with him—this small declaration felt like crossing a true and permanent threshold.

Doing it in front of Tegan was practically a proposal.

And so, he'd done it.

Went to one coffee shop alone while Tegan and I waited in another. Her scrolling on her phone, me staring into a cup of tea I couldn't bring myself to take a sip of, neither of us willing to talk about what we were waiting to find out. Nearly silent, in fact, until my phone buzzed on the table with a text from Adam, who'd never make us wait a second longer than we had to.

Your mom wasn't sick. Be there in a few.

The hours since have been, somehow, both long and short:

plans changed, calls made, distances traveled, but all of it while I was in some strange, sped-up whirlwind. I listened, of course, when Adam told me what he'd learned during his interview: My dad's old doctor friend was willing to say that he had, in fact, seen my mother a decade ago, but not as a patient. He was also willing to say that she had been traveling with a man named Miles Daniels. But what he was pointedly—suggestively— *un*willing to say, was whether he'd seen Miles as a patient.

So I agreed when Tegan suggested we call Salem, nodded when Salem said we should skip Tulsa and instead meet in Santa Fe. I said driving to St. Louis made sense, the first direct flight we could get on from there early the next morning made sense, checking into a hotel near the airport made sense.

But somehow it all seems to have happened so *fast*.

"We could watch this," I say now, my voice sounding tinny to my own ears as I pause on the programming guide of the too-big-for-this-room flatscreen. Another rerun of *Friends*. I look over at Tegan, who's sitting on her turned-down bed. I'd never let her sit on a hotel room comforter.

"If you want."

I blink back at the screen. The sped-up feeling is still chasing me, even in this slowed-down hotel room. It's been hours and I haven't found a way to say anything meaningful to Tegan about what happened today; I haven't even been able to ask how she's doing. At home, when Tegan has a bad day, I can't help but hover, prodding her with questions, finding excuses to check on her in her room, asking for her help with things I can easily do by myself, if only to get her up and talking.

But right now, I feel too fast to hover.

Half of me wishes Adam were here with us, instead of in his own room next door, but half of me is mad at myself for wishing it.

Haven't I let him handle enough for today?

Aren't I already relying on him too much?

My body practically aches for comfort from him. A hug, a warm hand on my neck. His low voice in my ear while he holds me.

My craving for it is almost as terrifying as the rest of today has been.

I press select on the remote and go to my own turned-down bed, trying to let the sound of canned laughter calm me down.

"Jessie," Tegan says after a few minutes of us both watching in silence, and I tilt my head toward her. She's watching me, and I have the feeling that maybe she has been for a while.

"Yeah?"

She reaches for the remote on the nightstand between us and mutes the laughter.

For a long time, she doesn't say anything. She turns the remote over and over in her hands. Good thing I cleaned it with a Clorox wipe when we arrived.

Maybe I *have* still managed to hover.

"Did you ever wonder before today if Mom was . . . if she'd maybe . . ."

She trails off, not willing to voice any version of the word I know she's thinking.

Dead.

Died.

And that, finally, is what slows me down.

Because it's exactly the line of thinking I've been running from since my dad mentioned the doctor this morning.

My first, fast instinct is to pivot, to turn her away from this and find some way to not answer her. In my whole life with Tegan, that's been my way, whenever we've gotten close to my feelings about Mom, to my feelings about almost anything. During my own childhood, my mother too often treated me as a friend—telling me too much about her and my dad's divorce, crying dramatically on car rides to school after some boyfriend broke up with her, pulling me into a gleeful dance around the kitchen after her second date with Tegan's father. Back then,

I thought her relentless sharing of her feelings meant we were close; we were *best* friends; we were inseparable.

Later—after the first time she left—I realized it hadn't meant that at all.

I realized that most of the feelings she shared weren't the sort a kid was equipped to deal with.

After the second time she left, I vowed I'd never do the same to my sister.

Except when I look at her now, I can see so clearly that she's not a kid anymore.

It's strange, in some ways, to realize it here—in a nondescript hotel room that's another stop on this trip I never wanted to go on but that I can already tell has changed me forever. I look at her now and I think of the last few days we've spent with Adam and Adam's family, people who somehow manage to have big feelings with each other and also boundaries about it, calibrations they make for the youngest among them. I think of Mace hugging Katie after camp and telling her he sometimes gets stomachaches when he's nervous, too; I think of Adam telling Sam he'd miss her when he said goodbye this morning.

No one in the Hawkins house wields a feeling like a weapon, or like a leash.

So instead of pivoting, I look up at the ceiling and think about my honest answer. I offer it to her at the same time I'm admitting it to myself.

"I never did. I never once thought she might be . . . gone. Not until today."

"Me neither!" she says, an exclamatory, relieved agreement. "Not *once*. Isn't that weird? Isn't it weird that we didn't?"

When I look over at her, she's sitting up and facing me, her legs crisscrossed, her eyes bright and hopeful. I turn onto my side so I'm facing her, too.

"Maybe it's weird. But also—" I break off, swallowing, still unsteady in this sharing. "Also, I think it was easier for me if I only ever thought about the possibilities that made me more angry at her than I already was."

There, I think. *There, you said it.*

I check my sister's face, looking for some sign that I've crossed a boundary or calibrated it wrong. But if anything, she still has that bright and hopeful look on her face, mixed now with sympathy.

"Easier how?"

I shrug the shoulder I'm not leaning on. This part, I *really* don't want to mess up. I don't ever want Tegan to think I'm angry about being the one who takes care of her; I don't ever want her to think I resent her.

So I go back a bit further in time.

To a time before Tegan knew me.

"When Mom left the first time, with your dad"—I pause and check her face again, but she doesn't react to the mention of him—"I worried about her a lot. I'd tell my dad all these things I thought could've happened to her. Every terrible news story I saw on TV—to me, they were possible explanations. He'd kind of blow me off, tell me I didn't need to worry about those things. That Mom was fine."

"I bet you hated that," she says, a knowingness born from experience. I think of all the moments I told Tegan I was sure Mom was thinking of her, that Mom missed her. I know now I owe her an apology for every time I did it.

"But he was right. I didn't need to worry about any of those things, and he knew that, because he knew her. What I needed to worry about was what ended up happening, which is that she'd come back after things fell apart and try to pretend nothing happened. And then, at some point, she'd flake out and do it all over again. This time, to you."

She nods and looks down at her loosely clasped hands.

"Except she didn't come back this time," she says.

"Maybe things never fell apart with Miles. Or Lynton, whatever we're supposed to call him."

"Maybe." But I know both of us feel pretty doubtful about that after today.

Both of us have the sense now that the Miles Daniels we met a decade ago wasn't as hale and hearty as he seemed, and there's no telling what kind of shape he might be in today. Or if he's in any shape at all.

"Even though I never thought about it before today," Tegan says, her voice quiet now, "I sort of—well, for a second, I almost . . ." She trails off and shakes her head. "I don't know if I should say."

"You can say," I say, matching my voice to hers.

Every day since we've started on this trip, everything we've said around each other about our mother has been tied up in this story someone else is doing; everything has been weighted by this sense of being *observed*. But here, it's only me and Tegan, and there's tons of things we probably should've said to each other way before now. No weapons, no leashes.

"Today, for a little while"—she breaks off, and then she blurts, all in a rush—"I was almost hoping we'd find out that she'd died."

She lifts her hands and covers her face.

Then she bursts into tears.

"Oh, Teeg." I scramble up and go to her, sitting next to her and circling her awkwardly in my arms. She leans into me hard, as though she's forgotten she's no longer got the small-kid body that she had when she used to let me do this, when she was so raw and confused and heartbroken, when I'd murmur to her those half-truths about Mom missing her.

She sniffs and gathers herself but stays against me.

"If she were dead, it would be—I guess it would be *so* clear why she never came back. Kind of noble, right? Like she was sparing us some from watching her with some terrible sickness, or something."

I swallow and rub her arm, not disagreeing, even though I don't think it'd be noble at all. I think it'd be about as selfish and cowardly as a bunch of other stuff our mom has done. Today, when we were all sitting with the idea that she might have been sick, I kept thinking, *God. What an* asshole, *to not even let us grieve her.*

"And then, when people asked me, you know, 'What happened to your mom?' I could say, 'Oh, my mom died.' I think people would look at me different, if I could say that. I think it'd be better than how they look at me now, when they don't ask at all. Isn't that the worst thing you've ever heard?"

No, I think, squeezing her through her next rush of tears. *The worst thing I've ever heard is that people don't ask you. Probably because I've spent the last ten years making it seem to you like no one ever should.*

All my boundaries and calibrations.

I set them so, so wrong.

"It's not the worst thing. It's totally understandable that you'd feel that way."

She scoffs, a sarcastic, disbelieving sound.

"Tegan, I wanted to believe she'd been *kidnapped.* Or that she was in, I don't know. Witness protection, or something. I wanted to believe anything other than that she'd just . . . *left* me. I really get it."

She sniffles again and nods, rests for a while against me. It feels huge and heavy, this moment, and while I'm glad we're having it, I also feel so unequal to it. I'm frayed and overwhelmed by my own experience today, worried that I'm barely strong enough to hold Tegan up during this.

Before I can stop myself, I wish again for Adam. Tegan leaning against me, and me leaning against him.

That way, I could definitely handle it.

I wish I hadn't told him, in my haste, to give Tegan and me some time tonight.

After a few minutes, Tegan sighs and straightens, swiping at her face. She smiles ruefully at the damp spot of darker black on my black T-shirt.

"Sorry."

"Don't be. I've got another one."

Her smile widens and she laughs, and I feel slightly less un-equal.

Without words, both of settle back into her bed, side by side and propped up on pillows. Tegan unmutes the TV and we watch for a while, chuckling together at parts that are funny, groaning together at parts that aren't. It's so similar to the night before Tegan almost left me that note, the night before Adam and Salem knocked on my door, but also hugely different.

All because Tegan and I talked honestly about something we've—*I've*—avoided for years.

"Teeg."

"Yeah?"

"I'm sorry for how I've always been, about Mom. I'm sorry that I made it so you couldn't talk about your version of kidnapping or witness protection scenarios. I'm sorry that my being angry at her makes it so hard for me to talk about her. And I'm so sorry about the stupid postcards."

Tegan tips her head toward mine.

At first, I think what I must want her to say is some version of *It's okay*, or *Don't worry about it*, the kind of small absolution most of us get in response to the meaningless errors of our daily lives.

But I know the way I've been with Tegan about Mom is more than a meaningless error. Deep down, I know it's not okay, and also I know that we'll probably both spend a lot of our lives worrying about it, because what's happened to us with our mom is big and difficult and unusual.

Deep down I know it'll take a lot of different kinds of *sorry* to get us where we need to be.

So it means a lot more that she offers one of her own.

"I'm sorry I impersonated you and wrote an email to Salem Durant and agreed to tell our entire life story to a really popular podcast."

Both of us laugh. Big, real, *Isn't this all a little absurd?* laughing. The opposite of something canned.

When we start to trail off, sighing it out and wiping at eyes that were already wet with emotion, Tegan adds, "But it hasn't been the worst thing. This trip."

"No," I agree. If we never found out another thing about Mom, everything about this trip would still be worth it, if only for this moment. "It hasn't been the worst thing."

Of course, as soon as I say it, I think of all the other worth-it things about the trip, many of which I should *not* be contemplating in front of my sister. My neck flushes.

She nudges with her foot, her smile saying she sees right through me.

"I mean. You did get a *boyfriend* out of it."

"Oh my God, Tegan. He's not my boyfriend."

She giggles and nudges me again, and I think I might . . . I'm pretty sure I *also* giggle. It makes me flush in embarrassment to realize it. It is humiliatingly immature, and also humiliatingly pleasant, to think of Adam Hawkins as my boyfriend.

It is not-humiliatingly lovely to giggle about it with my sister.

I let her tease me about it for another ten minutes—her flopping dramatically against the pillows again and declaring that it's "*so* romantic," pointing at the pink splotches on my neck and her proud declarations that she "*knew* it," recounting every occasion where she caught Adam making eyes at me. When she asks, with waggling eyebrows, if we've kissed yet—she drags out the word, obviously asking about more than kissing—I poke her in the side and gently scold her, telling her it's time we get to sleep.

That, at least, is an easy boundary to set.

But a half hour later, when we're both clean-faced and brushed-teethed and pajama-ed, tucked into our respective beds, Tegan whispers my name again.

"Yeah?"

"If you decided to, you know . . . sneak out tonight? To see your *boyfriend?*"

I throw an extra pillow at her, and she squeaks a laugh.

"I'm just saying. I wouldn't judge you even a little."

I snort. "I'm not going to sneak out. Go to sleep."

But long after I hear her breathing turn deep and even, I lie awake in the pitch-black of our heavily curtained hotel room. I think about the ten years since I've seen my mother, and about how finding out she wasn't sick back then doesn't mean she hasn't been sick since. I think about New Mexico and where Salem says we'll start when we get there, at a place where she suspects a probably sick Lynton Baltimore might have taken himself—and his money—to. I think about being one step closer to the mother I thought I didn't care to ever see again, how it'll feel for me and for my sister if we find her or we don't.

When it gets so overwhelming that I feel a press of tears behind my eyes, I think about a starry sky and a field of night-cloaked flowers, strong arms and soft words and a feeling of safety I can't ever remember having before.

And then I quietly push back my covers, swing my legs over the side of the bed, and sneak out to find it again.

Chapter 20

Adam

The knock on my hotel room door comes at around midnight, so soft that at first I think I must've imagined it. Or maybe willed it into existence.

If I thought I was desperate for Jess to come down to my basement room after our first kiss a couple of nights ago, then it's clear I didn't truly know desperation.

Because for the last few hours—ever since I watched her and Tegan head into the hotel room next to mine, both of their expressions drawn and tired—I've practically been climbing the walls with worry for them both.

I'm at the door before I think much about the state of my room or the state of myself. When I swing it open, Jess stands in the hall in the same pair of pajamas she was wearing that night by the pool in Pensacola, but this time, with a pair of thick white socks pulled halfway up her shins.

She's blinking slowly at my bare chest.

"Hi," she whispers, to my sternum.

Obviously, given what Jess and I spent most of last night doing out in the open air, this shy taking-in we're both doing of each other's sleepwear is a little silly.

But not so silly that I can't appreciate how sweet those socks look on her bare legs.

Not so silly that I don't feel flattered about the way her eyes roam over me.

"Can I—?" she begins, at the same time I say, "Come in."

I take a step back and she takes a step in, and as the door swings shut behind her, I open my arms and she comes to me, pressing her soft cheek against my chest and sighing against it as if she's been waiting all day for this.

I drop my head, rest my lips at the crown of hers. I only lift my mouth long enough to ask her if she's okay.

She nods and links her arms tighter, low on my back. I lean my shoulders against the wall and just . . .

Hug her.

Hold her close.

We stay that way for a couple of minutes, her breaths tickling across my skin, her thumbs idly stroking along either side of my spine, and I can only hope it feels as good to her as it does to me. It isn't until right this second that I realize I haven't spent the last several hours worrying *only* for her and her sister.

I've been worrying for myself, too.

Worrying about what her dad thought of me, on that video call. Worrying about whether she would regret asking me to do it. Worrying about how I'd so readily agreed, even after promising myself I'd take a back seat on this story. Worrying about what's next, about where Jess's mother ended up, about whether Lynton Baltimore is dead, about what happens if I lose this job and Jess, all in one fell swoop.

Worrying about a hundred other things that have nothing to do with all this, because worrying is a runaway train.

The hug makes it better. Puts me back in my body, which makes my mind a quieter place.

"Tegan okay?"

She nods again, then lifts her head and sets her chin on my sternum.

In the low light of the room, her blue eyes look dark as they search mine. "Are you?"

"Yeah."

Her lips curve in a small smile, a private playfulness I only learned about last night.

"I snuck out."

"Did you?" I raise an eyebrow, playing along.

"Mm-hmm." The murmur of it vibrates against me, becoming a hum, a hunger in my blood.

Before I can adjust enough so that Jess doesn't have to be subjected to my hard-on while she's only trying to get a nice hug, she moves: her arms coming up to link behind my neck, toes pressing up to put her mouth closer to mine. I must move, too, because a half second later I'm getting that murmur of hers right against my mouth—her soft lips and seeking tongue, a scolding nip of her teeth when she thinks I might be pulling away.

That quick, things between us transform, both of us seeking a harder kind of comfort than a hug has on offer. It's unreal how I missed her—how I spent half last night beside her, *inside* her, sat next to her in close quarters for most of today, and none of that matters now that I have my hands on her bare skin again. I curl my fingers against her hips, walk her a couple steps forward to the opposite wall, lift her so she can brace her back against it and wrap her legs around my hips.

At first, her hands and mouth and hips move over me restlessly, a little recklessly. But even after one night, I recognize this—her haste a reflex, as though she thinks anything that feels this good might get snatched away from her at any second.

I doubt we have much time tonight, but still, I slow her down; I surround her.

I make my body the safest place in the world.

She moans when I get it right—when I've stripped off her

shirt and lifted her enough that I can get my mouth on her breasts, when I've tilted her hips so she can rub against me exactly the way she wants. Those shorts she's wearing are thin enough that that I can feel her warmth and wetness against my skin, and every time she tightens her legs around me to tug herself closer, I feel the soft ribbing of those inexplicably hot socks.

I run my teeth lightly against one of her nipples as I lift my head.

"You want the bed?"

She shakes her head no. "It's quieter here," she says, pressing one of her palms back against the wall, and I guess she's right. If we're on the bed, we're one thin wall away from her sister, and that's not how I want this to go, either.

So we do it a new way tonight: untangling ourselves only long enough for me to go into the bathroom and wrestle up protection from my kit, fitting ourselves together again when I come back to her, her face and neck flushed, her sleep shorts gone. She likes it this way—her against the wall, all the muscles I still keep strong bunched and working. She strokes her hands over my shoulders and biceps while I bend my head and keep at her breasts; she grinds the most sensitive part of herself against me; she gasps my name when I push the head of my cock one inch in, then another.

Another.

It feels too good then for me to do two things at once; I have to raise my head again and press my forehead into the wall over her shoulder and clench my jaw tight as she squeezes her thighs around me, pulling me the rest of the way in. I was better last night—nervous but more focused, more in control. Now that I'm inside her again, though, the day's stress bears down on me anew, different this time. I want my body to know what my mind didn't for the last few hours—that she's okay, that we're okay, that nothing from today destroyed what we built out on the farm.

"Adam." Her whisper is a contrast to her nails digging slightly into the skin of my shoulders. I press my forehead harder against the wall, breathe through my nose. "You can go harder. Please."

"I don't want to hu—"

"You won't. I can come this way."

Just hearing her say that, Jesus. My cock twitches inside her.

"I can move just right."

"Yeah?" I ask, but I think I might be past listening for the answer. It's one driving thrust and her pubic bone grinding against me and I'm done for—my hands gripping the backs of her thighs more tightly as I set a rhythm that feels good to me. I use my whole body to fuck her, faster and harder than any time I did last night, and I like the way she pants in my ear; I like the way she keeps getting herself off; I like the way I can feel her inner muscles tighten around me when she succeeds.

And I like that I'm only distantly liking all of that.

Because the biggest part of me right now is muscle and blood and movement. No thought, only driving need and a hot, promising tinder at the base of my spine.

When it explodes, I come with a groan, my body damp with sweat, flushed with exertion and pleasure and relief.

I come back to calm slowly, grounding myself with the sound of Jess's breathing and the feel of her skin against my hands. I knead her thigh muscles and she sighs in pleasure, flexing her fingers along my back. I don't know how long we've been this way, but it's long enough that when Jess lowers her legs from around my waist, she laughs softly at the stiffness that makes her wobble on her feet.

I coax her to take the first stop in the bathroom, awkwardly handling the condom while I wait my turn. When she comes out, I press a kiss to her mouth and ask her to stay for a while.

She blushes—or maybe she's still flushed—and nods.

When I come out again, though, I'm reminded of the fact that my room—the part that's past the hallway I just fucked her in—is a pretty solid indicator of my headspace for the few hours before she showed up, and I can sense when I come to stand next to her that she's taking it all in with a degree of concern. One bed is covered with my partially unpacked bag, my closed laptop, a half-empty bag of popcorn I bought from the vending machine in the lobby a little while ago. Next to it, the nightstand is cluttered: two bottles of water, one empty, one mostly full, my phone, my earbuds out of their case, my watch. The other bed looks as if I've been tossing and turning in it, which is a little misleading: After my shower, I shoved all the covers to the foot of the bed and didn't try sleeping at all. Mostly, I've been staring blankly at . . .

Shit.

Jess's eyes linger on the muted television.

"You're watching football." There's an entirely justified note of surprise in her voice.

"Yeah," I admit, my ears suddenly hot.

It shouldn't feel—based on what we just did, based on what we've been doing for the last couple of days, getting to know each other in this new way—that Jess standing here staring at my shitty hotel-room television is intimate.

But it does.

"You've discovered my secret," I add, trying to keep my voice casual.

"Why's it a secret?"

I shrug. "I've made it pretty clear to the world that I don't really approve of the game anymore. At least not how it's played now."

I look away from her and to the TV, where an old game, probably from a couple of years ago, plays onscreen. Every color bright, every move fast. I can hear the crowd, the play-calling, the announcers' commentary, even though I haven't turned that volume up even once. The sound of a game like this lives inside me, an echo of another life.

"You still enjoy watching it, though?"

"I don't know. It's hard to explain."

She doesn't say anything in response. But she does move toward the unmade bed, sitting down on it and slipping off her socks before tucking her legs, crisscross style, beneath her. When she looks up at me, she's asking me a question with her eyes.

I know instinctively that this moment is important for her. Jess is about as cautious about asking for information as she is about offering it. Even her curiosity is a secret she keeps from the world.

But not from me.

Not anymore.

"Cope really loved football," I say. "Playing it, watching it, talking about it. He loved the game."

"More than you." She makes it a statement, not a question, but it's inviting all the same.

"Football wasn't—it wasn't his entire personality. I don't want you to think that."

"I wouldn't."

I nod tightly, strangely unsure of myself. It isn't as though I've kept quiet about Cope in the years since he died, and I don't intend to keep quiet about him now or in the future. But I can tell already that talking to Jess about him won't be the same as talking to anyone else. In here, I'm not the guy who wants to tell the world about what football did to Copeland Frederick.

I'm just the guy who lost his best friend.

I let my eyes drift back to the television.

"The way he felt about the game," I tell her, as I track a pass sailing in a spiral down the field, "it was pure. You couldn't really tell him anything bad about it. He couldn't hear if you tried."

A heavy, familiar feeling presses against me.

"Adam."

There's something in her voice that tells me I got lost in the screen for a minute. That I was watching this old game, these players I don't know, and seeing someone else altogether.

I look back at her, and she's set her palm on the bed beside her, an invitation.

I've spent the last few years of my life making a study of all the ways you might get someone to talk to you about something that matters.

But I've never seen a single thing as convincing as the sight of Jess Greene's slender hand on the white expanse of unremarkable hotel sheets.

I cross to her, and it's a transformation not unlike the one in the foyer—we slip so easily from one thing to the next. Standing apart, then sitting beside her, then lying back and pulling her close. She's warm and soft and still beside me, the same hand from the sheets now on my stomach.

This mattress is two hundred times more comfortable than it was a half hour ago.

"I'm sure you read a lot about Cope," I say. "When you looked me up, or whatever."

"Only a little." Her breath is a soft puff against my skin, and the funny thing is, I completely believe her. I believe that whatever Jess looked up, she would've quickly walked away from: closing her browser, desperately trying to clear her mind of whatever she thought she didn't have a right to.

"You saw the stories about him having bipolar?"

She nods—quick, almost apologetic.

"He wouldn't mind you knowing that," I assure her. "He wasn't ever ashamed of it, once he got the diagnosis. He was open about it."

Too open, according to a lot of the people around him. Some of our coaches and a lot of our teammates, almost everyone when he went pro. His agent, too, this dirtbag guy who got a lion's share of my public rage after he posted a soft-focus black-and-white shot of him and Cope celebrating on draft day.

With a broken heart emoji.

"Our sophomore year, after the season was over, Cope had—he had a real tough couple of months."

I'm understating it, to be honest. He had a terrifying two months, and as his roommate, I witnessed most of it. Sleepless nights, lost time. Behavior that at first made me mad, then freaked me the fuck out.

"It was the first time he'd ever had anything that severe, that long-lasting."

I don't add everything from the whiteboard that lives in my brain all the time: everything I've learned about Bipolar I, about traumatic brain injuries, about the three concussions Cope had before his twenty-first birthday, and the ones he had after, too. I've read study after study showing links between mental health and brain injury, study after study about mood disorders and concussions.

The worst shit I've ever memorized.

"That must've been scary." She strokes her thumb back and forth against my skin slowly. It's as calming as the deep breaths I'm incapable of taking right now.

"His parents took him home for a couple weeks to see a doctor they trusted, someone who had nothing to do with the team doctors. They were—they are—really great, his parents. And that doctor. That's who diagnosed him, and who first prescribed something. It helped him a lot. You wouldn't believe it, how the meds helped him."

I realize, of course, that this is a meaningless thing to say to someone who never met Cope, who never had the chance to know him. But I guess I'm saying it because I wish she did.

"Except also, they didn't help him. With football. He said he didn't feel as fast or as strong. His hands would shake."

I clear my throat, stalling through the flash of anger that accompanies my thinking about this next part.

"And we had this one coach who—I won't say he told Cope to stop taking it. I won't go that far."

He said other things, though, and to Jess I repeat them all. I tell her how he'd relentlessly point out the changes to Cope's stats, how he'd go on and on about "mental toughness." His lectures on doctors overprescribing "happy pills," his complaints that "everyone today wants a quick fix." He'd go on and on about "training clean," as if over half the guys on our team weren't sucking down deranged ingredients in their "protein shakes" three times a day. He'd say the media had gotten "hysterical" over concussions. That "snowflake reporters" were trying to ruin the game.

I still hate him for saying those things.

I still hate myself for not realizing, until so much later, how truly damaging it all was. Cope was haunted by that shit for years, even though he only rarely admitted it. But he'd go on and off his meds, on and off, year after year. Even though the back-and-forth surely made things worse for him.

"Uff," Jess says, flinching slightly, and I realize with a start that's not a reaction to what I've told her—instead, she's winced because my fingers have hit a small tangle in her hair, which I've apparently been stroking over and over. It's fanned out on the bed behind her, a record of my mindless, mostly careful self-soothing.

"Shit, sorry."

I unwind my fingers from her hair, and she moves carefully, sitting up and turning toward me, taking the offending hand and holding it, pressing our palms together.

"It's fine." Her eyes are soft and, if I'm not mistaken, a little wet.

My own drift back to the television. I must have been talking for a while, because the game's not on anymore. On the screen, men in ugly sunglasses sit around a poker table, looking either bored or grim. I don't know why in God's name this is on a sports channel, but I guess it doesn't really matter.

"It's easy for me to forget," I say, concentrating on the feel of her fingers in mine, "that football was a thing that helped

Cope. It hurt him, a lot. But it helped him, too. He loved playing. He really did. And he was so good at it, and that . . . that
made him happy, to be good at this thing that other people
loved, too."

When I look back to her, she nods in understanding.

"So you watch it to remember?"

"I watch it—yeah, to remember. Looking back, I always focused on the negative stuff with him, once he went pro. I'd talk
about the hits he took, or the stuff I heard about him through
the grapevine, stuff that made me worry about how he was doing off the field. But if I hadn't only focused on that, if I'd made
sure to tell him I was proud of him, too, if I'd—"

"Adam. You know it's not your fault. You were worried about
him."

I shrug. "It not being my fault doesn't mean I couldn't have
done different. And if I'm going to do this thing, this story I've
been working on for so long, I'll need to do different. I'll need
to remember Cope's love for the game, because a lot of people
share it. I'll need to admit my own mistakes."

I can tell, as soon as this is out of my mouth, that I've changed
the temperature in the room. I've made it so I'm no longer only
the guy who lost his best friend, the guy who wants to share
something with the woman he's in a relationship with.

This thing, this story I've been working on.

This story I once thought about trading Jess for.

We haven't talked about it since the trampoline.

She's concentrating on our hands now, her lashes low, her
lips pressed together tight. It's good that she hasn't pulled away
entirely at the reminder, but it's not good how quiet she's gone.
It can't be.

Jess being this kind of quiet with me—that's an us from a different time. From before Florida, before the farm.

Before that tiny foyer in this hotel room.

"I'm sor—" I begin, but at the same time, she says my name.

She keeps her eyes down. Squeezes my hand gently.

"Yeah?"

She clears her throat softly before she speaks again. Twice. Stalling, same as I did, and I brace myself. The stress we've worked out from the day, from the new lead on Lynton—I've brought it all back to us. Reminded her of how we got here, and where we're going next.

She'll probably say we need to take a step back, or that it's time for her to go to her room. That she needs to stay focused on Tegan from now on.

Finally, she raises those lashes and looks me right in the eyes, and I brace myself.

But I'm not braced enough for what she says next.

"I'll talk."

The Last Con of Lynton Baltimore

Transcript Excerpt from Episode 5, "Modus Operandi"

Durant: It's clear to me you have a particular attitude about women.

Baltimore: Oh, is it? What's that, then?

Durant: You don't respect them. You don't feel empathy for them. You see them as weak, and that's why you target them.

Baltimore: ::scoffs:: Ms. Durant, you could not be more wrong.

Durant: About which part?

Baltimore: About all the parts, really. I respect women. I empathize with their struggles. I certainly don't see them as weak.

Durant: Hmm.

Baltimore: Take you, for example.

Durant: Oh, I don't think we need to do that. I don't think we need to take me anywhere.

Chapter 21

Jess

"It's not difficult to get people like this to talk to the press," Salem is saying as we make our way through the lush, cactus-dotted courtyard that leads to the entrance of the Kirtenour Healing Institute in Santa Fe. The air is hot and dry and it somehow smells like rocks, even though I never noticed before that rocks had a particular smell. My eyes feel so parched that I imagine they make a *plinking* sound every time I blink, and frankly, I've been doing a lot of blinking.

Because being around Salem for the last several hours?

It's being inside a tornado.

Or a sandstorm, I guess, if I want to be location-specific about it.

"People like this," she continues, as though none of us are even there, "think you're dying to hear about their heroics."

"Salem," Adam says, but she ignores him. We're only a few feet from the front doors. "Let's take a minute."

Salem slows her steps and then stops, turning to face the three of us, and there—there it is again, the strange and crackling energy that has shot through our little foursome ever since we were all reunited this morning in the Santa Fe airport.

It's jarring, is the thing—and that's coming from someone who's been jarred an awful lot recently.

But after last night with Adam, I feel unused to strange and crackling. Unused to being jarred.

At first, when I told him I wanted to talk, he resisted. Shook his head and said no, told me that he'd already made a plan of his own. He was going to tell Salem in person that he wanted to take a step back from the story; he was going to tell her that he was too personally involved.

"I wasn't going to tell her any details," he said, a little sheepishly, a little clumsily, both of us conscious of our half-dressed state, our position on his bed. "I wouldn't even tell her that my feelings are, you know . . ."

"Mutual?" I said, and watched with private, proud delight as the tips of his ears turned red.

But even in his shy pleasure he was quick to turn serious again.

He didn't want me to talk.

"I didn't tell you about Cope so you'd feel obligated," he said, gripping my hands in his, the warm, rough texture of his palms making my skin pebble in delight. "I told you because I wanted you to know him. And me."

At that, I couldn't stop from leaning forward and pressing my mouth against his.

"I can do this," I said, against his lips, but he was already shaking his head again, his brow lowering with a stubbornness I hadn't seen in him before.

"This isn't about what you can do. It's about what we agreed to on the farm. If you talk, Jess, that's not for the story."

He reminded me of myself, sitting in that hammock-chair at my dad and Bernila's house, determined to lay out my conditions. White-knuckling my way into controlling a situation I definitely couldn't control.

Seeing that expression on him gave me enough perspective to take a step back. To understand that he would never be okay with my talking unless we came up with a plan together.

So in that rumpled hotel bed, where Adam Hawkins told me about the worst loss of his life, we worked it out together. A series of compromises. He should tell Salem that *our* feelings had gone beyond the professional. He should tell her that I'm *considering* doing an interview, but because of the bit about our feelings, he shouldn't be the one to conduct it. He should make clear to her a new condition: If—we'd still tell her it was an *if*, since Adam insisted I take more time to think it over—I do the interview, she has to stick to the deal she made with Adam originally, and produce his podcast. We'd make sure to tell Tegan all about it.

Afterward, when it was settled, I kissed him again, soft and hungry and strangely relieved. I couldn't have ever imagined feeling relief at the idea of talking about Mom, but with Adam's mouth on mine, with his body pressing closer, I realized that the relief didn't really have anything to do with her.

It had to do with *me*. I was relieved to know I was capable of offering something of myself to someone other than my sister. Of being someone different than I've been all these years.

When I'd crept back into my room in the small hours of the night, I felt so confident. In the morning, I didn't even stumble through explaining to Tegan about the plan.

But once we got to the airport—once we saw Salem—it was pretty clear that nothing was going to go to plan.

She blew in with a laser focus in her eyes and a big chip on her shoulder. She said her daughter was "fine" and left it at that. She looked at the three of us as if we were sitting in her classroom, as if we'd been left for days in the care of a substitute teacher, and now she needed to pull us all back from the bad habits we developed in her absence.

She looked at Adam and me as if she *knew*.

She made it seem as though the only plan that mattered was her own.

And, admittedly, her plan did seem more pressing than ours, because she'd taken that one piece of non-information about Lynton Baltimore from my dad's doctor friend and made a meal out of it. By the time we piled in to our new rental—a cramped, compact SUV, this time—Salem had told us about her research, her contacts, her calls. Her belief that Lynton and Charlotte came here, to this for-profit "healing institute," newsworthy for the apparently overstated claims it's made over the years about its success rate at curing notoriously hard-to-treat cancers. She'd already secured a meeting with the CEO.

She hasn't told us why.

"Oh my God," Tegan had said, "do you think Lynton Baltimore got *conned*?"

Salem had merely shrugged, and started giving us our instructions.

"Do we all remember who we're supposed to be in there?" she says now, obviously only willing to "take a minute" if it means going over the plan.

"I'm the intern," Tegan says, and that figures. She's always been a solid student, a fact that usually makes me hugely proud.

Salem looks to me and raises an eyebrow, waiting for me to confirm my role.

"Research assistant," I say grudgingly, lifting the binder I've been given to help make me look more authentic.

"Hawk?" Salem says.

He sighs. "I'm just being myself, Salem. I don't need a reminder."

"Hmm," she says, as though he does, in fact, need exactly that.

Then she turns and keeps walking. Ready to sandblast her way into this new place.

I drag my feet, taking in my surroundings as I go. The place looks weirdly identical to the pictures on the website, which I figured must've been enhanced, or at least only showed the pretty parts of the campus. But everywhere I look is a vista; every building is clean and new-looking. If there are sick people, or people worried about sick people, I don't see them anywhere.

I feel strange. Torn between curiosity and trepidation. I want to find out what Salem seems to have figured out already, and I also want it to be two days ago, when she was out of the picture for a while.

My body already misses Adam's.

He catches my eyes as he holds open the door for us all to pass through, and the only comfort is that I can tell he's torn, too.

Inside, we're guided up an L-shaped stairway that overlooks a bright, be-cactused atrium and ushered into a sleek conference room. On one wall there's a gigantic flat-screen television that's cycling through some of the same pictures as on the website, the occasional staged-looking photo of someone in a white coat talking earnestly to someone who looks perfectly healthy. We're all so quiet together as we take our seats that it's as if we've come here to talk to someone in a white coat about something very bad.

It's unusual, but I'm the one to break the silence while we wait, prompted by a thought I'm surprised no one has had sooner.

"Hold on, aren't we forgetting something?" I gesture at my face. "If someone recognizes—"

"Then that gets us where we need to be sooner," Salem cuts me off impatiently. As though I was the ringleader behind any while-the-substitute-was-in-charge shenanigans.

Adam's hands still on the recording equipment he's setting up. He sends Salem a cool look before sliding his eyes to mine.

I shake my head the smallest amount, warning him off.

Salem's disappointed-teacher mode is extremely effective. If she'd been this way the whole time, I might've thought about talking way sooner.

A second later, the door to the conference room opens and a short, fit, bald man who's maybe in his fifties walks in. He has tanned skin and the brightest white teeth I've ever seen in my life. He's wearing a dark blue suit, white shirt, no tie. He looks momentarily caught off guard by the fact that there's more than one person in the room, and I brace myself.

But as his eyes scan over each of us, he doesn't stop for even one extra second on me.

Maybe Salem's instincts on this are off.

Maybe my mom and Lynton weren't here after all.

"Ms. Durant," the man says, putting a hand out to her. "Happy to meet you, happy to meet you."

"Mr. Kirtenour." She stands from her chair and takes his hand. "Thank you for seeing me on such short notice."

"Call me Dennis, please. And of course I'd see you. I'm honored to be considered for your piece."

I think my eyes might *plink* again. Piece?

I look toward Adam. Brow furrowed low, jaw tight. He has no idea what this is about, either.

And more than that, he's not happy about it.

He adjusts something on the recording equipment, leans back in his seat, and loosely clasps his hands in his lap.

Salem responds to Dennis with a light, airy laugh. "The honor is mine. Or ours, I should say! These are my colleagues; they'll be helping with note-taking and recording matters."

She gestures to us in a sweeping motion, but doesn't introduce us with names, and Dennis doesn't bother looking at us again. He takes the seat closest to Salem and leans forward, pressing a button on a sleek black strip set into the table and speaking toward it.

"Ashley, can you bring refreshments for five instead of two? Thank you."

But Salem doesn't wait for Ashley or her refreshments.

"So, why don't we start by talking about your mission for the institute."

Even though I have absolutely zero idea what's going on, I can tell it's a softball, the kind of question this guy has a long, rehearsed answer for. He talks about the limitations of traditional medicine, about healing from "within." There's a lot of variations on the words *positivity* and *optimism*. Every once in a while there's a science-y word tossed in, but mostly it reminds me of the stuff my mom used to love hearing about on afternoon talk shows.

If she came here with Lynton and met this guy, she probably got stars in her eyes. I am certain he could've conned her.

But surely not the notorious Lynton, right?

Salem is nodding along, asking follow-up questions, laughing at moments that don't even register to me as funny. Briefly, I wonder if she's had some kind of break with reality while she's been gone. The intensity, the sternness, the caginess—it's all at a different register than it was when I first met her.

We should have taken longer than a minute outside.

We should have taken hours before coming here and doing this thing that three of us have no idea about.

"Dennis," she says mildly, "let's shift gears for a moment and talk about your detractors."

I look toward Tegan instinctively, and can tell she's thinking the same thing as I am: Is this where Salem gets to it? Where she suggests this "healing institute" is some kind of scam that managed to catch Lynton Baltimore in its snare? Will she pull up a photo of him? Will she point to me and say, *Why don't you have another look at my colleague here, see if she looks familiar?*

But Dennis only chuckles at her prompting, as though he's been through this gear shift a hundred times. He mentions the doctors and scientists who have criticized the institute, speaking of them with a cloying, pitying niceness that suggests he's sorry they're not yet so enlightened. Salem presses him on the doctors who've left the institute after comparatively short terms of employment; he says that's always been the plan, so that physicians can take what they've learned here elsewhere. She hits him with a question about accusations of the profit motive in healthcare spaces, and he does an impassioned critique of insurance companies that would probably sway even me, if I hadn't already decided that his institute was selling snake oil to terminally ill people.

There's a soft knock on the door a second before it opens and a woman who looks about my age enters, wheeling a small cart that's loaded on top with a polished silver carafe, small white cups, and a teak box that I'm assuming has a tea selection. Beneath, there's another shelf with fancy boxed water, a basket of fresh fruit, and packages of gourmet trail mix.

"Ah, Ashley," Dennis says. "I was beginning to think you'd forgotten about us."

She flushes beneath her tanned skin, but smiles. "Sorry about that, Mr. Kirtenour. I had to rustle up some additional items."

Salem looks annoyed at the interruption, but Dennis has the same placid expression he's worn for almost the entire time he's been in this room. I watch Ashley set a cup in front of Adam. It's a dollhouse accessory next to his hand.

He is looking at Salem as if he doesn't know her at all.

Salem clears her throat, redirecting Dennis's attention back to her while Ashley offers Tegan a trail mix packet that probably costs as much as a car payment. Maybe I'll try to take the rest on our way out. The kind of souvenir I can get on board with.

"It must be difficult," Salem says to Dennis, interrupting my straying thoughts. She's pitched her voice in a different tone now, and even after so long I recognize it from the podcast— this note of tender empathy she often used on Baltimore's victims.

"To have so many people judging and criticizing as you do this work," she finishes.

"Ah." He waves a hand deferentially, humbly. "Throughout history, innovators have always—"

"What do you do to keep yourself grounded?" she interrupts.

Adam shifts in his seat, and Tegan and I exchange a look. Something has changed; we can both tell. Salem's posture is still easy, her voice still calm and sweet.

But somehow it's like watching an animal stalk prey.

"Well, I have my family, of course, my wife and three children. That's any man's most profound blessing."

"Of course. And your hobbies, yes? I understand you're widely known as a collector."

Dennis's expression flickers. A tiny, fleeting pinch of discomfort.

"It's what I tell our guests here at the institute; it's so important to have something outside of—"

"Antiques, I think I read? Mostly jewelry and precious figurines?"

Dennis doesn't respond. I am pretty sure I've leaned forward in my seat. I have a vision of myself from long ago, my phone in my lap as I drove, one earbud in so I could listen to the latest episode of *The Last Con of Lynton Baltimore*.

She's so good at this it's criminal.

"Dennis, I'm sure you know where I'm going with this."

Some of Ashley's cups clink together on her tray.

"And I'm sure you know why I don't want to follow you there," he says, his voice cool now.

"It's important for my audience that I address it. It's important to your history here. And if people have misunderstood, here's your chance to clear it up, set the record straight."

"Ms. Durant, this was—what, a decade ago now? I've set it straight. It was a small and insignificant matter. I paid all the money back to the clinic using my own personal funds within six months, and the board supported my staying on."

"And the necklace you purchased?" Salem asks. "Is it . . . still in your collection?"

Dennis stands. Ashley stiffens behind her cart.

"I think that's all the time I have for you today, Ms. Durant. I certainly don't know what this could have to do with a profile regarding my status as a 'healthcare disruptor,' but I hope you have what you need."

"Speaking of disruptors," she says, as though he hasn't told her the interview is done, as though he isn't standing stiffly, his face a mask of barely contained rage. "Can I ask who first brought you the neck—"

"Goodbye, Ms. Durant."

He turns on his heel and walks out.

For what must be the longest moment in recorded history, we're all completely silent.

And then Salem calmly says, "You can shut off the recording, Hawk."

"It's not on, Salem," he replies, in the closest thing to a snap that I imagine Adam Hawkins is capable of.

She blinks across the table at him.

"I'm not recording someone if you've told them it's for something else. What are you doing?"

She shrugs, and ignores his question. "Fine. It doesn't matter. It's clear enough from that exchange that he was here."

Lynton, she means, though I don't know if anything is clear enough, at least not to me. Or to Tegan, judging by the confused look on her face. Did Lynton Baltimore come here for some kind of treatment and then somehow run a fake-antique grift on the institute's CEO? Did my mother—

"Wait," someone says, and I'm pretty sure that all of us look up at Ashley with identical expressions of surprise. A foursome again, united by our forgetting that there's still a stranger in the room with us.

"*Wait*," she repeats, her eyes widening, lit with excitement. "You're . . . you're *Salem* Durant?"

Salem smiles.

"I am."

"Ohmi*god*, I am such a fan of yours; I must have listened to *The Last Con of Lynton Baltimore* like three times straight through on different road trips. It was so good! I'm *big* into podcasts, true crime all the time, and you basically started it all!"

She presses her lips closed and looks toward the conference room door, as though she's only just realized that her excitement might be out of place under the circumstances.

"We seem to have upset your boss," Salem says calmly.

I can tell the *we* lands uncomfortably with Adam, who stands and starts gathering the equipment he must have turned off as soon as Dennis Kirtenour mentioned being "considered" for some obviously nonexistent "piece."

Ashley looks toward the door again, cautious.

Then she says, in a near-whisper, "He's not really my boss. Or he is, but only for another week. I gave my notice last month. I'm moving to San Francisco."

Salem raises her eyebrows. Adam is shoving stuff in his bag haphazardly, those lips I now know the texture of set in a firm, implacable line.

"He's actually my uncle." She casts one more look toward the door and says, "He is a *nightmare*."

Even I can see that this is an opportunity. Salem leans forward in her chair, sets her elbows on the conference table. To her, Ashley is the only person in the room now. Or maybe in the whole building, because she doesn't seem in the least worried about us getting kicked out.

"Ashley," Salem says. "How long have you worked here?"

Ashley doesn't seem to catch on to the fact that she's being led somewhere. She rolls her eyes and says, "Oh, *forever*. Since I was nineteen. So I guess twelve years or so."

Did you ever meet a man named Miles Daniels? I want to say, which I guess means I've finally been swept fully into Salem's sandstorm. I don't know why it makes me feel as if I'm somehow betraying Adam, and I wonder fleetingly how long he's felt a divided loyalty like this.

"Look, Ashley," Salem says, speaking quickly now, "obviously, I brought up an unwelcome topic with—"

Ashley scoffs. "Oh, he's *so* sensitive about that thing with the necklace. No one in the family is allowed to talk about it, ever. So don't feel bad about his reaction."

Salem doesn't feel bad. But I guess Ashley wouldn't know that about her.

"I'm here following up on my reporting about Lynton Baltimore."

There's that wide-eyed, excited look again. Ashley is closer to my age than Tegan's, but they remind me of one another all the same. I try to picture Tegan, connecting the dots between our mother's boyfriend and that *Best True Crime* listicle she found. It makes no sense, given how I never wanted her to make the connection, but I feel oddly bereft not to have seen her do it.

"You think Lynton Baltimore was *here*?"

Salem cocks her head at Ashley. "I do. About ten years ago, actually. When the podcast was first airing."

Ashley deflates slightly. "I mean, I think I would've recognized him. I'm telling you, I was *obsessed* with your podcast back then."

"He may have looked different," Adam says, for the first time engaging in this interview-slash-ambush. "He may have been . . . ill."

Ashley's eyes *plink*. "Well, I don't have anything to do with the"—she pauses and lifts her hands, hooking her fingers in sarcasm-quotes—"'guests' here. So if he was here to get"— another pause for the quotes—"'treatment,' I wouldn't know."

There's a sharp knock on the half-ajar door of the conference room, the woman who brought us up here sticking her head in.

"Ashley," she snaps. "You can clean up the refreshments later. I need to show these people out."

These people. I bet Dennis Kirtenour is somewhere in a glass-walled office, pacing around and shouting into a Bluetooth. The woman doesn't leave. She crosses her arms and waits, as if she knows only-one-week-to-go Ashley can't be trusted.

Salem stands, all obedience, and looks at us, her "colleagues," her recalcitrant students. She says, "I guess we won't have a chance to finish our tea!" as though we're a happy family being rudely treated at a restaurant we've casually shown up to.

She shifts her gaze toward Ashley. "Thank you, Ms. . . . ?" She trails off meaningfully, asking a question.

Ashley says, "Oh, it's Maxwell. Ashley Maxwell."

To the impatient assistant, it probably doesn't appear to be anything more than politeness on Salem's part, and Ashley's, too. But I know that Salem's only asked so she can secure a new source.

So she can more easily find Ashley again.

Salem smiles. "Well, thank you, Ms. Maxwell, for the tea." She looks at the frowning assistant. "We'll be on our way then."

She sweeps past her, appearing almost comically unbothered. Tegan looks so shell-shocked that I nod toward Adam to go ahead so I can walk out beside her. The two of us are probably going to *plink* our way all the way back down the steps and out the front door.

But right as Tegan and I are crossing the threshold out of the conference room, Salem and Adam already several steps ahead of us, Ashley whispers, "Um, wait. You dropped your—"

I turn around, but she's not holding out anything to me. She whispers even more softly now. I want to tell her that she shouldn't risk it, that Salem will surely reach out to her soon.

But she's determined to speak before I can.

"Look, you should tell Salem it definitely wasn't Lynton Baltimore who scammed my uncle."

Tegan says, "How do you know?"

Ashley looks between us, and then her gaze settles—lingers—on me.

As though she might be putting something together for the first time.

Remembering something familiar.

"Because the person who got him to buy that necklace was a woman."

Chapter 22

Adam

"Let me see it again."

Jess continues to blink down at the screen of my phone, showing no discernible reaction to Tegan's request. After a few seconds, she lifts her hand from her lap and brings it up to the table, and I think she's finally going to pass the phone over to her sister.

Instead, she sets her thumb and forefinger onto the screen, close together, and then splits them apart.

Zooming in.

She blinks down at the screen again.

"Jess," Tegan says.

I look over at Tegan, who seems more concerned by Jess's silence than she is annoyed by it. When she meets my eyes, we have the same silent conversation we've been having since Ashley Maxwell sent the photo that Jess can't stop staring at.

Is she okay?

I don't know.

We seem to be alternating on who's asking the question, and who's answering it.

Tegan sighs. "I'm going to the bathroom." When Jess doesn't respond, she adds, "Maybe I can purchase some recreational drugs while there! Or meet someone who runs a desert commune!"

"Take your phone with you," Jess says, eyes down, obviously not registering anything other than *I'm going to the bathroom.*

Tegan rolls her eyes at me. But she does take her phone with her. I watch as she makes her way across the rooftop bar where we've been sitting for the last hour or so, ever since we checked into this hotel. It's the nicest place we've stayed since this trip started, and it's not too crowded in here yet, but still. I have a feeling that if Jess weren't still in shock at seeing her mother in this photograph, she'd watch Tegan, too.

"She looks so different," she murmurs now, and I'm not even sure if she's talking to me or to herself. Tegan's made it to the restroom, the door swinging shut behind her, so I turn my eyes first toward Jess, then toward the photo.

Charlotte Caulfield sitting at a small, round restaurant table with Dennis Kirtenour and his wife, Lisa. Her hair is dark brown, cut to her shoulders, straight and shiny. She's looking directly at the camera, smiling without teeth.

"She didn't ever wear clothes like this," Jess says.

It looks like money, what she's wearing. A cream blazer with a silky shirt beneath it that's the exact same shade. A slim, yellow gold necklace, dotted with what I'd bet are diamonds. Matching earrings. Her left hand rests on the tablecloth, and while it's hard to see much detail, I can tell she's wearing a wedding band.

"And she didn't drink wine," Jess adds, referring to the glass of red that rests by the wedding-banded hand. "It made her face turn splotchy."

The woman in the photo doesn't look splotchy. She looks perfectly in control. She's running the show at that restaurant table.

Beneath the one we're sitting at now, I set my hand on Jess's thigh, squeeze gently.

"Hey."

Finally, she blinks up at me, as though she's waking up after a long sleep, and I feel an inconvenient tug of longing. I haven't woken up with her yet. And if I was waking up with her, I'd want her to look softer, safer than this. I wouldn't want to see something haunted in her face, wouldn't want her to look surprised to find me there.

"I'm sorry," she says. "I—"

"Don't be sorry. It's a lot to take in."

Charlotte Caulfield, running a con. Or at least we think so, according to the information Ashley Maxwell provided us about her uncle's greatest personal and professional embarrassment. According to Ashley, Dennis met the woman who sold him what turned out to be a nonexistent necklace when she came to the institute to find a potential solution for her brother, recently diagnosed with lung cancer. She was an antiques dealer, she'd said. She'd only recently returned from Europe, and only because she wanted to care for her brother. She was elegant, sophisticated. Dennis apparently thought she was the most brilliant and refined woman in the world.

"Ashley said she had an accent," Jess says. "Did you hear her say that? My mom definitely didn't have an accent. Just a Midwestern one, same as mine and—"

"We don't have to talk about this right now."

She blinks and then nods, her eyes going down to the photo again. "Right, right. We should wait for Salem."

I clench my back teeth together, unaccountably frustrated. First of all, I'm fucking mad at Salem. And more than that, I'm even less comfortable with Jess talking now than I was when she first offered to do it last night, fresh off our conversation about Cope. I want to take my phone from the table and throw it across this bar. I want to haul Jess into my lap and make her look at me, make her talk to me about how she feels.

Not like she's my interview subject, but like she's my . . .

I don't know what. *Girlfriend* seems too insignificant for what she is to me already.

Across the bar, I see Tegan emerge from the bathroom, and she pauses to give me a meaningful look, a *Should I come back yet?* look. It's such an automatic, easy gesture of trust and closeness.

I try to think of a word for what she is to me now. *Source* is too small; *friend* seems too simple.

Family, I think, automatically.

I shake my head at her, unsure at first if she can see the small movement from where she is. But she nods and points to a lounge chair in our sight line, and then plops down to scroll her phone.

I turn back to Jess.

"I don't know if talking to Salem right now is a good idea," I say.

Now, I've got her attention.

"Why not?" she asks, but before I can even answer, she goes on. "I told you before, I can do this. I'm fine doing this."

I gently squeeze her thigh again, desperate to slow her down. The truth is, I don't think what she told me before—in that hotel room where we'd been so intimate—can be counted on. It's too soon since our relationship changed, too soon since I told her about Cope, too soon since the shock of meeting Dennis Kirtenour and seeing the photo Ashley Maxwell found buried deep in a camera roll from an old, long-forgotten phone, shoved in the back of one of her dresser drawers.

But I have the feeling she won't take well to being told she's not ready.

So I try a different tactic. It's not really a lie, even though it's not the full truth.

"I don't think Salem's ready."

Jess's eyes widen a fraction.

"You see how she's been since we got here. You saw what she did with Kirtenour today. She's not herself."

It's not quite what I mean. She's herself, turned up to eleven. In the months I've been working with her, I've seen her be cagey, impatient, willing to push boundaries. I saw it in the weeks we were first working with Tegan, back when we thought she was Jess. But since she returned from Boston, there's something desperate about her. Something that worries me.

"She is being . . . a lot," Jess says.

She pauses, and I feel her thigh tense slightly beneath my hand until she looks across the room and spots Tegan. She relaxes again. Or at least she relaxes as much as she can after staring in a trance at a photo of her mother in disguise for the last hour.

"But I'm fine. I'm fine."

Again, I get that sense where I can't tell if she's talking to me or to herself, but I guess it doesn't really matter. I heard it either way, and I can't make myself believe her. This version of Jess—the one who wants to talk, the one who only hears half of what Tegan says, the one who wants to *wait for Salem*—isn't the one I know best, or maybe at all. To me, she's the same as that woman on the phone screen.

I can recognize her, but she looks so different.

"I want to do it. I can handle her."

I blink down at my drink, disoriented. It's the hot, dry air or the fact that I haven't eaten enough or the cumulative upside-downness of this entire day.

It's the fact that Jess Greene and I seem to have entirely switched sides in this fight over whether the story of her mother gets told.

"I still need to talk to her," I say, meeting Jess's eyes again. I'm desperate to remind her of the plan, the one we made together last night. In bed. After sex, after me telling her things I keep mostly to myself. As close as I've ever felt to anyone. We negotiated this like we were a team, a couple, and Jess had been . . . she'd been so *with* me. Open to me in a new way.

But I can tell this photo changes things for her, and I'm afraid to ask how much.

She nods, then looks down at my phone again.

"Can you send this to me? AirDrop, or whatever?"

Before I have the chance to answer—the chance to say, *Once I offered to AirDrop you a travel itinerary and you looked like you wanted to stab me through the heart*—Salem's voice cuts in from behind us.

"Sorry," she says, as she moves around our table to pull out a chair. "That took longer than I thought."

Jess stands as soon as Salem sits, and my hand, obviously, falls away from her thigh.

"I think Tegan and I are going to go take a walk. See some of the city."

I'm pretty sure what that means is that I'm meant to talk to Salem about the plan. To make it so Salem gets prepped to do the interview I don't think either of them seem ready for.

I watch her go. A black and cream and spun-gold column. Already I miss her enough to make my gut clench.

"I'll have a gin and tonic," Salem says to the waiter who I didn't even see arrive. "More gin than water and more limes than ice."

She dismisses him by turning her sharp gaze onto me.

"How's Pen?" I preempt her, because I'm not ready to talk about the plan.

"She's frustrated." It's more forthcoming of an answer than the brief, sharp *fine* she gave us all at the airport. "She has a long road of physical therapy ahead and she's afraid she won't ever be the same as a dancer."

I nod, opening my mouth to say something reassuring, but Salem speaks over me.

"Patrick can handle it for a few more days," she adds, which I guess means both her daughter's physical therapy and emotions. Either way, she's got that look in her eyes, again, the one that says she's not interested in talking about this anymore.

"Obviously, you've made progress in my absence," she says.

I swallow, feeling sick. *Progress.*

"Jess trusts you, that much is clear. She—"

"I'm involved with her," I blurt, because I doubt I could stomach whatever she'd planned to say next. "You don't need to know the details, but you do need to know that. I'm involved with her in a way that's not professional."

I'm sorry, I almost add, automatically, but I clamp my lips shut. I'm not sorry, I guess except for the fact that I am right now not back in Missouri, before this goddamned story caught up with us again.

"And?" Salem finally says.

"And what?"

"I know you're 'involved' with her, Hawk. In case you missed it, I am not only an investigative journalist; I am also a person with eyeballs. I assume what you mean is that you've slept with her or something close—don't give me that look; we're both adults here—but the truth is, you've been involved with her since she first opened her front door to us."

Obviously, I can't argue with that.

"You see the problem, then."

She shrugs as the waiter sets down her drink, murmuring her thanks to him before turning back to me. "Not really."

"Not really?" I echo, the anger and confusion I've felt at Salem all day slipping into my tone. "What is going on with you, Salem? You show up here this morning and drag us all to that institute like you wanted it to be some kind of clever surprise. And the surprise turns out to be you lying to a source? Now you're saying you don't care that I've fall—" I cut myself off, my ears heating, especially at the way Salem's mouth curves up knowingly. "That I'm in a personal relationship with one?"

She takes an indulgent sip of her drink, looking bored.

"I had a lot of time in the hospital to do research. But not a lot of time to text or call or to write you an email to tell you what I found out about Kirtenour. Which, I'm thinking, turned out to be fine, since you seemed to make good use of your days. Or nights."

"Jesus, Salem."

I push my drink away from me, leaning back in my chair. When we started this trip, I could have never imagined speak-

ing to her this way—in frustration, in censure. But she and I
have changed, too, both of us seeing parts of each other we
probably didn't plan on. She's not just my boss anymore, and
I'm not just her employee.

"Nothing I've done with Jess in the days since we've been off
were about progress, or making use of anything. You need to
understand me. I am not in this with her because I want something out of her."

"Well. That's hard to say for sure, isn't it?"

I stare at her, shocked by being on this side of her coolness,
her self-assuredness. She says things in a way that makes me
doubt my own truth. I want to say, *No, it's not hard to say*, but
when she's looking at me this way—it *is* hard. It's hard to untangle the pieces of me and Jess that exist outside of this story.

It's hard to be certain about whether there are any.

"Quit talking to me like I'm a source," I say.

She swallows a gulp of her drink, still unbothered. She
shrugs. "You could be. It's an angle."

I can't believe how far afield of the plan I am.

"An angle?" My voice sounds like it's being dragged across
pavement.

"Look, Hawk, I respect you. I think you're good at this work.
But you're green at this work. You want to disclose to me that
you're in a relationship with someone we're hoping to talk to
for our story, fine. But you know as well as I do that we're not
out here exposing government corruption or some kind of
billion-dollar corporate coverup. I could open my podcast app
right now and show you ten shows—*popular* shows—where the
host has a stake, where the host *is* the angle. *My parents raised me
in a cult; here's our story. My older brother ran off to live in the Alaskan
bush; here's my twelve-episode series about what happened to him. Ten
years ago a girl from my high school was murdered; I'm a guy with basic
podcast software and here's who I think did it.*"

She pauses, and I know—I *know* it's for effect.

It's to make sure I have a second to register what she's going to say before she says it.

"My best friend died, and I blame football, a sport I also played for years. Here's why."

"Jesus," I mutter.

"None of this"—she waves a hand, gesturing at the air around us—"passes whatever smell test you learned about in J-School, I can promise you that. I don't care that you're in love with Jess Greene, Hawk. I care about whether she's going to talk for my story. So, is she?"

I don't say anything. I can't say anything, not yet. My rib cage is a pinball machine; Salem's words a cold and polished steel ball, banging into the flashing, reactive pieces of me. If only it'd stay still long enough, I could see my distorted reflection in its shiny silver surface.

Not that I'd want to at this particular moment.

"She is, then?" Salem says, my silence all the answer she needs.

I grasp desperately at the plan.

"She's considering it," I say, which was true last night, and not as true today. Today, obviously, she's more than considering it.

Salem narrows her eyes at me. "Considering it?"

If my molars survive this day—this argument—it will be a miracle.

"I'm certain I don't know Jess as well as you do. But I'm also certain she wouldn't appreciate someone—even someone she's *involved* with—misrepresenting her wishes."

I clench my fist and tap it lightly on the table. Fighting with Salem is like fighting with one of my sisters. It's as if someone drew her a map to all my sore spots.

"I don't want you to do it. The interview with her, I mean. Not when you're acting this way. She doesn't deserve to have you come at her the way you went at Dennis Kirtenour."

The way you're going at me.

"You can't deny that you're different," I add. "That something's changed since you went home. Did something else happen? With Pen, or with Patrick?"

For the first time since this conversation started, I can see something in Salem falter. It's tiny, fleeting. But if I was the sort of person who kept a map of her sore spots, I'd be drawing an *X*.

She clears her throat and pokes at the limes in her drink.

"What's happened is that my daughter is still injured, and Lynton Baltimore is probably dead. If I seem impatient it's because I am. I want this over with."

I shake my head. "I don't believe you."

She shrugs again. "Believe what you want. Look, we've gotten what we can out of Ashley Maxwell. What we need now is all the information we can get about Charlotte, who apparently is going to be a bigger part of this story than we thought. If you don't want me to do the interview with Jess, fine. You do it, then. I'll handle the recording. At least that way I'll be able to trust it gets done."

"I can't," I say, automatically.

But when she looks at me, I know she's only waiting for me to realize the corner I've backed myself into. I've succeeded in earning Jess's trust; I've succeeded in getting her to agree to talk. I think I'm too close to do it myself, but I also think Salem will go too far.

I do it, or Salem does it.

Because either way, Jess has decided she has something to say, and it wouldn't be right to stop her.

I take a deep breath.

"Salem, you need to know. If she agrees to this, to me doing this, I'm not going to push her. Not even once, no matter what. I'm not going to hurt her."

For a long time, she doesn't say anything. I'm not looking at her, but I figure she's probably working up to another metaphorical roundhouse kick to my face. I haven't even mentioned her promise to produce my podcast about Cope, and now I can't bring myself to. That promise must've been made a million years ago; that podcast must be a million years away.

But then Salem sets a hand on my forearm, and when I meet her eyes, there's no fight there.

"Adam," she says, using my first name for the first time in our entire history. "Trust someone who's been there. If anyone gets hurt by this, it'll be you."

Chapter 23

Adam Hawkins: You're comfortable?

Jess Greene: Yeah, I'm good. This is fine.

Hawkins: Do you need—

Salem Durant: You've got water here, Jess.

Greene: Thanks.

Tegan Caulfield: ::dramatic snoring noise::

::indistinct shuffling, quiet laughter::

Hawkins: ::clears throat:: Why don't you start by telling us about what you remember from the time right before your mother left.

Greene: Which time?

Hawkins: Well—ah. Do you want to talk about the first time?

Greene: The first time she left, it was also for a man. So it might be relevant.

Hawkins: Okay. Let's talk about that first time, then. If you're comfortable.

Greene: I mean, I should say. Brent—that's who she left with the first time—he wasn't like Miles, not at all. Or Lynton. Should I call him Miles or Lynton for this?

Hawkins: Whatever you want.

Greene: Well, Brent was— ::pause:: Tegan. Do you care if I talk about him?

Caulfield: ::snorts:: Not even a little.

Greene: Brent wasn't really . . . he was into basically three things. His truck. Fishing. BW3. That's a wings place, if you didn't know. Like a sports bar.

Hawkins: I know what BW3 is.

Greene: Right. Right, that was silly. Sorry.

Hawkins: Don't be sorry. You're doing fine.

Durant: ::groans::

Hawkins: Salem. Leave it.

Greene: Well, anyway. Miles was . . . very different. He drove a Camry. He liked to cook. He loved the library. Cookbooks from the library. He actually took my mom *out*. To places other than BW3, I mean. So it isn't as if she had a type. As far as I know, Brent wasn't a criminal. Well, I guess except that he didn't pay child support. But my point is, they were different.

Hawkins: But was—what I wonder is, was your mom different toward them? Do you think she felt the same about both of these men, since they both convinced her to . . .

Greene: Leave her kids?

Hawkins: ::clears throat:: Yeah.

Greene: I guess, the thing about my mom is—probably any man could have convinced her. Any man who wanted to go, and have her go with him, I think she would've gone.

Hawkins: Because . . . because you think she didn't like being a parent? A mom to you and your sister?

Greene: I don't think she disliked it. I think . . . it's what Tegan said before. She wanted to be loved. Romantically loved, I mean. When she was with a guy, she—I don't know. She kind of disappeared into him. With Brent, she went fishing. She ate hot chicken wings. She said his truck nuts were "just a joke." Even with my dad, he wanted a certain kind of life—house in the suburbs, kids, stability. A wife who'd stay home. She was that, for a while. When I was really young, before they split, she always had dinner on the table when he got home from work. She kept a cleaning schedule on the fridge. That sort of thing.

Hawkins: And then what? She didn't want to be that anymore?

Greene: It's hard to say what she wanted to be. My dad left her. Brent left her. Other guys left her, too.

Hawkins: Who was she when she was single? When she wasn't seeing someone?

Greene: I don't really know. She was always looking for something. The next someone. I guess I'd describe her as inconsistent. Fun when she was around, but inconsistent.

::long pause::

Greene: That's all I can think of to describe her right now.

Hawkins: Okay. Would you say she was interested in money? Was she motivated by it?

Greene: No, never. Or not . . . I don't know. Not when I knew her. When my parents split, it was my dad who really kept offering her more, probably out of guilt. I'm sure his lawyer hated it. But he left her the house; he supported her financially until she left that first time with Brent. And even after, he helped her when . . . ::pauses::

Caulfield: You can say it. He helped when I came along.

Greene: ::clears throat:: Right, my dad helped her with some things after Tegan was born, too. But I mean, if you're asking whether she wanted really nice things, or whether she tried to date men with money—the answer to that is no. Miles certainly didn't seem as if he had money when she met him. I think he said he was a . . . what did he say he did?

Caulfield: Building inspector?

Greene: Oh yeah. For the city, I think. Obviously now I doubt that he ever inspected a building in his life, unless maybe if he broke into one. Anyway, she wasn't some kind of user. And she—she didn't care about fancy things. Clothes or cars or jewelry or anything.

Hawkins: Okay. That's helpful.

Durant: ::heavy sigh::

Hawkins: ::slight cough:: To your knowledge, did your mother ever break the law?

Greene: Not to my knowledge. I mean, sure—speeding, illegal parking, the sort of thing everyone does. ::brief pause:: Wait. Can you take that off the recording?

Hawkins: Yeah. Don't worry about it.

Greene: If you're asking whether I'm surprised that she apparently faked an entirely new identity and convinced some rich guy to buy an antique necklace that wasn't real, my answer to that is yes. I never knew her to do anything like that. Honestly, the fact that she even cut her hair makes me . . .

::long pause::

Hawkins: Makes you . . . ?

Greene: I don't know. I don't know what it makes me. She . . . she *really* loved her hair. I'm sure it sounds stupid to say—

Hawkins: It doesn't.

Durant: Well, I mean. Maybe let her say it first, and then you can decide.

Caulfield: Jeez.

Durant: All right. Excuse me. I'll stop. Carry on.

Greene: What I was *going* to say is, she never changed her hair. She changed a lot of things about herself for guys, but not that, you know? It was maybe the one consistent thing about her. A non-disappearing thing.

Caulfield: Maybe it was a wig.

Greene: That's true. Maybe it was a wig.

Hawkins: I suppose I wonder—if you're comfortable answering, I mean—you've said your mom wasn't motivated by money. That she didn't have a criminal background. But do you think she was capable of this? Running a con?

::long pause::

Greene: I guess if you would have asked me before I saw that picture, I probably would have said no. Once I realized the man she'd left with was Lynton Baltimore, it's not as if I thought she ran off with him because she wanted to do crimes. I thought she ran off because she was in love again.

Hawkins: But now you see it differently?

Greene: I suppose I always saw that when my mom was in love with someone, she was capable of doing terrible things. Leaving me. Leaving Tegan.

::long pause, indistinct shuffling::

Hawkins: Do you want to stop?

Greene: No. I'm fine.

::glass clinking::

Greene: ::clears throat:: I guess after seeing that picture, I think—I think when it comes to being in love with someone, maybe my mom was pretty much capable of anything.

Chapter 24

Jess

One thing I love about doing hair is, I almost always feel tired at the end of the day.

Physically tired, I mean. Feet, arms, back, shoulders. It's standing all day, sure, but it's more than that. It's a lot of bending and pulling and crouching; it's mixing color in the back and doing shampoos when it's busy and helping with cleanup, too. I like the movement of it; I like how I get into the car when I've finished for the day and roll my neck in relief. I'll think to myself, *I'm going to sleep so good tonight*, and it's almost always true.

But when Adam, Salem, Tegan, and I finally decide to take a break, after hours of mostly me talking—talking about things I usually hate talking about, hate thinking about—I feel a kind of tired I try to avoid.

Mentally tired. Emotionally tired.

Tired straight down to my soul, and the truth is, I doubt I'll get any sleep tonight.

"We can try again after we eat," Salem says casually, standing from the honey-colored leather armchair she's been stationed

in for most of the afternoon. We're in her hotel suite—I can
tell Adam is still appalled that she's gotten an entire deluxe
suite—and the early evening light has cast everything in the
room faintly rose gold, which I could probably appreciate if I
wasn't so wrung out.

"Something might come to you after a meal," she adds.

Across from me, in the other armchair, Adam cranes his neck
and looks up at her, jaw set. All day, he's been this way with her:
one-word censures or tense looks of frustration as he ran the
interview. I don't know exactly what happened between them in
that rooftop bar last night, but I know he's not happy about it.
I certainly know that nothing in New Mexico has followed our
carefully constructed plan, because Adam hasn't taken a back
seat to anything.

"We can call it a night," he says tersely. "Let her get some
sleep. She might remember something with fresh eyes."

Inwardly, I cringe.

He might as well be working security for me.

"I could eat," chirps Tegan from beside me. We've sat together
on this small loveseat almost all day, her presence both a comfort and burden. On the one hand, it's easier between us now;
it's as though we're finally on the same side, and a few times
today during the interview, she even broke the tension with a
gentle joke or a complementary memory or an announcement
that she suddenly had to pee.

But on the other hand. On the other hand, sometimes, as I
talked, I could feel her watching me with a rapt, unblinking attention that flushed me with renewed guilt.

She's so desperate to know anything about Mom.

"Like, I could really go for a pizza," she adds, sounding totally unbothered, and that's something, at least.

Salem clucks her tongue. "We're not eating pizza in Santa
Fe. I want to try this sopaipilla place the concierge mentioned."

Tegan shrugs and stands, too, and Salem starts tapping on
her phone.

I feel strangely outside of myself. On the rough-hewn slab of wood that's functioning as the suite's coffee table, my mother's five postcards sit, all but one—the one we've been puzzling over for the last hour or so—picture-side up. They stay flat now, their curtain-rod hiding place not even a shape memory anymore.

"Jess."

When I meet Adam's eyes across the space, I get the sense that he's had to repeat himself more than once.

"I'm sorry," I answer. "I missed that."

It's awkward, overly polite, but the interview was like this, too. The whole time, I held within me a separate but inescapable worry that had nothing to do with talking about my mother.

What if someone would be able to tell? I kept thinking. *What if someone could tell by the sound of my voice on this recording how I feel about the man who's asking me these questions?*

What if they'll be able to hear something that's so private to me?

Even to my own ears, my voice had sounded strange as I'd talked. Stilted and slightly robotic.

"Do you want to go get something to eat?" he asks.

I stare at him. Stubble along his jaw, faint purple half-moons beneath his eyes. What I want is to be alone with him. To crawl into his lap and tuck my entire self into the ledge his body makes for me. I want us to talk to each other in voices that hide nothing about how we feel.

"Why don't Salem and I go?" Tegan says. She's moved over to stand beside Salem, who obviously has been showing Tegan a menu on her phone screen. "We can bring it back here, try again after we get some food in us."

My eyes drift down to the Olympia postcard. The writing-side-up one.

Dear Jessie, I can see. The words beneath blur in front of me, as though my eyes have decided they're not participating in this find-the-grifter game anymore.

"Or we could be done for the night." Tegan's tone is gentle now. Concerned.

Probably Adam gave her a look to get her to change her approach. My cheeks heat. I don't want him bodyguarding me with my own sister.

I shouldn't want him bodyguarding me about anything.

"No, I'm—I'm good. A break to eat sounds good."

I start to stand, but Salem stops me.

"I think Tegan's right. She and I can go. You and Hawk deserve some quiet time, after all the work you've done today. We'll bring back whatever you want."

When I look up at her, I expect to see what I always see in her: something shrewd or calculating or smug. I expect her to raise an eyebrow, an *I'll bet you want some* quiet time *with him* expression.

Instead, though—maybe for the first time since I've met her—there's something compassionate in her expression.

Something almost . . . maternal.

I swallow back a terrifying swell of emotion. Embarrassment or annoyance or maybe longing.

"That's fine," I say quickly. "Tegan, pick something for me. I'll have whatever."

"Sure, same for me," says Adam. "Whatever you pick is fine."

In a distant part of my brain, I register that I no longer have the impulse to telegraph a warning as they go. Salem's getting her purse and Tegan's taken to looking at her own phone as she waits by the door, but I don't say anything like, *Be careful* or *Don't talk to her about the story while you're gone.*

I just sit on this little sofa in a very nice hotel suite, the kind of tired I try not to be. I feel as blurry and indistinct as the words on that postcard. My mind shuffles restlessly through the information I shared today: the boyfriends Mom was with before Lynton Baltimore, the few part-time jobs she'd held, the two or three casual friends that she never seemed all that invested in, the passing of both her parents—her only close family—well before I was old enough to remember them.

None of it really explains how she could so easily become

someone else, or how she could become convincing enough to run a simple but still sophisticated con on Dennis Kirtenour, or why she and Lynton Baltimore would have gone to Olympia afterward.

As soon as the door snicks closed behind Salem and my sister, Adam stands from his chair.

He shoves that slab-of-wood coffee table aside as if it's as light as a piece of lint on his clothes.

Then he drops to his knees on the terra-cotta tile floor in front of me. He sets his big, warm hands on my thighs and I feel less blurry.

He looks at me until I meet his eyes.

"I'm sorry," he says roughly.

"What for?" I ask, and I mean it. He didn't do anything I didn't agree to. And he was so careful the whole time. It was like watching a giant tiptoe his way through walled and narrow streets, wincing every time he accidentally flattens a car. "You were doing your job."

His face goes stern and his fingers curl into my muscles gently. Briefly.

Do that again, I want to say, but I don't. I don't know how to explain to him that his rough touch brings me back into focus. That it reminds me that I'm not just the lens we've spent the day trying to see my mother through.

"I didn't—" He sighs, bows his head and shakes it back and forth once. "This isn't how I wanted to learn things about you."

"Mostly you didn't. You learned things about my mom."

He raises his eyes to mine again, opens his mouth and then closes it, as if he's thought better of whatever he planned to say.

I set my hands on top of his, curl my fingers around his wrists and tug gently.

"Come up here. That floor can't be good for your knees."

He makes a self-deprecating noise, and I'm relieved that it breaks some of the heavy tension between us, reminds us both of the ways we know each other outside of anything I said today.

When he sits next to me, he takes up so much space that we'd be touching even if we didn't choose to.

But right away, we choose to.

Adam puts his arm around my shoulders and I lift my legs to hook over one of his. He pulls me close against his side and I rest my head against his shoulder.

I think, *I know why they call it a love seat.*

I close my eyes and try desperately to sink into the quiet, for however long I have until Salem and Tegan get back. I'll eat whatever they bring me and afterward I'll try again with the postcard.

But then, after what must be only a minute, Adam says, "I don't think we should keep going tonight."

It's something in his voice that has me sitting up to look at him. I don't quite know how to describe it except to say that it's not his bodyguarding voice. It's not the voice where he says I need to rest or that I've done enough for today; it's not the one that says all he cares about in the world is the conditions I set, or keeping me safe.

It's more . . .

It reminds me of Salem's voice, I suppose. Incisive but distant. Professional. There's a knowingness to his tone. A *We've gotten all we're going to get* assessment. I have the sense, somehow, that he's saying more than we should stop for the night.

I have the sense he's saying we should stop the interview altogether.

"Why not?" I ask, strangely insulted.

He doesn't answer right away. He rubs a hand over his brow and looks pained. I think about that night in St. Louis, when he told me he wanted to take a step back from the story. That he wanted to protect this thing between us.

A warm flush of affection rises in me.

"I know it wasn't what we planned," I say gently, reassuringly. "But it's better that you're doing it, in the end. If it were Salem, I'd be—"

"It's not that."

I think it's the first time he's ever interrupted me, and it stings. He leans forward, setting his elbows on his knees and bowing his head again. He gusts out a heavy sigh.

"It is that, but it's also not. It's—"

He breaks off, and I watch the muscles in his back expand again as he inhales.

"It's what?"

"You're having a hard time," is what he finally settles on. I can tell it's a settling. An inadequacy. "Talking about your mom."

I blink at him. "Of course I am," I snap, absurdly wounded. He's talking about how I sounded, I'm sure. The stiltedness, the roboticness.

I almost say I only sounded that way because of him, because of how I feel for him. But I can't bring myself to blame him for it.

It's me, after all, who doesn't really know how to live a feeling out loud.

"I told you everything I know," I say instead. "I answered every question."

I might as well be talking to a cop. I hate it so much that I stand from the love seat, pacing over to stand behind the chair Adam asked me questions from. I cross my arms and look down at him, waiting for him to explain himself.

I'll be the cop.

"I know you did. This isn't about whether you answered the questions. But you're not . . ." He trails off, clears his throat. "There's places you won't go."

I'm in freaking New Mexico, I almost say. *I've gone to four different states since I met you.*

I definitely know that's not what he means, but also, I don't want to admit that I know what he does.

"Remember the other night when you—when you came over to my hotel room?"

Of course I remember. The plan, sure, but more than that—

the way we'd clung to each other in that tiny vestibule, the way he'd pushed into me so strong and selfish and perfect. My neck heats, the warmth spreading down and all through me.

"When you caught me watching football."

Oh.

"Yeah," I say, my voice soft now. I think of his eyes on that television. His rough voice as he told me about Cope.

I wish I hadn't gotten up from the love seat.

For a few seconds, he doesn't do anything but look at me, something loaded in his gaze, and then . . . then, I realize what he's getting at.

Okay. Maybe it's good I got up from the love seat.

"My mother isn't football," I say.

"I know that. Of course I know that."

"But?"

He sighs again. "But you have a hard time talking about her outside of the basic facts. Outside of her leaving, and the men who she left for."

"No, I don't."

But even I can hear it has the ring of untruth.

"The questions were about her leaving," I say. "About Lynton, and the guys who came before."

He doesn't respond, and that's because he doesn't have to. If he lets me replay it all in my head, he knows I'll remember. Some of the questions were about other things. Who Mom was when there wasn't a guy in the picture. What kinds of things she liked, when it was only her making the choices. Whether I learned anything from her, when it came to raising my sister.

Every time I avoided giving much of an answer.

"What I said about Cope the other night—that I focused on all the negative things."

"I don't do that."

He nods once, but it's definitely not in agreement. When he leans over toward the coffee table and picks up the Olympia postcard, my stomach swoops anxiously, as though I'm watching someone pull them out of the curtain rod. I have to remind myself that they're not a secret anymore, that Tegan and Salem and Adam have all been looking, for weeks, at these little four-by-six artifacts of my mother's abandonment of us.

He looks down at it, and I can see his eyelids move across it as he reads it again. I can follow along, even from here, because it doesn't really matter if the words are blurry on the page. They've always stayed pretty crystal clear in my head.

> *Dear Jessie,*
> *The Pacific Northwest is a dream come true. People say it's rainy here and it is, but I barely notice. Water is just part of the beautiful landscape that surrounds us. I think even Miles likes it!*
> *I am thinking of you and Tegan. I know you are doing a great job with her. I have no doubt about that. I love you both!*
> *Mom*

"It doesn't even say anything," I tell Adam. "It's sightseeing bullshit. The *weather*. There's nothing there."

Nothing there except the line that'd made me so angry that I'd torn all the remaining clothes off her hangers while Tegan was at school.

I have no doubt about that.

I have every doubt, I'd thought, as I'd yanked shirts away from their cheap plastic hangers, as I'd kicked everything into a rumpled, tangled ball on the carpeted floor of her bedroom, my eyes burning and my throat tightening. A blind, bottomless rage. *I am twenty-one years old and I am made of doubt.*

"There might not be," says Adam. "But the way you see your mom—"

"Do you see something there that I don't?" I snap, impatient.

He lifts his eyes from the postcard, and everything is so confusing. I don't know if he's my Adam or Salem's Hawk right now. Him knowing me for himself and him knowing me for this story—it's so mixed up now. Impossible to untangle, which is exactly what he was afraid of.

"Jess. Please come back here and sit with me."

I linger by the chair for a few seconds, fighting with myself. My stubbornness, my standoffishness, my obsession with keeping parts of my life secret for so long. It was so much easier before Adam Hawkins knocked on my front door.

But it was so much harder, too. It was lonely and scary and small.

So when he sets his hand on the cushion beside him, I uncross my arms and go to him. When I sit, he lifts his hand from the cushion and sets it on my leg, exactly where I want it. So I can feel it: He's still my Adam. Not Salem's Hawk.

He passes me the postcard.

I take it with shaky fingers, swallow thickly, and look down at it.

"It would've been okay with me if you hadn't talked today. You know that, right?"

I nod. I do know that. Adam always says I can say when. With everything, he's always said I can say when.

"But you seem—since we met Ashley, you seem like you do want to. Or at least, you want to do what talking might lead to. You want to find her."

I turn the postcard over and over. Picture, writing, picture, writing. I do want to find her, and it's not only because it's what Tegan wants anymore. It's as if seeing that photo of Mom looking so different—not looking anything like me anymore—finally made it okay for me to want it, too.

It's as if I can make it so I'm looking for someone I never knew at all.

"You're looking at that postcard and you're not seeing your mom anymore," Adam says. "You're seeing her only through Lynton, now. You're trying to see if you can decode something about whatever con they ran. But if there were something about

Lynton or the con, Salem or I would've found it, the same way I found MacSherry, or the way she found Kirtenour."

I stop turning it over. Focus on the writing. He's right. Deep down, I know he's right. I let the words blur in front of my eyes again.

"She wrote those postcards to you, Jess. If there is anything in there that might help us in Olympia—and there might not be, we can't really know for sure—I think you have to remember that. You have to remember what she meant to you. What you meant to her."

I think it's pretty obvious I didn't mean anything to her, I almost say, but somehow, with Adam next to me, I can't.

Instead, I can think about Mom behind me in the mirror, brushing my hair. I can think of the times when she was in between boyfriends, when I had the feeling that she and I were a real team, just the two of us. I can think of the time she let me pick out books at the library that other moms said were "too old" for girls my age. I can think of a Saturday afternoon she spent coloring with me, *really* coloring with me, putting up her own finished page on the fridge right beside mine. I can think of the time she told my first-grade teacher that if I wanted to go by Jess, she expected everyone to call me Jess and nothing else. I can think about the sound of her laugh and the curve of her smile. I can think of all the movies she loved, because I watched them when she was gone with Brent. I can think of how, when she came back, watching movies was one of the only things I'd let myself do with her when I visited, because at least while they were playing, she didn't try to talk to me.

I can think of tons of things about Mom when I let myself, and the things I hate to think about the most are the things I didn't hate about her at all.

Part of me wants to gather up all the postcards now. Shove them in the nearest curtain rod. Adam would let me, I think. He might even help, if I asked him to.

But another part of me knows I need to read them all again, keeping in mind the hair-brushing and reading and coloring and defending me to my teacher. I want to make a list of every movie we ever watched together and remember all the parts of them that made her laugh or smile.

In the end, though, I don't have to do any of that.

In the end, all I have to do is look down at the first few lines of Mom's postcard from Olympia again, my heart rattling the whole entire cage of my body.

A dream come true
I barely notice
Water the landscape
Even Miles likes it

"Holy shit," I whisper, not even sure whether I'm talking to Adam or to myself. "Holy shit, I think I know where we should look in Olympia."

And what's worse?

What's worse is that I'd bet anything she's still there.

Chapter 25

Adam

Olympia is . . . heavy.

It's the only word I've been able to think of since we got off the plane yesterday morning, the sky gray with low, tight-packed clouds, the tall evergreens that seem to surround so much of the city, dark green and sagging with moisture. Far off, Mount Rainier looms in the distance, a view you can only see from certain spots in town, and only if the sky lifts itself long enough to let the earth breathe, but somehow you feel its presence anyway.

Maybe another time, I'd appreciate it, find it beautiful. Striking, at the very least.

But it feels all wrong to me right now.

Surely the hotel room I'm in isn't helping. Heavy like the outside: dark drapes, comforter, carpet. It's a cheap shock after the unexpected luxury of the rooms we had in New Mexico, but it was the only place we could book with three vacancies. Jess's room is two floors above me, opposite side, and I hate to think of it: her pulling shut the curtains, her lying beneath this polyester weight.

She won't come to me, not when it'd take her so far from Tegan.

I roll over, stare at the blocky red-light numbers on an alarm clock the likes of which I haven't seen since my teen years. Three fifty-eight a.m., exactly seven minutes from the last time I looked.

It's me, is the thing. *I'm* the heavy.

I'm responsible for this, for us being here. For there being only a few hours until this whole thing might be over.

I told Jess to dig deep about her mom. Told her what her interview was missing. I did my job, better than even Salem could've predicted, and now here we are.

Because Jess found Charlotte Caulfield.

Salem would object to this claim, I'm sure. After all, she's the one who spent all day yesterday out, visiting every marina within fifty miles of here in the compact rental we picked up at the airport. Pictures of Charlotte on her phone and a promise to be discreet as she asked around.

"I won't approach her if I find her," she told Jess and Tegan, before she left. "I remember the conditions."

Jess and Tegan couldn't go, of course. Too risky if anyone saw Jess and recognized Charlotte in her face, too risky if one of these small marinas ended up being home to Charlotte after all. One glance out a small window, maybe, to spot your two daughters, and you'd know someone had finally found you. You'd know someone finally let themselves remember a movie you loved once, how you watched and decided that your dream home, if you could have whatever you want, would be a houseboat.

A dream come true.

Water the landscape.

You might be inclined to leave before they could find you.

I could've gone with Salem, I suppose, not that I'm the sort of guy who makes it easy to be discreet. But I could've gone. Split the work, ask the sort of questions I knew she'd spend the day asking.

I'm in town looking to rent a houseboat, I could've said. *Mind if I have a look around?*

My aunt has a houseboat here, I could've told a passerby, a picture at the ready on my phone. *I'm supposed to meet her, but I'm lost trying to find it.*

I could've done all the things an investigative journalist is supposed to do.

Instead, I acted as if it wasn't even an option.

I stayed in the hotel all day and waited, same as Jess and Tegan. Sat—a little awkwardly—between them on one of the beds in their room, my laptop warm on my thighs as it played the movie Jess had remembered and that Tegan had never seen.

"Tom Hanks?" Tegan said, a confused expression on her face. "She had a thing for Tom Hanks?"

"She didn't." I didn't need to look over at Jess to know she had the same weary, wary expression she'd had ever since she shared the memory in Santa Fe. First with me, then with Salem and her sister. A memory of her mother that had nothing to do with the men she dated, or the one she eventually left with.

"She had a thing for the houseboat."

"Weird," Tegan had answered, a little numbly.

But any time that houseboat was on the screen of my laptop, Tegan seemed to lean forward a little. She thought the Seattle in the movie seemed better than the Olympia we'd shown up in, I could tell, but Salem's pretty sure she's solved that particular inconsistency.

Lynton Baltimore ran a con in Seattle once.

He maybe wouldn't have wanted to go back. Olympia makes a nice substitute, when it comes to Charlotte Caulfield's dream.

4:01, those red-light numbers blare at me. It's still nearly five hours before we plan to leave: to pack ourselves into the sedan and drive back to the northwest side of Budd Inlet, where there's a midsize marina with a good number of liveaboards, where there's a small, well-tended, pea-green houseboat with— you have to zoom in on the picture Salem took to see it—a wooden sign near its back door.

THE BALTIMORE, it reads.

I try to imagine what'll happen when we go, but I can't seem to do more than the basics. Jess and Tegan first, and then Salem and I to follow. We'll get answers about Lynton—about Charlotte—or we won't, and I can't seem to care either way.

Mostly I'm heavy with thoughts of what'll happen after.

I give up and reach for my phone. It's way too early to text, but since she's got Tegan with her, she'll have turned her phone to silent. I try to be comforted by the fact that I know that—that I know lots of things about Jess now that have nothing to do with whatever is on that boat.

Are you asleep

No, comes her near-immediate reply, which tells me all I need to know about the state she's in. She doesn't even *like* her phone. If she's up scrolling on it, she must be struggling.

My thumbs hover over the screen. There's a dozen potential texts crowding my brain, all of them too big, overweighted with worry over what she and I don't have settled between us.

But this sleepless night isn't about that for her, and I know it.

So I type, **Want to go for a walk?** and press send.

Watch her typing bubble appear, disappear.

Reappear again.

Two minutes, she replies.

IN the lobby, I wordlessly hand her the sweatshirt I brought down with me, because this place doesn't feel like any kind of July I've ever experienced. When she takes it, she holds it up in front of her, and it's basically a blanket.

She smirks, and it feels as though I've managed to flatten the whole entire world for her, if only for a second.

But after she's tugged it over her head—even though it falls almost to her knees and she has to shove the sleeves way up—there's no trace of a smirk, only the sense that every part of her is being pulled down by the same weight I brought her out here to escape. If anything, seeing her swamped by a piece of my clothing makes me feel worse. Everything about me is too big right now. My body, my boss, my job.

Most of all, my feelings for her.

We venture out into the misty air and are confronted by the bleak, boring outdoors of a chain hotel parking lot: too-bright lights overhead, the unnatural glow from the nearby strip mall's signs in the distance.

I look over at Jess, who's watching her feet at she walks beside me on a blacktop sidewalk that runs along the road into the hotel's entrance, a few newly planted, spindly looking suburban trees lining the way, unnaturally perfect circles of mulch surrounding their thin trunks.

I wish I could take her anywhere else.

"You okay?" I ask her, desperate to break the silence.

She gives me a quelling look.

Of course she's not okay.

"What can I do?"

She shrugs.

Can't fix her, I hear my dad saying, and I have to shove my hands in my pockets to hide the fists I automatically make at the memory.

"In a way, it's a relief," she says, but I've never heard anyone say something in a less relieved tone. It's as though I can hear her jaw grinding through the movements required to get this lie out.

Still, I play along. "Yeah?"

"It's what we came for," she says. Then she corrects, "What Tegan came for."

I make an effort to match my steps to hers. I say—knowing it's a risk, but unable to stop myself—"You're not curious at all?"

"No."

284 • *Kate Clayborn*

Another lie. I'm pretty sure she said it through her teeth.

We're out here together, but I can feel her getting farther away from me with every step we take, talking to me as if she has to hide herself away. Half of me thinks if I looked over at her right now, I'd see the start of her dissolving into the scenery.

I can't take it. I'm desperate to remind her that I'm something else to her now.

"Jess. It's just us out here."

She slows her steps and her shoulders sag. I stop, and she does, too. She reaches up and rubs both her hands over her face. When she finally drops them, she keeps her head down.

"I used to rehearse what I'd say to her," she says, so quiet I have to take a step closer to keep hearing her.

"Just in my head, when I was doing mindless stuff around the house, or when I was driving home from some parent-teacher conference where I could tell everyone was thinking that Tegan got the real short end of the stick, being left with me."

I clench my teeth to keep from correcting her. I doubt that's what *everyone* was thinking. I bet there were even a few people along the way who were pretty impressed by Jess Greene, people who would've been happy to help her out if she'd only asked. Whatever jolted Jess into this stubborn, permanent privacy— whether it was her mother leaving the first time or the second, her fear of the podcast or her fear of what people would think of how she was raising Tegan—I bet it's stolen more from her than she's ever realized.

"God. The things I'd say to her in my head," she adds. "Awful things."

Jess lifts her head, but doesn't look at me. She turns it out toward where I'm pretty sure that mountain sits in the distance, brooding and remote. A safer audience for all those awful things in her head.

I clear my throat. "You could say them to me. If you wanted to."

She keeps her face turned toward whatever's out there. She doesn't respond for so long that I start to wonder if she didn't hear me. If she's tuned so totally into those speeches she's rehearsed for the last ten years that she's forgotten I'm even here.

"I don't want to," she finally says, and I'm not only thinking of what my dad said now. I'm thinking of what Salem said, too. *If anyone gets hurt by this, it'll be you.*

Jess looks back, and she must see something in my face, because her own softens, and she steps toward me. Steps into me, setting her palms on my chest.

"I mean—"

"You don't have to explain."

She curls her fingers, fisting my shirt. She waits until I raise my eyes to meet hers.

"I don't want to have those things in my head. When we go there, I mean. If I say them now, I don't know if—I need to be calm in there. Focus on Tegan."

I know her enough now to know: There's no arguing with her about this, no fixing it at four fifteen in the fucking morning on some shitty sidewalk outside of a hotel we've got separate rooms in. I've got that too-big, heavy feeling again. I want to tear apart the world for putting her here, for putting *us* here. I want to beg her to reassure me that when this is all over, she'll tell me every awful thing she's ever thought, because when this is all over, she'll still want me there to hear it.

But this isn't about you, I remind myself firmly.

"I get it," I say. I lift my hands and cup her face in my palms, lean down to kiss her once. Soft and reassuring.

But those fists against my chest tighten again and she pulls me closer, kissing me harder—hungry and desperate, a kiss I can tell she wants to get lost in. And I let her—stroking my tongue against hers, getting my hands in her hair and grunting when she nips at my bottom lip. I curve my body into the shape that works best for kissing her this way, no wall to lift her against. I try not to think about the hundred other ways I haven't kissed her yet.

When she finally pulls away, she presses her forehead against my chest, both of us breathing fast. I rest my mouth against the top of her head, inhale the scent of her, take pleasure in the way it's mixed with the smell of my detergent on the sweatshirt she's wearing. Ignore the insistent, aching hardness between my legs.

Her muffled voice vibrates against my sternum.

I lean back. Set my hand against her cheek and tip her face up. I'm not missing anything she says to me.

"What?"

"I wish," she whispers, then purses her kiss-swollen lips and swallows before continuing, "I wish you could go in with us. Right from the beginning."

I stare down at her, something huge and hopeful and fragile in my chest. A bubble you could pop with even the slightest disturbance. It's the opposite of heavy.

I say nothing.

"I know it's against the rules," she says.

"You set them."

You can change them, I don't add. *I'll come with you. I'll keep you safe.*

"I know I did."

She takes a deep breath, and the bubble quivers inside me. I want her to say it: *Forget the rules, forget Salem, forget the podcast. Forget everything but you and me, because we go beyond all that now.* I know I can't be the one to say it first. It's too much pressure on her, for me to say it first.

"I'd want you to come in, if—if things were different."

I suppress a wince at the feeling of that bubble popping.

"Sticking to the conditions—it's the right thing. For Tegan to have some privacy for this. And also for . . . it's right for you, too. Your job, your future. You need to go in there as Salem's colleague, not my—"

I could finish that sentence for her in as many ways as I could kiss her.

Your boyfriend, your protector, your person . . .

Damn this bubble, swelling up again.

But she doesn't fill in the blank.

"Adam," she says instead. "Listen to me."

I manage a nod.

"It matters that I want you there. My wanting you there is a lot. It's . . ."

She smooths a palm over my shirt, rests it where my heart still beats in time to our kiss.

"It's a *lot*," she repeats, and there's something in it—a note of vehemence, of desperation. I think back to what she said, about not telling me all that was in her head about her mom before she goes in there to meet her. That she wants to stay calm, focused.

I think Jess is telling me about as much as she can manage this morning.

A half-truth to give me hope for the whole.

So I pull her to me again, wrap her in my arms, hide her away from the parking lot lights, the waiflike trees, the big brooding mountain on the horizon. I hold her close and lower my head, put my lips close to her ear.

I give her a half sentence, a half-truth of my own.

"The way I feel about you . . ." I murmur, and she nods, knowing that's all for now.

And with her standing here against me, these half-truths said, I work to reassure myself. We'll get through today and we'll tell each other the rest. We'll figure it all out: how we met, how we don't live in the same place, how getting through today is only the first part of getting through the whole entire experience of Salem releasing her podcast into the world.

We'll figure it out.

But when I've almost convinced myself—when I'm loosening my hold on Jess so we can go back inside and start getting this part out of the way—she bands her arms around me tighter.

"One more minute," she says, that desperate note back in her voice.

So I hold tight again, too.

One more minute, I repeat to myself.

And I try to believe it's not an omen.

Chapter 26

Jess

Up close and in person, the pea-green houseboat isn't nearly as charming as it might initially have seemed: the siding cheap aluminum, the porch railings grayish-white and rickety, the windows dirty around the edges. The sign by the front door— the one emblazoned with the name of the man Mom left us for—is easy to overlook, because the rest of the space is cluttered: a broom leaning against the wall, a pair of shoes next to a faded welcome mat, a terra-cotta pot with no plant that I can see growing inside it.

It's certainly no movie set, but I guess it's a fine place to hide.

"We should probably go up," says Tegan from beside me. "We're kind of lurking out here."

Her voice sounds good. Not upbeat, really, but not nervous, either. It sounds normal, which is a relief.

But I still can't look over at her, not yet, and I doubt she wants me to. We've been avoiding each other's eyes since this morning, when she stepped out of the hotel room bathroom. Her hair smooth and curled carefully at the ends. Mascara on to darken her pale lashes. Glowy pink on her cheeks. This morning, she took more care with her appearance than she has on this entire trip, and I knew she didn't want me to notice, let alone to comment on it.

I don't really know if all teenagers are like Tegan. But I do know that sometimes, the hardest, most heartbreaking moments with her are the ones where I'm reminded that all her flintiness, all her toughness and sarcasm and attitude is only a front. A cover for her tender vulnerability, a cover for the fact that there's a part of her—a big, beating part—that's still desperate for approval.

From a woman who left her ten years ago.

Right this second, I'm so raw and angry and sad over Tegan's curled hair and dark lashes and sparkling cheeks that I hardly trust myself to go inside this little houseboat.

I breathe through my nose, determined to calm down. I've already decided that Mom doesn't get any of my emotions today. I decided to leave them all in the parking lot before sunrise. I think of Adam's arms around me, strong and steady; I think of his low voice in my ear. *The way I feel about you . . .*

It gives me a strange sort of courage to remember it. As though everything I'm overwhelmed about is stored somewhere safe for now. I can take it all out and look at it later.

"Sure," I say to Tegan now, relieved about the normal sound of my own voice.

But when I take a step forward, to the small ramp that crosses the water and leads up to that cluttered front porch, Tegan doesn't move.

I turn to look back at her, have another of those heartbreaking moments. I knew her hair would have trouble holding up in this humidity.

"You okay?" I ask her. It sounds as silly as it did when Adam asked me.

"Yeah, I'm good." But her eyes are locked on that porch. "There's two chairs. On the porch."

I briefly look over my shoulder. I guess I didn't really notice, but she's right. Two plastic chairs.

"That doesn't mean anything."

About Lynton, I mean. He's almost certainly dead, and even if he's not, Salem doesn't think he's here. She asked around yesterday.

"It means she probably has a friend. At least one friend. Someone who comes over. Someone she talks to, or whatever."

I shrug. "I guess so."

"That's so shitty, you know? That she like—has *friends*."

Beneath her sparkly blush, there's an added flush to her cheeks now. It's hitting her now, maybe: After all this time, the frustration she's had toward me is finding a new target in Mom. Probably I should revel in it, be glad that we're finally fully on the same page.

But there's really no revelry about this.

"We don't have to go in there. We don't have to have anything to do with this. We've led them right to her, and that can be enough."

She nods. "I know. But I still want to go."

"Okay."

She still doesn't move, though. She keeps her eyes on those two empty chairs.

"I think we should get Adam and Salem."

I blink at her. "What?"

She finally brings her gaze back to mine. "We should go get them. Tell them to come in with us now. It's stupid, that they're sitting in the car waiting for us to call."

I swallow back my instinctive reply: *Absolutely not. That's not part of our deal.*

I know, deep down—in a way I wouldn't have known when we first set off on this trip—that this isn't the moment for me to be big-sister Jess, substitute-parent Jess, boss-of-her Jess. I know I need to listen to her, the way Adam listened to me this morning, when I basically told him the same thing. *I wish you could go in with us.*

So I say, "You'd want them there? When you see her for the first time?"

I'm asking her for real. Curious, not condescending. Not *I know better than you how this whole thing should be handled.*

Her mouth twists as she chews at the inside of her lip. Heartbreaking. God, she's so young.

Then she says, "Why should she get to have us by ourselves, you know? Why should she get that, after all this time?"

I answer her honestly. "I don't know, Teeg."

"They don't have to start their recording at first. But they could be with us. They should be, I think." She takes a breath, seems to get a little taller where she stands. "I think it's what's fair."

I'm not sure what fairness has to do with it. But when I look at Tegan standing there—really look at her, the whole messy, flinty, fragile, figuring-it-out truth of her—I'm pretty sure it doesn't matter.

I'm pretty sure what matters most is that I let her make this choice for herself.

"It's whatever you want, Teeg," I say. "We'll do this however you want."

It's way too small for all four of us on the porch, so when Tegan and I step on board, Adam and Salem stay on the ramp behind us. Both of them are intensely, purposefully silent. Maybe it's out of respect, or maybe it's that they're both still surprised that we asked them to come.

Adam wanted to talk about it—I can feel him back there, *still* wanting to talk about it—but there wasn't time. There *isn't* time. Now that we're up here, in front of this closed front door, I half expect we'll find out that she's not inside anymore. That she saw us standing around, and somehow bolted. I can't really picture her jumping overboard, but then again, before this trip, I couldn't picture her turning into a con woman, either.

"Ready?" I ask Tegan, under my breath.

She nods, and I lift one hand to the door. With the other, I grab hers.

She wraps her fingers around mine and squeezes.

When we hear a creaking noise inside in response to my knock, I think we must take the same deep, bracing inhale.

Then the door opens, and there she is.

Mom.

Like I remember her.

Long hair like mine. A face as familiar as my own. She's older, but then again, so am I.

Every single thing I've ever rehearsed to say to her—the furious rants, the dispassionate censures, even the occasional name-calling—flies right out of my mind.

Mom, is all I can think. *Mom*.

It must be the same for Tegan, who's also saying nothing. And eventually I realize it must be a version of the same for our mother, too. She's looking back and forth between us, but she's not said a single word.

From behind us comes a quiet but insistent throat-clear.

It's paddles placed on my chest. Shocking me back to life.

I cannot let Salem get the first word in.

"Mom," I say, the word more curt in my mouth than it was in my head. "Can we come in?"

For a second, she looks completely lost—her mouth opens and shuts, she blinks rapidly. It's as if I'm watching a movie of myself from two weeks ago, opening the door to Salem and Adam.

When she recovers, she takes a step back from the door. She raises an arm in an ushering gesture and says, "Of course, come in," but she's clearly caught off guard when she notices we're not alone.

Tegan points and says, "That's Adam Hawkins. Jess's boyfriend."

My eyes widen. But what am I going to do, correct her? Briefly, I look toward Adam. His throat bobs in a swallow, but he's definitely not going to say anything. I'm pretty sure he's holding to his own condition, now: Don't speak unless spoken to, not until someone—me or Tegan, probably—says it's okay.

"And this," Tegan continues, pointing again, "is someone who's been looking for you for a while."

"Hello, Charlotte," says Salem, because I don't think she ever waits for someone to tell her what's okay. "I'm Salem Durant."

Mom tips her head to the side the slightest amount. "I always wondered what you looked like in real life. I've seen a few pictures."

"Have you?"

Tegan and I exchange a glance in the silence that follows. The vibe—as she would say—is extremely off.

Not that it was ever really on, I guess.

I take the first step inside, just to break this new layer of tension.

And it's . . . it's sort of sad in here.

Outside the many windows, Mom was right: water is the landscape, and it's surrounding you. On a clear day, I bet it's beautiful. But on a day where it's gray and threatening rain, it only reminds you of how determinedly *inside* you are, stuck in this small, cramped space. Everywhere I look, surfaces are cluttered, covered. Books, newspapers, shipping boxes. On a low, long table beneath the TV, I count five picture frames.

Tegan and I aren't featured in any of them.

Mom and Miles—Lynton—in every single one.

"We can sit here," Mom says, gesturing to a small, square table off the galley kitchen. There are four compact chairs, and Adam's already crossed his arms and leaned against the wall, hunching slightly. He has to, in a space this small.

He watches my mother with wariness. With a sort of warning in his eyes.

Salem pulls out a chair and sits, leaving her bag—recording equipment inside and completely off, if she's following the rules—at her feet, and Tegan follows. For a long second, Mom and I look at each other from opposite sides of the table. She scans over my black jeans and tee, the same way she used to when I was a teenager.

I dare her with my eyes to say something.

She blinks and turns toward where Tegan and Salem sit. "Can I get you some water?" she asks, pleasant and polite.

I can't make myself sit down. I can only think of how strange this is. How I'm standing here, ten feet from my mother while she fills two glasses with tap water, as though this is a normal visit. How strange that you can see someone after all this time, and there're still these passing human niceties to observe. Come in, sit here, have water.

"Lynton is dead," Mom says, I think to Salem, as though she could read my mind about the niceties. As though she decided to cut right through them. "Six years ago now. So. If that's why you came."

Tegan blinks, and I can tell she's a little stunned. Maybe she didn't notice the five picture frames. Maybe she forgot that we've never been Mom's first priority.

Salem says, "We gathered that. We've been—"

"I found your postcards," Tegan blurts. "We went to all the places you sent them from."

Mom sits down, pushes the glasses toward Salem and Tegan. "I wondered if you would," she says. "Someday."

I swallow, grateful that Tegan didn't tell the whole curtain-rod truth. But when Mom flicks her gaze up to me, I have the uncomfortable sense that she can discern a version of it anyway.

My lips press tight together. I don't know why *I* suddenly feel as though I'm in danger of incriminating myself. As though *I* have something to be ashamed of.

"So like," Tegan begins, wetting her own lips before she continues, "how have you been?"

Salem's hands clasp together more tightly where they rest on the table. Mom smiles, not showing teeth. An indulgent smile.

"I've been okay. I work at a local greenhouse nearby, keep busy. The people here are friendly."

What the fuck, is all I can think. *What the fuck, what the fuck.*

I strain to hear Adam's breathing. A life preserver in this watery landscape.

"You look so grown-up, Tegan," Mom says. "You're beautiful."

Tegan flushes anew. I can tell she's concentrating on not touching her hair; she hardly ever wears it down for this long. She says, "I'm going to college next month. I was going to major in biology. But now I'm thinking about journalism."

Don't tell her that, I'm thinking. *Don't tell her anything. Remember what you said, about what she deserves to get from us after all this time.*

There's silence, and I realize it's because Mom has shifted her attention to me. She's looking at me expectantly, as though I might also offer something about my life. My career or whatever other thing she must think is normal to talk about after all this time.

"You can't be serious," I say.

Mom only looks sheepish for a second. "I am happy to see you. I know you won't believe me, but I mi—"

"Don't," I snap.

I can't hear her say it, that she missed me. She used to say it a lot, after she came back the first time. My dad would drop me off with her for a visit and she'd come out to the driveway and open her arms for the split-second, perfunctory hug I'd give her. She'd say, *I missed you, Jessie!* but she must've never really meant it. Not even back then.

Mom's gaze drifts over my shoulder at the same time I feel Adam's warmth at my back. He's not touching me, but I know he's gotten closer all the same.

She looks back at Tegan.

"Of course I understand you're angry at me."

Tegan blinks again, and Salem cocks her head, looking at my mother with a sharp, predatory curiosity that suddenly, to me, seems the only appropriate behavior in the room. Better than Tegan's shock, than my tenuous self-control, better even than Adam's stoic silence.

If anyone would have told me two weeks ago that I'd be almost desperate for Salem to take over a conversation, I wouldn't have believed them. But right now, I want to watch her do her worst. Ask a question about every single month my mother spent away from me and Tegan. Make her really feel how many days it was.

"Six years?" Tegan says.

All of us shift our eyes to her. The flush in her cheeks has faded; the shock in her eyes dimmed. Maybe the journalism major would be a good idea for her, not that I have time to think about that now.

"You said Lynton has been dead for six years?"

"Six years ago next month," Mom says, in a way that suggests she marks the day. Probably she lights candles around her fucking picture frames.

Tegan's brow furrows, and I'm pretty sure mine does, too. I'll admit, ever since Adam talked to Dad's doctor friend, or at the very least since New Mexico, I figured Lynton hadn't lived for long. I figured it even more since no one Salem talked to yesterday remembered ever seeing him around.

"Did you get married?"

Mom shakes her head. "No. Well, not legally."

I don't know what that means. I'm pretty sure there's only the one way to be married. Then again, maybe when you're wanting to marry a guy with multiple identities, it's not—

"So you just lived here with him? On a boat? And then he died?"

Behind me, I feel Adam shift on his feet. I wonder if he's thinking the same thing I am. I wonder if he's thinking about how Tegan's questions—and the lilting, casual cadence she's asked them in—is somehow more incisive, more wholly eviscerating, than any ask we've ever seen Salem present to a source.

Mom swallows. "It's not really that simple. I took care of him. He was ill. Lung cancer." She looks at Salem. "He actually was diagnosed while he was in prison. Stage one, at that time. I know he never mentioned that to you."

Tegan ignores that detail, drawing Mom's attention back to her.

"Right, but I mean. Were you taking care of him twenty-four hours a day? Was he . . . did he not let you call anyone? Was there—"

"Teeg," I say, before I can stop myself, but this time, she doesn't send me a withering glare for interrupting her. She acts as if she hasn't even heard me.

"Was there a reason you never called us?" she finishes.

Mom looks at Tegan, then at me. Then at Salem.

She says, "Are you recording this?"

"No," answers Adam. The first word I ever heard him say.

In response to the very same question.

Mom swallows again, lowers her eyes. Taps one of her fingers against the table.

"I was taking care of him," she says quietly, and for a second, I think she'll stop there. This is all we'll get about her absence, her total silence over the last ten years. All of it to take care of a man she'd only known for a few months. Her own flesh and blood nothing but a memory, not even worth a phone call, let alone a picture frame.

But then she looks up. Not at Tegan this time, but at Salem.

"I was taking care of him," she repeats. "But also, I was working for him."

The Last Con of Lynton Baltimore

Transcript Excerpt from Episode 10, "The Last Con"

::indistinct café noise fades in::

Durant: What time do you have?

Ari Raskin (co-producer, *The Last Con of Lynton Baltimore*): 3:26 p.m.

Durant: Hmm.

Raskin: Should we try the number he gave us again?

Durant: I doubt it's become operational in the last—what did you say, 3:26?

Raskin: 3:27 now.

Durant: I doubt it's become operational in the last nineteen minutes, then.

Raskin: ::clears throat:: Maybe it's time we pack it in.

Durant: No.

::long pause::

Durant: No. We wait.

Chapter 27

Adam

It's not that she's said it.

We knew, after all, since Ashley in Santa Fe. Since Dennis Kirtenour and his nonexistent necklace.

We knew.

But it's the *way* she's said it.

A slyness to it. A sense of pride.

And most important: that she's said it so directly to Salem.

I'm stunned in a way I wouldn't have expected, not after the last two weeks. I've listened to every word Jess has ever said about her mother, and maybe more important, I've watched, too. I've seen every tight line in Jess's brow when Tegan has said something hopeful about this very meeting, every shadow that's passed over her face when she's had even a split second of letting herself wonder how it would go. I knew that Jess's memories of her mother, her anger at her, her doubts about her, were real. Deeply felt and fully justified.

But maybe I'd started to think too much about the Charlotte Caulfield Jess was a little more willing to talk about over the last two days. The woman who wanted someone to fall in love with her, the woman who liked romantic movies. The woman who dreamed of living on a nice houseboat someday.

If that woman still exists, I don't see her here.

I see a woman staring across the table as though her two kids who she hasn't seen in ten years aren't in the room at all.

A woman who has the look of having spotted a rival.

I don't know when I moved closer to Jess. But I'm nearly beside her now, close enough that her shoulder blade grazes one side of my chest as she breathes. I look down at her, and she must sense it, turning and lifting her head to meet my gaze. I don't dare say a word, but I try to tell her with my eyes that I'll get her out of here now, if she wants me to.

She shakes her head once, almost imperceptibly.

Wait, she's saying.

So I do. Still, I move a little closer.

At the table, Tegan is looking between Salem and Charlotte, and I'm pretty sure every internal gear she has is turning. After a few seconds, she makes a move—small but telling. She turns slightly in her chair. Away from Charlotte, and toward Salem. It's permission, or an invitation.

She's saying with her body that it's Salem's conversation for now.

"We did gather that," Salem says, hardly missing a beat. "We met Dennis Kirtenour recently."

"What an interesting man," Charlotte says, then shrugs. "I mean, his ideas about treating cancer patients leave something to be desired, don't you think?"

Salem purses her lips. Annoyed to be asked a question by this woman.

"Is that why Baltimore marked him?"

Charlotte doesn't respond. She only smiles, and I immediately, instinctively hate it. I think it must be the worst smile I've ever seen in my life, and it only takes me a few seconds to figure out why.

It's because it reminds me of Curtis MacSherry's smile. But this time, that Cheshire-cat expression is on lips that look so similar to those of the woman who's standing next to me. The woman whose real smiles—small and honest and cautious smiles—I've worked so hard for.

I set my hand low on Jess's back. I do it slow, so no one can see me move.

"Maybe you'll tell me he had some kind of Robin Hood phase at the end of his life," Salem says. "Steal from the rich. Give to the . . . ?" She trails off, prompting.

But Charlotte still doesn't answer. One thing's for sure: If Lynton Baltimore were still alive and getting into trouble, he could count on this woman never betraying him.

"We know, for example, that you and Baltimore took some time to provide funds for his son."

Charlotte's placid smile transforms into something more earnest, her eyes lighting.

"Oh! Did you see my portrait?"

Salem blinks. "We did."

Suddenly, Charlotte shifts her attention our way. She looks right at Jess, as though she expects her to react with delighted commiseration. *Wow, yes, I saw that portrait; it looked exactly like me.*

Jess only stiffens—I can feel it low in her back—and stays determinedly silent.

For a few seconds, the two hold each other's gaze, and I can tell, Charlotte expects Jess to break. To respond in some way.

I feel a strange sense of pride swell in my chest.

I've always known Jess is a vault when she wants to be. When she needs to be. Now, her mother is getting to watch as she fully locks down.

No one deserves it more.

Finally, Charlotte looks away. Back to Salem, who tries a different a different tactic.

"I assumed your efforts with Mr. Kirtenour set you up here.

My understanding is that he paid quite a lot of money for that necklace you said you had. I assumed Lynton retired."

"I thought you knew him better than that, Salem. Is it okay if I call you Salem?"

Salem clears her throat. "Sure," she says flatly.

It's the same tone of voice I once heard her use on Cody, one of the associate producers at Broadside, when he argued that it was "bored housewives" who were responsible for the popularity of true crime in media.

"He talked about you a lot, you know," Charlotte says. "I do think he felt very remorseful. About never showing up for your interview."

Salem's lips roll inward, and even though the majority of my attention is focused on the woman standing next to me—on the subtle rise and fall of her body as she takes careful, controlled breaths in and out—I can still see that there's something unexpectedly tense between Salem and Charlotte. I can see that Salem seems to be a bigger part of this story than I ever thought.

"Well," Salem says curtly, "the show did fine without his participation."

"Oh, I know! We listened."

It hangs so long in the air that Tegan has time to lift her glass to her mouth and take a drink. To set it down and look between the two women on either side of her. I know Salem wants to ask. She wants to know what Lynton Baltimore thought of her story.

But I guess she too knows when to lock something away.

"So he didn't retire then," Salem finally says.

Charlotte shrugs again. "We adapted. We settled here, sure. But then I . . . did some traveling, at times."

"You did jobs for him. Away from here."

Charlotte isn't going to answer that, not directly.

"Well, he was more recognizable by then, thanks to you! And obviously, with him being ill—he got worse, as time went on, of course—staying here at home was better for him. But, you know, with technology—"

Tegan explodes from her chair. So sudden and so fierce that her half-full glass tips over, water splashing Salem's hands and dripping onto the floor.

"Are you *fucking* kidding me?" she yells. She *yells*. Full-throated with her fists clenched. Jess startles and steps toward her sister. I have to stop myself from gripping the back of her shirt and keeping her close to me.

"With *technology* you called him, Mom? You FaceTimed him, maybe? Checked in with him on how to *steal things* from people?"

"I never said I—" Charlotte begins.

"Gave him updates on what you made off with, when the job was done? You really *stayed in touch*, huh? While you were doing your *traveling*?"

"Tegan," Salem says, her voice quiet and cautious.

Jess is ghost white. I've followed her, taken the steps that bring me close to her again, but I don't think she notices. I don't think she's noticing much of anything right now.

"You are *disgusting*," says Tegan. "A disgusting person. You haven't seen us in ten years, Mom. You *left* us, and this is what you have to say for yourself? You want to sit here in your stupid *boat* and talk to a journalist about how you became some man's stand-in?"

I should be looking at what Charlotte is doing, should be cataloguing her reaction to this richly deserved onslaught. But all I can see is Jess. Her pale face and the fear written all over it.

All this time, I thought it was losing her privacy—Tegan's privacy—that scared her most. All this time I thought it was wanting to keep this story a guarded secret from the world. But I can see now, it's this—this is the fear that was lying beneath it all, always. The fear of watching her sister have her heart smashed to pieces right in front of her eyes, and she can't do anything to stop it.

Jess moves again, touching Tegan's arm. But Tegan shakes her off, a reflex more than a rejection.

"No!" she screams, and her voice cracks. I imagine me and Jess and Salem and Tegan as those compass points I first pictured on Jess's porch. When Tegan's voice cracks that way, I'm pretty sure the thin dome of glass that's been covering all of us cracks too.

I'm pretty sure we'll never find our way again.

"No," she repeats, quieter now. "I've heard everything I need to hear."

She turns to Jess, and her chin trembles slightly before she firms it.

"You were right," she says. "You were right this whole time, and I didn't *listen*."

Jess looks as if she might be sick.

"It's okay, Teeg. It's fine; it's—"

"You never forgave me for leaving with Brent, I know that," Charlotte says to Jess. "But with Lynton, it was a different situation. It—"

"You don't speak to her," I say, before I can stop myself, before I can remind myself that I promised I wouldn't interfere. My voice sounds unfamiliar to my own ears. Like I'm talking through the cracked glass of the broken compass that's been shoved down my throat. "You don't speak to her, ever."

If Jess is watching me, reacting to me, I don't know it. I'm staring down at Charlotte Caulfield and it probably looks as if I'm one word from putting a strip of duct tape over her mouth. But I'm not trying to intimidate her, watching her this way. I'm just memorizing every part of her face that's different from Jess's. I'm making it so I never have to connect the two of them in my mind ever again.

"I want to go," Tegan says, her voice thick. "We'll get a ride share. Let's *go*, Jess."

It's this that gets me to blink away from Charlotte, and I move toward Jess and Tegan again. I'm not letting them take a fucking ride share out of here, I'm not.

But Tegan holds up a hand, halting me. She looks between me and Salem, who's still sitting at the table, wet hands clasped, struck dumb or possibly thrilled to pieces about this dramatic turn of events.

"Every condition you have with us—you can forget about those now," Tegan says. "You two can stay and talk to her if you want, ask her all your questions for the story. But we're going."

I don't know how to describe it, what happens to the air in the room. It's not so quick as being sucked away. It's a slow leak. The oxygen getting thinner and thinner. Tegan doesn't realize it, but she's revealed something new to her mother.

Charlotte's gaze sharpens as she looks first at Jess, and then at me. "I thought you were her boyfriend."

Dread gathers in my gut—an indistinct warning. I don't know exactly what's coming from this, but I know it's going to be bad.

"He works for me," Salem says, probably thinking she's coming to the rescue. "Well, I suppose that might mean something different to you, given our conversation, so I'll clarify. He is also a journalist."

Charlotte tips her head back up to Jess. I guess she's forgotten my warning.

"Your boyfriend is doing a story on me?"

"That isn't—" I begin, but Jess snaps out, at the same time, "He's not my boyfriend."

I'll admit, it stings. But it's a wincing, insignificant thing, because I know what she's doing. I know she's trying to protect herself, and maybe me, too. The problem is, it's so clearly a lie. Her neck splotches pink, and I see Charlotte notice it.

The dread gains a new urgency in my middle.

I must make a noise. A grunt, a growl, I don't know. Whatever it is, Charlotte rethinks directly addressing Jess. She looks at Salem instead.

"Did he talk her into finding me? Into coming all this way?"

she asks. "Did he talk her into being part of some story about her famously disappearing mother?"

"No," I grind out, but I don't know if it's even audible. It's almost impossible to speak past that looming, dreadful feeling now.

Charlotte looks back at me. "Did you meet her before or after you knew she might have something to do with the Lynton Baltimore story?"

Salem says, "Look, this is not—"

"Don't say anything else," Jess interrupts. "Don't say anything else to her about me. She gets *nothing* else."

"You know, I always thought Jessie was the most like me," Charlotte says to Salem, as though Jess hasn't even uttered a word, as though she's on an entirely solo interview now. "Not just in looks! But she has a heart like mine. I could always recognize it in her. I always knew that when she fell for someone, she'd be like me about it. She'd do just about anything."

It doesn't matter that I know, deep down, that this isn't how it happened with me and Jess, or with this story. It doesn't matter because I know what the dread in my gut was about now—I can see it on Jess's face. It's not simply pale anymore; it's practically ghost white.

What her mother has said to her—in this cramped, mildewy boat, in the middle of all this mess and shock and her sister's furious sadness—there's a part of her that believes it.

I know what's happening here. I know what comes next.

"I don't ever want to hear from you again," Jess says to her mother.

But somehow, it sounds as though she's saying it to me. To Salem, too, but I can't get myself to care about that. Everything from early this morning comes back to me in a rush: the way she kissed me and clung to me before she whispered her wish. This is what she wanted, me in here with her from the very beginning, and I haven't managed to protect her at all. All I've managed in this room is to become a man her mother could use against her. A man her mother used to blame her for how this has all turned out.

I got her to do the interview. I asked the questions. I got her to connect her mom to this place, and I got her and her sister here.

"No postcards," she adds. "I'll burn them if they come, do you understand me? No phone calls. *Nothing.*"

"It's the same for me," says Tegan. She's holding on to Jess's hand, white-knuckled. "This is done."

They start to move toward the door, and of course—of course, I follow.

I have to get Jess to see the truth of this. Of *us*.

"Hawk," Salem says, and maybe I would've ignored her, except that Jess stills where she stands. As though hearing this stupid, awful nickname is an added blow, an added reminder.

"I'm going, Salem. I need to take them—"

Jess turns to look at me. She speaks quietly, but firmly. "Stay," she says. "Do your job."

This is my job, I think. *My job is being with you.*

I know as I think it that it doesn't make sense. Jess isn't a job to me in any kind of way, but I guess that's the problem. That's always been the problem, from the second I first saw her. From the second I fell in love with her.

She stares up at me, her eyes wild and desperate, and begs me—in a broken, private whisper that I'm sure I'll never forget the sound of—to let her go.

"Please, Adam," she says. "Please, just leave us alone for now."

Chapter 28

Jess

My heart is a clock.

It's been counting time since we walked out of Mom's front door. Seven minutes from when we stepped off the ramp to when our ride share arrived. In the car, it's seventeen minutes to the hotel, time enough for me to check and see that it's six hours, forty-three minutes until we can get on a flight in Seattle, and I'll need to build in the forty-nine minutes it'll take for another ride share to the airport.

Once the car drops us off at the hotel, it's under two minutes—cross the parking lot I walked through with Adam only this morning, hustle through the lobby where I put on his big sweatshirt, ride up the elevator that goes well past the floor I know his room is on—to the door of the one I've been sharing with Tegan.

Inside, it's twenty-four minutes that I sit on the bathroom floor with her while she gets sick twice, tears streaming down her face as I hold her hair and set a cool washcloth to the back of her neck, murmuring to her that she'll be okay, that this part will pass soon.

Afterward, when she's calm enough, when she's had water and when the trembling in her fingers has stopped, she takes a shower for nine minutes while I come right up against the credit limit on one of my cards to buy the tickets for the flight I found. She comes out in a cloud of steam, wrapped in a white towel with her hair wet and tangled, the mascara she put on so carefully this morning still a little smudgy beneath her eyes, and it only takes me six minutes to help her pack up most of her things, setting out a pair of leggings and an oversized long-sleeve shirt for her to put on.

Eleven minutes to comb out her hair, to put it in a thick French braid, while she sits on the bed numbly.

It's still two hours, ten minutes until we should comfortably leave for the airport, probably enough time to watch a movie, but she doesn't want to, same as how she doesn't want to talk yet. She wants to curl on her side and look out the window that shows a view of nothing special, so I lie down with her, and it's a full thirty-one minutes until she falls asleep.

When she does, I don't need to look at my phone to know how long it's been since we left Mom's.

Since I left Adam.

I feel every second.

I'm going to feel it for so long.

I tap lightly, silently, at the back of my phone. *Tick, tick, tick.* I tell myself I've kept it close in case there's some update about our flights, but really, I'm waiting. Either for him, or for me.

I won't just disappear.

I *won't.*

I could never do that to someone.

But I was right to walk away from him when I did. I had to walk away, for Tegan.

I close my eyes, feel a trembling, crumbling warning inside me—an avalanche I'm barely managing to keep at bay. If I let myself think about anything that happened on that houseboat, anything my mother said to Tegan, or to me, the whole thing will come crashing down. If I let myself picture the look in Adam's eyes when I told him to leave us alone, I'll get buried. I'll suffocate.

I set the phone down. I think fleetingly about bumping into Tegan and pretending it's an accident, because at least when she's awake my heart keeps time for someone else.

But of course, I'd never do that, either.

Especially not right now. Not after I've already failed her once today.

Not just today, a little wind whispers inside me, and everything rattles. Long enough for the thoughts to slide forward dangerously.

You should never have done the interview

You should never have looked at the postcards again

You should never have listened to Adam, when he told you to remember

You should never have let him and Salem see what they saw today

My stomach turns over and I have to sit up, scoot gently to the end of the bed and set my feet on the floor. If I get sick, too, Tegan will hear. I breathe carefully through my nose, out through my mouth. Wait for it to pass.

Wish for Adam's hand on my back. He did that first in Florida, I remember. When we saw—

Did you see my portrait? she'd said. As if we'd only been out on a pleasant sightseeing tour of her life after she left us.

I stand from the bed, desperate to steady myself, to plant my feet. Still, I look back over my shoulder to make sure Tegan's stayed asleep. Her eyelashes twitch slightly against the smudged-mascara skin beneath her eyes. She looks so young when she sleeps.

She looks like the kid I started taking care of ten years ago.

I reach forward, deftly swipe my phone from where I set it down. I'll text Adam. Tell him we're leaving. I'll tell him that when I get home, I'll want to talk about the voice actors thing he mentioned way back when I met him at my dad's house.

Another sliding thought: *When you set all the conditions that you didn't keep to.*

My fingers tremble as I navigate to the text box I have with him. See his message from this morning, and my reply: **Two minutes.** Maybe my heart was keeping time even then, maybe a part of me knew. I think of his big, warm arms around me, his quiet words in my ear, how I knew then that I'd fallen in love with him.

I think of how I begged him for one more minute.

I think of my mother saying I've always been the most like her.

You'll get buried, Jess, I tell myself firmly, sharply. *You'll get buried under this, and you'll disappear.*

I start to tap out a message: the time our flight leaves. That's all I can manage at first, even though I know it won't make sense to him. My fingers hover over the keypad, my brain still so sluggish and confused and shocked.

Tick, tick, tick, I think my heart is counting out, but then I realize it's not that at all.

It's three soft taps on the door, and I close my eyes, knowing already it's Adam.

THERE'S a distorted symmetry about it, the two of us standing here.

In a way, we met this way: on the threshold of a space I'm trying to keep him out of.

"Tegan just fell asleep," I say quietly, by way of explanation for how I barely opened the door a crack, sliding my body out into the hall sideways before guiding the latch on the handle closed so it would only make the barest snick when it shut behind me.

I've kept myself close to it. My back against the wall beside the door.

Across the narrow hallway, Adam looks less giant-sized than he did to me that first time. Part of it, I guess, is the way he's standing—his back against the wall, too, his feet planted a foot or two away from it, costing him a few inches of height. Another part, probably, is that he doesn't have his comparatively tiny, extremely tenacious boss standing beside him.

The worst part—the very worst part—is that even the tallest, broadest, strongest man you've ever seen will seem different to you once you've had your arms around him, once you've known him up close. Once you've seen how his heart works, and heard it beat against your ear while he held you.

He swallows. "Is she okay?"

"Not really."

He tips his chin down in acknowledgment, and the silence between us stretches. I can hear the muted sound of a television coming from one of the rooms, and the Jess of two weeks ago would definitely have the energy, the focus, to say that we need to go somewhere where we can be certain no one will hear us.

I'm not that Jess right now.

"I was going to text you," I say, at the same time Adam says, "I know you asked me to leave you alone."

Neither of us, obviously, smiles at the awkward overlap. Neither of us even bothers following up. I was going to text him; he knows he's not leaving me alone like I asked. It doesn't really matter now, because we're both out here in the hall, and I have a feeling we both know nothing good is going to come of it.

"I didn't stay," he says.

"What?"

"I didn't stay with Salem. I helped her set up some things for recording, and then I came here."

"Adam," I say on an exhale, shaking my head. "I told you to stay."

"I didn't *want* to stay." His voice reveals the first flash of temper. "If you think I wanted to stay even another second in a room with a woman who—"

"Please don't." I press a hand to my brow, hearing the sharpness in my own voice. But I cannot hear him talk about her. I cannot think about what he heard.

I always knew that when she fell for someone

"I got us a flight home," I blurt. "Tegan and me. We'll head to the airport soon."

His jaw firms. He's so frustrated.

I can't face that, so I change the subject again.

"Is she still there? Salem, I mean?"

"I don't know."

He sounds as if he has never cared about anything less.

"I assume someone will contact me. To tell me what the plan is for the story. Later, maybe we—or Salem and me, or whoever—can talk about the voice act—"

"Jess."

I look down toward my feet. I think I'll throw these shoes away when I get home. I can't see myself wearing them at work ever again.

"Is this it for us?"

I am terrifyingly close to tears at the plainness of his question. The artlessness of it. It's nothing like the questions someone gets asked in an interview.

I don't say a word.

I hear him take a breath. A sharp inhale. His own feet—the same boots he almost always wears, because there's not many shoes that fit him comfortably, a thing I know about him now—step into my line of vision, and I close my eyes, willing the wetness behind my lids to reabsorb.

"I will stop this, if that's what you want."

At first, I assume what he means is that he'll stop *this*—he'll stop coming for me, stop sticking close to me, stop trying with me.

It's what I should want; it's what would make this next, necessary part easier. But something inside me still howls in wounded protest.

But then he adds, "I will find a way to stop this from ever getting to air. The entire trip. Everything Tegan told us even before it started. I will find a way."

My eyes snap up to his, the howl inside me transforming into something more protective. My mind isn't so overrun that I can't remember what this means for him. What he stands to lose.

"No," I say, so forcefully that he blinks in surprise. "You cannot do that."

"I can. I'll find a—"

"Adam, no. Listen to yourself. You cannot burn down your job and your relationship with Salem. Your reputation with everyone in this profession. You cannot do that to yourself again."

The wince at this reminder of his past is infinitesimal. Barely a twitch. But I see it. It's easier this way, I realize—my thoughts clearer, every catalyst for that avalanche of feeling currently muted. I remind Adam to go back to work, remind him what's at stake for him. I get Tegan on the plane. I go home. I deal with everything else later.

"It isn't the same," he says.

"No, it's not the same, you're right. It's bigger. You need to finish this, whatever it is, with Salem. You need to keep on the right side of things with her and your job in general, because you have a huge opportunity. You need the chance to say all the things about Cope that you didn't get to say before. It's *important*, Adam. You know it's important."

His jaw works, tightening again. I get the feeling he's fighting an avalanche of his own.

"This whole thing, Adam—this is a means to an end for you. You can't—"

"Stop. Stop this *shit*, Jess. You're not a means to an end; you haven't ever been that to me."

He takes a step closer, close enough that I can smell him— mint and soap and the outside.

Why didn't you keep his sweatshirt? my fugitive brain whirs.

"Tell me you don't remember this morning. My hotel room in Missouri. Tell me you don't remember that field at night.

The trampoline. Tell me you don't remember every time you sat next to me in that van; tell me you don't remember how it's always felt between you and me."

He's lowered his voice now; he keeps these secrets for me. He knows it's what I'd want, were I in my right mind.

But I'm not. I'm not. I'm twenty-one years old again and I've just watched the fabric of my little sister's life get torn in half by our mother, and I cannot let myself forget it.

Not again. Not even for a second, no matter who shows up at my door.

"We are more than this," he says. "You know we are. You have to know, after all this—"

"I have to *go*, after all this."

Surely, someone in one of these rooms has heard me. I hope Tegan didn't, but either way, time is running out.

Ride share, airport, home. *Tick, tick, tick.*

Adam looks as though I've punched him in the solar plexus, but he only lets it stop him for a second. He's so fucking big. He's so fucking *strong.*

He swallows and straightens.

"This didn't just happen to Tegan."

His voice is gentle but determined, his eyes on me so *knowing.* Every thought I'm trying to keep at bay—every terrible thing I heard my mother say today, every fear I harbor about the truth of her words—he can see them. I know he can. I've *let* him know all these things, because I let him know me, and I am *terrified.*

You'll disappear into him. You'll turn out exactly like her.

"I'll come back with you," Adam is saying, but his voice is distant to me now, muted by the rumble that's gaining strength.

It'll be him that sets it off, if I let him. If I don't find some way to stop him before I get buried.

"I can help," he's saying, and that's when I know.

That's when I know how to stop him, even as I know how bad I'm about to hurt him. Even as I know I'm telling him another half-truth, the one that gets me out of this faster.

Huge Adam Hawkins, hardworking Adam Hawkins. Heart-of-gold Adam Hawkins.

I'd do anything for him.

So that's why I do this.

"You can't, Adam."

I make sure I make my voice firm. I make sure I sound like the Jess he met two weeks ago. Not the Jess from this morning, from his hotel room in Missouri. Not the Jess from the field or the trampoline. Not even the Jess that sat silently beside him early on.

"You can't help, because you're the one who brought this to my door."

Chapter 29

Charlotte Caulfield: Well. It's just us girls now, isn't it?

Durant: That's a strange thing to say.

C. Caulfield: Is it?

Durant: Yes. You understand that I'm here to interview you, right? That we're not friends.

C. Caulfield: Oh, I definitely understand that. But we have something in common, of course.

Durant: We do?

C. Caulfield: I don't think we need to do that, Salem. Lynton and I were very close, as I've told you. We were truly in love, you know? He was always honest with me about you.

::long pause::

Durant: I don't know what you mean by that. I don't know why you'd think he was honest about anything.

C. Caulfield: So you didn't have . . . a bit of an attachment to him?

Durant: I—

C. Caulfield: He had one to you; he always said so. He said you were the smartest woman he ever met. He said he barely had to explain a thing to you about his work. He missed you, when things ended.

Durant: By things, you mean the podcast?

C. Caulfield: Is that what you mean?

Durant: Charlotte, I don't really know what you're getting at. I want to talk to you about—

C. Caulfield: He was serious, you know. When he asked you to come with him. *That* conversation never made it into your show, of course! He planned to tell you about his diagnosis and everything, once he was released. It could've been you, sitting here! Not that you would've chosen a houseboat. But Lynton—he was a changeable spirit. He decided on another path.

::long pause::

Durant: Again, I don't know what you mean. I was married with a young child when I did the Baltimore story. Whatever he told you—

C. Caulfield: Suit yourself. I won't press the point. Do you want more water?

Durant: No. Thank you.

C. Caulfield: No one ever really saw me as smart. Even Lynton, he didn't think I was all that smart, not at first.

Durant: You seem very smart to me. I think you must be, to have been able to do what you did with Dennis Kirtenour.

C. Caulfield: ::scoffs:: Well.

Durant: You must take comfort, in some way . . . in feeling special to Lynton. To someone with his reputation, particularly with women. It must feel good, to be the only one.

C. Caulfield: The only one what?

Durant: The only woman he treated as a true equal. He never conned you out of anything.

C. Caulfield: Didn't he?

::long pause::

Durant: If you mean time with your daughters—well, from what I saw here today, it doesn't seem to bother you that you've been away from them all this time.

C. Caulfield: ::short, sardonic laugh:: If there's one thing I learned from Lynton, it's how to *seem*.

Durant: I beg your pardon?

C. Caulfield: But at the same time, he didn't really teach me that. I think I had a knack for it, in a way. I've always been good at seeming all sorts of ways. Maybe that's why he picked me, you know?

Durant: You're saying that what you just did to those girls—

C. Caulfield: Oh, it's "girls" now, is it? You almost sound like you really care about them.

Durant: You're saying that was all some kind of con?

C. Caulfield: I'm saying . . . I'm saying I know who I am. I know what I've done. And I know my daughters are a lot better off without me.

::recording stops::

Chapter 30

Adam

"There's no way to do it in a podcast space."

"I disagree. I think if we situate—"

In the second floor conference room of the Broadside office in Boston, my colleague Madhura—a senior producer with probably fifteen years of experience—cuts off my other colleague Cody—who only got hired six months before me—with a noise of strangled frustration.

"There's no way to *situate* it," she says. "You need *video* to make it work. Pictures, at the very least."

"It'll drive traffic to the website," Cody tries.

"Do you want to listen to a forty-minute podcast where someone's telling you every two and a half minutes to check the *website* for the big reveal? There's a reason HGTV exists! People don't want interior design in their *earholes*."

"We could use chapter art," someone volleys back, and Madhura—who is really mad, if she said *earholes* in a meeting—groans quietly.

"Chapter art is an idea," Cody says, absolutely clueless, and scribbles a note on his tablet.

Everyone around the table squirms in discomfort.

Everyone except me, that is.

It's Tuesday afternoon, and Tuesdays at Broadside are "trend report" meetings. They used to be in the mornings, which everyone knows is better for meetings, but our CCO, Emma— that's chief creative officer, a title Salem hates—likes "Tuesdays at Two." We get email reminders on Mondays with a stylized *T* in the body. Salem also hates those emails.

"Why don't we take a step back, hmm? What else is still working?" says Emma, in her typically soothing voice.

She's into "calm conflict," which probably she learned about on a podcast, and in general, I admire it. When Emma talks, everyone who was squirming only a second ago settles.

I stay the same.

I don't feel much of anything.

Not about trend reports, at least.

"True crime," someone says. "True crime is always working."

"There's been backlash lately—" Cody says. He's fine, I guess, but he's the kind of guy who wears a THE FUTURE IS FEMALE T-shirt while also making Madhura repeat the same points about videos and images every time he wants to talk about interior design podcasts again.

"Backlash or not," someone else chimes in. "Numbers stay good."

I want out of here. It's hot and this chair is small and I don't remember if I ate anything this morning. Or last night.

"Hawk?" Emma says. Calmly.

I look up at her. Judging by the set of her eyebrows she's said it at least more than once.

"Sorry. What was that?"

"Madhura was asking you a question."

Oh, great. I should go buy a SMASH THE PATRIARCHY keychain

on my way home tonight. Not that I'll go home after work, since I hate being there almost as much as I hate being here.

I give Madhura an apologetic smile that feels strange on my face. "I'm sorry. I'm a little distracted today."

Every day.

"It's fine," she says, waving a hand.

She thinks it's garden variety distraction, typical Tuesday at Two distraction. As far as I can tell, no one notices anything is wrong with me, which I guess is the benefit of not having worked here all that long. If I've got tells, they haven't figured out what they are yet.

"I was asking whether you'd been in touch with Salem about the Baltimore story?"

I swallow, press my thumb into my knee under the table. She's not the first person to ask me, but it's not getting any easier to answer.

"She should be back in a couple days. She's been a little off-grid."

"Of course," says Emma. "We know she's got so much on her plate with Pen's injuries."

I nod blandly, tuning out again. She does have a lot on her plate, with Pen's injuries.

But that's not why she's not back at the office.

That's not why she's taken the ten days since we got back from Olympia off.

I know it's not.

I can't say I was particularly observant, that day we left Washington. I can't say I even asked Salem how the rest of her interview went. I can't say I did much of anything but go through the motions, replaying every single part of that last conversation with Jess.

I can't say I could hear any words but the same ones I hear pretty much all day, every day since I last saw her.

You're the one who brought this to my door.

But distantly I'd realized Salem was almost as subdued as I was, her face drawn, her frenetic energy of the previous few days nonexistent. In the airport, while we waited for our flight—while I tried not to think about where Jess was right that very second—she'd excused herself and stood partially concealed behind a concrete pillar and spoken quietly into her phone.

For almost an hour.

When she came back, she said she was going to have to take some time off. That we'd work on the rest of the story when she was back.

She knew I wouldn't press her about it. I was in no shape to press anyone about anything. And anyway, we didn't even have seats together on the plane. I barely even saw her when we finally landed back at Logan, and the truth is, I felt strangely abandoned. Who else could I talk to about what happened, after all?

No one, that's who. Salem's the only other witness to what happened on that houseboat, the only other person who knows what led up to it, and I know it'd feel like a betrayal of Jess to tell anyone else. Three nights ago I looked up teletherapy services—just to get some of this *weight* off my chest—but then I realized I probably couldn't even bring myself to tell a professional.

It's too private.

"Pitches tomorrow," says Emma, wrapping up the meeting, which means I missed the last round of trends. She gives everyone one of her meaningful looks, which is her way of calmly telling everyone to get to fucking work on finding something that'll hit one of the trends we just finished talking about. "Looking forward to that!"

I stand from my chair, joints popping. I move slowly out the conference room door, dreading the next couple of hours of work at my desk. Back at my cube, my laptop has a folder named "Cope" with ten documents inside. One half-done pitch for every day I've been back. Not a single one is worth a damn.

You have a huge opportunity, I remember Jess saying. *You know it's important.*

It's an awful feeling, not to be able to work on it. Every time I try and fail—my head too full of Jess to focus—I get angry at myself. This *is* a huge opportunity, one that I've been working toward for years now. This is a tribute to my best friend; this is something that could help people. Two weeks with a woman who doesn't even want me with her, a woman who is always going to see me only as the man who turned the life she worked so hard for upside down, and I'm going to throw it all away?

Then, usually, I get a little angry at her, too.

Though that never feels right for long.

I'm not really mad at her. I miss her. I fucking love her. I never even got to say it.

I pass colleagues tapping away at sleek laptops, earbuds in, expressions of deep concentration on their faces. Maybe I should have taken some days off, too. I could've gone back to the farm, hid out with Beth and Mace and the girls. I could've avoided my dad's *told you so* looks, but then again, I guess I couldn't have avoided the fact that the farm is where everything changed for me and Jess; the farm is where I first—

I stop at the entry to my cube, see the familiar mop of gray-brown curls. She's sitting in my desk chair, legs crossed, hands clasped. Like she would've waited all day.

She looks me over and wrinkles her nose once, as though she's smelled something bad, which seems pretty unfair. I may not remember when I ate last, but I know for sure I showered this morning.

Still, when she finally speaks, it's a relief to hear her voice again.

"Hawk, I'm back. And you, unfortunately, look like absolute shit."

SALEM and I don't have to discuss the fact that we're not going to talk inside the office. Basically, I see her sitting there, I shove my shit in my bag, and we walk together out of the office and into the hot summer air. We go three blocks, past all the closest coffee shops our coworkers frequent, and settle on a café where Salem orders a full meal and stares at me in judgment when I say I'm not hungry.

Two weeks on a road trip will make you incredibly skilled at nonverbal communication with someone, I guess.

We're sitting close together at a cramped sidewalk table, which is probably a so-I-can-see-every-microexpression-on-his-face strategy on Salem's part. In contrast to me, she looks good: rested and polished, and her energy seems pretty much back to normal. She's lost the subdued mien from the airport, and definitely hasn't returned to the cutting, impatient intensity she showed up with in New Mexico.

She's pretty close to the Salem I started with. Maybe she's even a little more relaxed.

"Pen's doing good?" I ask, trying to get ahead of her.

She can see that, obviously. But she doesn't call me on it.

"Very good. Pat and I took her to Rhode Island, got a seaside cottage for a few days. I don't know if I mentioned."

I hope my face looks like that emoji with a straight line for a mouth. She knows she didn't mention. Also, she's been at a seaside cottage while I've been here in this hot, weird city that I still don't really understand unless I'm constantly looking at a map on my phone, licking my wounds and not getting any work done.

"I'm sure that was good for her," I say blandly.

"I can tell you're upset with me."

"I'm not."

"You have a terrible poker face."

"That's not the worst thing anyone's ever said about me."

You're the one who brought this to my door.

That's maybe the worst thing. At least that I can remember right now.

She sighs. Fidgets with her glasses, and then the napkin roll the server just brought over.

Finally, she looks back up at me and says—a little mechanically, as though she's been practicing it:

"I was not honest with you about my interest in the Lynton Baltimore story."

I don't say anything.

But in those distant parts of my mind, I'm prodded by the questions I know there are to ask of Salem. What happened after she went home during our trip, why she was so intense when she got back, what the hell was happening between her and Charlotte Caulfield on that houseboat?

If I'm honest, her jetting off to a seaside cottage in Rhode Island isn't the only reason I haven't asked her about it. I could've called her, emailed her. Texted her until she replied.

But I haven't done any of that, because I haven't wanted to think at all about Lynton Fucking Baltimore, and what he brought to *my* door.

And I'm pretty sure that's not fair to Salem, or to the job I've committed to doing.

"Do you want to be honest now?" I ask her, finally.

She rolls her lips inward. Steels herself.

She says, "It isn't that I was in love with him. Not really."

I lean back in my chair.

And then, Salem tells me.

That it wasn't that she was in love with him, but the thing was—she thought, for a while, that she might be. That she started the Baltimore story when she had a toddler at home, when she was miserable every day with the mundanity of childcare. She resented Patrick and the freedom he had to keep living his life when she was home. She was breastfeeding for months, and struggled with postpartum depression. She expected it to ease once Pen became less of a screaming, spitting-up blob and more like her friends' adorable toddlers, who had inspired Salem to have a kid in the first place, but the truth of it was, she didn't much enjoy the toddler stage of parenting, either. Her fights with Patrick about childcare were endless, and he resented her eventual decision to commit more time to her work.

The Baltimore story was a lifeline, a way back into the career that made her feel most like herself. A chance to reclaim that version of Salem, the one she felt she'd lost when she became a mother.

"He confused me," she says, and by the time she gets to this part, her food has arrived and she hasn't touched a bite. She has managed to fold and refold her napkin about twenty-five different ways. At first, I think she's looking at me, but then I realize she's not. She's looking slightly over my right ear.

"I knew his history of becoming someone else, the exact right person for whatever woman he was targeting. But when you talk to Lynton—when I talked to him, I started to think I was an exception, somehow. He . . . well, I suppose the person he became for me, at the time, was a person who respected me in my profession. Who had no interest in my life as a wife or mother. He became a person who seemed hugely impressed by my brain."

"He probably was," I tell her. "You've got a great brain."

"Nice try, Hawk," she snorts, deadpan. "You're not as charming as he was."

"I only meant—"

She waves me off, obviously embarrassed. Not so much by the compliment, I don't think, but by this entire situation. This confession. By how it fits into the whole puzzle of the Baltimore story, and of her behavior during our trip.

I think of what she told me in that rooftop bar in New Mexico. *Trust someone who's been there. If anyone gets hurt by this, it'll be you.*

"Were you trying to find him because you were hoping to . . . ?" I trail off, clear my throat. I don't think I'm a good enough journalist to ask this question. Or maybe I'm not a bad enough friend, and the thing is, I kind of think Salem and I are friends now.

But Salem's shrewd enough to know where I was headed.

"No, no," she says. "Once he didn't show for the interview, I—after a few weeks had passed, at least, I could see it more clearly. I was waking up from a spell, in a way. It's always been difficult to convince Patrick of that—obviously, he wasn't happy when I told him we had this new lead on Baltimore. We worked hard to keep our marriage together after it was over the first time, you know? We worked hard for Pen, and for each other."

She sighs, looks off into the distance for a second, gathering herself.

"But the truth is, Patrick has a point, even if he misunderstood my motivation for going back to this story. I'm over whatever feelings I had for Baltimore back then. But I've never gotten over it, really, that I let myself have them in the first place. I've never gotten over that I even for a second considered going with . . . well, never mind. I can tell you about that another time."

"What's wrong with right now?"

She folds her napkin again. Clears her throat. Waits.

"You want to talk for the story," I say, finally catching on.

She shrugs. "I am the last con, right?"

I stare at her, still surprised.

"I once told you this job was about the truth. Do you remember that?"

"Of course I do." I thought about that advice the first time I saw Jess. I knew even then that the truth for her was something different for me.

"Well, I'm no hypocrite. So it's time I tell it." She gestures toward me with her right hand. A quick flick of her fingers, and then I realize what she's suggesting.

"You want me to do the interview?"

"Who else would I want to have do it?" She says it as though I'm being absurd. As though there's no other real option.

"You're the one who brought the Baltimore story back to me in the first place."

I wince. It is a too painfully familiar thing for Salem to say to me. I think I mumble something about me receiving a random email not really counting as my bringing anything to her, but I can't quite be sure what she hears. Mostly I wish I had my own napkin to fold.

Mostly I wish for a million other things, and all of them have to do with Jess Greene.

In the silence, I can feel Salem watching me. Between the two of us, I'm pretty sure the name *Hawk* fits her better.

"Adam," she says.

I swallow, but don't say anything. It probably wouldn't be the worst thing in the world, for a six-foot-five former linebacker to cry a little in public. But I still don't want to do it.

"Have you heard from her?"

I shake my head. Jam that thumb into my knee, just in case.

"I didn't figure you would. I'll reach out to them in a few weeks, I think. Touch base with both of them after they've had some distance, you know? See what they're thinking about the . . . material we've gathered."

"I don't think I should be a part of that."

"Probably not."

Leave to it Salem to give it to you straight. Next up, she'll probably tell me exactly how many days it's going to hurt this bad. She'll be wrong, unless she says it's going to hurt every day. Forever. A new wound that's not ever going to heal.

Except then I realize *why* she would be wrong. I realize what she must think.

"It isn't the same, you know," I say. "Whatever you felt for Baltimore, when you got wrapped up in the story. That's not the same as how I feel about Jess."

I expect her to say what she said in New Mexico, or at least something similar—that it's hard to say for sure, that I can't tell because I'm too close to it.

But she surprises me.

"I know it's not the same."

"You do?"

She takes a big breath, blows it out slow.

"You know, Rhode Island is a good place to think. To talk to someone—someone you're married to—about stuff you should've talked about a long time ago. It's a good place to think about what it means to really love someone."

It's probably not so much Rhode Island specifically, I think. Probably it's the seaside setting. The distance from your job, being in a house that you don't have to take care of. The privacy.

"When I think back over our trip—I think I learned a few things I didn't expect to, being around Jess Greene. Being around you being around Jess Greene. I know you love her, Adam. I could see that."

Jesus, my knee hurts. Maybe I broke something in there, pressing on it so hard.

"And I know she loves you, too."

I clench my teeth against the immediate flush of hope hearing her say it makes me feel. I shake my head to drive home the point. What Jess feels for me—and I know she feels something—I don't know if she'll ever be able to get past how she first met me. I don't know if, like the Salem of ten years ago, she'll wake up one day in a few weeks and feel as though she's finally broken a spell.

"In Rhode Island," Salem says, and honestly, it's a lot about Rhode Island. I've forgiven her for abandoning me for a week and a half, but at the moment I'd prefer to go home and cry in private, rather than listen to more about her nice vacation.

"In *Rhode Island*," she repeats, like she's a teacher who caught me tuning out, "I also got to spend a lot of time around Pen. Hanging out, talking, doing puzzles. Helping her with her PT stuff. And you know, I don't think I ever forgave myself for those early years of her life. I don't think I ever forgave myself, for even thinking for one second about how maybe I wanted to escape from her for a while.

"I've always thought I was a bad mom to Pen, because of those years. Because of some of the things I let myself think back then, when I was in the grip of the Baltimore story. And maybe, on the scale of it, I'm not that good of a mom. Maybe I'm a mediocre mom."

"You're not a mediocre mom."

She smiles at me weakly, the kind of smile you give someone when you appreciate them but don't really believe them.

"But I am good to her, Adam. I love her, and I wouldn't have left her. I stayed with her and I taught her things and I listened to her talk about her friends and her dance classes and the teachers she loved and hated. I didn't ever manipulate her. I didn't ever abandon her needs to my wants."

"That's a good mom."

She shrugs. "That's not really the point. The point is, I always *thought* I was a bad mom. But I don't really think I ever really knew what a bad mom was until I met Charlotte Caulfield ten days ago."

She pauses, folds her napkin one more time. In the space of that fold, I see every terrible moment inside the houseboat in slow motion. I see every moment in the hotel hallway, too.

"I don't know what it'd do to someone, to have a mom like that," Salem says. "Someone who'd leave you like that. Who'd teach you that loving looked like that."

She leaves it there. Doesn't do much more than watch me for a few seconds. Like any great journalist, she doesn't just want to tell me the story. She wants to get me thinking. She wants me to keep seeing those moments, and a hundred other ones from the two weeks I spent on the road with Jess and Tegan, through this lens.

She wants me to remember that loving Jess Greene wasn't ever going to be easy.

She wants me to know I may have to wait.

"The interview has to be good, Hawk," she says, slipping straight back into work mode.

Maybe she can see I'm losing the fight against this lump in my throat. I feel like taking my phone out of my pocket and texting Jess Greene that I'm willing to wait forever.

But I guess doing that wouldn't really be waiting at all.

"I get it," I say. "I'll get my head on straight."

She nods, flicks a rogue fly away from landing on the food she still hasn't touched.

"You will," she responds, matter-of-factly, as though there's no doubt. "But what I mean is, the interview has to be good, because I'm not using a single second of that tape with Charlotte Caulfield if I can help it."

I stare at her, struck dumb. She picks up a potato chip and points it at me before she speaks.

"You're not the only one who cares about those women, Adam. You might be the only one in love with one of them, but you're not the only one who's going to try to protect them now."

Chapter 31

Jess

Is it too dramatic to say that therapy is excruciating?

Probably.

But also, sometimes, it feels pretty excruciating to me.

Tegan and I make our way out of the squat, unassuming office building where we've come twice a week together for the last three weeks. It's unusual, I guess, to get in to see a family therapist twice a week, especially when the first time is only four days after you've first called.

Four days after you've returned home from the most devastating family experience of your life.

But the convenient thing about Dr. Hobbs is that she hasn't been a therapist all that long, which means she's still building her practice up, and I happened to call when her book was still fairly open. I knew the exact number of days I had before I needed to take Tegan for dorm move-in and first-year orientation, and I figured, after all this time of leaving her without professional help, I ought to lean in. Take her for as many sessions as I could before then.

I admit, I didn't expect to do much in therapy. Like most of the stuff I did in those first days after we got home, I booked Dr. Hobbs with the same mechanical, force-of-will concentration I'd relied on ever since the houseboat.

The hotel hallway.

Get home, unpack. Sort through the mail. Call Dad; call the salon. Keep checking on Tegan. Sit with her in a therapist's office, and make sure all the focus stays on her.

Don't think about what happened. Don't dare think about Adam, and what I did to him.

What I feel for him.

But the thing about Dr. Hobbs—who I'm pretty sure is my exact age, though I try not to fixate on that—is that she is pretty good at her job, such as it is. And such as it is, is making Tegan and me talk about—and think about—hard things. Really hard things.

When we clear the door and make it out into the hot sunshine of the August day, Tegan and I both breathe in a lungful of fresh air, not looking at each other quite yet. I'm almost used to it now, the way both of us walk out of there every time a little sheepish, each of us needing a few seconds to shake off the session. I hear Tegan sniffle once, a remnant of the tears she shed inside, but I don't react or intrude.

I learned in a session last week that it bothers Tegan when I go into "fix-it" mode about her feelings.

In the car, though, she buckles her seat belt and leans her head back on the headrest. I feel, rather than see, her tip her head my way.

"Wow, that *sucked*, right?"

I snort a laugh, a fizz of relief in my middle that it didn't take her too long to bring some levity to the moment. Today was a tough one. We talked about the time right after Mom left, including the bed-wetting. I didn't know, but Tegan still feels so ashamed about it. Sometimes she still worries about it happening again, especially when she goes to college. She's embarrassed about how long she did it, but also about how many times it happened. How many times I had to clean up after her. How I'd never let her help me start the laundry or change the sheets.

It made me think of Adam. Him in that hallway, offering to help.

"Yeah," I say, meaning it. I snap my own seat belt. "Want to get fries?"

"Uh, obviously."

So, we do what we've done after the last five sessions. I start the car and Tegan pulls up a delivery app and we get two gigantic orders of fries and four different sauces from our favorite place. We never used to eat out much, before the road trip, but now we've got a taste for it.

Do something difficult; eat food you didn't prepare yourself.

By the time we get home—Dr. Hobbs's office is almost a full half hour away, far out in a northwest suburb of Columbus— our fries are on our doorstep, and Tegan hops out to get them. If she notices that I avoid that doorstep like the plague, only ever coming through the garage now, she hasn't said.

It looks empty to me, is the thing. All the time, it looks empty.

We're quiet as we eat. A couple months ago, I know I would've tried to fill the silence. I would've pressed Tegan on how her day was, asking her too many questions. Now I let her be alone with her thoughts, and I try to be alone with mine.

Adam, I think, the way I always do these days, and on Dr. Hobbs's annoying, excruciating, probably very good advice, I don't shove it away. I don't stand up to get more napkins or to start cleaning up even though I'm not done eating yet. I don't suddenly remember I need to check whether I paid the gas bill this month.

I just think about Adam, and how much I miss him.

How lonely I am without him. His warm, wrap-you-up body and his carved-from-stone face. His curiosity and his calm, his weird cracking bones and the quiet smiles he used to send my way.

I strain to imagine the life he is leading back in Boston, a place I've never been to, but that I've looked up on the internet more than a few times since we've been home. I try to cobble together a picture of his apartment based on the scattered, small details he shared over the time we spent together. I puzzle through a picture of the office he works in, based only on the scraps I picked up from listening to him and Salem talk about work. I remember that at dinner on the farm one night, he told his nieces about his downstairs neighbor who lets their cat wander all through the hallways and stairwells, and sometimes Adam comes home to gigantic, disgusting hairballs on his doormat. The girls had laughed and laughed.

I am a shell collector. I'm trying so hard to coat all these precious, fragile facts about Adam in something hard and firm and inflexible.

I'm trying to make a souvenir.

Tell me you don't remember

Tell me you don't remember how it's always felt between you and me

"Helloooooooooooooo," Tegan says, snapping two fingers in front of my face in dramatic, lighthearted interruption.

When I blink at her she rolls her eyes.

"You're a little gremlin after therapy," she says. "Just dead-eyed and hungry, eating your fries like an animal and ignoring me."

"I'm *processing*," I say, and she laughs again.

It's good she's laughing. She does it more, the last week or so. At first, she was so fucking sad. Cocooned in her room or on the couch. She didn't even really want to talk to her friends. She kept me close like a security blanket, a fact that worried me more than I expected. It didn't feel right anymore, for Tegan and I to do that to each other.

"Anyway, as I was *saying*, I think we should sort through that stuff from Target tonight."

338 • *Kate Clayborn*

I rouse my brain back to this moment, back to this place. It's good she's talking about the stuff from Target, too—a pile of things we ordered online for her dorm, working from a list the college sent over and from the many text conversations Tegan's been having with her roommate, a girl named Destiny who's also from Ohio. When the boxes finally arrived, though—on that too-empty porch—Tegan hadn't seemed all that eager to unpack them yet.

She was still so cocooned, maybe.

The college sent some material for parents, too, all about helping your student manage some of the anxiety that might accompany move-in day. I figure that not all of it applies to someone who's been through what Tegan has, but still—probably under Dr. Hobbs's influence—I paid attention. I know that it's important for me to show a lot of enthusiasm at this preparation stage. To help Tegan picture the room she'll be living in, with all the stuff we've bought all settled inside it.

"Yes!"

It comes out a shade too enthusiastically, and she narrows her eyes at me.

I take the opportunity to clear our plates, which is not what Dr. Hobbs would suggest, probably, but on this I've got to go my own way. I know Tegan's worried about me being here alone, and I don't want her to be. Part of that is because she doesn't need the extra pressure of concerning herself with what I'm doing while she's settling in at school.

But another part is that I can see now how I'd be lonely even if she were staying. I can see I'll be lonely even though I'm making a real effort out there, soft-launching efforts at being a person who needs friends. Who *wants* friends. On my first day back at work, for example, when poor, naïve Ellie asked where I'd been for so long, I surprised every coworker in the vicinity by giving her an actual answer. I said, "I had some family stuff to deal with," which basically felt like announcing my Social Security number to an auditorium. I've even been reaching out to

Dad and Bernila more. They invited me to a Labor Day cookout in a few weeks, and I'm pretty sure I'll go. I'm *determined* to go, because I know I can't keep living the next ten years like I've lived the last. I know I have to start taking back at least some of what Mom took from me.

Anyway, I'll keep making the effort, but I'll still be lonely.

The souvenir I make won't ever be enough.

Thankfully, Tegan decides to let it go for now, and an hour later we're in her room, up to our elbows in new bedding and towels and desk and dresser supplies, doing all the things that pamphlet suggested. We're planning it all out, picturing it, and Tegan's got tons of ideas.

"I can't believe it's so *soon*! Is it—is it okay if I say, I don't know. I'm getting really excited now. Is that okay?"

My arms drop from their lifted, towel-folding position. "Of *course* it's okay to say. Why wouldn't it be okay?"

She shrugs, avoiding my eyes. "I know it's sad."

I swallow. "It is sad. But remember what Dr. Hobbs said. We're allowed to feel sad about things. That doesn't mean we should avoid them."

"Listen to you!" she teases. "Therapy, am I right?"

"I hate it," I deadpan.

She laughs, but she quiets again quickly.

"Jessie?"

"Yeah?"

"I know we haven't talked about this yet, and maybe it's a thing for Dr. Hobbs, but . . ." She trails off, twists and untwists the scrunchie she's fiddling with. "But I don't think I want to say this in front of her. Not yet."

I swallow, immediately nervous. Have I missed something crucial, something new that's really bothering her? I figure it took a lot of courage to talk about bed-wetting in front of a practical stranger but if there's something—

"I've been thinking about what Mom said to you on the boat. Or, um. I guess she said it about you."

Oh.

I let the towel I was folding drop to the bed.

"You know, the thing about you being like her."

I don't even know if I nod. The truth is, I'm grateful Tegan hasn't brought this up in front of Dr. Hobbs. What Mom said to me—what she said to Salem—it's as bad as bed-wetting for me. Not just the content of it, but what it caused me to do.

Tell me you don't remember, he said to me.

His heart in his eyes. Begging me to listen to him, instead of to her.

Maybe I haven't managed to tell Dr. Hobbs about it yet, but that doesn't mean I can't see how I took Mom's words too hard. How Mom's hold on me about this is still so, so deep—way deeper than the distance I've kept between myself and potential friends, between myself and my father.

I know I wrecked something so important because of that hold.

"I know we're very united on the whole 'Mom sucks' front right now," Tegan says.

I can tell she's working to keep this light, which is maybe why I should better anticipate that she's about to say something incredibly heavy.

"But also. I kind of think she was right?"

It doesn't matter that she's said that last part fast—rushing it out as though she knows she might lose her nerve. It doesn't matter that I can tell she was so nervous to say it.

It still hurts. Like, I-should-go-shower-and-plausibly-deny-crying hurts.

"Uh, I mean—not *literally* right!" she clarifies, and I realize that's because I haven't managed to hide it, after all. Tears have immediately sprung to my eyes.

I don't know how you could be metaphorically right about this.

"Let me—okay, let me explain what I mean."

She sounds a little panicked now, and I swallow back the tears.

"Mom said that when you fell for someone, you'd do anything for them."

I know, Tegan, I want to snap, but I don't. *It is seared into my brain, what she said. I broke a man's heart, because of what she said.*

If I say any of that, I'll fall apart, and I don't think I'm ready yet.

"But I think that's because Mom really only thinks love is what she had with Lynton. Or my dad or yours, I guess, for the time that she was with them."

"Right, I know that."

We *have* talked about this with Dr. Hobbs. Mom's personality, her fixation on men. The limits to how she loved us. But I'm having trouble following what Tegan is trying to—

"I think what Mom doesn't get is that the person you've loved the most—the person you've been willing to do anything for . . . that's me, Jess. I'm the one you gave your heart to."

I pick up the towel again.

There's no time to run to the shower.

I press it right against my face. Right against the tears I can't stop from coming.

"Oh, *no,*" Tegan says, rushing over to me and putting her arms around me. "God, don't cry!"

And then, "No, wait! Definitely cry! Dr. Hobbs would say it's great to cry!"

I snort-sob into the towel.

"I'm sorry!" she exclaims. Obviously, despite therapy, she is not fully convinced that it's great for *me* to cry, and I get it. Dr. Hobbs would also say that new things are challenging.

I let the towel fall from my face, but only so I can clutch Tegan harder. I'm crying a lot now, but in the moment I can't tell if it's the same as falling apart.

"Don't be sorry," I manage eventually. "I'm crying because—" I lean back from her, untangling us so I can wipe my wet cheeks.

"I'm crying because that was so nice, what you said. Thank you for saying it."

She looks at me a little strangely.

"Okay," she says, an awkward note in her voice. "It's—the thing is, I didn't really mean it as a compliment?"

"Oh."

She tugs me over to her bed. I'm so stunned from the fact that I actually cried in a dry location that she can pretty much put me where she wants me, sitting sort of sideways so I'm facing her. I have a flash of her in her dorm room in a few weeks. I hope she and Destiny sit this way together, sharing secrets. Telling each other the kinds of things it takes to make new friends.

"Jessie. What I mean is—what I mean is, when Mom left, you . . . you became what I needed. Everything I needed, that became all you needed, too. Your whole life, you gave over to me. And you kind of disappeared, you know?"

I swallow thickly, my heart suddenly thundering in my chest. I . . . disappeared?

"When we were on the trip, I felt—sometimes I thought I was seeing you for the first time, when you were around Adam. I'd watch you watching him, and I'd think, wow, that's how Jess looks when she's interested in someone. When she wants to . . . *know* someone, when she doesn't feel responsible for someone. I don't think I'd ever seen that before, you know? And then, when we got to Missouri, it was . . ."

She stops, shakes her head. I can't decide if I want to know what she was going to say, or if it'll make everything worse.

Tell me you don't remember

"It was what?" I say, voice shaky.

She shrugs, her face flushed. "I don't know for sure, I guess, given all the stuff we've talked about with Dr. Hobbs. About our backgrounds, I mean. But I think I know, in a way. I think I know that what I saw with you and Adam—that's how love is supposed to look. That's how *you're* supposed to look. When you were with Adam, you couldn't disappear. He wouldn't let you."

Oh, *God.* Oh God, oh God.

"Give me the towel," I choke out.

She waits until I have it against my face to speak again.

"When we got to Mom's, you sort of did it again. I couldn't really see it, in the moment, because obviously I was pretty upset, too. But now, when I think back to it—you barely said a word. And you must be so mad at her. You must have wanted to say so many things, but you didn't."

"I didn't want to—"

"I know what you didn't want. You didn't want it to be about you. You wanted it to be about me, because I said that's what I needed. So you shut yourself away all over again."

"I'm sorry," I say into the towel, but I don't really know who I'm saying it to. I think maybe I'm saying it to myself, and to Adam, too.

Dr. Hobbs would call this a breakthrough.

"I'm always going to have your heart, Jessie. Because you gave it to me so completely, and yours taught me how to make my own. But I think—I think I need to give yours back to you now. I think you need it, because I think it's high time you get to share it with someone else."

I nod mutely, finally lowering the towel from my face again.

"I know you really love him. Not how Mom loved Lynton. Not even how you've loved me for all these years. I think you love him as yourself, you know? *For* yourself. I think Hawk is the first person in a long time who could really see you. Even when you tried to hide."

Of course I remember, I'm thinking. *Of course I remember that morning in the parking lot, your hotel room in Missouri. Of course I remember the field at night and the trampoline. I remember every time I sat next to you in the van, and I remember how it always felt between us.*

I remember everything.

"God, Tegan," I say, wiping snot from my nose. "You're really good at this. Is this a fifty-minute hour, or—?"

She laughs and pats my back, and I want to feel comforted,

but inside me there's a riot. Because Tegan is so good, and so right, and I was so, so wrong. I *do* remember everything, including all the things I could've done better.

"I really hurt him, Teeg," I admit.

"Well, you know what Dr. Hobbs says. Hurt people hur—"

I groan. It's a choking, soggy-sounding thing.

"Adam is a pretty smart guy," she says. "I think he could probably see what was coming there at the end, when it came to you. When it came to Mom."

"He tried to tell me."

"Well, maybe you could give him a call. Let him know you finally heard him." She pauses, nudges me. "Make sure you tell him I helped."

I nod, but it's feeble. The idea of calling him—I can't fathom it. I can't fathom ever knowing what to say to make up for the way I must have made him feel.

"Then again," she says, "calling might be kind of a weak move, under the circumstances."

I nod again, stare down at the tear-spotted towel in my lap. At the stack of bedding we've set out, at Tegan's new shower caddy and her little desk lamp. I cling to the picture of her new dorm room, and then I start making myself another one.

I set out all the little shells that have been living on a shelf in my mind. I look and look at them, and I don't coat them in anything at all.

I think of Adam, and I remember everything.

"Tegan," I finally say, newly resolved. Newly back in my body and mind. Newly reappeared. "Do you think there's any chance you'd be up for another road trip?

Chapter 32

Hawkins: When we first started working on this together, you said something to me about storytelling. You said that Baltimore's best trick was telling women a story they wanted to hear. What story do you think he told you?

Durant: I don't enjoy being on this side of you being good at this, I'll admit to that.

Hawkins: Sorry.

Durant: Don't be. ::pauses:: The story he told me, I guess, was that I could get the story. That I could get to the truth.

Hawkins: Do you think you have now? Gotten the truth?

Durant: ::chuckles:: Oh, probably not. Not about Lynton, at least. I don't know if there is a truth about someone like him.

Hawkins: About something else, then?

Durant: I think I've probably figured out some truths about myself. A good story . . . a good story can do that for you.

Chapter 33

Adam

When I shut off the recording, Salem breathes out a sigh of relief.

"All right?" I ask.

"Ask me in two days. I need to let it settle."

I nod and busy myself with tidying some of the equipment clutter on my coffee table, leaving Salem to her thoughts for now. I'm sure she's tired from the interview, but the truth is, I am, too. It isn't just that I've spent the last week preparing for this, keeping long days and late nights listening to tapes and poring over transcripts of conversations that never made it into Salem's original podcast.

It's that being dunked back into the Baltimore story—being steeped in it—means I'm constantly being reminded of what this story took from me.

I sit back on my couch, blow out a breath of my own. All through the interview, I tried not to look around much—tried to keep my focus on Salem or on my notes. I didn't want to think about the fact that we were doing this here, in my home, or wonder whether Lynton Baltimore might linger like some poisonous cloud.

But now that it's over, I'm back to wondering about it. Worrying about it.

This time, I brought it to my own door.

"Salem."

"Mm?" She's looking at her phone. Typical.

"Why'd you want to do this here, anyway?"

She sets her phone facedown on the arm of the chair I usually sit in to read. She looks absurdly small in it. She has to sit way forward so her feet reach the floor.

"Where else am I going to do it, the office?"

Fair enough. Salem and I haven't told anyone at Broadside yet about this piece of the story, on her request. She wanted to make sure this interview went okay first, and I'm sure when I'm able to take a step back from my worries over the poisonous cloud thing, I'll be able to see more clearly that it went better than okay. I'm pretty sure Salem did great.

"We could've done it at your house."

Salem snorts. "Listen, Patrick and I are doing pretty well these days. But do I think he wants me to talk on the record in our family home about that time ten years ago when I basically had an emotional affair with Lynton Baltimore? Not really."

Right. Patrick works from home, too. It would've been awkward.

Poisonous, if you will.

"Anyway, this worked out perfect!" she says, weirdly chipper.

Maybe she's feeling some kind of euphoria now that it's done. She must've been nervous, even though she didn't seem so.

"Your apartment is fine!" She picks up her phone, checks it again. "It's a little spartan, though. What do men your age have against hanging art on the walls?"

Jesus Christ. Since our lunch that day she first came back, I've gotten used to the fact that my relationship with Salem has slipped into a friendship, even though it's a friendship that's obviously been conditioned by our work together. And the experience of prepping for this interview—this interview that's about something so personal to her—has meant spending even more time together outside of the office, talking about things we never would have otherwise, probably.

But that still doesn't mean I want her commentary on the state of my apartment.

"I haven't lived here that long."

She makes an annoyed face. "You didn't even put out any snacks."

I stare at her. "We were recording."

She shrugs. Am I going to have to . . . get her a snack? I can't remember the last time I went to the grocery store. My eating habits since getting back from Olympia have been uneven at best. The truth is, I thought Salem would want to go right after we wrapped. I thought she'd want to be alone.

I want to be alone.

Still, I get up from the couch and make my way to the kitchen. I think there's an unopened bag of corn chips in the pantry. They're a generic brand and I don't have any salsa, so maybe when it's all I have to offer she'll decide to go. When she does, I wonder if she'll call Jess and Tegan, or if she'll wait a little longer.

I wonder what they'll say.

I don't know if I'm dreading or anticipating hearing.

The way I miss Jess—it isn't like missing someone I knew for a little more than two weeks.

It's missing someone I knew forever. Every day that passes, it gets harder to imagine waiting for her for much longer. I know I can't push her, but also—also, who's looking out for her? Who's helping her get through this?

I swallow, shove my hand in the pantry for the corn chips. Even better, they *have* been opened. They're almost certainly stale. Surely with this offering, Salem will be out of here in five minutes, max.

Except when I turn back to the living room, she's got her laptop out. Tapping away.

What the fuck.

"Okay, so I've been going over your latest edits on the pitch," she says. "Strong, but I think we can still improve this last part, about the joy of sport. It's not hitting yet."

I stay where I am for a few seconds, stale chips in hand. Breathe through the frustration of this. I can't be annoyed, because the pitch is maybe the one thing that's kept me from doing something asinine like buying a plane ticket to Ohio and flattening my way back into Jess's life. In the last week, I've made a lot of progress on the pitch, and a good deal of that is down to Salem. She seems excited about it, supportive about it, but she's also exacting. She presses me on the story structure, presses me to make it bigger, sends me links to more and more research she thinks I should read. I'm grateful for the distraction—for the way I'm pretty sure she's propping me up through a tough time—but I'm also grateful for how good the pitch is getting.

Much as I hate to admit it, I can see how much I've learned from the Baltimore story.

How much better of a job I'll do for Cope because of it.

That's what I always wanted.

That's what Jess wanted for me, too.

"I've only got chips," I say, crossing back to the living room and holding out the bag to her.

She doesn't look up from her laptop.

"Never mind, I'm not hungry."

The bag crinkles in my hand. Is she serious?

Her phone pings and she picks it up, looking at the screen for only a half second before she snaps her laptop lid shut.

"Anyway, I have to go!"

I blink down at her. Probably she's rattled from the interview. I shouldn't judge.

Still, now I'd kind of gotten it in my head that we'd work. I guess tonight I'll work alone. Or maybe I'll call Mace later. Beth says he's really going through it about Katie starting soccer, and I'm pretty sure his stress is at least partially my fault. At this point, I don't think anyone in my family has been spared my commentary on head injuries in contact sports.

Maybe I can tell him about the joy-of-sport stuff Salem's been wanting me to work on for the pitch. It might help.

Salem's sliding her laptop into her shoulder bag when there's a knock on my door, and I suppress a groan. It's definitely Karen, my downstairs neighbor. Her cat Peaches hairballed my doormat again today. If Karen could keep Peaches out of the hallways or, I don't know, modify the cat's diet or something, that'd be better than these every-few-days awkward apologies.

I think about telling Salem to be quiet and wait for a minute, pretend no one's home. She can leave when the coast is clear. But before I can say anything, she's already going to the door, as if she owns the place.

And then she opens it, and it's not my neighbor.

It's Jess.

Jess and Tegan, at my front door.

"Uh," I think I say.

"Hi!" says Tegan brightly. "We're here!"

"God," Salem says. "I've been stalling forever. He didn't even put out snacks."

I'm still holding the bag of corn chips. I haven't managed to say or do anything else.

Jess.

Jess is there on my doorstep. All black as usual.

Beautiful, as usual.

I think I might be dreaming.

Except then, Salem leans forward casually and hugs Tegan. When she's done, she does the same to Jess, who doesn't even seem all that bothered. Only the slightest hesitation.

I could never have dreamed that.

"Jess missed a turn," Tegan says, I guess by way of explanation for why Salem had to stall so long. "Her nerves! What a nightmare."

Jess's cheeks flush. She hasn't taken her eyes off me. Not even during that awkward hug.

"All right, are you ready?" Salem says to Tegan.

Tegan looks to Jess. "You're good?"

Jess nods. Still flushed. She looks so nervous.

"Okay. Call me!" She holds up her phone, making sure Jess sees she has it. Then she looks at me. "Hawk, make sure she calls me!"

"Okay," I manage. Dimly I realize there's been some kind of plan in motion, Salem and Tegan and Jess working together for I don't know how long.

But I can't care. I can't care about anything except her standing there.

Tegan steps back from the door so Salem can make her way out. When she does, she stops long enough to look over her shoulder at me. "And you make sure you call me. We have work!"

Then she sets a hand on Tegan's shoulder and leads her away, and it's only Jess and me.

Two points in our compass gone, but it doesn't matter.

I'm still staring straight at my true north.

"Can I come in?" she says, and that's when I realize I've been staring for a shade too long.

I drop the chips, the bag obnoxiously, absurdly loud.

"Yeah. Yeah, of course."

She steps inside, closes the door gently behind her. Why *don't* I have any art on the walls? She's going to think I live like a college student. The corn chips don't help, surely.

But she doesn't seem to notice. She seems to have a plan, because she comes in only far enough to stand in front of the coffee table I just cleared off. She slides her phone from her back pocket and taps at the screen, a look of sincere, serious concentration on her face. I hear a familiar tinny ping, and then she bends to set the phone on the table.

352 • *Kate Clayborn*

She doesn't speak softly.

"This is Jessamine Greene," she says. "I drove all the way from Columbus, Ohio, to Boston, Massachusetts, to see Adam Hawkins."

She pauses, swallows. Keeps her eyes on me.

"To see you."

"Jess," I say, but she shakes her head. Gestures to her phone with a small, explanatory gesture.

"To see you, and to say how sorry I am for disappearing on you. To say how sorry I am for what I said right before I did. I know we haven't known each other that long. I know it was only two weeks, but it wasn't just any two weeks. It was . . . it was a really important two weeks, and I remember every single second of them, and I have thought of you—I have *missed* you every single day since I left you in Washington. And also . . . also, I'm in love with you."

Her voice wobbles, and she takes a second. Swallows and lets her eyes slide shut for a beat before opening them again. I don't dare make a sound.

I'm in love with you, she said, and it's all I want to hear for hours. For forever.

Until she speaks again.

"I love you, and I haven't loved many people in my life, so I don't think I've done the best job at it. But you said you'd help me, and I was wondering if that offer still stands. If you—if you can be patient while I'm working on helping myself. If you think you can love me, too."

"I—"

But before I can say anything, she bends down, taps the screen on her phone again. A couple of times, quickly, her face all concentration again.

From somewhere behind me in the kitchen, my own phone vibrates on the counter. A message received.

"So you'll have it," she says quietly. "On the record."

"Jess," I say again.

"There's other stuff I have to tell you, too," she interrupts quickly. "But it's not for a recording."

"None of it needed to be for a recording." My voice sounds thick to my own ears. "But I'm still glad you made one."

I'll save it, of course. I'll back it up to the cloud, put it on a portable hard drive. I'll keep it on every phone I ever own.

"Tegan said I needed a grand gesture. Her ideas were a little over-the-top. She had this one idea about balloons spelling out your name. But I was thinking, if I could—"

"Jess."

She clamps her mouth shut, as though she knows she's rambling. I've never heard Jess Greene ramble, not even once. It's about as beautiful as I bet that recording is.

I step forward. Shove my coffee table to the side with one of my legs. I walk right up to her, and I take the phone from her hands, toss it gently on the chair Salem was sitting in all afternoon.

I put my lips close to her ear. I say it only for her, which I know is how she'd want it.

"I love you, too."

She exhales a shaky breath, and sets her hands on my waist, over the fabric of my T-shirt. She leans her forehead against my chest.

"I'm so sorry, Adam," she whispers.

I wrap my arms around her, which is what I've been waiting to do since Washington. I hold her so close. I tell her at least a dozen things that I didn't practice for at all, that probably don't make any sense—that she's got nothing to be sorry for but also that I forgive her, that I'm sorry for what I brought to her door but that I'd never take it back if it meant never meeting her, that two weeks may not be long but two minutes isn't either, and I'm pretty sure that's all it took for me to fall for her. I tell her I missed her, everything about her, her hair and her tattoos and the stubborn set of her mouth when she doesn't want to talk and quirking edges of her lips when she does. I tell her I bought a set of black sheets at three in the morning one night last week, that I haven't been to the grocery store, and that I never thought I'd see a day when she and Salem gave each other a hug.

At that, she laughs a little and hugs me tighter, presses against me closer, and that's when I feel the moisture seeping through my T-shirt.

I lean back to look at her, cupping her face in my hands. I never thought Jess Greene could be more gorgeous, but somehow, like this—showing her whole self to me—she is.

"I do this a lot now," she says. "For the last couple of days, at least. My therapist is going to be thrilled."

"Your therapist, huh?"

She nods, a little sheepish. "One of the things that's not for the recording."

I lean down and kiss her. Her salt-soft lips that open to mine, and it feels so good that my knees nearly buckle with it. I wrap my arms around her waist and lift her a little, making it easy, making it good for us both, the remnants of her tears transferring from her cheeks to mine. I kiss her until we both lose our breath, until I'm seconds away from showing her those sheets. From begging to see her body against them.

"I'm sorry," I breathe against her neck. "I know I'm too—"

"You're not too anything. You've never been too anything, for me."

I smile against her skin. That feels so good, to hear her say that.

"There's so much I want to ask you," she says. "Have you been working on your story? Salem said she'd produce, right? Is there—"

"What is this, an interview?"

She laughs, quiet and happy. I pull back so I can see it.

"I've got a lot of questions for you, too, you know. The therapy thing, for one. But also, how you and Tegan and Salem pulled the wool over my eyes, and for how long. Like how we got to where you're good with Tegan and Salem going off to God knows where together."

She smiles at me, playful and mysterious. I love that smile on her. I have a feeling she's never shown it to anyone but me.

"They're going to Rhode Island for the night," she whispers.

"Let me guess. A seaside cottage?"

"Yeah, with Salem's husband and daughter. Tegan's really excited."

"You're okay with it? Her going?"

There's a little flicker of uncertainty in Jess's eyes, but she wrangles it quickly. She wouldn't be Jess without that layer of worry for her sister, and I get it.

But I also get what she's doing, too. I get that she's working on it.

"Yeah, I'm good with it. It'll be a nice break for her, and . . . um. Maybe for you and me, too. If you'd want to—"

I stop her mouth with mine, kiss her long and hard.

"I want to," I say, when I finally stop. She's flushed along her neck, her hands fisted in the fabric of my shirt. "I'd love to. I have to show you these sheets."

I don't even think she knows what I mean about the sheets, which is fair enough. I guess I'll have to explain when I get her in there. Which I hope is soon.

"Adam," she says, loosening her hold, smoothing the fabric she had crushed in her hands even as her brow creases with worry.

"Yeah?"

"We have a lot of questions to ask each other. Real ones. What happens when the Baltimore story comes out. What we'll do, living in two different places. How it'll be, when I'm being difficult and distant, or when I maybe start to disappear a little. What you'll think of me, when—"

"Jess," I say, taking her hands in both of mine. I bring them to my mouth, press my lips against the bumps of her knuckles before lowering them, holding them against my heart. "We'll have to answer stuff about me, too. What we'll do when I push too hard, or when I can't help but try to be the biggest thing in your life. How it'll be when we finally figure out the two different places thing, and I can't compromise about which side of the bed I want to sleep on or what time we get up on the weekends."

"You've got strong feelings about those things?" Jess says, eyebrows raised.

"Oh yeah. I'm a real nightmare, I'm sure."

She smiles again, different this time—a closemouthed, slightly embarrassed smile. "It's not the same as the stuff with me. It's so much more stuff, with me. Everything I went through with Mom, and with Tegan."

I press her hands closer against my heart. "The point is, these questions—we're going to answer them together. Tell our own story, okay? We're going to know this one only for ourselves."

She looks up at me then, her eyes filled up with happy tears, relieved tears. Any of her tears, I'll take.

"Only for ourselves," she repeats, and then, as if she's sealing a bond, she leans forward and sets her lips against my hands, where they still hold hers against my heart.

We stand that way for a while, soaking it in—the relief and the promise of it, the privacy of it.

But eventually, I get restless.

Eventually, I need more.

Jess's bare skin and her panting breath and yeah—the look of her on the bed I know she belongs in.

So I bend my creaking knees and I put my strength into my right shoulder. I push it against her stomach, as soft as I can, and then I have her up and off the ground, her laughing yelp a sound I'll have to settle for never having recorded. Her body folds over mine, one of her hands swatting my backside.

"You can't do this!" she says, as I start walking toward my room.

"I can. I'm currently doing it, in fact."

"No, I mean—you have to save your strength! For—um." She pauses, then taps insistently at my back with one of her fingers. "Listen, I didn't get to ask you one of my questions!"

I pause, set her down in the hallway outside my bedroom. *So close.*

I look down at her, her face all red from being upside-down, her hair a huge, spun-gold cloud around her face.

God, I love her.

"What's the question?"

She lifts her hands, tries to tame that mass of gorgeous hair I can't wait to feel against my skin. She shifts on her feet and clears her throat.

"I was wondering how you'd feel about helping me move my little sister into college?"

I smile down at her, but I doubt she has time to see it. In seconds I've got her over my shoulder again, and I don't bother saying a word.

This answer, I'll give to her with my body. With the beat of my heart.

Because whether Jess Greene knows it or not yet, whether she trusts it or not yet—it's the same answer I already know I'll be giving her for the rest of my life.

Epilogue

Jess

Eighteen months later

Tegan should be here any minute now.

I *need* her to be here any minute now.

Because I can't keep this ruse up for much longer, not on my own.

I need a partner in this project of distraction.

"You're sure you're okay?" Adam asks as he comes back into the kitchen, a concerned wrinkle in his brow. He's just out of the shower, changed into his oldest pair of jeans and a soft gray sweatshirt he only ever wears here at home. It's always the first thing he does, when he gets back after traveling for work.

"Oh yeah," I say, hoping he can't hear how forced my casual tone sounds.

I keep my eyes determinedly down on the bowl of cookie batter I'm mixing, which is certainly yet another clue that something is amiss. The truth is I've never made cookie batter from scratch. I've only ever bought it in those weird little tubes from the grocery. You don't even have to add eggs to those.

"Just concentrating on getting these right. So Tegan will have something homemade when she gets here, you know?"

"Hmm," is his only response, because I know he's suspicious. He's only been home for an hour and I'm blowing it. I practically jumped out of my skin when he hugged and kissed me hello—I think I stayed as stiff as a board, when usually I simply sink into him, into the relief that he's back.

I'm so *bad* at this.

"She's on her way?" he says, as he passes behind me to grab a glass from the cabinet. He sets a hand low on my back and bends his head, pressing his mouth against my neck, inhaling deeply. He's been gone for four whole days, wrapping up some loose ends before the holiday break, and all I want is to turn around and take a deep, calming breath of him, too. I want to slide my hands beneath his sweatshirt and feel his bare skin, and then he'll do the same back to me, and . . .

No, I tell myself firmly, probably stiffening again. *He* can't *do the same back to you, not yet.*

Not until Christmas.

Adam clears his throat softly and steps away. The next thing I hear is the quiet stream of the water dispenser inside the fridge as he fills his glass.

"So how was it?" I say, so he won't fixate on it, so he won't worry about it. "Salem's good?"

He moves to the other side of the counter, bends his big body to set his elbows on it. I have a feeling he's watching me close. But I am concentrating on this cookie batter.

I am *one* with the cookie batter. I'm practically becoming it.

"She's good. We got a lot done this round. After the new year, we'll bring it all to Emma. And then . . ."

He trails off, as though he can't quite believe that it's real, that it's finished, and now I can't help but look up at him. All my fixation on my probably doomed project of distraction dissipates, and Adam and I share a speaking gaze—nerves and anticipation and relief.

It's finally ready, his story. Cope and football and sport and mental health. It's earnest and complicated and sensitive.

It's exactly like the man who inspired it, and also exactly like the man who made it for him.

I'm so proud of Adam I could burst. He's been working so hard. He *and* Salem have been working so hard. Even in this new remote-collaboration setup, they've stayed so focused, so dedicated, even as they've filled their time with other, smaller stories, too.

In August—almost a year to the day that I showed up to Adam's apartment in Boston to tell him I loved him—Adam officially made the move here, to Columbus. To the house I raised Tegan in, to the house that feels more like home to me now than it ever did.

If I'm honest, I don't know if Adam and I will stay here for good, or even for all that long after Tegan graduates college. But after a year of doing long-distance—two weekends a month at first, gradually becoming more frequent as we grew closer in new ways, as I grew more confident and more open—we'd both wanted more time together.

We both want forever together.

My relocating to Boston had been part of the conversation we had about moving in together during one long weekend we spent away—in Rhode Island, at a seaside cottage, because Salem insisted. But honestly, it was never all that big of a part, and the conversation hadn't been all that long. Some of that was my reluctance—and Tegan's reluctance, too—to sell this house, to move away from the place Tegan had always known as her home while she was still away at college. I still wanted her to have a familiar place to be on her breaks, during her summers, for as long as that felt important to her.

I know she needs that kind of consistency, after Mom.

But some of it—just as much of it, really—was Adam, who'd never quite warmed up to Boston, and who liked the idea of being that much closer to his family in Missouri. It wasn't uncommon anymore for Broadside employees to work remotely, and Adam hadn't had a difficult time negotiating an arrangement, though the conversation with Salem had been a bit more strained at first. Until he officially told her he was moving here, I don't think Salem realized how much she'd come to rely on him at work, how essential he'd been to helping her through the release of the new Baltimore podcast.

It's been out for almost a year now, the five-episode "update" to *The Last Con of Lynton Baltimore*. One episode for every postcard, though Salem talked less about them than you'd think. In fact, she talked less about my mother than you'd think, and less about me and Tegan, too.

She kept the focus on Lynton, and on herself.

It hadn't been a huge hit, but by the time it released, that seemed fine by her.

She said she was doing it to close the book on Baltimore, not start a new one.

I admit—I was relieved that it wasn't a bigger deal, that it didn't get the kind of attention that would've meant every single person I met would ask me about it.

But even if it had, I think I could've handled it. I think I'm a lot better at handling it now. It helps, I'm sure, that I still don't get on the internet all that much.

It helps that I have Adam with me.

I lean over the counter, helpless not to give him at least a brief congratulatory kiss. But of course, it's easy to sink into it, especially when he lifts a hand to the nape of my neck, pushing his fingers into my put-up hair and probably loosening it from its bun. In seconds my mouth opens to his, my tongue sliding against his lower lip, and he groans in relief. There's a little alarm in my brain about my plan, the secret I'm supposed to keep, but I smash the snooze button. This is fine, with the counter between us; he won't be able to—

"Oh no, my eyes!" interrupts a laughing, familiar voice, and Adam and I jerk apart immediately.

The tops of his ears are bright red.

"I came in the back!" says Tegan brightly, tugging a huge duffel through the sliding door. "Who knew I'd walk into ol' mom and dad *making out* in the kitchen!"

I roll my eyes and Adam chuckles in spite of his embarrassment. This little mom-and-dad joke is one Tegan's been loving for months, ever since Adam officially moved in. I pretend to hate it, but really, I don't. I know me and Adam are nothing like Tegan's mom and dad, but her lightness about it, her happiness about us being together—it reassures me about all the things she and I have worked on since we got back from that fated road trip. Trust and honesty and transparency, and also the privacy we give each other, too.

I set down the cookie batter and come around the counter. I know she has more bags in the car, but for now, all I want to do is hug my sister.

She puts her arms around my shoulders to tug me to her but she's careful—because she's in on this thing with me, though she doesn't know all the details. When we're wrapped in a hug, she whispers in my ear, "Does he know yet?" and I shake my head quickly. I don't get to whisper back, because then Adam is there, too, wrapping us both up in his big arms.

I suppress a wince when he hits the wrong spot.

"Okay drive, Teeg?" he asks.

"Piece of cake," she answers, her voice muffled against him or me. It's hard to tell, pretzeled all together as we are.

He stands back—I breathe out a sigh of relief—and sets his hands on his hips, looking down at Tegan seriously. He looks like Adam Senior when he stands this way.

"You turned on the all-wheel drive?"

She rolls her eyes. "Yes, nerd. It's barely snowing."

Adam nods approvingly. He helped her pick out a used compact SUV this past summer, before she headed back to school. He took it so seriously. He takes everything with her so seriously: her classes and extracurriculars at school, her feelings, their relationship.

I'm so in love with him it hurts.

At the moment, it actually *physically* hurts.

"Okay!" I say, too brightly. "Adam, why don't you help Tegan get the rest of her things, and I'll put the first batch of cookies in. And then we'll have dinner!"

Oh *God*.

I sound like a different person. Adam is staring at me as if I've grown a second head, but thankfully, my sister has my back.

She tugs on his sleeve and pulls him toward the partially open back door.

But when he's out, she turns back to me, giving me a co-conspirator's narrow-eyed warning.

Be cool, she mouths, but I have a feeling that ship has sailed.

DINNER goes better.

That's down entirely to Tegan, who keeps Adam almost totally distracted. This fall, she took her first journalism course at the college, having spent her first year mostly filling in some general education requirements and focusing on acclimating to campus. Throughout this semester, she's kept Adam posted about this particular course, and now she's given him a full rundown of her final project—including her best guess at the grade she's going to get. Once she finishes that, she goes straight into what is basically a ten-question series about Adam's life right now, including about the parts I'm pretty sure she already knows. Salem, Pen—who Tegan texts with regularly—the whole Hawkins family, who we'll be traveling to see in a few days. Already our second Christmas with them, and I can't wait to hug them all.

364 • *Kate Clayborn*

But when the table is cleared and the kitchen is all cleaned up, Adam starts to head into the living room to settle on the new, much bigger couch we bought when he moved in. Adorably, Adam loves to sit by a lit-up Christmas tree at night, and if I go in there, he'll want me sitting in my usual spot, cuddling up, my left side pressed to his right.

I look at Tegan in panic.

Her eyes widen briefly, and then she improvises.

"Oh, no you don't!" she says, too loud, and Adam pauses.

"What?"

"You can't stay out here."

He blinks. "I . . . can't?"

Tegan shakes her head. "Jess and I need to . . . ah. Well, I've met someone!"

His brow lowers. "You've met someone?"

"I can't talk to *you* about it yet! It's too new! This is girl talk, *okay?*"

He stands with his mug of decaf in his hand and looks between us. The expression on his face is half-surprised and half-wounded. He was really looking forward to hanging out tonight.

He's been saying so for days.

My heart gives an aching thump. I can't do this. I'm going to—

"Very *private* things," Tegan says.

Adam's expression clears gamely and he nods. "Sure, sure. I'll just . . . go do some reading. I guess it is a little late."

It's barely nine o'clock, but whatever.

I stay awkwardly rooted to the spot while he makes his way to us, giving Tegan a quick half-hug before bending to give me a quick kiss on the lips.

"Love you," he whispers into my ear.

"Love you," I say back, squeezing his hand once before he heads toward the bedroom.

Tegan and I look at each other in shared apprehension.

"You are never going to make it until Christmas."

I groan and hang my head, shaking it.

She's so right.

Still, she does her best to stall, hoping if we stay up talking long enough Adam will fall asleep, and that at least buys me one more night. And even though Tegan and Adam and I are a family who try not to keep secrets from each other, it's still good to have one-on-one time with my sister, to talk about her friends at school and the professors she likes and doesn't. We stay in touch when she's there, texting throughout the days, doing a video call once a week—separate from the ones we still do once a month with Dr. Hobbs—but it's different to catch up in person.

We laugh more together now; we're ourselves more together now.

When it's nearing eleven, we've grown quieter, a bit more contemplative, the twinkling lights on the tree blanketing us in cozy security. Tegan adjusts the blanket on her lap, looking like she's only moments from sleep.

"I wonder how Mom is," she says casually. It's not a false coolness, either—just an easy, unbothered musing.

I shrug. It's hard to believe there was a time that this simple statement from Tegan would've sent me into a tailspin. But now I know that for Tegan and me, Mom will always be an absent presence, a person who'll get huger and more damaging to us if we never acknowledge to each other that she's out there.

"I hope okay," I say, and I mean it. I hope she is okay, doing whatever it is she does.

For now, hoping that seems like a huge achievement.

"Yeah," Tegan says, yawning.

I sit with her for a few minutes while sleep takes over, and soon enough, she's snoring softly. I probably shouldn't have let her get so far gone, should've nudged her toward her bed. But this couch is nice and she looks cozy here under the blanket, by the tree. She'll probably wake up in a few hours and shuffle to bed. She'll probably sleep until noon tomorrow.

How am I going to stall Adam on my own until *noon* tomorrow?

Maybe we'll go out for pancakes. He loves pancakes.

I stand, shutting off the overhead sink light in the kitchen, my side pinching with discomfort when I stretch to close a partially open cabinet door.

I bet Adam is asleep.

Surely he's asleep, right?

I move quietly down the hallway to the bedroom, and open the door so, so carefully.

And he is not asleep. He's sitting up in our bed—the California king he moved all the way from Boston—a book held in his big hands. As soon as I come inside, he closes it and sets it on the nightstand. Then he clasps those hands in his lap and looks straight at me.

Dammit.

"Show me," he says.

I lift my chin. "I don't know what you mean."

His lips quirk.

"Jess."

"How do you *know?*"

The quirk turns into more of a grin.

"You've been favoring your right side."

"Maybe I fell! Hurt myself, or something."

"You also left cling film on the shelf in the bathroom."

I blink at him, then my shoulders sag. I drop my face into my hands.

"How am I so *bad* at this?"

I hear him move from the bed, and then he's standing before me, pulling my hands gently away from my face. When I look up, he's still got that triumphant grin.

"Maybe you're not bad at it. Maybe I'm just that good."

I blow out an exasperated breath.

"Observant," he adds. "A hawk."

I can't help but laugh.

"It was supposed to be a *surprise*. I was going to show you on Christmas morning, before Tegan got up."

He maneuvers me toward the bed, pulling me carefully onto his lap when he sits. "You thought I'd be able to keep my hands off you until Christmas morning?"

"It was such a bad plan," I acknowledge. "I was trying to time it just right, but I couldn't—"

Adam is tugging at the hem of my shirt, and I squirm away halfheartedly. "What about the surprise?"

"I hate surprises."

I snort. "No, you don't. You just want under my shirt."

He leans in, gets his mouth against my neck again.

Oh, this is going to be impossible.

This was always going to be impossible.

"You're observant, too," he says, his low voice vibrating against my skin. "Come on, honey. Let me see. Please."

I give up the battle I'm not really fighting anymore. I stand from his lap and take a step back, and then I lift my sweater over my head. Surely I've left my hair a static-y mess; surely I'm splotchy with stress and embarrassment now.

But none of that matters when I have Adam's eyes on me. When I turn slightly to the left and lift my arm, showing him the spot on my ribs where the feather tattoo used to be.

A new one covering it now.

I hear Adam's careful breathing, feel his warm, rough fingertips reach out to touch gently around the edge of the shiny film I'll need to keep over it for the next few days.

"Oh, wow," he whispers.

I stay still while he looks close. He traces his eyes over the slim black lines of a delicately drawn field of flowers. A crescent moon above. Tiny stars the punctuation.

"Do you like it?"

He doesn't answer. He just brings me closer, enough so he can kiss all around it, slow and so careful. As he does, I slide my hands into his hair, press my mouth to the top of his head, his temple. I bend to catch the edge of his ear between my teeth, a move that makes him suck in a breath of pleasure.

After that, it certainly becomes clear I wouldn't have been able to keep my hands off him, either. I'm pulling off his T-shirt as he unhooks my bra, pressing against his bare skin even as he moves me and his own hands in such a way that avoids my new ink. He kisses me and kisses me, lays me back onto the bed and moves over me, murmuring his thanks and praise in between breaks from my lips, in the middle of perfect, caressing touches that make me warm and wet between my legs.

"I got you other presents," I breathe out, at one desperate point, when he has his fingers slipping through my sex, when I'm trying so hard not to get too excited, too soon.

"Yeah?" he says, moving his thumb in a perfect, slow circle, ducking his head to lick at one of my tight, aching nipples.

"Yeah," I echo, not sure if I'm answering him or encouraging him. "You'll still have surprises, I mean. On Christmas."

He doesn't answer for a long time; his mouth is too busy.

But when he eventually lifts his head, his eyes bright and his cheeks flushed with impatient desire, his fingers still teasing me, holding me in perfect, aching suspension, he simply says my name.

"Mmm?" I respond, my eyes slipping shut again, my legs and hips restless and rolling.

He doesn't say anything until I look at him, meeting his green, knowing gaze.

"I have to tell you a secret," he whispers.

I shudder in pleasure. "Tell me."

He lowers his head again, licks across my collarbone, up my neck. Puts his lips against the shell of my ear.

"I'm glad you can't hide from me."

My lips curve in a smile—pleasure and happiness and the

perfection of him finding out about the tattoo this way. It could only ever be this way.

"Me too," I answer, and oh—oh, do I mean it.

Adam, the person who always sees me.

The person who makes sure I'm always seen.

"Me too," I repeat, against his lips this time, and then, for a little, private while, we let ourselves disappear safely—perfectly—into each other.

Acknowledgments

Sometimes, writing a book means pulling a bit of a disappearing act of your own. Long stretches of time where you're not as available as you'd like to be, where you're hiding yourself away to get words down and to commune with these characters who live in your head.

But if you're lucky, you get people who don't let you disappear . . . at least not for long. And I've got a lot of people like that in my life to thank.

I want to first say an extra-special thanks for this one to my agent, Taylor Haggerty, who truly believed from the beginning that I could make *this* idea work, even though it was big and different and scary (for me, at least!). Taylor, thank you for the way you held me up throughout this writing process, as you always do, and thank you for giving me the extra encouragement you knew I needed to make Jess and Adam come to life.

Similarly, my editor, Shannon Plackis, was a crucial source of support for me, especially as I drafted this book during an intense time. Shannon, thank you for your patience with me and your confidence in me, which made it possible for me to keep writing. Thank you, too, for your keen eye—this book is so much better for your feedback. It feels so special to have the opportunity to work with you . . . especially since that keen eye of yours was the first to spot my work! I am forever grateful.

My gratitude to Shannon extends to everyone at Kensington Books, who have worked so hard and so tirelessly to bring my books into the world. I am especially grateful to Lynn Cully, Jackie Dinas, Vida Engstrand, Tory Groshong, Lauren Jernigan, Kait Johnson, Alexandra Nicolajsen, Kristen Noble, Jane Nutter, Carly Sommerstein, Adam Zacharius, and Steve Zacharius. That my books have found such a devoted readership is thanks so much to all of you, and to your enthusiasm for these stories.

Kristin Dwyer and Molly Mitchell from LEO PR always insist in the most calming and supportive of ways that I absolutely *not* disappear when it's time to get the word out about a book I've written, and without them, I would be totally lost. Thank you for the calendar, for the reminders, for the calls and texts . . . and for your boundless excitement for every win. You two are my shining stars.

So many devoted friends support me in myriad ways when I'm writing, including in making me leave my house occasionally or reminding me that I sometimes need to walk away from whatever I'm working on for a while. For this one, I owe exceptional, especial thanks to my friend AJ, who was hugely enthusiastic about my "con man" book, and who—in addition to reading everything as I was writing it—never, ever let me get too scared to keep going. Jennifer Prokop, who I am fortunate to call my friend *and* my freelance editor, helped me at crucial brainstorming and drafting stages; her knowledge of how story works, how the genre works, helped me to balance all the parts of this narrative that mattered so much to me. I could not have finished without her.

Thank you to my dearest Lo, who always tells me my words

matter; to Sarah MacLean, who goes full gremlin with me during deadline time; to Esi, who keeps me laughing and keeps me connected; to Jackie, Elizabeth, Joan, Amy, and Sarah, people who know me by heart and who love me anyway. To my family, who inspire and support in equal measure. To my husband, who doesn't care if his "Best writer ever!" chant is true or not; he'll say it to me every day anyway. Every one of you makes it possible for me to do this work, and I love you so.

Finally, to every reader, blogger, librarian, bookseller, to every book enthusiast out there who takes the time to post and share and review and participate in the reading community—I thank you so much, most of all. What scared me most, when I started writing, was showing something of myself to the wider world. But so many of you have seen to the heart of me, and have shared your own. Your messages, your support, your excitement, your book recommendations and book thoughts—they have kept me here. I'm glad we can all disappear together, for a little while, into the pages of the books we love.

Visit our website at
KensingtonBooks.com
to sign up for our newsletters, read
more from your favorite authors, see
books by series, view reading group
guides, and more!

BETWEEN **THE** CHAPTERS

Become a Part of Our
Between the Chapters Book Club
Community and Join the Conversation

Betweenthechapters.net

Submit your book review for a chance to win exclusive
Between the Chapters swag you can't get anywhere else!
https://www.kensingtonbooks.com/pages/review/